OPERATION CINDERELLA

Previous books by James Douglas

Breathless to Casablanca

Zero Philadelphia

OPERATION CINDERELLA

A THRILLER

JAMES DOUGLAS

Welcome Rain Publishers
New York

Operation Cinderella

Note: This is a work of fiction, and the events and characters here are products of the author's imagination or are used fictiously. Any resemblance to actual events, places, or persons are coincidental.

Library of Congress Cataloging-in-Publication information is available from the publisher.

ISBN: 978-1-56649-395-6

First US Edition: August 2015

PROLOGUE

Even in hindsight, it was hard for the chronicler of these events to fully grasp the unbelievable nature of what had happened to him that rainy night, in the cold late autumn of 2005. There had been no compelling reason to stay off his usual route and take a third-rate road that led through a relatively deserted area with hills, forests, and ravines. He would have been making good time. Maybe the traffic he was sure to encounter along the freeway motivated him. Maybe he was simply following his intuition...

Lost in thought he drove through the lonely countryside into the swiftly approaching night; looking forward to the party, his loved ones, a gathering of friends and interesting women. In his mind he saw the château, the tree-lined path leading up to it lit by silvery moonlight, the symmetric jewel of a garden with a glittering pond at its heart. The gravel driveway that led to the main entrance, where the hostess would be waiting in an enchanting crepe-de-chine dress, ready to greet him with a gentle kiss. Then dinner by candlelight—his stomach growled at the thought...pleasant conversation, sweet nothings, exquisite wine, all intermingled with soft music. Nothing could have kept him from the château, and the night of pleasure and passion that it promised. Nothing, except another woman.

The road descended toward the bridge in a wet, glistening curve. In the sparse moonlight he started to make out the black, languid river. Then he saw headlights that seemed oddly out of place. Their fixed cones shone straight into the nocturnal nothingness. *They weren't on the road*! No doubt: something was very, very wrong here! Instinctively he brought the car to a rough halt, jumped out, threw himself against the balustrade to stare down at a car. It was tipped grotesquely on its side in the murky riverbed, its lights ominously piercing the night sky. He moved fast, screaming as he slipped down the steep muddy embankment, calling out garbled questions. Not a soul answered.

Her head rested on the steering wheel. Her blond hair gleamed as it washed around her face in the water. He inched his way forward, holding on to the side of the car, the cold current rising up to his chest.

After struggling for long minutes that seemed like an eternity, he managed to pull her limp body from the car and drag her back up to the road. She lay lifeless at the top of the embankment, sunk deep into wet ferns. His mind raced frantically. A call for help? His jacket was in the river, along with his cell phone. Later, he had no idea how he had managed to pull it off. It seemed like a dream, but the contusions that covered his entire body told the story, lacerations on his hands, bloody scrapes on his forehead, all tangible reminders of the last minute rescue.

He forced air into the woman's lungs. Again and again. Somehow, he was doing it right. His military training lay years back, but it had given him skills so deeply entrenched they were visceral today. Finally, at long last, she showed signs of life. Their eyes met for a split second. A stunned expression crossed her face. She coughed, started shaking. He helped her up and into the car, found the plaid blanket, the hip flask half-filled with whiskey. Both worked. As she warmed, her voice came back, to tell him where she lived.

He cautiously drove her home: *Le Milieu de la Fin*, a rusty sign proclaimed. *The Middle of the End* turned out to be a moonlit hollow with a farmhouse that now appeared as little more than a dark shadow.

A man stepped into the dimly lit doorway as the car pulled to a crunching halt on the gravel. "Bill," she breathed weakly. He fixed the chronicler, who was carrying the man's wife over the threshold, with a blatantly hostile look. "What happened? What did this guy do to you? Where's your car?" His tone was low, agitated, as he used two fingers to rub the ugly scar that ran the length of his nose. She started explaining, calming him down.

Later, all three sat in front of the blazing fireplace. Bill had reluctantly made tea. He wanted to call the police. She shook her head. He gave her a sullen glance, then totally stopped talking. A little later, he left the house without a word, holding a camera up in front of his bearded face to signal his intentions.

"Why were you driving through this area?" she asked. The embers were glowing powerfully, spreading more warmth.

The chronicler was at a loss for an answer. *Fate*, he thought, shrugging.

"There's a lot more to this," she sighed, still thawing. After midnight, Bill had not returned, she started to tell her story. "It was just before 9/11, 2001, in New York. My name was Leslie Palmer then. I had two wonderful kids, twin sons, a fabulous career, an almost perfect life. Then everything came crashing down..."

"I will tell you this under one condition only, James," she said firmly. "You have to promise to respect my anonymity, including my present name and where I live. You can do with the story what you want, but you must protect my privacy. Absolutely and unconditionally!"

Before she could continue, Bill returned. He looked beat, camera hanging from his neck, his closed features frowning with deep skepticism. Sizing up the scene, he mumbled something and clomped up the narrow stairs.

The night literally flew by, her gripping story taking them into the early morning hours. Finally, looking exhausted, she told him she would have to get some sleep. He was welcome to stay, he could sleep on the couch.

"So why are you telling me all of this?" he said, as they stood in the kitchen next day, cutting vegetables for a *salade niçoise*, Bill having once again set out, this time with a neighbor and his tractor, to retrieve the wreck of the car.

"And why did you come along and save me?" she countered mysteriously. "I believe in a higher order. There are times in life when we have to listen to our inner voice. Can we really know who sends our saviors out into the dark of night?"

James ended up staying on the farm for a week. Bill remained remote and austere. Still, sometimes they sat outside at night, smoking, gazing up at the stars above *Le Milieu de la Fin*.

The story told in the following chapters is Leslie Palmer's account of the events that occurred during those fateful days when the United States swayed in the wake of the terrorist assault on Manhattan's World Trade Center, then only narrowly escaped a treacherous attack on its government.

PART I

01

. . . Rick Bronx had killed for his government before. In Afghanistan. The thought that he would kill again stirred nothing in him, not even for an instant. This was strictly business, to be executed in a meticulous manner following certain principles: simplicity came first, along with a gathering of mental and physical energy. After that, it was a matter of watching one's back at all times.

He had left Langley, Virginia, behind ten minutes ago, taking the Georgetown Pike east. About four miles down the turnpike he reached an interchange with the Capital Beltway, which took him across the densely tree-lined Potomac River on into Maryland.

Traffic was moderate. He followed Exit 38 north to the I-270, near the town of Rockville.

Bronx saw himself long ago, a young hothead in Aden, lobbing a bomb that he had made with his very own hands into a Yemenite Maoist gathering place. He felt the same arousal now.

The right choice of weapon was always a crucial factor. It had to be as natural as an extension of his own arm, so that there was no chance of even the slightest uncertainty jeopardizing his success at the moment of truth.

Twenty minutes later the navigation system alerted him that he was approaching Exit 18. Allowing the car to slow, he left the highway, shot a quick glance at the map, crossed Frederick Road, and continued toward the small town of Clarksburg. He was well within his schedule. Ahead was the gently rolling, tree-filled landscape of Little Bennet Regional Park. Golden, mowed fields gave way to the green meadows of Montgomery County, as he slowly entered a light forest resplendent in fall colors.

Bronx looked grimly determined as he checked his appearance with a cursory glance in the rear-view mirror. The corners of his mouth, cast in a sinister smirk, deep furrows on a brow above a prominent nose, generous eyebrows and, above all, his gray-blue, piercing eyes. All of that lent this somewhat stiff, middle-aged man a provocatively interesting appearance. Women often gave him quick looks of appraisal, mixed with a hint of admiration. Men envied him because, despite his rough appearance, or perhaps because of it, his seemingly natural charm won people over. These attributes were almost certainly among the reasons why his career had advanced with astonishing speed from well-versed field agent based in Hindu Kush to the upper echelons of the notorious Central Intelligence Agency. His rapid rise through the ranks was further aided by the fact that Bronx had neither wife nor children. Being, as he was, a confirmed bachelor and loner meant that he didn't need to concern himself with cumbersome family obligations.

A low wind from the northeast drove a few wispy strands of clouds across the treetops. Just before the rural road took a dip toward a river after about three miles, Bronx turned onto a narrow trail that lost itself between tall, silvery trunks. He drove ahead at walking pace until he reached a small clearing, found the spot, then reversed the dark blue Ford with Washington DC plates to stop next to a small, derelict shed.

Bronx had systematically gone over the variations of the kill even as he drove. Strangulation? Pretty clean, of course, but potentially problematic—a struggle could leave telltale signs. An explosive charge? Not enough time. Car bombs were best planted in parking structures. A staged car accident? He had immediately dismissed the idea with a contemptuous frown. It was absurdly complicated. So it was down to the firearm. A shot to the head was quick and final—brutal, yes, but in his line of work any sort of sensitivity was the beginning of the end.

Howard Young reached the meeting place, which was located some distance from the hiking trails and parking spaces, almost exactly on the minute. At first Bronx heard only the sound of an engine cutting off in the distance. Then silence. He stared intensely in the direction from which he expected his contact to appear.

"Hello?"

Bronx spun around. A slender young man with blond hair was coming toward him from behind, his gait confident. His expression was serious as he awkwardly fingered his tie, as if it was a bit too tight for comfort. Then his lips curled in an impish smile. It seemed he was proud of his little surprise.

Not as wet behind the ears as he looks, Bronx noted calmly.

"There are too many beech trees in this forest," the young CBP customs agent gave the code sentence. He raised a briefcase in front of his face, as if it were a lantern he was using to cast light on his CIA counterpart.

"Right, beeches deprive the saplings of light. Rick Bronx, CIA."

"Howard Young. Pleased to meet you, sir. Pretty desolate out here."

He squinted at his surroundings as if trying to make out enemy spies.

"Solitude is the agent's favorite bride," said Bronx in an assertive tone. "We're safe here, I know the area."

He got to the point. "You did some good work, Howard. Only, I wonder why you didn't find it necessary to inform your commissioner right away."

The Chief of Customs and Border Protection was an old dog little inclined to cooperate with the CIA. He considered the spooks at Langley to be a degenerate band of lawless snitches and licensed killers left over from the cold war. Consequently, Howard's answer came as no surprise to Bronx.

"You see, sir, I didn't even try. My boss has no fine-tuning when it comes to this sort of thing. His affinity for Secret Service operations is about as fervent as his love of cannibals. So I did what was necessary and created my own file. Here, sir, this is it."

Howard handed the CIA agent an oblong, yellow manila envelope, which he had extracted from his slender briefcase. Bronx hesitated for effect.

"And you think it's acceptable for these to fall into the hands of the CIA with no regard to official channels? Surely you've made a copy for the CBP archives?"

Howard put on a sorrowful face as he shook his head.

"The thing is, sir, our intelligence department leads a woeful existence. And changes are slow to come. So I figured the CIA had to be told before it's too late. You Langley folks know what needs to be done. Our people aren't interested in cooperating with yours; they'd rather sit on the information in the hope of some future glory."

Bronx seemed to be weighing Young's words. That Howard may have copied his information was a risk that he was going to have to take. On the other hand, he saw no hint of duplicity in the man's youthful face. And he was rarely mistaken in such matters.

"Tell me about it, Howard!" he said, the pleasure in his voice now genuine. "You're right—one of these days intelligence rivalries could lead this country into ruin. You did the right thing, coming to us."

"Thank you, sir. Can I count on your discretion? If our CBP people catch wind of this meeting, they'll hang me high."

Bronx liked the camaraderie in Young's tone. He put his hand on the man's shoulder in almost fatherly fashion.

"No worries, Howard. Not a soul will know. I'm silent by nature. You can count on me to be as tight-lipped as a clam."

Howard seemed relieved.

"You know, sir, the thing is I'm newly married and my wife and I are expecting our first baby in October. You understand, I can't afford to lose my job, so..."

Bronx took a step closer and looked directly into the young man's bright and guileless eyes.

"Howard, you can trust that I will remember your name. Langley isn't immune to change. Our organization is constantly adapting, particularly since measures to counter terrorism are becoming more important every day. People with your kind of initiative, the go-getters, have a bright future. Well, then!"

He grabbed Young's arm with both hands, squeezing his hand firmly as if to take his leave.

Howard stammered a few words of thanks, then couldn't help asking: "Sir—*hmm*—don't you want to see what's in it?"

Freeing himself of the older man's grasp, he motioned toward the envelope that Bronx had stuck under his elbow.

The CIA man nodded affirmatively a number of times, an appreciative smile appearing at the corners of his tense lips.

"Of course. Enormously interested, in fact. You mentioned the issuance of suspicious visas when we spoke on the phone. Not very cautious of you. Could anyone have been listening in? Who else have you mentioned this to?"

He carefully extracted the stack of papers from the envelope, stepping toward the dark, yawning entrance of the shed.

"Not a single word, sir," said Young, hastening to keep up. "I had to be careful. Our agency is full of intrigues, and..."

"Well done, Howard," Bronx praised as he wiped a sleeve across an old sawhorse, stirring a cloud of dust into the semidarkness.

"You'll...ahem...see, sir," Young coughed. "The visas were issued by our embassies in Saudi Arabia and Pakistan."

Bronx spread the papers on the moldering wood, his foot meeting with a hard object on the ground as he did so. Specks of dust danced like gnats in the ray of sun that fell through a narrow gap in the roof.

"These men are attending flight schools in Florida and California...," he heard Howard say as he bent to inspect the ground.

The wooden handle of an axe lay half-buried in caked earth and rotting foliage. The handle felt solid. It was firmly attached to the heavy iron blade. Rising, he casually leaned the handle against the sawhorse, then started scanning the documents.

"I was able to make one of them out," Young chatted innocently on.

Bronx could barely believe his eyes as he took in the explosive content of the document before him, illuminated by a thin, glaring sliver of light. His breath halted as he read, his hand slowly grasping the axe handle.

The basic question, one he routinely asked himself, was whether it would really be necessary to take that final step. And in this case, in these seconds, the answer was inescapably clear. Right now it was his head on the plate. Either him or me—this was Afghanistan all over again. Right now he could not afford to hesitate or waver!

"The name even appeared on an APB issued by the FBI," Young

continued. "They all entered the country without any difficulty. I think that surveillance would be wise, especially..."

Bronx's sharp gaze turned to the young agent.

"Yes? Especially *what*?"

"Especially because there are rumors of possible airplane hijackings making the rounds at our agency."

"Really? What have you heard?"

"The usual. Al Qaeda issued a threat that was broadcast by Al Jazeera. It was said that there would be a massive attack that would destroy the myth of American invincibility. None of our people are willing to pay attention."

"I understand," Bronx said quietly. He was now leaning on the hard wooden handle. Like a walking cane, it reached up to his waist where his 9mm Glock, safety mechanism disabled, sat securely in its holster.

"You're dead right, Howard. Langley has been looking into this theory for quite a while. I mean terrorist attacks here, on home soil. Suicide killers."

"So you don't think my informing you of these three visa cases is an overreaction? The details are all contained in the documents. You'll be amazed."

The look in Young's crystal blue eyes was tinged with more than a bit of enthusiasm and pride. Bronx nodded in assent. He didn't doubt what Young was saying for a moment. Young had no way of knowing the explosive effect that the occurrences he had stumbled upon would have on national security in the near future.

Bronx leaned forward. He seemed to be studying the papers intently. His hand held the axe in an iron grasp.

"Tell me, my friend, does your wife know where you went?"

Howard shook his head emphatically.

"I don't talk to Beth about work."

"Good. Very good," Bronx mumbled.

They were definitely alone. Only a sparse amount of light managed to make its way through the mighty crowns of the tall evergreens. The shade fostered copious undergrowth; joggers and hikers sought out paths in lighter areas, where they could enjoy the spectacle of foliage turning all shades of red and gold, sparkling streams, and the almost cloudless sky of a departing summer. Park attendants had no reason either to patrol the remote part of the forest that Bronx had chosen.

"I was wondering, sir, I mean professionally—how did you pick this spot for a meeting place?"

Bronx sensed a challenge behind the question. He straightened up.

"Routine, I guess. This location is outside UAV parameters."

"UAV?"

Howard looked curiously at Bronx, whose features now seemed extraordinarily harsh in the half-dark of the shed.

"Unmanned Aerial Vehicles. We employ them to protect sensitive targets. Their systems are on alert 24/7. Langley, Washington, D.C., Dulles Airport and their surroundings are all within the drones' deployment radius."

Howard made a slight involuntary ducking motion. He squinted through the shed door and up past the treetops.

"Forget it, Howard. Those things fly at such an altitude that you wouldn't be able to see them. That aside, there aren't any out here. We're safe. But if there were any around, they could read your license plate number. Even in the dead of night."

Bronx motioned with his hand.

"Let's go back."

As Young turned, Bronx grabbed the axe handle with both hands. As so often, he had reached his final decision on impulse.

"Thank you very much, sir," said Howard, as he preceded Bronx out of the shed, "I truly appreciate your trust."

Bronx hauled back with both arms. The blade of the heavy axe met the back of Young's blond head with disastrous force. The man keeled forward onto his knees, then crumbled without uttering a sound.

"Sorry, Howard," Bronx gasped.

In a fraction of a second the axe had split the cranium, divided the brain, permanently severed the nerves that gave rise to all perception, and killed Young's scream before it could leave his throat.

The killer dragged the lifeless body back to the shed by its feet. He surveyed his work, grunting as he looked at the gaping skull. He carefully wiped the axe handle with his handkerchief before going systematically through Young's pants and jacket, pocketing his car key. Neither clothing nor briefcase held any indicators that could be linked to the secret meeting. Howard's small Toyota was also clean. As a final measure, Bronx took the time to erase the route last taken by Young from the memory of the navigation system. He strode past a grouping of beeches on the way back to his car. Autumn's first dry leaves crackled between the gravel and his feet.

"Beeches deprive the saplings of light," he muttered under his breath. That had been the code.

He was suddenly overcome by a hoarse cackle at the thought of his choice of words. He had, indeed, been forced to fell a promising sapling. It was unfortunate. But things could have started to unravel. The big plan could not be allowed to fail. No matter the cost!

His breathing had already slowed down; his heart rate was, perhaps, still slightly elevated. Bronx lit a cigarette. His hands were steady. He was in no particular rush. A few minutes later, an inconspicuous, dark blue Ford made its way on to Route 123 north, crossing Little Bennet Creek.

Bronx then followed the Interstate 270 further north and back to Langley. He sought the comfort and privacy of his own office in order to study a woman's file. Leslie Palmer—one of those talented, overbearing women known in Washington as 'power swans.' She was hot, with—fortunately—a few less than benign weaknesses that, with his characteristic finesse, he would use to his advantage. Pictures of the shed, the axe, and Young's gaping skull flashed through his mind. That, too, was an act of finesse. He chuckled wryly to himself. But now this Palmer woman had moved to the top of his list.

02

Had Leslie Palmer known what awaited her over the coming weeks, she would probably not have bothered to get up and go to the office. She would have cancelled her appearance at the little theater, would have fled to somewhere safe. But she didn't know, of course. She started her day open to what might come, just as she usually did.

Leslie woke to the sound of howling sirens on the street below: an urgent staccato that climbed to a nerve-shattering crescendo, suddenly interrupted by the sputtering sound of a bass horn.

She stood up, her bare feet touching a fluffy, lime green carpet that felt like satin, walked slowly into the living room. It was large, with three wide windows that afforded a view of the street. A generous glass dining table surrounded by four armchairs looked inviting; she used it mainly to spread out books and magazines. She looked out of the window, absent-minded. A few people rushed along the broad sidewalk, a yellow cab turned onto the street and stopped for a moment, allowing a pack of greyhounds attached to a gaunt woman to cross to the other side. The noise subsided.

Almost eight! Realizing the time, Leslie hurried to the bathroom.

The sound of the sirens somehow lingered in her bones. Something disturbing lay in the air. Not that she was superstitious; she had a strong dislike of occult spells and black magic. It was just these premonitions that came to her as inevitably as the break of dawn. They crept upon her, sometimes raising her spirits, sometimes, like today, causing her to get lost in thought.

Her sixth sense had a lot to do with the illustrious career she had built for herself: a career that would soon take a dramatic turn.

After today nothing in her life would ever be the same as before. Her head had begun to throb gently. Signs? A warning?

She was unable to decipher their meaning, and would not have accepted it had it been revealed to her. No doubt she would have brusquely rejected the absurd notion that she would soon be entangled in a colossal, deadly conspiracy.

The living room telephone buzzed like an aggressive hornet. No caller ID, it turned out. She picked up hesitantly.

"Hello?"

Her boy's voice. Her heart sank.

"Mom, Craig. It's *me*... Hey, how're you doing? Can you send some money? Alex got himself in trouble."

Leslie held her breath. Her heart pounded in her chest. Please, dear God, don't let this be terrible news!

"... He got into a fight with some guy. He doesn't look too hot right now."

"Oh, for heaven's sake! Can't you two ever stay out of trouble?" Leslie's voice was raised in agitation. "Who was this guy? Are the police involved?"

"I don't think so. We haven't heard anything. It was kind of weird."

"Why?"

"Alex swears the guy had been following him for days. So can you send us some dough, just in case... I mean, in case Alex needs it. The guy will probably want to get paid."

Leslie understood. Her son was calling from Gstaad, Switzerland's answer to Aspen, where the rich and beautiful basked in the splendor of snow-covered mountains and glaciers, and grand chalets exuded their conservative charm.

"Listen, Craig, you're getting money from Monsieur Mercier, aren't you?" She said this in her soft, slow, Southern lilt.

"Mom, Alex doesn't want Paul to know."

She was impatient. She wanted to be at the office by nine at the latest. She had to rehearse the presentation for the chief negotiator at the United Nations. It was crucial that she gauge the Chinese statesman correctly.

Craig sounded tense.

"Mom? You still there?"

Leslie's breathing was more even now. But her maternal instinct still called for a firm reaction.

"Just a moment. So, your dear brother got into a fight. Is he hurt?"

"A shiner. Otherwise he's okay. But you should see the other guy."

"Alright. I want you to listen to me. Just wait and see what happens," she said, turning to her pragmatic side. "Keep me posted. If anything needs taking care of, I'll take care of it. But you'll need to call me later, I've got to run. And one more thing, Craig. Don't get yourselves into any more damn trouble!"

She ended the call irately. Her heart was still beating fast as she took the elevator downstairs. Its rhythm accompanied her across the street, past the movie theater and the café, to the corner of 68th Street, and down a narrow staircase to the subway.

Why had Craig even called about something so trivial? She knew her boys weren't that inept. Was there something they weren't telling her? Leslie tried to conjure soothing pictures of the Alpine landscape—the white peaks, the lush green lawn in front of Paul Mercier's Villa. The rattling and shaking of the subway wouldn't let her focus. She felt riddled by guilt. The twins needed her attention, not just financial handouts. On the other hand, they were very independent—brilliant students, great athletes. Leslie's heart grew warm as she thought of how handsome and dashing they were—her two sweethearts.

03

At nine that morning, the WTC Plaza appeared large, clean and light as always. The mighty Twin Towers stood so tall that, when viewed from a certain angle from below, they seemed to touch in the sky. In their shadows, droves of pedestrians crossed over from Wall Street and onto the square, with an occasional VIP limousine passing by. Soon a mass of tourists from all over America, Europe and Asia would be posing for souvenir shots, before crowding into the South Tower elevators. The view from the dizzying heights of the observation deck was intoxicating. Leslie had once stood up there with Alex and Craig. Together they had made out the restaurant under the Brooklyn Bridge, where they would be dining that night and looking back up at the top of the massive landmark they were looking down from.

She sighed. Something was bothering her as a limousine flashing a blue light glided to a stop. The fountain partially obstructed Leslie's view, but the person who exited and walked around to the other side of the vehicle was obviously eminent. A giant with the characteristic mannerisms of a professional bodyguard escorted her to the building entrances.

"...the First Lady...," she caught a snatch of comment. She tried to catch a glimpse of the familiar face as she stood patiently waiting her turn at the coffee stand, wondering all the while what might have brought the First Lady to the Towers at this early hour. A youthful, resonant voice coming from behind her interrupted her thoughts.

"Hey Leslie!"

She turned. Shelley from the Analysis Department was grinning down at her from his impressive six-foot-three frame.

"Ah, Shelley, good to see you."

She gave the avowed bachelor with the giant stature of a well-trained heavyweight athlete a warm smile. She read politely restrained desire in his dark eyes, which strayed to her breasts for just a moment too long. She saw no reason not to enjoy this unforeseen opportunity for a bit of flirtation.

"The First Lady, did you see?"

Shelley casually motioned with his head. Leslie took her coffee, put down some change. By the time she looked over, all she could see of the party was the limousine and its black chauffeur.

"So what's Provincial doing in the big city, I wonder?" Shelley scoffed, as he paid for his coffee. He placed his hand, gingerly, on Leslie's hip. "Shall we?"

"Probably doing some smart investing," Leslie ventured an airy guess.

"Watch out, the dame will probably end up paying us a visit," Shelley said, grinning. "Hey, you don't happen to have time for a drink, do you? After work?"

Leslie shrugged her shoulders in a noncommittal manner. Both in good spirits, they sauntered across the Plaza together. For no reason, she glanced up at the tops of the Towers, which seemed to be slicing through plump white clouds to make their way up into the blue sky. *Movement analysis is my life, Shelley,* she impulsively felt like calling out. But there was something off about this majestic picture. Something was in the air.

"Sure, Shelley. Anything's possible, right?"

With a smile, she pulled away from the charming analyst.

"See you later. I'm going to get my newspaper."

Premonitions were usually difficult to pin down, Leslie knew. They were elusive, with an unreal, dream-like quality. Their interpretation was all-too-often clear only once it was too late.

She pondered the possible meaning of the ominous feeling that had come over her. But then, the *Wall Street Journal* now clutched under her arm, she suddenly wanted to laugh about this seemingly random notion.

Watch out, the dame will probably end up paying us a visit, Shelley's remark echoed in her mind. And why not? Still wearing an amused smile, she entered WTC 7 moments later and took the discreetly swooshing express lift up to her floor.

Concern over Alex and Craig made a sudden reappearance. The boys were always up to something; however, thoughts of the safe haven of Switzerland always soothed her mind. She reassured herself with visions of her offspring lounging around on the terrace of Paul Mercier's dark old chalet: Craig dressed casually in knee-length shorts; Alex, the taller of the two, in tight jeans and a washed-out Polo shirt. She could see them standing there, tall and lanky, with their backs to the Alps, the sun silhouetting their ample blond hair. A pair of really smart kids—nineteen in October. The whole world at their feet. Leslie Palmer smiled, lost in thought... *Her boys*! She would have done anything for them. Absolutely anything...

04

White blinds in the 17th center conference room discreetly blocked the glare of the morning light reflecting off the silver façade of the gigantic North Tower, which loomed above the building in which Ms.

Palmer had been working for the past few years. Here, some two dozen people, predominantly men, patiently awaited the movement analyst. Leslie Palmer, meanwhile, had slunk unnoticed into the mailroom, where Danny sat, blissfully chewing on a juicy New York bagel.

"Danny, I have a plan and I need your help," she said in a conspiratorial whisper coupled with a naughty smile. His eyes grew large and he grinned.

"Sure thing, ma'am."

Leslie rummaged through the cloakroom, found what she was looking for, and disappeared into the ladies room—while her audience upstairs was beginning to grow restless. Ms. Palmer was always on time, her tardiness at half past ten this morning was peculiar. Someone was flipping through a newspaper. Shelley was casually telling someone else that he had seen the First Lady this morning. Yet another person interjected that she had often been seen around town lately.

Suddenly Danny from reception stood in the doorway, waving his hands dramatically. His long, well-groomed hair tossed wildly around his classic Asian features.

"The... the First Lady, the First Lady of the United States is here!"

An index finger held crooked and shaking in front of his chest, lips pressed together tensely, suggested imminent catastrophe.

Those waiting stared blankly at the clown. Someone laughed.

"Quit messing around, Fung Ku!"

Another burst out: "Screw the Frost Lady!"

And, just then, she appeared, where Danny had stood. Her neck arched in typical manner, her features taught. "Who said that?" she asked coldly.

The agency director stammered, completely beside himself.

"It's... Are you... *you?*"

It was her, alright. No doubt about it. The men in the room bolted to their feet, some stealing incredulous glances at each other. The wife of the president of the United States walked confidently into the briefing room, her stern gaze making every one of them feel like the culprit.

"I'm waiting. Who said that?"

The group joker was the first to crumble.

"Bill Clinton, ma'am?"

The First Lady stepped up amid the suppressed laughter and turned to the director. "Mr. Wagner, sir," she said sternly, "I am led to understand that your department is over budget."

The man addressed looked as if he had just been struck by lightning. He finally found his voice to make an attempt at a gallant recovery: "Well, er, allow me to say that we are extremely honored by your presence. Welcome to the Navy Intelligence Agency."

"Don't try to change the subject, Wagner," the First Lady responded tartly. "It has come to my attention that you have an extremely competent woman by the name of Leslie Palmer working for you. Is she present? I do hope that you intend to give this talented lady a raise in pay?"

"I will certainly consider it, ma'am," Wagner answered, confused, "but, if you will allow me..."

The First Lady interrupted him rudely.

"I certainly hope so, or you can count on me to personally hand you your balls. *Sir!*"

The men stood dazed for a moment. The silence was broken only by the buzzing of some decrepit computer at the far end of the room. Shelley alone was leaning back with a serene smile. When Leslie sensed that the men were starting to realize what was going on, she pulled the wig off her head with both hands, laughing heartily.

"Okay people, just a little diversion. You have just seen a demonstration, gentlemen, of the power of gestures and appearances. Which also happens to be the topic of our meeting today."

She strode to the lectern and started to make adjustments to the overhead projector, a triumphant smile on her face.

Everyone was still acting a bit shell shocked. Only Shelley offered some glib praise: "Well done, Leslie, that was first class! By the way, rumor has it that Clinton actually did say *'Screw the Frost Lady'* when Hillary found out about the Monica Lewinsky cigar incident."

Leslie deflected the salacious comment with a superior smile.

"Men!" she sighed, then got straight to her topic:

"The Chinese president, gentlemen"—she pointed to the projected picture behind her—"has a number of notable weaknesses, which we should be able to take advantage of during negotiations."

Her colleagues had still not quite recovered.

"Any ideas what I'm talking about?" she asked, in order to get them involved.

"Arrogance?" Shelley suggested.

Leslie shook her head.

"That's not a weakness, Shelley. Just an expression of exaggerated confidence."

"The man is not capable of listening," she said after a moment of silence. "You will need to tell him what you want to tell him in no more than two sentences. Limit yourself to independent clauses if possible. Have exactly what you want to say neatly arranged in your head. Put as little as possible on paper."

"How do you gather that?" asked someone from the State Department.

She nodded to her audience, looking to see if anyone wanted to venture an answer. When nobody did, she started a video recording.

"Look at his hands," she instructed. "He has them both on the table. Now he is raising his fingers to show his palms. See?"

"Like a shield," Wagner suggested.

"Exactly. And now watch: shield up, shield down, and then back up again. The man is not open to being told anything. What does that tell us?"

"He plays with facts and emotions. He can go from harp to slingshot, so to speak."

"Not bad, Shelley," Leslie praised. "The man is repressed. The right environment, the Chinese Gardens for instance, will literally help to loosen his physiological and psychological armor."

"What makes you say that?" an intelligence analyst asked incredulously.

"Wait and see."

She started a film sequence in which the Chinese statesman approached a group of women.

"The man is a hugger—someone who wants to draw everything in," she explained while her audience concentrated on the scene being shown. "This head of state craves recognition. He wants to feel that he is loved. So go heavy on the harp."

"Recognition?" an African American man said. "He's number one already. He has everything!"

"Wrong," Leslie disagreed. "Our president has everything, too. But he still wants recognition. He wants to hear that the speech was great, the initiative was well received, his jokes during dinner were funny, and so on. See how Mr. Epicanthus can hardly keep his arms still?"

"Epicanthus... *what?*" interjected a stern-looking career woman.

"The epicanthus is the characteristic Asian eye-fold. That would be 'slant-eye' in the vernacular."

Her wit was rewarded with laughter.

"It's true," the State Department guy marveled, "about his arms."

Leslie mimicked the shielding hand motion.

"So, remember to surprise him with a familiar environment, and with people who admire him."

"Not so damn easy," Wagner grumbled.

"But not impossible. And don't forget: he wants to embrace everything. I mean that in a geopolitical sense."

"You're thinking Taiwan? An offensive move?"

Leslie shook her head.

"I'm thinking India and Iran. I believe that China wants to consolidate bilateral relations with Iran, to compete for our position. I read all of this from his body language."

She rewound the film, showed a few more key scenes. A lively conversation about body language ensued. Time passed quickly.

"Let's take a break," the agency director decided after about an hour.

Danny from reception wheeled in a coffee cart. He gave Leslie a conspiratorial wink. Talk of her success as a double now dominated the conversation, as the group gathered around the coffee with their paper cups. Shelley complimented her: "You and the First Lady really are almost identical. I can't believe I hadn't noticed."

Leslie fluttered her eyelashes theatrically.

"I think that the real First Lady is not publicly present enough. This means that she cannot evolve into an object of desire, like some adored movie star. The truth is, you don't actually know what she looks like. It's easy to explain, psychologically speaking."

Shelley nodded thoughtfully.

"Make-up and hairstyle add a lot. I am similar to her in type, but I don't want to look like her."

She drew her hand across her face, as if wanting to erase the other woman's image.

Wagner wanted to know if her performance today had been improvised. He offered her a cup of steaming coffee.

"Sugar? Have you ever acted on stage?"

"Thank you, no. You mean because of the First Lady bit? I did imitate her on stage once, just for fun."

Shelley was curious: "So, not only can you imitate, but you can read physical expressions and body movements to draw conclusions about a person's inner being?"

"Exactly. My love of dance turned into what I now call my career. The psychology of movement. Analysis of gestures and human motion."

She halved a large croissant.

"Here's an interesting fact: President Reagan was among the first to use these tools during his term in office."

She took a bite. She knew she had their attention.

"It was during the eighties, when NATO was stocking up on cruise missiles. Gorbachev traveled to Geneva to get Reagan to back down. The president's staff assigned Uri Geller, the parapsychologist, with keeping a close eye on the Russians during the negotiating process."

She took a sip of her coffee. The façade of the North Tower shimmered in the mid-morning sun. It was going to be one of the hottest late summer days according to weathermen across the stations.

"Geller gave our people some very useful tips. He also claimed to have bombarded the Soviets with positive thoughts."

Wagner assumed an innocent expression.

"Were you serious about the raise?"

"Well, it does seem to be the First Lady's personal wish..."

Everyone laughed as she pointedly raised her eyebrows.

When the conference ended a short while later, Leslie cleaned up and returned to her bright corner office.

She called Switzerland again, then spent the next hour and a half sorting through mail, magazines, and memos from other departments. She issued a check to the name of Craig Palmer. Her work instruments consisted of three large monitors, all in a neat row, and two television sets equipped with hard drives.

The middle screen showed the Chinese head of state standing on a junk, a classic Chinese vessel, in front of an enormous dam. Leslie played the sequences back and forth as she examined his body language. First his hands, then his arms, and the way he held his head. Torso involvement, the posture of his shoulders, the movement of his legs.... She hardly noticed time passing by as she entered notes on the appropriate computer. The digital clock clicked to noon. Normally it would have been time for lunch. She leaned back with a contented sigh.

She was in a better mood now than she had been this morning. Everything was more or less as it should be. Alex had called from Switzerland, where he was studying at the acclaimed École Polytechnique Fédérale de Lausanne. He had downplayed the disturbing brawl. The plan was for both of her sons to be in New York over the holidays. Was it the thought of Christmas that had put Leslie in a dark mood, or even the thought of her twin sons? She shook her head, unsure.

A short while ago she would have given anything for a nice, steady relationship. It was certainly easier said than done. "My girl," her father had recently joked, "you need a man with intelligence, a man with money, a man with...Actually, it would be nice if you could find one with all three." He had winked roguishly, as if he considered himself to be the last of this rare breed. Leslie believed it, too. It was hard to pry herself loose from the opposite sex. Had it been up to her, she would have had a man at every fingertip. She needed men like she needed oxygen. She wanted to be the focal point of desire; a lion tamer bidding her will to the animals on her leash.

And then this Ben had, almost literally, fallen into her lap from out of the blue. He should be here any minute now. Leslie felt the excitement mount in every fiber of her youthful body. Had she completely lost her mind? Or was she just a healthy, passionate, middle-aged woman?

Down on the plaza a homeless man pushed a stolen shopping cart that was hung with three bags bloated with empty cans and bottles, like a grown child pushing his dolls. An old transistor radio played a tinny song.

Ben Heller tugged at the waistband of his casual pants and looked up to the windows behind which he knew Ms. Palmer waiting in eager anticipation.

05

Ben happened to be a piano virtuoso, and he was just as versed in specialized computer software. Leslie frequently found herself annoyed over junk mail, which she tended to innocently open when it contained deceitful references, such as *Craig* and *Alex,* in the subject line.

"Let me have a look," Ben suggested.

"It's always nice to watch," she whispered in his ear.

Now he was tapping away on her keyboard.

"Strange," he said ponderously. "Someone wants to stick you with a Trojan. Now, who would want to do a thing like that?"

She leaned on his broad shoulders. Without waiting for an answer, he put his memory stick into the port.

"I'm downloading my special software. If anyone hassles you again, just let me know. My program will find the swine."

"Synxx," Leslie read. She brushed her lips lightly against the nape of his neck.

"What does it do?"

"You'll see. It's a user application that enables you to place free phone calls via the Internet."

He lowered his voice.

"You have to keep this strictly confidential. This program is going to spread like wildfire, because it's very attractive. Who doesn't want to make free phone calls? What users don't know is that they will be giving Synxx automatic access to their servers. It's simple and ingenious. The codes are encrypted to U.S. federal security standards."

"Is that legal?"

He shook his head.

"Illegal, but extremely useful. We are working under orders of..."

He stopped.

"Doesn't matter. At any rate—call me if you're being bothered, or shall we say, if you want to practice retribution. My program will access other people's computers as sure as Casanova spread women's legs."

"I love your program," she said with a smile, although she didn't understand exactly what he was getting at. *Retribution?*

Leslie wasn't really in the mood for computer technology chatter. Her lunch break was limited, and so when Ben showed signs of wanting to start in on further minutiae, she pressed her fingers on his lips. Then she took him by the belt, pulled him into the old, unused newsroom and locked the door from the inside. Ben had been a lucky catch. Not just because he developed hypersensitive offline surveillance software for Synxx, but also—and especially—because he allowed her to experience greater passion than she had ever felt.

A large, old oak conference table, dimly lit by an ancient green lamp, was the only piece of furniture. Dusty blinds kept all outside light from penetrating the mysterious room. Once a long row of telex machines had lined its walls, spitting out a constant stream of data from the carrier groups all over the world.

Her meeting Ben had to do with the fact that she liked to jog, and that she had a habit of stretching afterwards. She innocently chose to overlook that her skin-tight, red workout shorts, which had an inner seam of all of two inches at most, tended to draw more than just passing attention from any virile man who happened to be in the vicinity at the time.

It had been a pleasant Sunday morning in the park, around nine a.m. Leslie had run her laps and was capering down the few steps that led from the old reservoir building to the planks of the wooden bridge.

The sun was painting bright spots on the well-worn wood, a clear blue sky spread over the tall sycamores. Two equestrians rode along the sand track under the bridge; one of the horses whinnied. Other than that, all sounds were far off and muted.

What an incredible morning! Leslie took a deep breath before she gracefully lifted a slender leg onto the iron railing, stretching her arms toward the tip of her running shoe. After a certain amount of time—she had the slightly eccentric habit of counting: curbstones, steps, seconds—she switched sides to stretch the other leg. This was when she first caught sight of Ben, his sinuous body stretching against the rail at an almost right angle. His dark blond, curly head lay against the metal, as if he had put it there to rest. The man grinned broadly at her, unabashedly displaying his pleasure at the sight of her tight, red shorts.

She returned a mechanical smile, really little more than a twitch of the corners of her mouth. It was the slightly disdainful kind of smile that smart women often display when they want to drive their suitors half out of their minds.

"Hey," he said.

"Hey," she replied, bending her right leg and pressing her heel to her behind.

Not bad... Not bad at all, she thought to herself with a hint of insolence. I hope he doesn't spoil the picture when he opens that pretty mouth again...

She called it her lunch position. It was pretty risky to consume her sweet lunch in the middle of a business day, with her colleagues just on the other side of the door. But she just couldn't get enough of him. He was young, beautiful, and insatiable. His mess of blond hair, full lips, and deep blue, innocent looking eyes drove Leslie crazy.

The lunch position. Just the thought of it sent a rush of blood to her thighs. There was little time. She roughly tugged up her skirt, pressed against him. His lips passionately met hers. His hands groped her thighs, tore down her panties. She panted shamelessly.

"Got it out already? I want you to give it to me... I want you... *now!*"

She threw herself, freely, back onto the table. The feel of the cool wood on her hot, bare behind added to her excitement. She leaned up on her elbows, wanting to watch, no, *having* to watch. It turned her on beyond belief to see him entering her with his superb dick—almost painfully slow, as she had taught him—then hard and deep, then teasing her again, with his tip. Then that deep, pounding rhythm. It was almost more than she could bear.

"Red suits you," he had said back then, in Central Park, and then added with a grin. "What else could I possibly say, from this vantage point?"

She had to admit that his direct approach had caught her off guard. With a provocative look she sized up the man, who had now drawn himself up to his full stature.

"It sounds like you want to invite me to something? Brunch?"

"I'd love to. I live on 67th Street. We can meet at . . . at . . ."

He couldn't think of the name of the restaurant, so Leslie suggested a popular brunch place on Columbus, on the other side of the park. Before they parted ways on the bridge, she pointed to his legs.

"You didn't really stretch, Ben."

He looked somewhat perplexed.

"How come . . . why do you want to know that?"

"Your true intentions speak through your body. And your intentions, my friend, were commanding you to be straight and stiff, not limber and supple. I know my way around body language. See you later!"

And with that, she left him standing there.

Later, after brunch, Ben insisted on showing her his grand piano, hitting a bull's-eye in terms of arousing her curiosity.

"I have to get back," she breathed into the old, bare newsroom.

He had gently withdrawn and was now looking down at her with deep desire. She stroked her breasts, then suggestively moved her palms down her stomach, on to the insides of her thighs. She opened her mouth slightly and let the tip of her tongue glide around her wet, shining lips. In one smooth motion reminiscent of flowing silk, she turned on her stomach. Ben had only a moment to admire her flawless body from this perspective, then she arched her small, tight ass up toward him and commanded him, in a quiet, dark voice, to take her. Now. He obeyed, following her order silently, slowly pushing his hard member into that tight, dark place. The beautiful woman beneath him uttered a guttural, sensuous moan; a sound that was ageless and timeless, that made Ben involuntarily catch his breath.

She felt his strong, steady hands firmly grasping her hips, just like he had after brunch, when he had played so enchantingly for her, his fingers moving effortlessly across the keys, gently summoning a waltz by Chopin. The romantic music had roused her desire, had made her deepest wishes sway, as hypnotized, to the sound. Her senses had been adrift, the gentle motions of his body had promised complete fulfillment. Her soul had given itself unconditionally to his music. She had taken off her blouse, pulled her skirt up, and drifted across the parquet floor to the rhythm, eyes closed, light as a feather... There were things in her life that had left an indelible mark on her. Like that piece: Chopin, Opus 34, number 1...

They were both exhausted now. He pulled her close and stroked her cheek.

"Leslie, Leslie... you... are so exquisite!"

He looked at her, in the wake of their passionate lovemaking, and saw a wild spirit. No—a beautiful wild animal. *His* animal!

She slid off the table, stood unsteadily for a moment, and smoothed her clothes. Then she carefully opened the door, just a crack.

06

Ms. Palmer was in high spirits that evening as she exited the subway at Hunter College. Then she crossed 68th Street and saw a man standing in the entrance to a clothing store. He seemed to be looking at her, a grim expression on his face. There wouldn't normally be reason for someone to be skulking in an entryway like that, unless it was raining. Leslie began feeling ill at ease.

She cast her eyes down and stepped up her pace as she crossed the pedestrian crossing, heading for Third Avenue. Her apartment was just a few blocks away, and it was still broad daylight, the sky clear blue.

She sensed that the man was following her, and began walking even faster.

"Excuse me, do you have a moment?"

It really was the guy from the store. He was wearing an ill-fitting, shabby brown suit. Leslie hurried on.

"I work for the government."

He pulled out an ID badge to convince her. Leslie took in his repulsive green tie, his posture, all at a glance. Something was off about the way he was moving his arms.

"What?" she snapped, not slowing her pace.

He showed his ID again. That was it! He was holding his hand like someone begging on a street corner. Why wasn't he holding the badge at eye level?

She had almost reached the corner. She rebuked him, harshly.

"Anyone can say that. Back off!"

The guy finally came to a stop. A taxi repeatedly blared its horn. When she looked back, she no longer saw him. She felt relieved as she walked up the few stairs that led to the entrance of her apartment building.

Making a cheap pass, she thought to herself, annoyed, as she unlocked the door. But in truth she wasn't entirely convinced by her own explanation.

Leslie's apartment on the third floor faced south. She stepped up to one of the tall windows, pulled the lace curtains aside, and peeked over to the street corner. People were streaming from all directions. There was no sight of anyone wearing a brown suit.

She undressed, stepped into the tub and turned on the shower. Her thoughts drifted. She saw herself in Ben's embrace, laughed quietly about her little stunt, flashed back on her amorous tête-à-tête in the Navy newsroom, thought with concern about her sons in Switzerland. She didn't hear the phone immediately. Its ring didn't startle her until she was already standing at her dressing table, appraising her well-trained body. *Craig and Alex*! It was already approaching midnight in Switzerland. She hurriedly wrapped the towel around herself, ran into the living room and eagerly snatched the receiver.

"Hello!?"

Not her children, unfortunately.

"Mrs. Palmer, it is imperative that I speak to you. I'm with the government."

Leslie caught her breath: "So you've said."

"Listen! Mr. Charles J. Palmer is your father. Is that correct?"

Leslie was suddenly wide awake.

"He is. What about him?"

"Well, that's what I want to speak to you about, in private," said the mysterious voice at the other end of the line.

"And I want you to leave me alone!"

She hung up. Another cheap pass! Then she nervously dialed a number. Could something be wrong with her father? Something to do with Vietnam? Had his research led him to some sort of military secret? Some atrocity? One never knew. She let the phone ring ten times. No answer.

Half an hour later the doorbell rang, startling her. She wasn't expecting anybody. But it was only the Chinese delivery boy bringing dinner. Leslie breathed a sigh of relief.

07

Riding up in the South Tower express elevator on her way to a meeting with Steinberg, she had already all but forgotten the incident with the would-be government official. The filthy rich, handsome tycoon's offices strangely occupied the fifty-sixth floor of the WTC. Certainly not the most prime location. All of eighteen stories of Morgan Stanley and Dow Jones towered above Steinberg & Friedman. But there were whispers that the slightly chubby real estate agent wasn't overly fond of heights, which is why he mainly dealt in luxury co-op apartments on Park Avenue, between 60th and 90th Streets: the so-called Gold Coast.

"You should go into politics, Leslie."

He had invited her to take a seat on an elegant Italian designer couch in his corner office.

"Thank you," she answered politely but almost curtly. "I work for the government. That's quite enough for me."

"The point is, you can assess the President like no one else in the nation."

He put his feet up on the valuable antique salon table, a gesture inviting her to do the same. She looked at him questioningly.

"So, Mr. Steinberg, what are you getting at?"

"Spike. My friends call me Spike," he said amiably. Just for a moment he stared at her knees, which were not covered by her tight skirt. "I would like to invite you to our convention."

"Convention?"

"The Democratic National Convention."

"And what business might I have there?"

He reached for a paper lying next to him on the couch, cast a glance at it.

"You were a brilliant professor. A real steel magnolia. Your voice still carries a lot of weight."

"Well, Spike, my parents always taught me to do things right." She caught herself speaking with a certain buoyancy in her voice—*a pretty nice guy, this Spike.* "They always thought very strategically. They wanted me to excel at everything I did, be well prepared, and hold my own as a woman in a man's world. They did a very good job."

There was a pause. Spike's smile was a little strained as he repeated himself.

"You know the President."

She moved her shoulders. Spike didn't need to know that she knew the First Lady even better. She had invited Leslie to the White House at the beginning of the year.

"We want you to run a couple of analyses for us, you understand?"

Leslie raised her brows. She didn't understand much at all yet.

His index finger pointed through the window in the direction of Leslie's staff unit on the twelfth story of the neighboring building.

"I know what you do over there. You are an expert in body language. You are able to read aggression, detect weaknesses, and devise communication strategies, all by reading the posture and gestures of your subjects. Right?"

Leslie motioned her head in a manner suggesting deliberation; as if she were considering the grammatical correctness of his statement.

"It is true that part of my work deals with analyzing heads of state negotiating with the United States."

Spike's voice rose with excitement.

"Right, exactly. We want to open the American public's eyes to just how ambivalent and impulsive he is."

"Who?"

"The President."

"Oh... well... *Spike,* you are aware that I earn my living working for Marine intelligence. The president that you would like to have me disassemble is my commander in chief!"

The way Spike pursed his lips and moved the corners of his mouth, he almost seemed to be savoring her objection. His face was soft and personable. Leslie was the kind of woman who was always, at least subconsciously, on the lookout for good men. Her eyes fell on his strong thighs. His masculine sensuality distracted her a little, just for a moment. Spike made a new attempt.

"Perhaps I was being too pointed. What we are looking for is a behavioral study. We want answers to questions like: does the President believe in what he says? Are his statements genuine? Is he spinning us?"

"And I am quite sure I know what your opinion is," Leslie interrupted him sharply. His grin seemed unconcerned.

"My bias, perhaps, but at least it is an actual opinion."

"Mmm, and you want me to supply you with the ammunition you need?"

"No," Spike said, his face now more serious, "we want to credibly counter the puppets of the mass media."

"I quite understand what you're saying. But you can count me out."

"Leslie, please. You have access to a ton of analytically relevant material. Footage of television appearances, his speeches, campaign reports, visits abroad—almost everything imaginable."

"He's been abroad?"

Spike shot her an appreciatively amused glance.

"And I hear that you also have plenty of footage on the First Lady. Why, if I may ask?"

"Who told you this?"

"You see, Leslie, your boss, Martin Wagner, is actually on board with the idea. As long as it's off duty. I have spoken to him."

She shook her head emphatically.

"But the fact is that I am always on Marine duty."

Spike motioned as if to brush her misgivings aside.

"Martin would be happy to give you a little time-out."

Leslie had been playing it cool. In truth she had no inkling about any plans for a scientific hiatus.

"Martin reckons if you were to go without pay—if you were no longer under his command, or that of the commander in chief…"

Acting indignant was not hard for her at this point.

"So Wagner is in on this? What is going on here?"

"Martin and I are old pals. He won't get actively involved, but he supports my idea."

She shook her head emphatically.

"Next you are going to tell me you pay well. At least twice as much, I presume?"

"Well caught, Madam. Yes, my company will pay you—*three* times as much, in fact. It is pure commission work. No conflict of interest and we protect our source by all means necessary."

Leslie swallowed a few times. She got up and walked to the window, feeling Spike's eyes on her curves. Events in her life seemed to be spinning out of control. She turned back to face him.

"Did Martin tell you *everything*?"

"What do you mean?"

"I mean my sons. I mean that I have been thinking of bowing out of the service in order to devote more time to them. Did you know that?"

She hung her head. "I have neglected them. I'm afraid I've been a terrible mother."

When their eyes met again, she knew he was not lying when he said that he had had no idea.

"Are your boys at school here?"

"No, at a boarding school in Switzerland."

He had walked to where she stood, and now placed a hand on her arm. His lips were tensed, as if concentrating on the next step.

Leslie gave herself a jolt and made a motion toward the door. She had no idea how she was going to handle her future. Her research was not progressing, her work for the government had become routine, she lacked a mature, reliable man in her life, and she constantly struggled with the guilt of abandoning her sons at a crucial phase of their development.

Spike had moved with her, and she could not deny a powerful energy. She felt the urge to throw her body against his; to unite their magnetic fields. As if he had read her like an open book, he spread his arms, temptingly.

"Sleep on it, Leslie, we'll pick this up..." he hesitated, obviously unsure, "...when I'm back from California. I'm picking up my new jet. A nice little bird, if I say so myself."

He walked over to his desk and leaned over his laptop.

"Does the ninth of September sound good?" he asked. "Here in my office? Steinberg & Friedman, the fifty-sixth floor?"

She shook her head. She knew that her calendar was marked for a conference in Newport News that day.

"The tenth?"

"No. Busy, too. But I'm open on the eleventh."

Spike studied his electronic calendar, stroking his smoothly shaven chin.

"9/11 it is. Shall we say for a morning cup of coffee? Is eight thirty too early?"

She laughed for the first time.

"Please, sir. I work for the Navy."

It was a deal. A week would allow her to gain some clarity. She would be on more solid ground. She was sure that accepting his offer would not be an actual possibility; but it couldn't hurt to talk about it. Spike was nice, and she found him very attractive. Hell, he owned a private jet. If that wasn't sexy, then what was? The elegant man in his mid-forties accompanied her past employee offices that were arranged like shoeboxes, to the elevator hall.

As the elevator door opened to reveal a dozen indifferently staring faces, Spike skillfully pulled out the last little card he still had up his sleeve.

"By the way, are your still interested in that West Side apartment?"

She stopped abruptly and stared at him.

The elevator door jarred against her hip. *Of course she was; and how!* The tenant committee had been in the process of rejecting her application, or had now probably already done so.

"How do *you* know about *that*?"

Her tone was exasperated. He may as well have asked her about the details of her monthly cycle. He gestured vaguely.

"Oh, I happen to know the chair of the tenant committee. You know how it goes. They're always looking for reasons to reject people…"

He faltered—half the people in the elevator were now staring at him with open hostility. He gently pulled her away from the elevator door, back into the hall.

Leslie protested: "I gave the board my complete CV, the interview went well, I have no pets, I certainly don't throw any wild parties. I'm a single mother…"

"And then there was the question of your line of work?" He said this in a teasing imitation of her tone.

She nodded repeatedly. He raised his left hand, setting out to explain.

"Exactly. These narrow-minded folks think you are a Secret Service agent. It makes them nervous to think they may have a snoop in the building, you understand? A good reason to say *Nyet*."

She snorted in disgust, marched over to the door marked by a lighted green sign indicating the way to the stairs. Her eyes fixed on the black silhouette of a walking person. For a moment she was tempted to follow its lead, head straight for the emergency exit and run blindly down the stairs.

"Come on, Leslie. I can offer the committee a guarantee. Only if you want, of course. I really think the apartment is one of the better ones, and the price has come down."

Leslie saw her chance. Why not! She had waited for two years—done everything she could to get her hands on the four-room apartment that overlooked the park.

Another elevator arrived.

"Okay, we'll talk about it when you get back. Honestly, this was a lot to digest for one day."

"I'll see you on the eleventh, then!" He called as the elevator door slid shut behind her, closing on the image of his warm smile. It was a smile that was still very much with her as she stepped onto the plaza outside, and later, as she exited the subway and crossed Columbus Avenue, strolling past clothing stores and beauty parlors on the way to the park entrance. This was just what she needed—a mature, reliable, filthy rich man with a promising smile.

08

The amateur stage of the *Much Ado about Nothing* theater-lovers group was situated in an old apartment block on SoHo's West Broadway that once housed a somber Salvation Army meeting hall. The high-ceilinged room on the first floor contained about fifteen tightly packed rows of chairs that were filled but for two, shortly before the beginning of the performance. A man in a sports jacket without a tie, wearing a baseball cap, had taken a seat all the way in the back. When a couple gave him a friendly greeting before sitting down next to him, his face remained dour. The lights went down shortly thereafter. A grand crescendo of music swelled and swept over the waiting audience as the curtains opened ceremoniously.

A lanky man seated behind the grand piano lowered his head and began to rhythmically pound on the keys.

It was a modern piece, supposedly written by some Miller. Arthur or Henry. The unshaven spectator with the baseball cap couldn't have cared less.

Fortunately for him, the piece rapidly progressed in just three acts. A pretty dumb play, it seemed to him. But then he was pretty ignorant, culturally speaking. The only type of art that he knew anything about was martial. The leading actress alone was of any interest to him this evening. She was the only reason that he had come out here and grudgingly sat himself down in the back row. A complete waste of time. She was playing the role of a mother who hovered over her daughter like a hawk. The manner in which she transformed herself into a would-be female rival to test the faithfulness of her daughter's fiancé required sophisticated acting. The fiancé, played by the lanky piano man, was unable to resist temptation and threw himself at the other woman like a two-timing rat. It was all lost on the guy in the back row.

The one thing he did notice was that the pianist kissed the lead actress with a fervor that suggested they were not just lovers on stage.

For just a moment the spectator was cast into the role of voyeur, and was overcome by a sweetish stirring that did not fit in with his usual, cold-blooded temperament. He found himself distracted by passion and jealous craving.

For Leslie Palmer the stage in this former branch meeting place was a natural sequel to her previously hotly pursued passion for acting. But tonight she felt that her engagement here was slowly but surely growing to be too much for her. She also felt that her diction was no good tonight, but she simply had no time to devote to taking up speech training again. Given the choice, she would rather go back to dancing. She was determined to inform the director of her decision tonight: *Fred, you know how demanding my job is*... Pathetic! *Fred, I'm quitting. I need you to accept my decision.*

The audience gave a standing ovation. Way in the back a man pushed his way toward the exit.

"Can we talk, Ms. Palmer?"

"No interviews," she said curtly. "Fred is our spokesperson." She turned to leave, but the man was not giving up.

"This isn't about the theater."

She turned, surprised.

"Why . . . ? Oh. It's you! What do you want from me? Are you stalking me?"

She had spoken loudly; heads were turning. Uncomfortable, she searched for Fred. The man in the sports jacket and cap leaned over. She felt his breath.

"I'm CIA."

"So what? Do you have something you want to accuse me of?"

Leslie's indignant voice had risen; people passing began to stop in their tracks.

"Not here, please," the CIA man appealed, then whispered hoarsely, "Everything is fine. Your sons, Alex and Craig, are doing great in Switzerland."

Leslie froze. She stared in disbelief at the man in the stupid cap, with two days of stubble on his face. Her mouth half-open, she slowly began shaking her head. *Her sons? Something as intimate to her as her family—it was outrageous!*

She grudgingly followed him to the edge of the sidewalk, next to a black Explorer with tinted windows.

"Special agent, CIA." Again he flashed his badge. "Call me Bob."

She had to laugh. It sounded unnatural, even to her.

"*What the hell is wrong with you*? Are you spying on my sons?"

"Simmer down, Ms. Palmer," Bob said calmly. "Our intentions are completely harmless. Get in. I'll drive you home."

Skeptically, Leslie tried to squint through the four-wheeler's darkened windows into its roomy interior.

"Leslie, is everything alright?" A tall man with a white shock of hair and sharp features wanted to know from the top of the stairs. He looked down appraisingly at the vehicle. "You're going already?"

She waved at him, smiling.

"Thanks, Fred. I'm good. No worries. Really, thanks a lot. I'll see you for rehearsals."

The man who called himself Bob opened the passenger door for her with feigned gallantry.

"You're pretty hard-headed," he grinned.

Her sons in mind, Leslie got in.

"Unfortunately I wasn't allowed to contact you openly," Bob explained as he got behind the wheel. The starting engine swallowed something that sounded like *"strictly classified."* The man slowly eased off the brakes.

"We know that you started working on a Secret Service program at the beginning of this year, Ms. Palmer. We want to suggest that you take on a similar job for our agency now, in the nation's interest."

He examined her from the side, then looked in the side mirror as he calmly maneuvered out of the parking space.

"I have a job. Thank you," she said, irritated.

"I know. We can fix that." The Explorer pulled into traffic.

"Your work for the War College won't suffer. Everything has been discussed with your director."

"Then he knows way more than I do. That's just wonderful," Leslie said, a sarcastic edge to her voice.

She felt that she had sounded uncertain and defensive. She rarely resorted to cynicism. The guy who called himself Bob was suddenly acting embarrassed.

"No, no. Not really. Wagner hasn't been briefed on any details, of course. As I said, the assignment is strictly classified, which is the reason for us contacting you like this."

Leslie's demeanor switched to sharply condescending.

"So, what do you want? Don't they teach you to ever get to the point, up at Langley?"

Bob steered the Explorer easily past pedestrians and double-parked cars.

"You practiced as a double for the First Lady. We want you to continue this job, under my supervision."

His eyes were fixed on the road. Traffic on Houston Street was denser now. He directed the car onto the lane headed for the FDR Drive, which would take them along the East River. Leslie realized that her hands were shaking.

"What's the catch? Why the CIA?"

He stopped for a red light. Light from a brightly illuminated façade entered the car and fell onto a white envelope on the center console. A letter. He looked up, waiting for the light to change, casually waving toward the envelope with his right.

"National Security."

As a matter of habit, Leslie took a closer look at the envelope and registered the address that was printed on it: Mrs. Amira al Raisi, Dushanbe. The writing was clearly legible. The return address on the upper left corner read Rick Bronx, 178 Braodway, Brooklyn, N.Y. 11211.

Leslie was facing stiffly forward, but her eyes were straining to take in every detail of the envelope: *Du-shan-be. Rick Bronx... Braodway... typing error.*

The light turned green. The car took off; the letter slid back. Bob reflexively caught it, without seeming to take his eyes off the road. He stuck it into the compartment on the driver's door.

Leslie pointedly directed her gaze up at the passing buildings. *Amira al Raisi.* A lovely name; almost lyrical. *Was she a girlfriend? A daughter?*

FDR Drive proved to be clear all the way up the East River. Bob picked up his train of thought.

"As I was saying: national security. You'll get a clearer picture once we discuss the details. For now I need your acceptance of the assignment, and your signature on a statement of confidentiality. Then you will immediately receive your first payment."

Her knees had now also started to shake which is why she made an effort to react in an unimpressed, deliberately vulgar manner.

"You can stick that where the sun don't shine, mister. I'm really not in the mood for any of this shit. Up front there, Exit 12, make your turn! Sixty-first Street."

He hit the indicator, slowed down.

"Fine, Ms. Palmer. We'll give you time to think. Do not speak to anyone about this conversation. I mean that literally. *Not to a living soul!*"

He gave her a short and shamelessly direct look.

"If you do not follow my instructions—whether you accept or not—your sons could suffer."

It wasn't the sharp corner that turned Leslie's stomach. Her whole body was shaking now. She pressed her palm against her forehead and said, almost stammering:

"My family is none of your damn business!"

Bob seemed unperturbed. His tone was businesslike. Cold.

"You have two sons. Twins. We know everything about your family. Without exception."

"What about my mother?"

Leslie's lips barely moved as she spoke.

"Died. In Texas. Very unfortunate, I'm sorry."

"That was over thirty years ago."

"I know. You were still a child. Your father is currently living alone, in Brooklyn Heights."

"And? What else?"

"What do you want to know? Your life history? Schools? Your time at Taft University?"

He turned onto her street.

"Oh," she virtually hissed, "I know your type. A real, bona fide asshole is what you are! How about my many convictions?"

"What are you bluffing for? We both know you're absolutely clean. Not one skeleton in the closet."

Leslie took a deep breath. Good. She had begun to fear that he had really spied into the depths of her private life. Fortunately the guy didn't seem to know anything about her Jennifer. She decided to go with a mixture of insulting and judicious.

"Okay, I'm impressed. *Asshole.*"

He shrugged slightly.

"We do what we must."

That's what they all say, these dicks . . . No. She'd better control herself.

She would bide her time, as she had learned to do. The man got out.

"Just moving my legs a bit," he said, as he methodically took in her building, the dimly lit entrance, the windowless door, the fact that there seemed to be no curious doorman. He produced a deliberately easygoing smile for her benefit, as he got ready to leave.

"By the way, my name is Bronx. And it's not Bob—*Rick* Bronx. "

Leslie waited at the top of the broad entryway stairs until the sound of the eight-cylinder motor had faded. Then she used the code to open her building door. She heard the click of the lock and entered.

"*Dushanbe,*" she muttered. "Dushanbe . . . Dushanbe . . . ," as the elevator took her up to her floor. In her kitchen she quickly scribbled the name she had read on the envelope onto the first piece of paper she could get her hands on.

Half a chicken sizzling in the microwave, Leslie opened a bottle of Cabernet. She carried a full glass into the lounge; started up her laptop with hands that had not stopped trembling. She couldn't put it out of her mind.

Dushanbe. Capital of Tadzhikistan. Fifty percent of the country's landmass at 3,000 meters above sea level or higher . . . Leslie looked at the bookshelves, scanning for her atlas. . . . The East of the country is dominated by the Pamir Mountains and a large part of the Pamir highlands . . . It is home to the country's highest mountain, 7,495-meter Ismoil Somoni Peak, once known as Peak Communism. . . . Leslie shook her head in reluctant amusement. She learned that glaciers covered about 1,200 square kilometers at what seemed to be the top of the world. She felt chilled again at the thought of tonight's recruitment effort. *The CIA, of all goddamned agencies!*

She stood up. *The Great Randell Atlas* gave her a clearer picture of the country's geography. The northernmost borders of the range of fold mountains were part of Kyrgyzstan, the eastern borders extended into China, the southern borders into Afghanistan, and the rest were part of Tadzhikistan.

The microwave sounded. She hurried into the brightly lit, windowless kitchen, put her half of a chicken on a plate, and removed the pre-packaged salad from the fridge.

While she ate she studied the mail that had accumulated, sorted it, and decided to spend the rest of her evening organizing her bills. Screw Communism Peak and everything else! Her cell phone vibrated loudly. *Ben?*

She walked into the kitchen; stared down at the display. It wasn't Ben. Her stomach started to tighten. "Expect you tomorrow 6 p.m. at the newsstand on WTC Plaza. Bronx."

This was more than she could take. She had to get out. Leslie rushed into the bedroom, rummaged through drawers, and decided on an alluring outfit. She draped a scarlet scarf around her neck as a finishing touch, turned off the lights on her way out the door.

I have no intention of going weak-kneed like an idiot, she said to herself. She needed to take the bull by the horns! She slowly raised her hands. The shaking had indeed subsided. She felt herself smile in relief. And speaking of bulls... Hmm... Perhaps a dynamic young man could help her regain her energy, spunk and sense of imagination...?

09

Ben, who was approaching thirty, liked to consider himself an extraordinary young man who had successfully completed his computer sciences degree, was very cultured, and generally quite superior to others—or, depending on the moment, a somewhat base kind of guy who lived by his unwavering instincts—slightly off-beat, devious, and carefree.

"I'm from Virginia," he chatted. "My father was a respected judge. I was fortunate. My parents were both generous and tolerant. And Mom had a flair for networking the social circuit."

"Yup. A country bumpkin," Leslie said a bit mockingly. "Just like me."

"Why? Let me guess. Georgia?"

"Texas. Odessa. It's to the west. Ever heard of it?"

Ben shook his head. He hadn't.

"My dad was a doctor. I went to Odessa College, and because I was valedictorian I was picked for a spot at Taft University." She rolled her eyes. "Highly prestigious."

Ben acted duly impressed, kissed her on the cheek. He spoke softly, as if practicing a song.

"I never regretted growing up in the country. Quite the opposite. I didn't have everything handed to me, like some of my friends at university." He laughed easily. "I always felt I had one up on those spoiled city brats."

Leslie nodded.

"I also learned to stand my ground early. Later my father moved to New York. Do you get the History Channel?"

Ben nodded.

"My dad directed military history programs for them."

Ben looked up, surprised. "As a doctor?"

"He did two tours as a staff surgeon in Vietnam." She straddled him tomboyishly. "When he returned, he authored a standard reference on army surgeons working under combat conditions. All the way back to World War II, Stalingrad or something."

She wrapped her arms around his neck. Ben held up to her kisses, amused by their ardor.

"And... oh... what did... uhm... your dear mother do?"

Leslie tossed her head back.

"Died young. I barely knew her. Are your parents still alive?"

He nodded silently. Leslie looked at him with an air of playful coolness and confidence.

"You honor your mommy, don't you?"

"Er... well... I guess I do, why?"

She laughed and kissed him on the mouth.

"Because you clearly have a thing for mature women!"

She continued to kiss him, to head off any possible protest. *She's got that right,* Ben thought, grinning with admiration. He also had a particular fondness for blondes. If they were beautiful, he felt the need to try to impress them with his many talents. He had an appreciation for good style, and became all but submissive with awe when women exuded power—be it in commerce, politics, or because they were successful in show business. Leslie perfectly fit this image.

Her whisper deliberately tickled his ear.

"So, what do we do now?"

He pulled her tighter with both arms, stood up. She wrapped her legs around him and allowed him to carry her across the parquet floor. In the bedroom, he placed her gently on the bed.

"Pretty please," she whispered, "*music.*"

He stepped to the window, lowered the shades. Then he started to adjust the stereo. Barry White's resonant bass baritone filled the room. Ben lay down next to her on the bed.

She impatiently grappled with his waistband as he unzipped her skirt and pulled it down with able hands. He stared, dumbfounded, at a pair of red vinyl panties with white dots.

"I love to undress you to discover that you are dressed underneath," he said in a teasingly knowledgeable tone. "And I'm really turned on by the toadstool look."

"I deserve pretty underwear," she laughed, flattered by his appreciative tone, and began to pull at his pants. His shorts had the perfect fit, as was to be expected. She slid her hand beneath the tightly ribbed cotton, grasping the warm, firm yet silky tip of his fully erect cock. *Men really are so simply built,* she thought to herself, aroused. *Simple—and so damn practical!*

"I love erotic misdemeanors," she admitted hoarsely and turned to sit backward on his chest. Her ass, with those two very attractively placed dimples, was slightly raised; the little mound of her vulva, barely covered by the scant vinyl slip, right before his eyes. Leslie, for her part, found herself hungry to take the proud, hard staff of his manhood into her mouth. To suck on it; to stroke it with the palms of both of her hands. First gently; then harder. To grasp, then lick, his taut balls; until she felt so turned on that she was carried upward by a sweet, brimming swell, and she came.

Then it was her enduring man's turn. Leslie lost all sense of time and space.

Somewhere, in the depths of this other existence, a strong heart was pounding rhythmically. It was Ben, and it was her, now moving as one to his pulse, which was becoming her own. When he spilled into her with deep, rasping breaths, she came again. This time it was not like a swell of the ocean, running its course on the sand, but like a river being released, finally, into the sea.

It was only much later that she admitted to herself that Ben had helped her rediscover her sexuality. The almost divinely beautiful boy had set her ablaze, awoken all of her secret desires. He had startled to life all of the erotic cravings and pleasures that seemed to have gone asleep some time after the birth of her sons. He had made her feel lust, had really given it to her the way she needed it. No, he had just completely satisfied her.

That passionate night in his apartment, after all of that stress, that night in which soft red light, Barry White's deep voice, and even that frivolous poster of Madonna dressed in leather, hanging over the head of his bed, had lent his bedroom a certain illicit whorehouse appeal. All of that had cloaked her in a warm sensuality that stayed with her for a long time afterward. It let her forget; it softened the contours of all that was disquieting in her life.

10

The next day, as announced, Rick Bronx was waiting next to the newsstand, from where he had a good view over the plaza. Leslie came alone. They strolled across the square to the fountain. Bronx did not waste any time putting her under pressure.

"Listen, Leslie, we need your decision by next Tuesday."

She contemplated. Tuesday was the 11th of September, and that was when she had her meeting with Spike.

"What is your problem? What's the hurry? Why the *panic*, for heaven's sake?"

"I know. It must seem harsh. But we are protecting the country from terrorism. Extraordinary times call for extraordinary measures."

"Terrorism? What exactly do you mean? We're safe here on home ground." She looked around as if seeking reassuring confirmation of her inviolable world on the sunlit part of the plaza, half-shaded by the mighty Twin Towers.

"What exactly do you think is supposed to happen to us?"

Bronx sighed.

"That's just the point. We need to ensure our safety so that nothing *does* happen. And that is precisely the reason why we have security precautions in place to prevent terrorist acts."

"Oh, please. We're not in Chechnya, after all."

Leslie stopped at the fountain.

Bronx saw the reflection of the Twin Towers. The water's rippling surface made them appear to be wavering. An icy shiver ran down his back. It was as if the sight had made his blood turn suddenly very cold.

"Of course not," he said, getting a grip on himself. "But who can read the future? What we do know is that you are under oath as a government official. We are dealing with national security. This project is of the highest priority."

"All *I* know is that you are putting me under pressure, and I would like to know what the rush is."

Bronx sighed again, this time in a worldly fashion.

"God created time, Madam. And the devil created timetables."

She raised a brow in amusement.

"Next you're going to tell me you're a man of faith."

He gave a disparaging shrug.

"I am a Muslim, but not a fanatic. I believe that the United States is a great and powerful country. Ever heard of a man named Osama Bin Laden?"

"How could I—when I was obviously born yesterday."

"Then perhaps you know that he was behind the bloody embassy bombings in Dar es Salaam and Nairobi. He is also responsible for the destruction on the USS *Cole*. We are a naïve and happy-go-lucky nation. We see some funny-looking Arab with a long beard, and we don't think we need to take him or his fatwa seriously."

Bronx held his arm in front of his chest, his hand turned up.

Now Leslie *was* looking slightly stumped.

"Fatwa?"

"His command, which makes it every Muslim's holy duty to kill Americans."

She tapped on his chest with her finger.

"People like you!"

Bronx's fierce reaction dumbfounded her.

"Do not poke your finger at me," he yelled, angrily, as if she had pierced his core.

Had she insulted his religious beliefs? But Bronx had already recomposed himself, was mumbling contritely: "It's fine. I'm just saying, we really need to be prepared!"

"Nonsense. Those are just sound bites meant to stir the masses. This is New York, man! We are a superpower, remember? What do you think these little turbaned fanatics are going to do to us? Spread nerve gas at Grand Central during rush hour?" She condescendingly flicked her hand at the thought of such absurdity, and added: "You clearly watch too much television."

Bronx seemed disproportionately agitated. He had instinctively raised his arm to shoulder-height, in a shielding gesture.

"When it happens; *that's* when people are going to start taking us seriously!"

Leslie caught up to him, feeling she might have detected a subliminal threat.

"Are you telling me that you have concrete evidence?"

"We have our leads. Your only part is to take on the role of the First Lady, should national security call for it."

"Oh. Is that *all* then?"

Her jeering tone seemed to annoy him.

"You are the only viable person to take on the job. Your looks are practically identical—a couple of cosmetic touch-ups will turn you into her spitting image. We will instruct you on the finishing touches. You will be doing more than just impersonating her. You will *be* the First Lady."

Leslie looked around uneasily. Hundreds of people were streaming across the plaza, some strolling at leisure, some looking businesslike. She knew that the president had doubles on call, supposedly for his protection, or to mislead the enemy—but the First Lady? What was the security rationale behind that?

"The president's wife is also a political target," said Bronx, as if he had read her mind. "For murder or kidnapping. It would be catastrophic."

They reached the stairs. Leslie's tone almost dripped with sarcasm.

"A real black day for the CIA, right?"

"Scoff all you like, ma'am. We have our orders, and they will be followed to the letter." He stopped abruptly. "Are you going to commit?"

"I take it that I will be discussing everything with her one-on-one at the White House?"

He seemed to flinch at her words.

"What for?"

"What do you mean, what for?" she shot back. "For a big CIA man, you sure are slow on the uptake! It's perfectly natural. I will almost certainly have to discuss the assignment with the president, also."

Bronx had pulled himself together enough to shake his head.

"I'm going to say this one last time, Ms. Palmer. Nobody except you and I are to know anything about this mission. That goes for everyone. Including the president."

She broadened her stance and looked obliquely into his blue-green, deep-set eyes from under contentiously lowered brows.

"I need time to think."

"You don't have any."

"I beg your *pardon*? I'm going to... I mean, I will give this a good amount of thought before I..."

Bronx interrupted her sharply.

"Who were you thinking of consulting?"

His eyes were narrow slits. His rough voice had taken on a threatening undertone.

"Come."

She followed him past the stairs and over to the pedestrian bridge in silence. Thoughts were tumbling through her mind. *What was in this for her? They would have to offer her a fair sum of money. It really wasn't a very difficult job,* she told herself. *In a sense, it was tailor-made for her. And what the hell did Bronx really know about her previous assignment for the First Lady?*

She didn't get around to asking. Beneath them heavy traffic roared along the Hudson Parkway, as usual. Bronx stopped at the end of the passage. The office towers of the financial district rose against the slate-gray sky. On the other side of the Hudson, New Jersey lay covered by the smog of its industrial facilities. The river formed a glistening divide between the two. Bronx wordlessly produced a picture the size of a postcard and held it in front of her eyes.

Leslie felt stung.

"My... Those are my sons! Where did you get that picture?"

Instead of answering, Bronx dug out more pictures—razor sharp, black and white photographs.

"Look, here, riding a bicycle. Monsieur Mercier, if I'm not mistaken, right? And the marathon runner—he's training with Craig. And here we have Alex, the model student in Lausanne..."

Leslie exhaled sharply. Her insides seemed strange and completely hollow. Bronx had pictures of her sons, as if he had been traveling around with them! Playing sports, at the lake, in the mountains, in front of the boarding school, at the station...

She took a deliberately slow, deep breath, managing to control the rage that was mounting within her only with extreme difficulty. "How did you get those? Give them to me!"

She snatched them from his hands and pressed them against her chest. For all of the indifference that Bronx displayed, he could have been a completely uninvolved bystander.

"Madam, we are *protecting* your boys."

Was she hearing right? Her voice had grown frigid.

"Protecting them? From what?"

She suddenly grabbed his collar, then shoved him away with all of her might.

Japanese tourists shuffled to a surprised standstill, the obligatory cameras around their necks, and smiled like Japanese people smile in just about any situation. One raised his camera as if intending to take a picture. A bit further on, two police officers stood with their backs toward them. Their attention was focused on a coast guard helicopter in low, loudly sputtering flight over the Hudson.

Bronx adjusted his suit, stroked his hair back. He stepped toward Leslie, motioning with his arm in a placating manner.

"Leave me alone!" she screamed, clasping her hands to her head in clear desperation.

"Picture, please!"

A Japanese tourist was holding his camera out to her.

"Picture of tower, please?"

Leslie looked up, exasperated. Bronx stepped between the two, his broad back forming a shield.

"Look, Leslie, you really only have two options," he lectured calmly. "Either you're in or your boys, so to speak, are out."

She felt suddenly drained.

"What do you mean?"

"Exactly what I am saying. Your sons are our collateral. Whether it suits you or not."

"That is beyond blackmail. That's... it's... *criminal*."

"Call it what you want. We can make sure that your sons enjoy every advantage. Good universities, the best jobs. We take care of our own. That is my offer. If you commit, you'll be doing it for your boys."

"And if I don't?"

"If you shoot your mouth off, or start asking questions, or don't accept our offer... Well, your sons could suffer serious consequences."

Later, Leslie could not have described exactly what happened. The only thing that was vivid in her memory was the blind sense of anger that she felt rising within, then a stinging sensation on the back of her hand from where she had made contact with Bronx's face. Next she had found herself sitting, in despair, on a bench, staring at a shiny pair of black shoes under a pair of uniform pants, the weapon in the police officer's holster...

She shook her head, nodded, lifted both hands defensively.

"Thank you, officer, everything's fine!"

She looked up: Bronx was gone. She walked unsteadily to a side street, and waved down a cab.

Once at home, she pulled a dusty bottle of cognac from the kitchen cabinet and shakily poured herself a full glass. She took a big swallow. Shuddered. Her feelings of desperation mixed with anger would not subside. She wiped her face with a paper towel, swayed into the living room, and collapsed, exhausted, onto the couch.

This whole Bronx thing hung over her head like a sword. She had to do what he commanded, whether she wanted to or not. She tore her clothes off indiscriminately and headed, unsteadily, toward the shower.

The steaming water brought some relief. She breathed deeply. Yes, there was perhaps one person that she could turn to. There had to be a way out. Her father would surely be able to give her some advice.

Her lightly tanned skin was red from the heat of the shower, her hair dark and wet. She wrapped the bathrobe around herself and walked barefoot to the kitchen, looking for something to eat. What she found was a small piece of cheese and half a tomato. But she was too agitated to swallow a single bite.

"Get a grip," her father had often admonished her when she came home from school despondent and ready to blow everything off.

She eventually reached for the phone, hesitated before finally hitting the button.

The ringing went on forever. Of course. She seemed to find him out more often than not. There was a click.

"Palmer."

How wonderful it felt to hear his deep, benevolent voice.

"Dad! Hi. How are you? I have to talk to you. What? . . . No, not on the phone. Can you meet me for lunch? Tomorrow at Sette Mezzo?"

She could just see him. His large, bushy head of hair, the furrows on his brow, keen eyes, that funny mustache, his posture slightly forward-bent, a massive, corpulent frame. *The picture of a country doctor, just as Norman Rockwell would have painted it,* she sometimes thought affectionately, *almost a caricature.*

"What's so urgent? I could make it at one. Did something happen?" She felt herself breathing faster.

"Daddy, have you been contacted by anyone from the government?"

"Oh, those bureaucrats," he grumbled. "Yes, someone did call regarding some tax matter. Such nonsense! You remember. That money that's meant for you."

He had established a trust fund for her, which would ensure her a steady and significant source of funds after his death.

"No, no, Dad. This is about Alex and Craig. It's important."

The phone was silent for a few moments.

"Says who?" he finally asked, with tension in his voice.

"Tomorrow, at lunch, okay?"

"Sure, but don't worry yourself about anything now child, alright?"

Relieved at having made the right decision, she ordered vegetarian from the Chinese restaurant, dried her hair, and lay down on the couch.

Those words kept ringing in her head: *When it* happens, *that's when people are going to start taking us seriously!* And that arm motion. Something about this Rick Bronx seemed *really* wrong.

Her thoughts agonized, her mind picking apart the details of Bronx's gesture, she finally nodded off.

In her dream a man with strong arms carried her easily up the stairs in her father's house—*Ben*...

...how gentle and caring he was! Flames blazed in the study fireplace. Like always. All year round. Summer and winter.

They drank Champagne. A lobster crawled across the salon table.

Ben was slowly, sweetly arousing her. Leslie had slipped out of her buttoned dress; let the brightly colored suspender belt fall to the ground...Music began to rain from the ceiling, falling on her back like tiny pearls as she bent over the back of the couch, wantonly spread her legs and whispered: "Come now!"

It was simply incredible. Ben had a flair for creating an atmosphere, the passion to seduce her. He allowed her to experience new dimensions of life, and opened up a whole new world for her to discover. They had been out, visiting their favorite bars and restaurants...A waiter with a big mustache, wearing a white apron, and carrying a finely woven net, knocked on the frame of the door: he needed to catch the escaped lobster... Bronx stood behind him, grinning, and waving a stack of photographs. Leslie shrieked with laughter. Ben ripped his fly open.

"You're insane," he moaned.

His penis was aroused, and as he urgently pressed its head into the scarlet folds of her labiae it flooded with hardness, growing ripe and stiff... as a dainty, smiling girl wearing nothing but black lace gloves entered, carrying a bottle of Champagne.

He was in good shape, just right for her, she praised, breathing loudly as she stretched her ass higher up, throwing her head back as if she were in heat... She didn't push, remained still, suspended, leaving him the pleasure of being in control. As he thrust forcefully toward climax a piece of wood suddenly cracked loudly in the fireplace. The girl dropped the bottle with a scream; the lobster sizzled in the flames...

The cracking had been a shot. Bronx had shot Craig in the heart. Now he was raising a threatening finger. "In or out!" he said.

A piece of wood burst with a loud bang.

Leslie woke, her heart pounding. Where had the noise come from?

The light was still on in the living room. The dark windows locked the night outside. The apartment door was securely locked.

Unsettled, she slipped into her bed, pulled the blanket up over her ears. It was a long time before her disturbed thoughts gradually faded away and she slept.

11

The next day, Leslie was in a hurry. The rain was making it hard to find a cab on Fulton Street around midday. Father Palmer hated tardiness. He was almost certainly already seated at the table, and, charmer that he was, he would greet her by saying: The sight of you makes me lose all sense of time. I just got here myself.

By the time the taxi driver came to a halt on the corner of 70th

Street, the rain had stopped. As so often in this mercurial city, the dark clouds cleared within minutes and a bright blue sky spread over the rooftops on Lexington Avenue.

Charles Palmer appeared out of nowhere. His warm, burly hug said more than many words. Together they walked the few steps to *Sette Mezzo.* Oriente, having given them a warm Mediterranean welcome, led them to the round table by the window.

"How can you afford to eat in such expensive restaurants," Charles murmured as the lean Croatian waiter hurried up to their table, arranged some notes in his hand, wet his lips, and began to recite the daily specials.

Leslie loved the private, club-like atmosphere of this place. As a regular, she enjoyed the full attention of the predominantly European staff.

"Isn't that the Polo fashion guy?" Charles proclaimed and turned unabashedly to get a better look at an older gentleman with a full, white mane of hair.

"Daddy, please!" Leslie whispered admonishingly. "Do you know what you want?" She discreetly raised her eyebrows toward the waiter, who was standing at the ready with his sharpened pencil.

They ordered, the Croat noted, Oriente brought a bottle of Montalcino to the table. "Tenuta Argiano, smooth as silk and very seductive," he rhapsodized.

Charles allowed him to pour, tasted, and announced his verdict.

"Buono!"

His eyes showed signs of impatience, as if he wanted to get something off his chest, but didn't yet deem the time to be suitable.

"Pretty elitist place, this," he grumbled, dipping a piece of white bread in olive oil.

"That's right, you're not the only celebrity here," Leslie teased. "By the way, this is my treat, and I don't want a word out of you!"

He smiled at her benignly, then leaned closer.

"Alright, let me have it. What's going on?"

Leslie raised her shoulders slightly and cast a discreet look around.

"Well, to get straight to the point, I'm being blackmailed by a CIA agent. He is trying to force me to take on an assignment at the White House."

Charles chewed on another piece of bread drenched in olive oil.

"That's your line of business, isn't it?" he said simply.

She denied this with a vehement shake of her head.

"No, this is something completely different. This guy is threatening me. If I don't comply, he says that he will take it out on my boys."

"What? Did he really say that? Alex and Craig?"

Palmer's indignant tone swelled through the entire restaurant.

"Does this guy have any idea who he's dealing with? No Palmer is going to…"

He got no further. Leslie spoke slowly. Seriously.

"Daddy, listen, I have no choice."

He plucked at his mustache, glanced out of the window for a second:

"The CIA, you say! What do those imbecilic good-for-nothings want from my daughter?"

Leslie hesitated. She was battling with a decision. Should she really be telling her father about this? *Nobody except you and I are to know anything*, Bronx's warning echoed in her head.

"I don't know," she said, suddenly evasive. "I'm not allowed to talk about it."

"Come on, there's nothing on earth you can't tell your father. That's laughable."

He raised his glass.

"To us, Leslie!"

She joined in the toast reluctantly, took only a quick sip.

"They want me to double for the First Lady," she said, her voice hardly audible. "It's a matter of national security. Daddy, you have to promise…"

His reaction made her fall silent. His familiar, innocently humorous expression had become mask-like. He leaned back slowly. Stared at her for a long time, with eyes that had turned cold.

"What?"

Charles leaned forward and whispered hoarsely.

"What reason did they give you? Why did they pick you?"

Leslie looked at him, her eyes growing large.

"You're not surprised?"

He moved his shoulders and distinctive head.

"You have a fine talent for acting and, well, you resemble her. I've always known that."

"Fine, but they need to leave my sons out of it!"

Charles ignored her objection.

"Did the guy give you any kind of explanation?"

"An explanation is certainly not what I'd call it! And if you'd been there, you probably wouldn't either. I believe the word is *extortion*. Either I agree to play along, or there will be unpleasant consequences. Dad, I'm really scared."

He smiled a fatherly smile.

"Come on, baby. I've never known you to be afraid of new tasks. I know you better than that. You're a control freak. You wrap men around your little finger like bits of string. But tell me again—is he poking around in your past? What is his name, by the way? He needs to watch himself."

Palmer's eyes glinted menacingly.

A busboy brought the plates with their appetizer to the table. Leslie lifted her fork.

"Past? Mine? No, why should he?"

Charles seemed relieved. He poked around in the lobster salad as if it might contain an exit strategy.

"Oh, well that's fine then. So, are you going to accept? I would think it should be a cakewalk for you!"

But Leslie was not about to be distracted.

"Why the concern about my past?"

"You have always leaned toward a certain fatalism. You may control men; but you do not take charge of your fate. You let events run their course, in the unshakable hope that everything happens for some predetermined reason."

Leslie irresolutely turned her plate.

"Thank you for the psychological digression."

"What I *mean* is that you are usually open to suggestions, as long as they are made by an intelligent person. You take it all to be part of a dynamic process, and you go along with it. Out of curiosity; or call it a sense of adventure if you want."

"Okay. So you think I should just give in?"

Charles shrugged his shoulders, chewing.

"I do. You can't resist the challenge anyway, can you?"

She analyzed her behavior. Had she succumbed to Bronx? Did part of her actually want to be bossed around by him? It was always the same with men. Or were her instincts telling her that something was seriously wrong? She placed a newspaper article on the table. The caption of the short article read: First Lady in the Financial District.

"Have you seen this?"

"Is Jerry Moseley her financial advisor?" he read out loud, firmly shaking his head as he did so. "She doesn't have to fly to Manhattan to make an investment. When women go anywhere, it is usually for one of three reasons: to go shopping, to meet a girlfriend, or because they're having an affair!"

"You're an impossible macho!" She tapped the article with her finger. "My CIA guy hinted at something like that."

"Like what?"

Leslie cast a sharp glance to both sides before leaning forward.

"Do you know what he said? His exact words were: 'She has a relationship that we don't approve of.' Mysterious, don't you think?"

Charles said nothing. His characteristic, barely contained roguishness had disappeared. He pursed his lips, pensively stroked his mustache with his index finger and thumb.

"You wanted to tell me something about my childhood?" Leslie reminded him.

He turned his head away, his vigilant gaze scanning the busy street.

"Dad, hello! What's up?"

She followed his eyes. Traffic was piling up at a red light. Pedestrians walked by. He looked at her, his face working. Finally he spoke.

"Alright. There is one sensitive issue, but..."

"But what? No secrets please, I'm no longer twelve."

"Forget about it. If they don't know, everything's fine."

He put down his knife and fork. He looked as if he wanted to say more; as if he had something on the tip of his tongue that he had been meaning to tell her for a long time, but had not been able to. Something that he could not quite bring himself to reveal to her.

Leslie had suddenly lost her appetite. She left the buffalo mozzarella on her plate untouched. In a voice so low that it was barely audible, she asked.

"Does it have to do with Texas?"

He nodded, extended both hands across the table.

"These hands, baby, brought you into this world. It was an unforgettable night, to say the least. I've wanted to tell you for a long time, but..."

His sinister expression left her speechless. This change in demeanor was an ominous sign. Unfortunately, she knew this mask of his well enough to fear the worst. Palmer stared angrily out the window. The glass he was holding almost dropped from his shaking hand. He slowly raised his right hand, pointing with his finger.

"That guy over there...eh...I saw him outside of my house this morning. That can't be a coincidence."

She leaned forward to follow the direction of his gaze.

"Where?"

"Next to the blue bakery pickup."

"Are you sure? Those guys all look the same."

He raised his hands in a typical gesture that said 'Be still.'

"Dearest, I have an eye for anatomical details. Do you notice something about this character?"

Leslie took another, closer look.

"The ponytail?"

"Nah. Look carefully, will you—the guy has only one ear! Probably cut off by some Mafia boss in person."

Leslie acted as if she now saw it, too.

"Now he's getting behind the wheel," she reported.

"Then those goony, light-brown cowboy boots he's wearing. I saw those poking out of his truck this morning. No doubt. That makes three coinciding criteria. Now do you finally believe me?"

Charles Palmer's face had reddened.

"Why should it be the same guy?"

"They're shadowing me, Leslie. Your CIA spook is behind it all. Come, we're leaving."

He stood so suddenly that the glasses on the table clanged against each other, and stomped toward the exit so determinedly that his steps practically shook the ground.

She held him back by his jacket.

"Daddy, you wanted to tell me something just now!"

"Come by the house. Just wait, I'm going to give this guy what he's got coming."

He made his way through the door with the steadiness of a steamroller, held up traffic with one huge paw, and calmly crossed the street without altering his pace.

Leslie could hardly believe her eyes as she watched him impulsively haul the guy out of the driver's seat by his one remaining ear, pin him against the loading ramp, and slap him across both sides of his face in rapid succession.

After that, everything happened in a flash. Charles Palmer disappeared into the back of a taxi, and the cabby took off like a NASCAR driver. The blue pickup shot from the curb with screeching tires, hitting a white bread delivery truck squarely on the side, thereby tipping it and sending it crashing on two wheels into the corner wine store. Honking wildly, the blue pickup took chase.

Oriente stood next to Leslie. The chef looked alarmed.

"What happened?"

"An emergency," she whispered, horrified. She started moving slowly, mechanically. Reality was beginning to dawn on her. And the guilt she felt was dreadful. Had it been a mistake to draw her father into all of this? Why did he believe he was being shadowed?

She stopped by the laundry and picked up her blouses. When she reached her apartment a short while later, the red light was already blinking on her answering machine. The message was from Dad. "Leslie, my dear, I shook him off. Did you see? I sure showed him, *ha!* And I've been thinking about your other guy. Come out to the house around six. I'm uneasy about this thing!"

She speed-dialed his cell phone number—no answer. Typical!

That same evening, she drove over to Brooklyn Heights to see him.

12

"This Bronx guy doesn't want *you*. He wants control," Charles Palmer concluded. "What we need is a plan. But first let me get back to what I was saying this afternoon. It's possible that there's a connection."

The cozy room was paneled in warm, dark wood. Charles Palmer shoveled ice into a snifter, then poured a golden-brown liquid from a crystal carafe over the clinking cubes before sitting down in his leather, burgundy-colored wingchair with a satisfied grunt.

Leslie noted the flames flickering brightly in the fireplace. She had long grown used to this foible of his, but she still couldn't help teasing him about it: "You're just unbelievable! Lighting a fire in the middle of summer! And with the air-conditioning running."

Charles Palmer held his glass up to the fire, turning it slowly in his hand.

"I'm not about to stop my habits!" he droned. He gazed at the reflection of the flickering flames that lent his whiskey the appearance of liquid, shimmering gold. He took a swallow, began to talk:

"Baby, it was the worst night of my life. It was a life or death situation. The rain was coming down in torrents outside. The winds were howling so strong that elm trees in the park were bending fit to snap. The lights were flickering. Fabienne, who was almost due to deliver, suddenly began moaning in pain. Her face showed that peculiarly noble expression that women have when they're giving birth. I knew immediately that there was no time to waste. I remember Eisenhower on television in the background, on his election tour, furiously damning the Soviet invasion of Hungary in front of a crowd of cheering troops. Even today, those images remain crystal clear in my mind. I raced our old Chevy down Dixie Boulevard as fast as I could. You remember... near your college...

"...the city wasn't as big as it is today. The population explosion came later, with the oil boom. Odessa had only one hospital at the end of the Fifties. It was on 4th Street, where the giant Medical Center complex towers over everything today. The lights were out along the long driveway to the maternity wing. Rain was coming down in sheets on the windshield, the wipers couldn't keep up, the road was sporadically lit by lightning. I'm telling you, I had a hard time even seeing the dimly lit entrance. Of course, it was closed at two in the morning. There was no sign of life in the hospital. I got to the emergency entrance around the corner, my hand on the horn as if it was stuck there. Failing neon lights were crackling eerily on and off. Fabienne was brave. In the rearview mirror I could see her lips tightly pressed together, she was holding her lower abdomen. She stared at me silently, desperately, as if helpless in the face of her fate..."

Leslie gestured impatiently.

"And then, did everything work out?"

She was sitting across from him; her feet stretched out toward the crackling fire.

"Just wait, things hadn't even started to happen yet..."

...Charley Palmer had come to a careful halt in front of the awning of the ER entrance. He glanced anxiously to the back seat.

"Everything okay?" he asked lovingly. He got out and helped the woman out of the car. Holding her upright, he rushed her inside through the swinging door. The corridor was empty and bare. Their footsteps echoed desolately through the bleakness. Finally, they reached the reception, where a woman's pale face showed in the light of a single desk lamp.

"Julia, prepare delivery room one for us. Call Melissa!" Palmer called as he approached. The night nurse grudgingly shifted her attention from what she had been reading.

"Get moving!" Palmer barked as he reached the elevators.

Only now did she recognize the physician.

"Right away, Doctor," she called, startled.

"Who else is here? Do we have an obstetrician?"

Julia ran from behind the desk to the elevator, the door of which was just opening with a loud rumble. She waved an on-call sheet:

"There's only one resident here tonight. Ferguson. No attending doctor in the ER. No one from obstetrics is on-call either."

Her eyes were fixed on the ashen face of the pregnant woman, which contorted in pain as she pressed against her swollen belly, gasping for breath.

The elevator doors were slowly rumbling shut.

"And Kirkhoff?" Palmer yelled through the narrowing gap. "Get Doctor Kirkhoff here, Julia. Immediately!"

He squeezed Fabienne's arm reassuringly.

"Almost there. Everything will be fine, darling," he said, wanting to comfort her.

But his mind was racing. Ferguson was a licensed doctor receiving specialty training in internal medicine. He was a useful assistant, but he would not be much good if complications occurred... *Kirkhoff!* If only he had his expertise at his disposal right now...

The elevator shuddered to a stop. A scream stuck in Fabienne's throat. The doors opened to reveal a nurse, who was rolling a bed toward them.

"Melissa! Good that you're here. It's urgent."

One look was enough for Melissa. Together, they silently pushed the bed down the long, dimly lit hallway.

"It's Doctor Kirkhoff's day off, Charley," Melissa informed him, her voice tense. The doctor now spoke in the forceful commando tone that he reserved for true emergencies.

"Well someone needs to get him here; and I mean this instant!"

She raised a hand in resignation.

"He's at his country house. Julia is trying to reach him there. But I don't see him making it in less than an hour in this terrible weather. What now?"

Fabienne groaned fiercely. Palmer reached for her in fright. She reared up, her face mask-like, her eyes rolling back. Suddenly she let out a heartbreaking scream that ebbed into a gurgling stammer: "Oh, oh... Charley, help me!"

She sank back onto the pillow, all but lifeless.

"Caesarian. We need the OR... *GO*," Palmer yelled so loudly that his voice reverberated off the walls. Now running, they steered the bed past the delivery room down an empty side hallway. Palmer reached for Fabienne's neck, palpating.

"Her pulse is weak! Where the hell is Ferguson?!"

The lights came on in the operating room as they wheeled in the bed. A young doctor hurried in through a door, fumbling with his mask.

"Ferguson," Palmer called in a sharply commanding tone. "You are going to take over anesthesia!"

He leaned over her inanimate, beautiful face, his eyes wide in terror. He pressed his lips close to her ear and whispered, "Darling, Fabienne..."

"Ready to lift," Melissa announced, in a calmly professional voice. Together they lifted the pregnant woman onto the operating table. Melissa wheeled the instruments over and helped Palmer, who was already drying his hands, into a white apron.

The operation in the sparse, glaringly lit Odessa Hospital operating room began five minutes later. It was precisely 2:36 a.m.

Sitting in a different time, safe and warm in a book-strewn study in Brooklyn, Leslie asked tensely: "So who... may I ask... was Fabienne?"

Palmer was wearing tinted glasses that made his large, furrowed face with its broad double chin look more dashing. He turned his gaze from the fire.

"A French woman. Young, breathtakingly beautiful, full of spirit. The only woman I ever... never mind. She died that night."

Leslie stared at him, stunned.

"And the baby?"

She hugged her legs, chilled in spite of the flames.

He sipped at his glass and continued.

...Charley Palmer was a talented doctor, who had enjoyed excellent training during his surgical rotation at the Dallas University Clinic. He felt secure in performing Caesarian sections. In fact, he would not have been able to tell offhand how many such operations he had performed without mishap up until this fateful night. At any rate, it had been a long time since this procedure had caused him any kind of apprehension.

He was perfectly clear on the fact that the woman was not going to be able to give birth naturally. She had sunk into a softly whimpering state of apathy. Her confused eyes suggested that she might be about to lose consciousness. Her apical pulse was weak. She was battling, her body in crisis. Whatever the exact source of that crisis was, Palmer knew that time was of the essence. But his worst fears would dim in light of what was yet to come.

The preparations went without a hitch. Melissa kept excellent charge of the OR, and helped a nervous Ferguson with the anesthetic machine. She was worth her weight in gold, but as she handed Palmer the scalpel, she blinked in shock: the surgeon's hands were shaking!

"Is everything alright, Doctor?"

The inquiring look in those lovely, dark eyes stabbed at Palmer's heart. He pulled himself together, asked reproachfully: "Why shouldn't it be? Everything is fine, let's get going. Pulse? Respiration?" Routine questions. He made a meticulous incision, then another, asked for scissors...

"The uterus has ruptured," he screamed suddenly, and started to bark orders: "Clamp, stat! Suction! Prepare for infusion... Clips...! Hurry, for God's sake. What's taking Kirkhoff so long? We have to..." He broke off. Then declared tonelessly: "*Twins!*"

In front of the fireplace, Leslie started from her comfortable position.

"Twins?" she cried, surprised. "If she was carrying twins, then..."

Dad made a brushing motion with his hand, cutting her interruption short.

"We didn't know. Back then, doctors didn't have the benefit of ultrasound technology. And the patient was from out of town..."

He was visibly fighting for words.

"It was at that moment that I knew I'd lost her."

Leslie reflexively held her hand up to cover her disturbed expression. Only the gentle crackling of the fire broke the silence. Eventually Charles cleared his throat and continued where he had left off…

…He had been hectic, but nevertheless in control, as he delivered the two tiny babies from their mother's womb. He handed the precious newborns over to Melissa.

All emergency measures, all hemostatic efforts: clamping, tying, suctioning…were of no avail. She continued to hemorrhage; blood pulsing and escaping inexorably. It was every surgeon's worst nightmare. Palmer was forced to watch helplessly as the woman bled to death under his hands. And then, in the midst of this most desperate of situations, two babies began to emit earsplitting screams.

The twins were alive! They were screaming! The cold hand of death seemed suddenly to withdraw. New life flowed like light into the darkness, and Charley Palmer sensed a surge of energy that seemed to be emanating from the young woman, whose heartbeats were now growing weak and ineffective. Then her heart stopped entirely. The vital sign monitor sounded a monotonous, irritating alarm that signaled merciless finality. Palmer bent over the now peaceful face, a sense of despair rushing through him. He sobbed.

"I'm so sorry, so sorry…"

Brooklyn. The fire was slowly turning to ashes. Leslie's lips barely moved as she uttered the words.

"You *loved* her."

"She died under my knife," he said evasively. "It was terrible."

"What happened then? Did you blame yourself?"

He nodded slowly, took another swallow of whiskey.

"It had already happened before I made the first incision. The autopsy confirmed it. It was incredibly fortunate that the twins survived. But that was just the beginning of the catastrophe. Events took a further apocalyptic turn. That night in Texas, it was as if the entire world had chosen to conspire against me."

Leslie impatiently refilled her glass of water.

"Go on," she urged.

"Yes, it was a long time ago. You should know the entire story, my dear..."

...Charley Palmer had stood over the dead woman as if paralyzed, while Melissa diapered each of the twins, swaddled them in warm blankets, and placed them in separate infant beds. Somewhere, sirens were screeching. A short while later, footsteps and calls were heard in the room next door. Palmer remained frozen. The loss of his beloved had shaken him to the core. He had failed as a doctor; had failed *her.* The voice sounded as if it was coming from far away.

"Doctor Palmer?"

Melissa tugged carefully at his blood-soaked sleeve. She spoke in a voice that was soft, but that was nevertheless not going to accept any form of contradiction.

"Doctor, we have an emergency. *Please!*"

She pulled him gently away from the dead woman's body.

"What? Emergency? I know, it was terrible..."

"You can't help her anymore now," he heard her say. "Come, Charley." Ferguson stood at the door, a look of horror on his face.

"The woman is delivering, she has started to push!" the young resident yelled, clearly beside himself.

"Need to diagnose..." Palmer murmured, mechanically setting himself in motion.

The woman was positioned on the birthing chair, her legs spread beneath white sheets. Palmer wanted nothing more than to turn and run.

"Doctor Kirkhoff is on his way," Melissa informed him hopefully.

"We can't wait any longer," said Ferguson, looking worriedly over to birthing chair, where the dark-haired woman had closed her eyes, as if sleeping. "I had to sedate her."

"Are you *insane*?" Palmer burst out.

He was in the process of examining the woman when her labor pains returned.

She struggled and pushed, panting and moaning. She screamed in pain. The baby was not descending! Palmer did not need to speculate on the cause for long—the baby was in a transverse position. The logical solution, the inescapable answer, was a Caesarian. But Palmer found himself unable to move.

"I was traumatized, Leslie," he spoke into the snifter, in which he was slowly swirling his whiskey. "I just stood there, staring at her cervix, and I couldn't budge. It was just like one of those terrible dreams, when you find yourself driving toward a precipice, your foot wants to feel for the brake pedal but your muscles aren't working, nothing is moving. That's exactly how I felt."

"You were scared that..."

"...I was going to botch the operation again, you can say it," he finished what he was sure would be her sentence. "Yes. Of course. I couldn't muster the courage to cut again, after the bloodbath that I had just experienced with Fabienne. Terrible. Unbelievable, right?"

She placed her hand on his arm. Asked if he was certain that he wanted to go on.

He looked up, as if awakening.

"Don't be silly, why not," he laughed. "That was so many years ago."

He stood up, went to the bar to replenish his glass from the heavy, crystal whiskey carafe. He took a deep swallow.

"You're going to hear the rest of the story now." He hovered obliquely on the edge of the table. "Whether you want to or not."

...It had taken a weary Charley Palmer until four in the morning to deliver the baby. When he did, he immediately noticed the tragic fact that the infant was not breathing. No scream, no sign of motion. Palmer protectively held the tiny, lifeless body close to his. His broad back shielded it from Ferguson's gaze. Then an idea suddenly shot into his exhausted mind. Looking over at Melissa—the seasoned, composed, best of all nurses—he commanded: "A towel, quickly!" Melissa helped him, her eyes betraying nothing. She assisted him calmly, professionally. Palmer took off for the operating room with the bundle in his arms.

"Reanimation!" they heard him call, before the door slammed behind him.

It had grown dark in Charles Palmer's study. Leslie switched on the floor lamp. Her voice was intense.

"You were able to save the baby, I hope?"

"It all happened in a matter of minutes. I didn't know what was going on inside of me. It wasn't until later, much later, that I thought about what I had done: it was sheer insanity. It was profoundly criminal, Leslie."

"Criminal? What do you think was immoral about anything you did? Every surgeon experiences operations with undesired outcomes."

Her father shook his head. He proudly raised himself to his full stature, and said with the deepest conviction: "What I did next was crazy. It took a lot of chutzpa, and..."

"And what?" Leslie's eyes grew large. "Tell me, please."

...When Nurse Melissa had the courage, after a few apprehensive minutes, to open the door to the operating room, she found Palmer standing at the instrument table. In his arms, he lovingly held a newborn. He was speaking to it in whispers, his head bent forward. He answered the nurse's questioning look with what seemed like a relieved nod. Melissa looked around curiously, then stepped up to him, and held out her arms to receive the baby. Their eyes met.

"A girl," Palmer said hoarsely.

The infant breathed, twitched, scrunched up its face. Melissa carried it silently over to where its mother lay, spent, and placed it in her arms, just as a portly Kirkhoff came blustering into the delivery room, sweaty-faced and panting.

"What, all done?" he teased. "Well, well. What have we here?"

He bent cheerfully over the new mother, playfully poked at the baby's arm with his index finger. "Aren't you a beautiful baby? How sweet!" Turning to Ferguson, he asked brightly: "Is Master Palmer still here? Where's that boy hiding himself?"

Following the head nurse's gesturing arm, he rushed into the operating room.

Palmer turned from the scrub basin, calmly drying his hands. The operating table was empty. In the background, a sheet covered what could be seen to be the contours of a body. Shiny, stainless steel containers were overflowing with traces of the operation in the form of blood-soaked cotton, rags, and bandages. All of which more than covered the bundle containing the dead baby.

"Exitus in tabula," Palmer admitted soberly, before Kirkhoff could open his big, buffoon mouth.

"Oh, I'm sorry. Who was it?"

"A young woman. Gave birth to a healthy girl. Ruptured uterus."

"Pre or post?" the obstetrician wanted to know.

"She was already hemorrhaging profusely when I opened her up."

"Good for you," ruled Kirkhoff, immediately following with a casual motion of his hand: "Off to the medical examiner!"

Leslie now stood facing her father, her feet in a wide stance, chest heaving. She searched desperately for words. He guiltily raised his eyebrows. He spread his arms, as if wanting to sweep all the intricacies of his past in to one comprehensive package that he might be able to explain.

Leslie leaned forward, almost as if she was intending to climb backwards into the fireplace.

"You told this Kirchhoff it was *a girl*? You didn't say *twins*? Who was the other woman?"

Palmer raised his hand to calm her. It looked as though he were getting ready to be sworn in.

"Kirkhoff asked me the same question," he said, almost mischievously. "I had no idea either. I asked him to finish the paperwork."

Leslie was still staring at him in disbelief.

"You had no idea who the other mother was? You helped her, I mean, after all that horror. And you didn't know her *name*?"

Palmer pensively swayed his wise, gray head. "I didn't care," he said simply. "I had a lot to digest before I could grasp much of anything. Can you understand that?"

Confused, Leslie pushed on: "But wasn't there something else?"

She was trying hard to find the thread, but Palmer interrupted her thoughts in an authoritative tone.

"Fine. You're right. The story does have a little sequel. But it's getting late. I'm tired, and you shouldn't be driving home too late. And knowing you, you don't want to sleep over, right?"

She signaled with a smile and a wave of her hand that she was not going to stand for his evasiveness.

"You can't torture me like that. It's not fair. You're going to tell me the rest of the story, now!"

He remained relentless.

"I already have everything written down and documented, and..."

"Documented?"

"Of course. For you. It's in the drawer in the bedroom upstairs, where I keep the revolver... never mind, my cuff links... you know the one. There's a red envelope with a few important records that we need to take some time to go through. Next time. I'm tired now."

As if to prove his point, he rubbed his forehead and closed his eyes.

And so she said goodbye. With an extra kiss.

"I love you, Daddy."

She left the room with a smile, began walking down the stairs. Behind her, her father cleared his throat.

"There was one more thing, Leslie. Melissa... Melissa took..."

She spun around. He read in her eyes that she knew what he was going to say. "Melissa took the other baby girl. Later we married and..."

His voice halted. Leslie grasped her temples with both hands and completed the sentence: "Fabienne is my birth mother! And you were the father of her twins... *twins*..."

She ran back upstairs and sank onto the chair. He passed her a drink. The cognac burned at the back of her throat. She managed breathlessly: "Then Melissa was... my *foster mother*?! Why did you never tell me?"

She looked up at her father, her eyes broken-hearted. He put his hand on her shoulder in a comforting, fatherly gesture.

Much later that night, in a taxi Charles had called, she rode smoothly across the dully-shimmering Brooklyn Bridge, the mighty Twin Towers of the World Trade Center glittering distantly against the night sky. She tried to order her thoughts. Her mind was still in a shambles as the driver left FDR Drive and turned into the lively Upper East Side. Her rational brain was telling her, as if from a great distance, that this story still had a few loose ends.

Finally at home, she took a tranquilizer and went to bed. For a while, she lay breathing quietly in the dark, waiting for the pill to take effect. Soon, without realizing it, she had sunk into a deep, dreamless sleep.

13

The last light shone across the long, dark-green ridge. The sun was low and would soon disappear behind the mountain range. The typical, early evening bustle started up in Gstaad's pedestrian zone, which was paved exclusively with expensive, finely ground granite. Cowbells rang sporadically in the distance, climbers made their weary way along the traffic-free promenade. At the Rialto, Maggie—a waitress from Toronto—was serving a guest wearing slacks with crisply ironed creases and a Polo shirt a glass of white wine. All the while, two guys at a table nearby stared silently.

The church bell announced the half-hour with two deep clangs. One of the observers wore a floppy hat. The other suddenly thrust a hand inside the right pocket of his pants and retrieved a cell phone. He listened, chewing on the end of a matchstick, looked at his companion from behind a dark pair of glasses. He nodded. They got up, disappeared effortlessly among the strolling pedestrians. They stopped in front of a store selling clocks and watches. One clock was set to New York time: a quarter past noon. At the train station, the men got into a black Montero and quietly drove off.

Once they reached the rise of the gently sloping hills, they turned toward a chalet that seemed to be crouching at the base of the steep mountains to its rear. Their car was well hidden where they parked it, next to the house. They walked up to the front door. The guy with the floppy hat looked around. His gaze fell on a piece of pasture that had been grazed to the ground by sheep, across the valley, and into the mist that had settled over the large village.

The dark-skinned one, his sunglasses perched on his forehead, started on the lock. It was a task that barely raised a sweat on his smoothly shaven head. Two short scratching noises later, and the deep green door adorned with a pattern of red flowers stood open. The men stepped into the generous entrance hall and looked around. Mail lay on a side table, a copy of *Newsweek* magazine, two letters addressed to Craig Palmer.

The man with the floppy hat nodded in a satisfied manner and made for the parlor. The dark-skinned one searched through the bedroom, cast a disparaging glance at the tiny shower. He then went on to the kitchen, where he sat on a small stool with his back to the window and scrutinized the snap-shots of crazy snowboarders, catapulting wildly through the air, which were stuck to the refrigerator door. He grunted darkly as he rubbed his fists in primitive anticipation…

The bus stopped further down along the main street. A tall, slender young man stepped out and walked back up the road. Craig inhabited the little guest apartment on the ground floor of Monsieur Mercier's chalet. For a moment he hesitated in front of the ornate door to his apartment, then on second thought put down his sports bag, went up the stairs and reached for the key on top of the doorframe. He opened the door hewn out of matured timber and stepped into a large, modernly furnished room. He hit the flat light switch. Recessed lighting came on above the windows, casting a warm glow up toward the ceiling from which numerous, small spots shone down onto the light parquet floor.

Craig stepped through the narrow hallway that was paneled with antique wood, and into the bathroom that Monsieur Mercier had had installed for his rare guests, and that he, himself, barely used. Craig, on the other hand, very much enjoyed the large shower stall behind the glass wall, which featured an entire panel of jets and showerheads. Just a moment later he stood naked in front of the mirror. His body still glistened with sweat from the workout that he had just put himself through. Almost an hour of advanced spinning with rapidly changing speeds, simulated inclines and sprints with increasing resistance had pleasantly worn him out. He loved his body, with all of its raw energy. His arms and thighs were lean and muscular. He was proud of his washboard abs. The only thing right now that did not fit in with the picture of an athletic man of steel, a macho who drew the admiration of countless girls, was his limp penis. His brother Alex, although a few inches shorter than him, was no less popular. Alex had been living on campus at the EFPL Lausanne for a while now.

The water pleasantly massaged Craig's body. He turned to enjoy the feel of it on his back as he washed his hair. Then he opened the glass door, reached for a red terry cloth towel, and dried himself. When he walked into the living room to get his clothes... he stopped in mid-motion.

There was another knock on the door.

"Paul?"

No answer. He wrapped the towel around his waist, turned the key in the lock.

The door slammed into his face. He stumbled backwards. Two men rushed the room, grabbed the struggling Craig by the arms, and rained blows on him without uttering a word. The one with the floppy hat held him down, the other punched his face, kneed him in the groin, and landed a brutal hook to the chin of the defenseless youth.

Then he bent over Craig with a pleased sneer. He lit up a cigarette, as the one with the sunglasses continued to kick Craig in the back. Groaning, Craig tried to field the blows to his head and body with his arms. Blood was now pouring out of his mouth and nose. The one with the floppy hat took off a shoe with stitched edges, held Craig's right hand to the parquet floor, and proceeded to beat his fingers with the hard heel as Craig groaned dully. His buddy, meanwhile, stuffed Craig's shirt in his mouth to make sure that his whimpering and weakening screams would not be heard.

When they were finally finished with their victim, the dark-skinned one, grinning, took a few pictures with a small digital camera. Then he gave a nod, signaling it was time to leave.

14

Around the same time, Leslie Palmer took an elegant, yet powerful swing.

"Well done, Les!" Harry praised.

The white ball flew in a wide arc, high above the Hudson River and toward New Jersey—at least that was how it appeared.

"Nice distance," Harry announced, as the ball descended a good two hundred meters down the Pier 59 practice range, to land on the green target area surrounded by high nets, rolling to a halt amid a white sea of balls.

It was two o'clock in the afternoon. Leslie often visited Chelsea Piers, where she had once taken dance classes, on Sundays around this time, to practice her drive. People could come here to scale massive climbing walls, sprint around a quarter-mile Mondo track, and meet plenty of interesting New Yorkers in the process. Leslie loved the casual, unconventional atmosphere of the place.

Harry, who filmed everything in order to later analyze the details of her swing with her on a screen, spurred her on.

"Keep it up, that was perfect."

The next ball rolled automatically onto the tee. Leslie concentrated as she addressed it, did a careful practice swing, and adjusted the positioning of her feet. It was just then that she sensed a movement to her rear. She stopped just short of taking the swing and turned, slightly annoyed.

There he stood—Rick Bronx. With that dumb grin on his face. The man was definitely getting on her last nerve. Had he announced that he was planning on coming?

She inhaled sharply, swung back angrily, and hacked down on the ball as if she was picturing hitting Bronx right between the eyes.

"Hmm, zilch," Harry commented, not very charitably. Her club had come down hard on the mat. The ball jumped, took a short, crooked course through the air, and rolled off to the side.

"Shit!" Leslie hissed.

She stomped, huffing, toward the unwelcome intruder, grasping her seven-iron fiercely.

"Go to hell, Bronx!"

He raised both hands in a gesture that was part conciliatory, part appeasing.

"Sorry, ma'am. I'll wait next door." He added in a whisper, "We have to talk!"

What choice did she have! The creep had her cornered. Talk?

She shrugged apologetically at Harry. The pro understood. Many of his regulars appreciated his discretion at least as much as they did his coaching.

"No problem, Les."

He strolled, whistling softly, to the next tee. Bronx was casually playing with a ball until Harry was out of earshot. Then he got straight to the point.

"Listen, Leslie, I want to emphasize again that your mission calls for the highest level of secrecy. You are not to talk to anyone about it; not even the President. *Especially* not the President."

Leslie waved her club in front of her slightly spread legs.

"Why on earth shouldn't I talk to him about it? After all, he's my husband, isn't he?" Her tone was short, she now swung in earnest. "We sleep together, don't we?"

Bronx drew back, his face flushing darkly. These women with their liberal logic were going to cost him his sanity one of these days! He managed to put on a calm tone.

"The fact is, Leslie, that the president is simply not reliable as far as we can tell."

Leslie hit the ball perfectly. It took off on an ideal trajectory with a light, satisfying whack. Her follow-through elegant, she followed the course of her projectile with visible pride. Bronx seemed unimpressed.

"Our Number One is a blabbermouth. His office is a rumor mill, with gossip flying around all over the place. Fragments of his undigested opinions circulate behind the scenes, and the next thing you know, one of his brainiacs is digging around, elaborating on stuff, and leaking it to the public. It's a recipe for a really bad mess. Do you understand now?"

Leslie leaned on her club. She was not clear on why, theoretically speaking, the disappearance of the First Lady should represent such an affair of state. What did the woman do, after all, besides occasionally receiving women's groups and looking decorative at charity events? She looked at Bronx as if ready to yawn.

"And why should the public not be informed in case something happened to the president's wife?"

Bronx could hardly believe his ears. The woman was annoying the hell out of him with her obstinacy.

"Ms. Palmer," he lectured in the condescending tone of a head teacher, "national security is at stake here. We are not naïve, and we have a collaborative strategy with the FBI and Secret Service in case the President, or his wife, falls prey to assassination."

He paused and bent down to place a ball that had rolled off the tee back in its place. She positioned the head of her club in front of the ball, as if contemplating her angle.

"I don't know. I'm sure that people would respond to such an event with a wave of sympathy for the President. A tragedy like that would only unite the nation, wouldn't it?"

Bronx waved her remark aside.

"This is not about the President. Our actions are aimed at the nation's highest interest."

Leslie swung. Bronx followed the ball with half-closed eyes until it landed around the 180 mark.

"This is a key psychological issue that we have analyzed thoroughly over a long period of time."

She slipped off one of her golf gloves, dangled it in an ironic gesture.

"You don't say, Mister!"

"If the President realizes that you are not his wife, then he will almost certainly drop you like a hot potato. In any case—it doesn't matter. His actions would almost certainly compromise you and your mission. And you know what to expect if you fail."

Leslie stared at him with wide eyes.

Bronx calmly extended a red cell phone.

"I really just wanted to bring you this."

"And what am I supposed to do with it?"

She returned the clubs to her golf bag. Bronx had thoroughly ruined her interest in the game, and more. She felt ready to throw up!

"From now on, you are to use only this secure phone. All of your calls will be automatically encrypted. It's user-friendly, but..."

Without a word she snatched the phone from his hand and marched off.

He waved a postcard size, color photograph between his thumb and forefinger.

"Hello, Madam, one more thing..."

Leslie's eyes were angry slits. She understood the nasty message at a single glance. There stood her sons, in front of a sunlit country house adorned with flowers. It was Paul Mercier's beautiful old chalet. Paul stood, smiling, between the two boys. Crosshairs had been drawn directly above Craig's head in red ink, marking him as a living target. It was almost ingenious in a dreadful, diabolical way! As a mother, she was mortified.

"Is... is he... What is this supposed to mean? Have you gone insane?"

Bronx shook his head.

"Obviously someone wants to convey a warning to an arrogant lady mother."

Leslie was ashen.

"Why Craig? What does he have to do with anything? I must speak to him."

Bronx looked around before whispering: "If you do not follow everything I tell you to the *letter*, Leslie, your boys will be taken care of. Both of them."

He looked at her with steady, ice-cold eyes.

Was this some kind of wild fantasy? The man was mad. She had to be dreaming! But Bronx was clearly standing in front of her like the devil incarnate. The only thing missing from his brutish mug was a set of horns.

"You and I both know that you're lying! You can't say something like that. Did you really just imply that my sons would be killed? *Killed?*"

He nodded. A completely casual nod. Leslie's eyes suddenly gleamed dangerously.

"You bastard! I'm going to the police, I will see your director in person. Yes—I will have you put behind bars... I work for the government, I have contacts, the President will hear about this all the way in the White House. You can bet your life on it. You...you dirty, rotten *bastard*!"

Bronx looked at her until she returned his gaze. Held it.

"Do whatever you want," he said coldly. "No one is going to believe you anyway. What kind of proof do you have? And if you go to the police, or to anyone else, you're just asking for trouble!"

Once again he raised the picture with the ominous crosshairs, held it right in front of her eyes.

Later, as she left the complex, she had to avoid a film crew shooting a scene in front of the entrances to the piers. She thought she recognized John Travolta. *How would* he *handle a predicament like this?*

It was no use thinking of revenge, even though she was boiling with rage. Her situation was hopeless. She just wanted to get home as quickly as possible, so that she could call Switzerland. *Why had Alex not called yet? And Dad! Yes, Dad would help her do the right thing. There was no other way. She would have to tell him everything.*

Hadn't John Travolta played the President once? The thought was somehow reassuring, as if she was in good company. She rushed through the Chelsea District, which was cluttered with pre-war houses, on to the 34th Street Subway, from where she would catch the N-line back home. The short walk did her good.

A group of motorbikes rumbled past her at a civilized pace. The men, riding easily on their colorful machines, took up the entire width of the street. PLEASURE CRUISE RIDERS, it said on the backs of their leather jackets. Leslie wanted nothing more than to be able to ride around like them, apparently without a care in the world, destined for a place where there were no obnoxious monsters like Rick Bronx... or that everything happening to her were just part of a movie with her the female lead... and good old John Travolta as the romantic hero. No—not Travolta! The man she needed was *Ben!* No question—when it came to comforting her, Ben was her very own Mister Perfect.

15

By the time she got home Leslie was quite despondent. As she hurriedly climbed the stairs to the entrance her head was filled with all Bronx had drummed into her. Her burdensome thoughts rode up with her in the elevator. Sighing, she placed one hand on the doorknob, picking her keys out of the side pocket of her blazer with the other. She was surprised to find that the key opened the security lock on her door with just a quarter turn clockwise. *Not what you'd call secure. Had she perhaps forgotten to lock up properly?* She took a few cautious steps into the entrance hall. Like an animal sensing danger, she immediately knew that she was not alone. Should she run? Turn on her heels and get the hell out? She advanced hesitantly.

"Anyone there?"

Of course she'd been mistaken. Panic. Paranoia. She threw her bag into the wardrobe recess, looked forward to the bright, warm light of her living room.

They stood in the middle of the parquet floor. Two men, their feet slightly apart. Leslie's heart pounded in her throat. One was larger than the other: a real meatball, with a fat, dark, sweaty face. He held his head aslant, as if resisting a strong wind. He was grinning.

"Hello, Ms. Palmer. My name is Leon. This here is my partner, Chenny. We thought we'd stop by and pay you a visit."

"Get to know each other," the smaller one grunted, sizing the place up as if he were taking measurements for a complete renovation—the olive colored wallpaper, the beige sofa, the Le Corbusier armchair. He had a very pale face, and a thin, straight mustache that didn't jive with his crooked, narrow eyes. His chin and jaw line appeared hard. Leslie stared at the fat one.

"Who are you? How did you get in here?"

She seriously asked herself whether they were out for sex. Disgusting, the way in which they were violating her beautiful apartment with their dirty presence. Calling the police? It was the little one with the crooked eyes who spoke.

"We don't mean any harm, honest!"

To prove it, he raised his hands reassuringly in a peaceable gesture that suited his skewed, angular face.

"We work with Mister Bronx," Leon explained, his greasy grin still in place.

Wonderful! So Bronx had a bunch of goons to do his dirty work! Leslie pretended to be impassive.

"If you don't leave this apartment instantly, there will be trouble," she threatened, taking a few steps toward the bedroom door. With lightning speed, she had put together a plan that should work. She just had to find an excuse to go to the bedroom, where she hid her service weapon.

"Of course you could call the police," the meaty one said. "It's not even like we wouldn't understand, right, Chenny? We did kind of come in uninvited."

With a nasty grin the little one perched himself on the edge of the glass table.

"But Mister Bronx will be very angry if you call the police. And we want to avoid that; because when he gets angry, bad things can happen. Very bad things."

Leslie couldn't believe her eyes. The brazenness of their intrusion seemed like it might be only the beginning of her worries. *And that midget thinks he can just sit his ass on my dining table!* She turned suddenly and made a dash for the bedroom. The surprise maneuver worked. She slammed the door behind her, took a deep breath, and ran to her large, broad bed. She kept her weapon under her mattress for protection. It was positioned in a way that would allow her to grab it easily in case of emergency—even if someone were to surprise her in her sleep. In her sleep—what a joke! These days gangsters apparently had no qualms about doing whatever they wanted in broad daylight. Unbelievable! *Just wait. I'm going to have them by the balls.* She lifted the side of the mattress, reached under it—her hand was met by emptiness. Only cold fabric. Her heart skipped a beat. Where had she put her damn piece? She reached again, lifted the mattress higher, looked under it. Nothing!

The door opened slowly. Leslie straightened up. The one with the crooked eyes stood in the door—*in her bedroom!* He raised a hand to reveal her gun. He grinned at her scornfully, allowing it to dangle by the trigger guard, through which he had cockily stuck his index finger. "Looking for anything special, Ms. Palmer?" he asked with a sneer as he motioned gruffly toward the parlor.

His fat friend, Leon, had made himself comfortable on the couch where he sat, legs bent wide apart. His jacket hung off his bloated gut like a piece of cardboard.

Should she just run? Leave the apartment to get help? That was hardly going to work. The little one's scabby hand was still playing with the revolver. "Safety off and loaded," he noted with a disparaging twist of the corners of his mouth, as if he had been able to read Leslie's thoughts. The fat one spoke, wearing an expression of deep disappointment on his face:

"Really. We only want to help you, you know. You can't have a problem with that, can you? I mean, we just want to make sure that you don't make any mistakes or something."

Leslie's voice sounded as sharp as a scalpel, with which she would dearly have liked to slice into his massive paunch. Lengthwise.

"Bronx sent you? What exactly do you want?"

"Well, see, your sons could suffer if you do anything rash. We just wanted to make that clear."

Her eyes stared emptily at his words.

"What's that supposed to mean? What do you know about my sons?"

She sank into the armchair by the glass table.

"Oh, we know everything we need to know. We are just concerned about their safety."

Fighting for composure, she still managed to counter.

"And just what do you think you can do? My boys are in Europe."

"Don't get us wrong here. We just want to help you, so you don't do nothing wrong. We want to make sure you follow all of Mister Bronx's directions the way he wants you to."

"And that you don't talk to anybody about any of this," added Chenny, who was looking into the muzzle of the gun in a bored manner.

Still seated on the edge of the table, he leaned forward. His face came closer to Leslie's.

"Listen, babe. If you let us down, Craig and Alex are quickly going to be slaughtered like a pair of pigs, get it?"

At these words, the fat one slapped his own forehead with the flat of his hand. "Oh, darn—I almost forgot."

He pulled a piece of paper that was folded down the middle from the side pocket of his jacket, holding it out to Leslie.

"This digital photo was taken a few hours ago. In Gstaad."

Gstaad. Gstaad, he was saying. *Unbelievable!*

"Give me that!" she barked at him.

She would have been better off not looking at it. Craig lying in a pool of blood, his face contorted in pain. Leslie's mouth felt dry, her lips were pressed together tightly. She started feeling dizzy. A dozen dull heartbeats later, she had finally collected herself enough to raise her head. She struggled to find words, but the little nasty man beat her to it.

"Yeah, girlie. Your Craig is still alive. Emphasis on *still.* He's short a coupla teeth and—err—has a couple more broken fingers than he had before. Don't take it too hard, baby. It's just a little reminder. A *little* one, mind you."

"Yeah, that's it," the fat one confirmed, "a little reminder, nothing more. If you do whatever Mr. Bronx expects from you, nothing else will happen to your boys."

"And... if I don't?" she stammered, even though she was already well aware of what the answer would be.

"Then we'll kill this one here, won't we. And if you still don't play nice, it'll be that one's turn."

He produced another color picture. This time Leslie recognized the person on it immediately.

She reflexively drew her head in. There was no question—it was her Alex, wearing a woolen cap and a large pair of goggles, and whirling high up in the air on a snowboard. The picture of her boy swam before her eyes. Somehow, she had ended up in a world that was surreal! *What she had just heard had to be a figment of her imagination.* She wiped a hand across her cheek, which was wet with tears. No. The shock she had suffered, seeing Craig in that picture in a pool of blood, was making her delirious...

"Alex!" she managed. "You...pigs...Miserable, filthy *swine*...Bronx's henchmen—paid torturers! *Ugh—you disgust me*!"

She spat right in the middle of the fat one's face. He wiped her spit away with the back of his hand, shook his head—as one does, when someone whom one is trying to help seems determined to continue to head for disaster.

"Aw, well. There, there!" he said, calm as could be. "We're something like partners, you and us. Bronx did write to let you know that we were coming, by the way. Like people do when they're polite. Why don't you go ahead and check your email?"

"Uh-huh. We already turned on the computer in the study," said the little one, his voice dripping with irony. "Just like I said, girlie, we're really doing our best to be helpful."

Leslie swayed to her office area more than she walked. Her thoughts were beginning to spin wildly. Everything was still in its place, only the monitor was on. Her email account was, indeed, open. It showed that she had received a new message. She clicked it open, and read:

"Leon and Chenny, my partners, will be visiting you. Be nice to them. Bronx."

Nice! That's all she needed. Leslie reproached herself. Her behavior had been stupid and cowardly. Why was she putting up with all of this? But she knew the answer before she had finished her thought: Bronx had taken Alex and Craig hostage. She had no other option; not the slightest choice!

The tub of lard finally heaved himself up off the couch. He nodded at the little one.

"So, be careful, Ms. Palmer. And everything will be fine."

He nudged Chenny, who shrugged his shoulders muttering *Alright, alright then,* out of the door ahead of him. Leslie yelled like an animal that had been shot in the belly.

"That's right—beat it, you...you...*pigs from hell!*"

Raging, eyes dark with hatred, she hurled the thick brass paperweight. It crashed into the door, just as it clicked shut behind the two.

16

Nassim Hassan reclined comfortably on the ultimate biker showpiece: an old Harley on which, it was rumored, Elvis himself once rode. He rumbled down Houston Street at a leisurely pace, before turning onto the broad Avenue of the Americas.

When the lights turned green in a row that stretched into the distance, Nassim opened the throttle and roared past a bus and across the intersection. The long, six-lane street lay before him like a racetrack. There was little traffic. The engine droned. The towers of the World Trade Center sparkled in his side mirrors. Sandy's curls blew into his field of vision. She sat behind him, wearing a black, tightly fitted helmet, like the ones worn by English soldiers in WWI trenches.

The other bikes came closer after about half a mile. Riding in loose formation, they occupied the entire width of the road. Gleaming, full-face helmets hid the faces of the men who roared up, majestically, on their machines. Sandy waved easily.

Noise filled Sixth Avenue. The lights turned yellow. Nassim raised a hand on which he wore a fine, black leather glove. Engines revved down; wheels slowed, turned toward the curb.

Whenever Nassim removed his helmet with the red Superman tail, Sandy was taken aback by the fullness of his hair and mesmerized by his sparkling, black eyes.

The look he returned was a mixture of villainous cunning and gentle caring. That was Nassim—a ruffian with charm.

The other Pleasure Cruise Riders heaved their massive, chrome adorned, colorfully painted machines onto their kickstands and gathered around Nassim. It was greeting and backslapping time.

"So, when are you finally going to get rid of this piece of junk?" the gaunt one said with a grin.

Nassim's Harley was known amongst connoisseurs as a masterpiece with a lot of years on its back. Over one hundred thousand miles on the road had worn at its mechanics and engine: Nassim really was thinking of selling.

"This machine is in excellent condition, mate," he played along defensively. "It has dignity, boy, not like that zucchini-looking Suzuki of yours. Someone offered me twelve grand for it on e-Bay, no shit."

They sat down at the street café's metal outdoor tables and ordered.

Only one man was missing. Other than that, everyone of the inner circle of the Pleasure Cruise Riders had followed the summons of their leader. Nassim raised his hand importantly, tossed his long, tethered hair over his shoulder.

"The rally is on the 11th of September. We meet on Fulton Street, as planned. Where we always do."

Long Bill blew a pillar of cigarette smoke into the air.

"When's the new one coming?"

"Pretty soon, I hope. Should be right in time for the rally."

A swarm of bike riders wearing black sunglasses droned closer, their modified helmets styled after the German Wehrmacht 1943 vintage headgear shadowed their pale faces above worn leather jackets. Almost as one, they raised their fists against the Pleasure Cruise Riders, and drew protesting honks from a cab as they swerved in loose patterns across the entire avenue, smirking broadly as they passed.

"The Rommels," Long Bill remarked dismissively.

The Pleasure Cruise people avoided them. They themselves did things in style. Most of them either had good jobs, or were independent. Long Bill, who had the brawny build of a college football player, was the managing director of a packaging plant in the Meat District. Ronnie, a pudgy, bald-headed man with a mustache, excelled as telematic specialist, who always kept the group up on the latest gadgets, having in depth knowledge of all of the tricks of illegal interception.

Nassim was the oldest of their group. He also seemed more seasoned, not to say devious, than the others. He was usually unshaven, smoked pink cigarillos, and could be downright despicable. He was, no doubt, the most interesting one of the lot—certainly as far as women were concerned. They tended to think of the eminent surgeon as a real catch, possibly also because he had a stiff leg, was never at a loss for sexist comments, and downed a constant stream of painkillers that only appeared to add to his allure. What seemed to be the man's injured soul almost irresistibly drew out women's caretaking instincts. They couldn't wait to stroke the divorced loner's ego, and anything else that needed it.

Nassim was not just a bike enthusiast; he also loved soaps and gambling. And when he put down one of his well-tuned saxophone riffs, he may just as well have been opium as far as all of those willing, would-be nurses were concerned. As a senior surgeon at the Medical Center's Bellevue Emergency Room he patched up victims of beatings and shootings with sovereign competence. The solemnly dramatic demeanor of the gaunt, youngest man of the group, on the other hand, might have been that of a televangelist. But Martin Luther, as the man of supposed German heritage insisted was his real name, successfully ran a mundane plumbing workshop, where an old Ferrari was jacked up right next to an assortment of toilet bowls. The fourth group member was—what else—a lawyer. There were so many of those running around New York that being of the profession wasn't even noteworthy. But Chuck Browne, a young junior district attorney, prided himself on standing firmly on the side of the law—or what he took for it.

They had one distinct feature in common—the color of their skin. They were not pitch black, like the Senegalese from whom they had apparently descended; nor were they light brown, like Puerto Rican half-casts. They were a bit darker than that, say the color of the famous brown bags that Manhattan stores handed their customers their merchandise in.

The Rommels had returned, circled in front of the café like sleek sharks, and then jerked their beasts over the curb and onto the pavement, obviously looking for a fight. One of them swung a Budweiser bottle in his fist like a grenade.

"Hey, you rich little city pricks, wanna race? You're just crapping yourselves already, aren't you?" the one in front on a black BMW bawled.

Behind him, a broad-chested man got off his bike and stepped up to Nassim with a rowdy attitude. Nassim put a pink cigarillo between his lips and casually lit up. The Rommel blustered on.

"Did you say something, cripple? You don't like us much, do you?"

"Not here, Rommel boy," Nassim answered, coolly blowing smoke up in his face. "We'll see you at the Bogey Dump. Just the right place for you washed-up punks."

The Bogey Dump, an abandoned garbage dump close to Long Island Air Force Base, was a hotbed for the motocross crowd.

The eyes of the man wearing the Wehrmacht helmet narrowed to slits. He was obviously contemplating whether he wanted to deck the arrogant asshole or not, but he thought better of it when he looked into Nassim's hard face and cold eyes.

"Ha. You hear Mister Bigmouth, here?" he spat. "These weekend wanna-be bikers would like a race! Fine, you losers—the Bogey Dump it is!"

A scuffle suddenly broke out around Long Bill. Fists started to fly. Long Bill had one of the punks in a headlock and was heaving him around in circles, so that his frantically kicking legs kept the others at bay.

The situation was dangerous. Knives could be drawn at any moment. Nassim was still contemplating his next move when the cops came racing up, blue lights flashing.

The Rommels stepped back toward their bikes and acted innocent. The men from the New York City Highway Patrol stepped up in their heavy boots. They chained the Rommels' bikes together and then took their time examining registration papers, driver's licenses, and proof of insurance. They called the data through to headquarters. A sloppily dressed plain-clothes cop checked the VIN numbers on the machines with a flashlight. The Rommels were on their best behavior. They stood there, whispering, their shaven heads stark white against their dark leather outfits. Half an hour later the Pleasure Cruise Riders were still continuing their club meeting, undisturbed and apparently not much interested, when the humbled braggarts meekly took off again.

"I'll be riding my new Honda on the eleventh," Nassim crowed. He stood, patted imaginary dust off his leather jacket. "Don't forget where we're meeting. The Rommels avoid the Plaza—they won't hassle us there."

Sandy was reverently polishing the galvanized cylinder with a red cloth when Martin Luther stepped up to her and casually, yet gently, patted her stomach.

"You think you'll be able to hold out until the eleventh?"

"Hands off, you monster," she said, laughing. "First of all, I am retiring my Honda for now, and secondly, I'm not due until the end of November."

She stroked her stomach softly. Sandy was the official Pleasure Cruise Riders caterer. A job her service team, high up in the South Tower Windows on the World restaurant, managed with ease.

The sun shone in a glorious Indian summer sky. A scheduled airliner flew high above the glistening Twin Towers, drawing a thin line of condensation through the cloudless blue. Nassim made a casual turning motion with his slightly raised, black-gloved index finger. The Pleasure Cruise Riders mounted their bikes, revved their engines once, twice, and roared off. This was America. Home of the free.

17

They were sitting in Leslie's workspace. Ben had run Bronx's email through his program and gained access to the sender's server just minutes later. He scratched the back of his head.

"Funny, Les, these messages that your guy is getting... I'll be damned if I know what to make of them."

The Synxx spyware program projected an ocean of data onto Leslie's screen.

"Show me!"

Leslie moved her chair up closer and looked at the pieces of text interrupted by series of apparently random numbers.

"The faculty of economics... the faculty of life sciences..." he read aloud. "Here, the faculty of medicine, the faculty of law... What is this all about? Has he got something to do with the educational system?"

"Who's sending him these emails? Can't your ingenious program tell us that?"

Ben furrowed his brow.

"Sure, sure, I can find out, later maybe—see, these are encrypted messages. You should be up on this kind of stuff."

She kissed him briefly on the cheek.

"I decode body language, sweetheart. *Hang on!*"

She suddenly froze, her lips a thin line.

"What is it? Cracked the code already?" Ben teased.

She rose, shaking her head, and began to pace slowly back and forth. There had been something else! Yes, Bronx's right arm. Leslie recalled his gestures, remembered how he held it, stiffly, in front of his upper body—like a defensive boxing move. Standing up, walking…his hand clenched in a fist. He wanted to prove something. The know-it-all? No. The dogmatic one. Maybe? The destroyer, yes, the…

She drummed her fists against her temples, sat back down.

"I just can't put my finger on it."

"Les, this guy is with the CIA, isn't he? So—the faculties may stand for…countries, or towns…companies. It's possible, isn't it?"

She nodded, waiting.

"This is the really odd message: *Submission deadline for all faculties: September 11, 2001.* Isn't that weird?"

"There are such things as enrollment deadlines, Ben," she suggested.

He brushed her comment aside, as if she had understood nothing, then spoke firmly.

"If I were with the Secret Service, my alarms would be going off like crazy right about now. Of course this is only my insignificant, amateurish opinion, but I believe that September 11 is code for triggering of some kind of operation. Maybe to blow up these so-called 'faculties,' or to rob financial institutions that these guys have labeled as faculties."

Leslie remained skeptical. "Those CIA spooks may be all kinds of things, but they aren't bank robbers."

"That's not the point. What we need to know is, what these

faculties stand for? That is the analytic million-dollar question. Aren't you counterintelligence?"

She motioned both hands in denial.

Ben leaned over the screen again. For a while, all was silent except for the tapping of keys.

"Listen... a certain Mohammed is studying economics, Ahmed medicine... Hassan... here, a real tongue twister... all Arabs. Terrorists, if you ask me."

"Now you're just seeing ghosts, Ben. Bronx is at the Middle East Desk. His informants happen to be Arabs from there and not Mayans from Guatemala." She theatrically suppressed a little yawn. "So they send him this junk in coded language, it's the way to do things. By the way, September 11th is this coming Tuesday."

Ben took an indifferent sip of champagne.

"I'll tell you one thing..."

"Go ahead!"

"Champagne is excellent for your complexion."

She threw a paperback at his head in feigned indignation. Ben caught it easily and threw it back.

"Boomerang!" he called boisterously.

Leslie gave him a dark look, as if he had insulted her terribly. Ben began an unworried apology.

"Wait—I've got it," she cried. "He is the rejected one, lusting for revenge. The rejected one, turned destroyer! That's it!" Excited, she jumped up and clenched her fists, punching the air.

"He's fighting back!"

"Who? Sure you're all right?"

"Never mind, forget it. It's just, his gestures... I see it... psychology of motion is my field of expertise!"

Her wild shadowboxing had made her feel trancelike. She saw a clear image of Bronx in her mind's eye—misunderstood, rejected, humiliated, not taken seriously. He sought to annihilate symbols of power in an avid thirst for revenge... Maybe even the USS *Cole*... the destroyer... and the embassies in Africa..." Yes. Yes, that had to be it!

"He's an Al Qaeda mercenary, Ben," she declared, alarmed.

And now what? Call Jennifer? It made sense. Maybe she still had her mysterious job and knew the right people inside the CIA. People who might know more about Bronx. Yes, she would call.

Right now, however, Ben was stopping her from doing so. He had put his arms around her from behind and maneuvered her toward the living room couch. She freed herself and gave him a shove making him plop onto the sofa. Laughing, she straddled his lap and kissed him passionately. The heat of the moment made everything else fade into nothingness. The thrill of anticipation let her forget everything but him. And what if the world went to the dogs! Her hand strayed across his body to find the only hard truth that mattered in this sensuous moment.

The U.S. Ambassador to Tajikistan smiled a forced smile from Leslie's other monitor. Ben's fingers searched for the sleep mode button. The smile died unceremoniously. He gathered Leslie in his powerful arms and carried her lithe body to the bedroom, where he let himself fall with her onto the generously proportioned bed. Being a man who appreciated order, he noted with amusement that a certain structure had snuck into these midday rendezvous. It gave them both the emotional security they needed to give themselves utterly and completely to their hot lovemaking.

And so Leslie had fallen into a satisfied slumber when Ben went to the kitchen to grab a beer out of the fridge, then quietly crept back to her office space. He opened the page, copied the encoded messages, compressed them, and sent them to his own email address. *Done!* He would take his time finding and researching the senders of the suspicious messages once he got home.

Before closing the page, he made sure that he had not only transferred all of the IP data correctly, but that he had complete access to all of the key data that his Synxx software had cited—including server ID's, passwords and access codes. He checked his watch. Four thirty. He stuck the copies in his jacket, snuck back to the bedroom door and cast a last glance at his lover.

Leslie had thrown her left leg over the sheet; both of her breasts were exposed. Her dark, shiny nipples were hard, even in her sleep, while her facial features were relaxed; almost liberated. She had a faint smile on her lips. Oh, *baby!* He stepped back, moved silently to the door, and snuck out. *Baby, baby, baby!*

18

The World Trade Center Path station was bustling with people. Thousands of commuters coming from work headed to their trains to bring them home. Leslie rushed up the escalator to the large shopping mall, stopping in front of a long row of public phones. She huddled into the narrow opening and dialed the number that she had not called in over a year.

The phone in Maryland seemed to ring endlessly, then a voice. Leslie's maternal heart beat in anguish—three, four times.

"Jennifer? It's me. How are you?"

The answer was also a while in coming.

"I'm fine, but I suppose you're not. Otherwise you would hardly be calling!"

Leslie pretended not to have heard the rebuke.

"I'm fine. Health-wise, anyway. But I have to speak to you. Can you fly over here?"

She waited. Jennifer was clearly not enthused by Leslie's request.

"It's important Jennifer, really. You have to believe me; someone is after us. They want to finish us. They beat Craig terribly."

Leslie sobbed. Jennifer's voice suddenly sounded compassionate.

"Mom, I'll call you right back."

Jennifer was stunningly beautiful. She had that flawless, slightly brown skin-tone, a soft, narrow face with high cheekbones, deep-set, tranquil eyes, silky black hair, and sensually curved lips.

No wonder—her father had been an exceptionally good-looking man, and intelligent to boot: Pandar, a highly talented molecular biologist.

Jennifer was Leslie's first child, and also her best kept secret. Her lover had been married, and she could not afford a scandal at the time. She would have been thrown out of college immediately. Leslie gave birth secretly, stated *father unknown* on the birth certificate and cared for the child until she gave it up for adoption. She hated herself for it, but her career—Pandar had implored her—was on the line. She had simply not been ready to raise a child. She sighed. Jennifer was not officially listed anywhere as her daughter. Neither her dad, nor Craig and Alex, knew of the beautiful half-sister, now 24 years old, born on September 11. It was her birthday next week. And Leslie, who sent her a check from a special account every three months, would top the next one with an extra amount.

19

Having arrived at his apartment, Ben sat down behind drawn shades, turned his printer on and printed two copies of the messages about the faculties. Next, he typed up two short letters, printed those on plain, white paper, and stuck them into separate envelopes, each with a copy of the mysterious emails. He addressed one to the CIA, Langley, Virginia, the other to the FBI, Washington, D.C. He carefully considered everything one more time. The government agencies would be able to determine that Ben had accessed the emails by hacking into the account of a certain Rick Bronx, and would no doubt follow up on the matter. Or should he actually serve up Bronx's contacts for them on a silver tray? He hadn't really reached the point at which he was willing to do that. First he wanted to find the senders of the secret messages for himself. At any rate, he had done his duty as a good citizen, even if they could accuse him of performing an illegal act by fishing emails from secure servers.

His cell phone chortled—it was Leslie: stressed out and short-spoken. She was on her way to her father's in Brooklyn. In a soft tone, she promised Ben she would call him again later. He took a sweat jacket from its hook and left. The early evening was mild; the first lights had begun to sparkle from the high-rise façades. He hurried along 67th Street, across

Third Avenue and over to Lexington, his steps light. There, he hailed a cab and headed over to 42nd Street. It was in this bustling area around Grand Central Station, which was as lively as it was blemished, that he stepped into a FedEx office and sent the two letters by express delivery.

As he strolled past Grand Central and onto Third, deciding that he would walk back home, he suddenly realized that he had put Leslie at risk by using her computer for his hacking purposes. Anyone with the necessary interest, and patience—and of course the extensive knowledge of an ingenious Synxx programmer, such as Ben—would be able to localize the fishing source. In effect, they could even extract Leslie's home address from the data pool.

Still, Ben was not seriously concerned. Rather, he was hoping that his letters would rouse the powers-that-be. He had no problem picturing himself a celebrated hero on the front page of the *POST,* under a bold heading that read something like Hacker Prevents Terrorist Attack. No problem at all.

20

After her conversation with Jennifer, Leslie entered the WTC 7 underground parking lot of the Naval Intelligence Agency and pressed the key on her car remote. Her platinum colored Audi lovingly blinked its headlights at her in response. *At least one thing that could be depended upon!*

She carefully curved her way up into the fading summer-evening light. Soon deep in thought, she hardly noticed that she had made it through thick traffic all the way to the Brooklyn Bridge. Her head was completely occupied with thoughts of the conversation she had with her father about his dramatic experience at Odessa Hospital over forty years ago. Her curiosity simply refused to die down. No amount of distraction was helping. *Her father had told the obstetrician, Kirkhoff, about one girl. Singular! He had foisted the second baby, her twin sister, off on the woman who had suffered a stillbirth. Who had that woman been?* Over the next couple of hours, her father would finally lay his cards on the table and reveal the last remaining secret of that tragic night. Smiling to herself—her heart almost stopped.

Startled, she hit the brakes. The wheels screeched as the car skidded to a stop. The man jumped aside, wearing a look of horror. The red light! She had been so deep in thought that she hadn't even seen it. How embarrassing! She gestured wildly, grimacing apologetically. At first, the guy stared at her angrily, then his face relaxed into a grin and he continued on his way. "I'm fine," he mouthed. Leslie heaved a big sigh of relief.

Turning onto familiar Cranberry Street, where Charles Palmer had acquired one of the sought-after houses in Brooklyn's historic district years ago, she had another terrible fright.

An entire armada of blue and white police cars stood flashing outside of the house that had served as a backdrop for *Moonstruck* with Cher several years ago. It was hard to forget the trailers, utility trucks, lighting equipment, and all of the other stuff with which the film crew had barricaded everything. Now the brownstone with the broad stairway was completely taped-off with yellow police tape. There were uniformed cops standing around everywhere. The red and white beacons of their patrol cars flashed eerily. A news team had positioned itself next to a police van. The reporter was sticking a mike into some plainclothes bigwig's face. People stood in dazed clusters; some had pushed their way up to the tape.

Leslie honked frantically, parting the shocked crowd with her car until a uniformed policewoman blocked her path. She jumped out, rushed at the woman, screaming, "I have to get in there. What happened? Let me through immediately!"

Not waiting for an answer, she shoved the officer aside, ran up the steps.

A big civilian with a wild mane of hair, wearing a motorbike jacket, stood in the doorway. He raised a hand in a calming gesture. "Hello, please! I'm District Attorney Chuck Browne, are you . . . ?"

Leslie reflexively yanked out her Naval Intelligence ID badge.

"What has happened to my father?" she panted.

Browne cast a practiced eye on the badge, then said calmly, "Come with me, Ms. Palmer."

He put a protective arm around her shoulder and guided her into the house.

Charles Palmer's corpulent body lay at the foot of the stairs that led to the bedroom on the second floor. The junior district attorney lifted the white sheet from his face. Leslie suppressed a scream. His white head lay in a pool of dark red blood, the eyes stared at her coldly, their light extinguished.

His arms were stretched obliquely to one side, as if he had been trying to break his fall.

"Daddy…" Leslie broke down, sobbing. She leaned over him, grasping his arms. "Daddy, Daddy, Daddy!"

Crime scene investigators padded around silently.

"I'm sorry for your loss," Browne mumbled.

Leslie had to gather all of her strength in order not to howl with pain. Seeing her father this way broke her heart. She took it all in, her eyes dull: his supine position, the angle of his legs, the checkered sports shirt, his black jeans. For a long time, she was unable to shift her gaze from all of this unspeakable sadness. Her heart clenched. She felt an evil foreboding rising within.

Then she gently closed his eyes. In a strained voice she asked what had happened.

Father's head was unnaturally twisted. It seemed to her that his face bore a peculiarly mysterious expression, as if he were intent on telling her something. Something like *Be careful, my girl. They're after you!*

"…skull fracture," she heard the district attorney saying.

"And? How did it happen? Do you have any idea?"

Leslie was breathing in bursts as she fought down waves of nausea.

"You mean, was it an accident?" Browne asked.

She nodded. Someone who introduced himself as the medical examiner said, "The body has not been released yet."

Leslie's voice suddenly sounded very sober.

"My father was murdered!"

The men stared at her. She had composed herself.

"What are your findings, Doctor?"

"The head wound was caused by a hard, blunt object. Could be the stair rail."

"The stair rail is made of wood," Leslie countered.

"We can't rule out assault," Browne said carefully. "Did your father have any enemies?"

Leslie did not need to think long. *Of course, this was Bronx's doing. The CIA shut Dad up!* Her thoughts raced. She finally shook her head in denial.

"Are you sure—there are signs of a break-in," said Browne. "Would you be able to tell us if there are any valuables missing?"

"Yes, I would!"

She numbly mounted the stairs to the bedroom. *In the drawer, where I keep the revolver... there's a red envelope...*

The dreadful disarray in the bedroom did not fit in with father's disciplined lifestyle. Leslie recognized at a single glance that the room had been searched. Hastily, she kneeled down and rummaged through the open drawers. Her hand found the revolver under old, woolen socks, touched against metal cufflinks, groped the naked wood searchingly... Nothing! *The other drawers, the study! She had to look.*

She searched in vain, no red envelope surfaced. It was gone! Disappeared! Exhausted, she sank down next to her father, and gently pressed her dry lips against the curve of his forehead.

His face looked as if he were just asleep, dreaming peacefully. There was no sign of suffering. She slid her fingers softly through a silvery curl that had strayed—and felt something—a piece of glass. She looked more closely: crystal. She jumped up and ran to the bar in the study, where she froze. "It's not there," she said tonelessly to Browne, who had followed her in alarm.

"What isn't?"

"The crystal carafe!" Leslie breathed. She pointed to the leather wastepaper basket under the desk.

One of the investigators pulled the heavy crystal receptacle from its hiding place, looked up at the carved molding along the ceiling as if looking for inspiration, then inspected the blood and hair stuck to the glass. He vaguely muttered something about unmistakable evidence. Leslie all but jumped on the man.

"So it was murder! Do you know who did it?"

The detective vacantly moved his shoulders.

Later, as Leslie stood under the hot shower in her apartment, the spray from the massage showerhead soothing her abused body, the realization hit her without mercy: she herself had killed her father! She bore the sole responsibility for his dreadful death. She had defied Bronx's strict instructions and thoughtlessly let her father in on what was happening, thus sealing his fate. In complete despair, she threw herself onto the bed, naked and wet, hiding her face in the pillows.

It took a while before she realized that her cell phone was vibrating. It was the district attorney.

"Ms. Palmer? It's Browne. I just wanted to inform you that we were able to lift prints off a cup in the kitchen. It'll be a while before we have a suspect profile. But this has brought us a big step further."

She thanked him and saved his number. She liked the man—he was one of those people she would classify as "no-nonsense." A front line soldier in the fight against evil. A crying jag seized her. It took a while before it subsided into soft sobs.

21

The following morning Leslie walked over to Madison Avenue, and past the Whitney Museum. She stopped in front of the Carlyle Hotel. The fresh breeze soothed her battered soul. She had time before her meeting with Jennifer, so she pulled her phone out of her bag and sought refuge from the street noise under the protective cover of a public call box. As the call went through to her office, she watched a man looking at the display of a maternity store window. Sheer force of habit made her note his appearance: the short, black hair, the dark-blue turtleneck sweater. There was nothing new at work, and Wagner knew how to get a hold of her. There was something annoying about the guy! *MotherCare? Why was he interested in maternity clothes? His large nose was not pointed at the wares he was supposedly looking at, but remained raised, as if he were following a reflection in the window. Whatever.* Her growling stomach led her to the cafeteria diagonally across the intersection.

A short while later she was nibbling at a bagel, drinking a cappuccino, and checking her cell phone for messages. The display showed a missed call. Curious, she checked the number. Browne, the district attorney! She hit the call button. The elegantly designed phone automatically dialed his number. After Browne politely inquired as to her wellbeing, he came straight to the point.

"Muhammed Jannos, that name mean anything to you?"

She shielded her phone with one hand.

"I assume you're going to tell me he's my father's murderer. What about him?"

"Well, Muhammed Jannos has been incarcerated in a high-security New Jersey prison for almost ten years," she heard Browne's pleasant voice say through the babble of voices at the restaurant.

"So he was on prison leave when he killed my father?"

The line was silent.

"Hello, are you still there?"

"I am," Browne replied, sotto voce. "Jannos is dead—shanked in prison the day after your father's death. He hadn't been out since the day of his conviction. He had no existing family members. He was a loner. Someone faked the evidence, Leslie. The prints on the cup were planted..." He broke off.

Leslie clutched her forehead, her voice was shaking.

"You will find out who's behind this, Browne. I am going to help you."

If you do not follow everything I tell you to the letter, Leslie, your boys will be taken care of. Both of them... Bronx's warning stabbed at her heart like a dagger.

"I've been removed from the case, Leslie. I'm sorry. I can't talk right now. Thanks."

The phone cut off.

Leslie stared at its red casing. Should she call Bronx? Wasn't it more important to contact the undertaker? At some point, she would have to take care of the house, sort through her father's files and the papers on his desk. Manuscripts? What was going to happen with the furniture, the old brown, round dining room table that he never ate at, but used to work on his reports? There was an overwhelming amount to do. She sighed, put a few bills on the table and made to get up. Her cell chimed.

Leslie's heart sank. Bronx! His cold voice rasped into her ear.

"It was murder, Leslie. The evidence leads to a derelict black guy from Harlem. His motive was robbery." When Leslie remained silent, Bronx lowered his voice, "I'm very sorry about your loss, really. My condolences!" She felt her throat constrict at his feigned compassion. Struggling for air, she burst out, "I don't believe a word you're saying, Bronx. You're a damn liar!"

"You violated my strict orders," he countered. "You blabbed and told your father about the mission. That was bad of you. We know everything, Leslie. Not that it matters anymore."

Bronx's hoarse, threatening tone stabbed at her with every word.

"I just wanted to say, think of your sons. As long as you do a good job, you won't regret it. We'll take good care of them. Just like the Mafia takes care of its own, I'll see to it that they have everything they need. I think we can all learn a lesson from the Mafia, especially when it comes to payback, right?"

This maliciousness cut even deeper into her tortured soul. Bronx's voice now seemed to be droning in her ear from a distance.

"If you screw this up, Leslie, then I don't give a shit what happens to your two idiots. I don't give a shit whether they live or die." Rick Bronx used what seemed to be his favorite word again, his voice rising alarmingly, "Not a *shit,* I'm telling you... if you don't wise up, I won't be able to protect Alex and Craig. Think of your Daddy."

The line went dead.

She tasted bile in her mouth. She stood up, swayed out of the coffee shop. *If Bronx had meant to lay down an ice-cold ultimatum, he had succeeded*; she choked inwardly as she waved a taxi down. She got in, her face ashen.

"York and 72nd."

She stared straight ahead, as she touched her hot cheeks.

Bronx was applying the thumbscrews. He had her by the throat. Now it was going to be an eye for an eye, a tooth for a tooth...

22

"I'm going to take this guy down," Leslie ensured her daughter grimly. "I am going to expose that pig. Whoever, or whatever, he is. A double agent working for Al Qaeda? An out-of-control freelancer? An evil criminal, abusing his power?"

"Come on, Mom, you have to know that's crazy. He's CIA. There's nothing you can do."

They stood at the end of 72nd Street, looking out onto the East River from the platform overlooking FDR Drive. A barge plowed against the current of green, shimmering water with its broad bow. A sightseeing boat approaching downstream sounded its dull horn.

"He killed Dad. Craig and Alex are next. He has to be stopped. It's true, I want to finish him. That is my goal. And nothing is going to stop me."

"I've been looking into this," Jennifer countered, calmly. "Rick Bronx is both trusted and respected."

Leslie waved both hands wildly, but Jennifer remained firm.

"Mom, keep your fingers off Bronx. The CIA is more than you can chew. Threatening is a routine thing in their business. But the wet job days are long gone."

"Wet job?"

"Governmental killing. Something like that can't move forward without authorization from way up the chain of command. Not anymore. During times of war, maybe. But we're not at war."

"Jenny, I bet you this son-of-a-bitch is plotting much worse than just that. I know it. I can read his demeanor like an open book—a very evil book."

Jennifer leaned against the railing.

"What he's asking of you, that you don't talk about your mission, that's completely reasonable. You know that very well yourself. Whatever he is implementing has been signed off at the highest level. You can count on it."

"I want to fight," Leslie said, defiantly. "That's how I was raised. Dad always used to say, 'Fight back, before it's too late.'"

Upset, she began to pace. Jennifer looked at her earnestly.

"Alright, I have a few pieces of information for you. But you need to know that I'm sticking my neck out here. Is all of this really as important as you think?"

Leslie made a small gesture of complete helplessness.

"I'm afraid, Jen. This man murdered Dad. He is blackmailing me with Alex and Craig. You have to know that I'm done if anything goes wrong. These people are merciless. This person, this Amira al Raisa, is my only lead. And my gut tells me I'm on the right track."

"Look, Mom. Bronx's position within the CIA is undisputed. He is involved in the Middle East. It seems that he has his informants over there. He is what we refer to as an *eagle*, which means that he is an agent with certain liberties. His mother is Arabian. She lives in the capital of Tajikistan . . . Dushanbe?"

Leslie avoided a skateboarder who was curving toward her.

"I know where that is," she snapped.

"Bronx's mother has freelance status with the CIA," Jennifer continued, unperturbed. "No big deal. She reports to the station chief. Takes care of little odd jobs. Bronx sends her a check every month."

"Is that all?"

"That's a hell of a lot, Leslie. Now you know his weak spot."

"Bronx's?"

A helicopter suddenly sputtered over the roofline of an adjacent high-rise.

"Of course," Jennifer yelled into the noise, nodding repeatedly.

"You mean . . . ?"

"Oh, please! Don't play naïve," Jennifer said, visibly annoyed, as she followed the receding machine with her eyes. "I'm only doing this because you're practically one of us. Naval Intelligence. If anybody asks, it's a simple matter of information exchange."

They parted from the railing and took a leisurely walk back to York Avenue.

"Sure, that's all I know," Leslie promised. "Do you have the mother's address?"

Jennifer rolled her eyes in a dramatic show of resignation.

"*Hello!* Who do you think you're dealing with here? Of course I have it—here. And I can count on you not telling anyone about any of this?"

"*Hello!*" her mother countered smilingly. "And how did you get a hold of it?"

"My boss, Ken Cooper, knows a few people in counterintelligence. His security clearance is high—level three, at least. That gives him access to certain data."

Leslie grabbed Jennifer's arm.

"Do you really think Bronx is clean?"

Jennifer shook her head.

"No. He spent a long time in Afghanistan, speaks Arabic, is familiar with the Koran, his mother is Muslim." She stepped off the sidewalk, raised an arm. The taxi pulled over. "Bronx is secure in his position, but would I *trust* him? No, certainly not. I don't trust any of those guys."

Leslie leaned her head to one side.

"When will I see you again, Jen?"

"Don't know," her daughter said evasively, as she got into the car. "Maybe Christmas. Are Alex and Craig coming home?"

She pulled the door shut behind her and turned to the driver. The taxi did a U-turn. Jennifer gave a quick wave through the window, her expression serious. Leslie kept her eyes on her daughter for a while, dropped her waving left hand. Then, with long, energetic strides, she set off on the short walk home . . .

23

. . . Her steps began to slow. It was with a feeling of emptiness that she now walked past a row of clothing boutiques, then impulsively changed direction after a few buildings. Her thoughts focused on revenge, on Tajikistan, she hardly noticed how she got to 82nd Street. She stopped, undecided, in front of a large bookstore on Lexington. *Should she take the subway back?* Then, through the window, she suddenly saw a young man perusing a book table. Ben? What a wonderful surprise! She entered the bright store with a sense of buoyancy, made her way through mountains of books, and finally reached her lover.

"Ben?"

A stranger's face turned to look at her. Disappointed, she sought out the quiet corner with the comfortable chairs.

There was a table with glossy magazines, one of which captured Leslie's attention. She sat down, began to page apathetically through the luxuriously arranged articles. Every once in a while, she lifted her gaze as if she had not quite given up on the elusive hope that Ben might appear after all. And there it was! A broad, ragged, brown valley with shimmering, silver river branches: *Tajikistan*. She read the captions to the breathtaking photographs, diving deep into that far-off, exotic world. She soaked up its strange names like a sponge: Dushanbe, Pamir, and the eastern highlands where the most revered Imam of all Imams, the Aga Khan, ruled. The helicopters, the pilots . . . it was fascinating.

Leslie looked around furtively, then ripped out the pages, coughing loudly to muffle the sound. Nobody took any notice. Exhilarated, she rushed home with her find. A plan was beginning to take shape.

Ben? She wanted Ben. She carelessly dropped her bag and jacket as soon as she entered her apartment, kicking her shoes off on the way to the phone.

"Ben?"

His taped voice vibrated through her body. She left a message, and contemplated. *Could Ben help her? The piano player, computer freak, software specialist, skier, angler, pizza delivery boy... what all else? Lover—no—gift to womankind!*

But her geographic interests prevailed. She called again and left a message on his machine.

"Ben, I need information on Tajikistan, Pamir... I mean, what's over there? What goes on there? How would one get there?"

This question seemed pretty stupid to herself. She sat down at the computer, opened Trip Advisor.

Nothing. Destination unknown. Just a moment—there...

...There was a Tajikistan Airlines. No flights from New York, only from Munich and Almati.

Munich, departure 17.40, arrival at 05.50 the next morning, local time. A long flight with a stopover in Istanbul.

She ended her research just before midnight, and finally switched first her computer, then herself, to *sleep* mode...

24

The next day, she hurried back to Brooklyn from the funeral home. One more time, she thoroughly searched all of the rooms in the ghostly silence that pervaded her father's house. Still, she was unable to locate the red dossier. She half-heartedly ate some of the sushi she had brought along, then quickly dialed the number in Switzerland. She had to tell Craig and Alex about their grandfather's funeral. Since no one answered, she settled on sending a text message: Funeral Tuesday, 4 p.m., Greenwood. Then she locked up.

The taxi was waiting out front. Without any nerve-racking traffic jams along the way, she made good time to the flag decorated entrance of the United Nations building, where she arrived at the very last minute. Panting, she reached the U.S. delegation's conference room on the 21st floor.

"Everything's ready," good-old Shelley murmured, discreetly handing her the laser pointer. Clearing her throat, she stepped up to the podium.

"Hello, people, time to get serious," she called out cheerfully. "I hope you haven't had too much sushi for lunch, like I have, because I am going to require your full attention. There's coffee in back, in case anyone needs a pick-me-up."

The first picture showed the bottom of a pair of pants legs, and patent leather shoes. The approximately twenty negotiation team specialists grinned. Ms. Palmer remained earnest.

"I'm glad you're all amused, but the positioning of legs and feet really does give us an often underestimated amount of information."

Not far from the UN building, in the imposing, high-ceilinged hall of venerable Grand Central Station, Rick Bronx leaned between two counters at the old, octagonal ticket booth. He looked grimly up at the clock with the four brass-framed clock faces. Holding his cell phone to his ear, he shifted his weight back and forth between his feet, the corners of his mouth sagging unpleasantly. Leslie's phone was turned to voice mail. Bronx angrily hit the end-call button and entered a text message.

"We don't only analyze words," Ms. Palmer meanwhile lectured the select audience of experienced diplomats and negotiators who had been invited to attend. "We consider gestures, behavioral expression—in other words, body language in its entirety—in order to determine character or behavioral patterns. Suppressed libido—to name an often misjudged and displaced example—a suppressed libido can convert to hatred and sadistic tendencies in reaction to withheld love. Repressed desires lead to a characteristic tensing of musculature—in the neck, mouth, or pelvis. This is how the body expresses constraint. What we will see is drawn shoulders, stiffly extended legs..."

Her phone vibrated.

"...so if you encounter a person with a raised ribcage, who is not breathing freely, and shows evidence of a stiff, hollow back, you should be highly alert. Body language that uptight often signals a propensity for unpredictable actions and reactions."

Bronx had entered a time and meeting place and hit send. His two partners remained in sight, hanging around the newspaper stand. Chenny, the Chinese-American, wearing a flat hat with a narrow rim, was buying pretzels; Leon, the fat black man, was pretending to be checking out the latest paperbacks. Only a trained eye could have detected their conspicuously inconspicuous behavior in the constant coming and going around them.

Bronx was in no hurry. The plane that the Palmer boys were on would only be landing in a few hours. He would use this time to prepare the last details of his plan.

At the UN building, the lecture titled *Emphasis on Body Language Analysis of Negotiating Partners* continued undisturbed. The audience of approximately two dozens male and female listeners seemed entranced by her discourse. Time flew by.

"People who have been plagued by feelings of discrimination and inferiority throughout their childhood, and repeatedly throughout their lives, be it because of their skin color, origins, religion, or for other reasons, will develop a self-destructive, all-encompassing hatred..." she explained with authority, "...this also goes for people who feel they are not taken seriously. Their dangerously destructive attitude, marked by antipathy and mistrust, will express itself in physical tension, particularly around the mouth. Think of the lips..." she theatrically drew the corners of her mouth down with her fingers in an exaggerated frown "...you know, twenty-past-eight on the dial. Those real sourpuss faces," she said to general amusement. "This usually signifies an ominous hardening that you can also detect in other parts of the body if you are schooled to notice these things. You've all met a few of those proverbial 'uptight asses' in your time..." another salvo of laughter. "Well, all of that holds true. Unfortunately, some of the highest-ranking people in our nation, in agencies such as the CIA, for instance, show signs of this personality type..." she critically assessed her audience for any visible reaction—"...CEO's, male or female, of course, or people in governmental positions of power."

She clicked to the next slide, allowed the pictures of various faces to sink in, before asking, "What do you see here?"

"Pictures of statesmen," someone called out.

"Faces that speak volumes," a young female diplomat, who introduced herself as Melanie, opined.

"Good. Very good." Leslie turned to the screen. "Now you just tell me: 'tense' or 'relaxed.' Ready?"

Her listeners nodded enthusiastically.

"Over here!"

Her laser pointer centered on a picture of Hitler.

"Tense. Anal retentive," came the calls.

"This one? Do you know him?"

"Yes, Schmidt. The former German chancellor," the female diplomat called. "His prominent naso-labial folds suggest tension; a twenty-past-eight..."

"Alright, alright," said Leslie, laughing. She pointed to the image of a broadly grinning President Reagan.

Calls of hmm, and ah.

"Freshly shaved and relaxed," someone commented. "Totally at ease, a detached showman," another said.

Leslie nodded her praise.

"And here, who is this gaunt, emaciated general?"

There was a moment of silence.

"He's a picture of frustration," said the delegation leader, "I wouldn't trust him as far as I could throw him."

"Dictator Franco," Leslie noted, moving her pointer to the face of a man wearing a jauntily slanted cowboy hat. "And here?"

Spontaneous laughter.

"He has a bit of both," the female diplomat ventured. He has an easygoing look about him, but there's also something edgy, as if he's on the lookout for adversaries."

"Good analysis, Melanie," Leslie said into the merriment.

Then she moved on to a picture of a young Khrushchev.

"Pretty sovereign, confident," said a woman wearing glasses, seated next to the delegation leader.

"Okay, not bad. And here? What do you see when you compare Putin with de Gaulle?"

The audience contemplated the projections of the two heads of state for a long time before a hand went up.

"Both have a problem with their past."

"Why?" Leslie asked, encouragingly.

"I don't know," said the man, a young intern. "De Gaulle's face seems to be looking back; and the mask-like features of the Russian seem to be hiding some unpleasant legacy from the past—torture, or murder by poison, for all I know..."

Leslie remained serious in spite of amusement in the room.

"You have a good eye there...er...?"

"Ron," the man said, delighted to be singled out. "And I'm totally fascinated by your talk."

Ms. Palmer's audience clapped in lively approval.

"Thank you, Ron, thank you all. Let's stick with it for a moment longer. I'd like to pass out a little handout about body language that should help you to better assess your opponent at the bargaining table. That's it, then. Thank you for your participation, and for your valuable time."

Another round of applause. Stimulated, everybody got up, some crowding to the front.

Leslie accepted compliments, including the ones offered by Shelley, who had coordinated the visual sequencing. Two female audience members besieged her with questions about gender-specific body language; the delegation press spokesman also waited in line—the corners of his mouth facing, of all things, prominently downward. Leslie noticed herself getting impatient.

Today was the tenth. Her meeting with Spike was scheduled for tomorrow; she wanted to arrange a festive funeral for her father, and to arrange her study for Craig and Alex. Fortunately, her father had been organized enough to reserve a niche for himself in the urn columbaria at Brooklyn Greenwood Cemetery. Leslie had already spoken to the funeral director on the phone, and agreed on the order of the ceremony. Finally, her boss had invited her to lunch in the Village. Wagner wanted to discuss her downtime, but she seriously doubted that she would be able to juggle all of this.

"Yes, you're absolutely right," she agreed with the woman wearing glasses and a business suit that was a bit on the tight side, "Reich considered the orgasm to be an autonomic process, which triggers release once the impulses of arousal have streamed down to the genitals, and effects complete relaxation in women—in men, too, of course... If you would excuse me..."

Leslie cast a panicked look at the time. Smiling and nodding, she began to make her way toward the door. Before exiting the enormous, shiny chrome elevator, she had checked her text messages and learned, to her disappointment, that her sons had declined her offer.

We'll be staying at Mark's loft in Greenwich Village, read the sobering announcement that occupied Leslie until she got onto the 101 bus on Third Avenue.

It was September 10. She mentally checked her calendar. Her meeting with Spike in the South Tower was at eight thirty tomorrow morning. And Bronx, that damned plague of a man, had ordered her to the South Tower lobby at nine. She wondered what the heck he wanted now! She was going to have to meet him and find out. She had no choice. *How did I get into this limbo? Wrong question!* she corrected herself. *What I really need to know is: how do I get out?*

25

Rick Bronx had found out without great difficulty that Charles Palmer's cremation was scheduled for September 11, in the late afternoon. According to the airline's automatic phone service, Swissair flight SR 100, coming in from Zurich with the dead man's two grandsons on board, would be arriving at JFK on time today, at 4 p.m.

Tomorrow is September 11, and after that, nothing will ever be the same, Bronx ruminated happily, as he stepped lightly to the newsstand, bought a copy of the *Times*, and gave his two partners the nod that they had agreed upon as a sign.

"Well, ladies and gentlemen, many roads lead to Rome," Ken Cooper was busy explaining at CIA headquarters in Langley at around the same time. "Inside sources, double agents, listening devices, fishing for documents, satellite reconnaissance, then computer analysis of all the collected data. We don't know where their leaders are hiding. If we had an agent up high enough in the ranks of AQ, we would be in possession of that information, and we would have sent intelligent bombs out to pulverize the terrorist manipulators a long time ago."

A group of analysis specialists had gathered in the small conference room to follow the elucidations of the accomplished CIA man, who had been put in charge of special missions by the director.

"I'm sure someone is about to interject that we had very precise intelligence on the terrorist leader's location in the Hindu Kush mountains. And you may be asking why we never got to him with our bunker busters. How come our special forces found their concealed hiding places, but none of the ringleaders?"

Ken looked around expectantly. As head of the Innovation Section under the newly established Directorate of Science and Technology (DS&T), he did not enjoy as much prestige as the so-called tough guys involved in secret intelligence gathering. Like Rick Bronx, a man on the front line, whose office just happened to be right above the auditorium.

"Next, you will come to the conclusion that the target was informed on the plans for our mission. *Isn't it obvious?* you will ask. We had the right coordinates. Our projectiles hit home, pierced the concrete, burned and destroyed everything inside—but the person we were gunning for managed to escape. One week later, he's on the Arabian TV station scornfully swearing revenge. You, my dear ladies and gentlemen, are frustrated. And you have every right to be. I am, too."

Ken Cooper switched the projector off. The panoramic photograph of the Tora Bora cave complex disappeared from the screen.

"If only things were that easy!" Cooper murmured.

"Thank you very much, sir. But what do we do now?" Jennifer, who supported him in all of his unmanned reconnaissance aircraft projects, asked brightly.

"We stick to what we know. We deliver cutting-edge target reconnaissance technology. That is my core competency. Perhaps next time we'll be able to head the informant off at the pass."

Ken Cooper was firmly convinced that Al Qaeda had a spy in the States—one that was close to the people responsible for mission planning. At the Pentagon, or in the Central Command of the armed forces, or even within CIA headquarters. At any rate, this mole had to be someone who knew his way around Afghanistan.

He took the next half hour to explain his reasons for extending the deployment radius for drones over Washington, D.C.

"Experience tells us that preparatory criminal activity usually takes place in close proximity to the scene of the crime," he expounded. "I'm thinking along the lines of appropriating vehicles, and so forth. Therefore the extended radius for UAVs—it's of great potential benefit for targeted investigations. We have already evaluated the first photographs, and are going to run them through preliminary analyses to test their accuracy."

Once the rest of the group had left, Jennifer placed her attractive right curvature on the edge of the table, poking her sharpened pencil in Ken's direction to emphasize her point.

"Why don't you talk to Rick Bronx, or to the director in person?"

Cooper looked at her for a couple of beats.

"First of all, my dear, counter-espionage is not my line of work. The bosses have absolutely no appreciation for people who butt into their business. Secondly—always assuming I do want to lose my job by all means—I would need proof. Solid evidence. Rumors flourish where information is lacking. And rumors can come back to bite you in the ass."

"And you're certain there's a rotten egg in the nest? That there's a mole digging around somewhere?"

He nodded, smiling boyishly. Which turned out to be the starting move to his asking her out to dinner.

What Bronx in the intelligence division couldn't know, was that Cooper had changed the UAV surveillance radius just a couple of weeks ago.

Before his rendezvous with the beautiful Jennifer, Ken stood lost in thought, staring at the Orbiter model on his desk.

Something about it bothered him. He wasn't able to figure out quite what it was—a fact that continued to plague him until he gave way to one of his intuitive hunches, rummaged through his electronic address book, and found the name he was looking for. He hit the dial with a smile of anticipation.

The phone rang in a New York City apartment.

"Please leave your number," said an accented voice. Ken did as it asked, hung up, and picked up the paper he had saved.

On page three, the *Washington Post* reported on the unsolved death of a Customs and Border Protection employee in Maryland. Cooper read the article, which had been marked in red, once more. He was familiar with Little Bennet Regional Park—a friend who worked for the department of covert intelligence gathering had talked him into joining him there on a fishing trip last spring. A pursuit for which Ken had neither patience nor enthusiasm. He had gone anyway, because he had seen it as a good opportunity to try his new titanium bike on the park trails. He deemed the drive into the countryside forty miles north of Langley, on the other side of the Potomac, to be just within acceptable range for a chatty excursion.

And speaking of range. . . ! What was the dead man's name? The paper didn't say, of course, since the investigation was still ongoing.

In a sense, Ken really didn't care much about the man's death. Around here, hardly a day went by that someone wasn't murdered. According to FBI and Cosmopolitan Police crime statistics, 262 murders had earned the Washington district the questionable reputation of being America's "Murder Capital," just ahead of Detroit and Baltimore.

But this case is within range of my drones, Ken reflected, *better check whether the evaluation of our aerial photographs yields any clues.*

The buzzing of his cell phone interrupted his thoughts—Avi Leumi, returning his call.

26

Leumi was a lean, quick, dark-haired Israeli who, disguised in an army uniform, led a military police mission targeting an abandoned hospital north of Aden in 2000.

Back then, he had earned his living as a covert special agent for the Mossad. The Israeli secret service had received word that preparations to attack the *synagogue* were under way in Yemen. In Al Qaeda speak, *synagogue* stood for Israel at large; just as *Americans* stood for the entire United States.

The hospital hadn't given him any direct cause for suspicion; there were no curious telephone connections or electronic data traffic. But Leumi had a nose for trouble, and something about this hospital, which had ostensibly been rented out to a group of investors, didn't smell right. Once the military police had penetrated the building there was a skirmish—and then, among a group of Arabs this American agent surfaced, apparently busy to recruit men for an operation. To Leumi the matter appeared rather fishy, he started taking pictures and focused his investigative eye on the leader of the group, who was later identified as Rick Bronx. He had provided the LEO (Low Earth Orbiter) spy satellite with the GPS coordinates. One month later, the Mossad was in possession not only of sharp black and white photographs of Bronx, but also of thermal imaging that captured evidence of underground gatherings—so-called chthonic activity. Avi had stowed his involuntary meeting with Bronx in Yemen away in his files. Bronx was CIA; and the Mossad was not in the habit of monitoring clandestine CIA operations—just as Langley would not have thought of shadowing the Mossad. The agencies knew and respected one another, always there to back each other if the situation called for it.

Nor did the attack on the USS *Cole* in October of 2000 give Leumi reason to direct any attention toward Rick Bronx. The Israeli's acutely structured sense of reason did, however, leave a splinter of contention in his mind, which reminded him of the Yemen incident occasionally. But it was only when he came to Washington as a technical advisor for the new Orbiter exactly six weeks ago, that the name Rick Bronx surfaced again, for real.

Inevitably Leumi came in contact with Ken Cooper, who was in charge of a CTU. Cooper had established the Counter Terrorist Unit first as a trial structure against the will of CIA bureaucrats. He had equipped it with the latest tools: supercomputers, drones, Internet codes—state of the art technology on every level.

"That's what makes the new Orbiter so sophisticated," Avi now explained with visible enthusiasm. "You can enter a GPS camera position for data evaluation, and it will provide you with data from the vicinity. Let's have a look. You don't happen to have a grid square? That would be helpful."

"Does a frog have ears?" Ken countered with a grin and placed the grid on top of the map of Bennet Regional Park. "Try P 9!"

"Okay—*Papa Nine,*" Avi repeated. There was stillness for a while, then, "Negative. No feedback."

"One moment, Avi, hold the line!"

Ken double-checked the electronic map. The police files made no note of the exact location of the crime scene where CBP Agent Howard Young's body had been discovered. But Ken remembered that a woman collecting berries had reported making the horrifying find only because a fox had fled from a shed as she approached. Shed? He zoomed in on the section. And was, indeed, able to localize a blurry spot.

"Try R 10, Avi," Ken called, "can you see a shed?"

"*Romeo Ten,*" Leumi confirmed. A short while later, the speaker resonated with a cheerful voice: "One shed, two vehicles. One moment, I'm zooming in."

"What's it showing?"

"Well, there's a dark sedan next to your shed, the license plate reads..."

"You can read the plate?" Ken interrupted, thrilled. "Like hell you can...!"

"Down, boy. It's going to take a few seconds. The car is taking off and, here, you can see it in the light. A perfectly sharp picture!"

"Can you pull the driver up?"

"No, the angle is too acute. But I think you'll agree that the Orbiter is unbeatable. Its range and clarity are unique. I do hope your connections to whoever is in charge of CIA acquisitions..."

Ken interrupted him sharply.

"The number, Avi! Can you transmit the plate number?"

"No problem. Done. Who does the crate belong to?"

Ken checked the bottom of his screen, where the message had now appeared—a government code, IA-G, one from the car pool. He entered the number into the CIA vehicle index.

"No listing..." he read.

"And what does that mean, exactly?"

"Most of our agent's cars are unlisted, even internally."

"But somebody has a list somewhere, right?"

"I would think so. Listen Avi, I'm going to need your help analyzing this, okay? Your application program reads like it's written in Hebrew."

Cooper hung up with a grin, and hit the radio link button.

"Jennifer, do you know someone from the car pool?"

"You mean the CIA vehicle fleet? No, but I've had cars from them every once in a while. Why?"

"Come over, I'll explain."

An hour later, Jennifer crossed the large parking garage in the basement of the CIA complex and approached a small office booth close to the exit.

The parking attendant, who was leaning up close to his computer screen, was an elderly gentleman who wore his well-kept uniform proudly.

"Howdy," Jennifer said with a smile. "I'm Jennifer. I have a bit of a problem."

She looked into his bright eyes. His even, furrowed face might have been that of an aging actor. Lowering her gaze, she read the gold-framed nametag on the starched chest of his uniform. The man smiled. "And what might that be? Have you lost your key?"

"No, *Jack*, the thing is that the people from accounting are on my case. It's about expenses for a business trip... One moment."

She laboriously angled a piece of paper out of her tight trouser pocket, while Jack looked on benignly.

"Darn bureaucrats," Jennifer sighed, "there, I have it. The license number is 456 IA-G."

Jack sat back down at the computer, hit a couple of keys.

"The date, Madam?"

Jennifer gave it to him. It was the date of Howard Young's death.

Looking around the white wall, she suddenly called out, "Wow! Is that your car, Jack?"

"Just a second, almost there. Pardon?" He looked up, smiled. "You mean that old jalopy there. Yes, that's mine. Aston Martin DB 5, built in 1958."

"That's so cool. It reminds me of Goldfinger and James Bond. You even look like Sean Connery, Jack!"

He laughed and shrugged, as if he had heard the same compliment often.

"Well, unfortunately I don't make his paycheck. There we are. Your name's not on here—look."

Jennifer leaned forward, her blond hair tickling his cheek. He didn't draw back. Her story may have been a fake, but her intensity was not.

"There we have it. Those people from accounting want an expense report from me, including mileage and all sorts of things, and I didn't even have the car that day. This cheap agent—*what's his name?*—did."

"Bronx, from intelligence," Jack read willingly. "He ordered the car and brought it back the same day. Would you like a printout for your documents?"

"Thank you, those nitpickers won't give me any peace otherwise. Isn't it amazing, Jack, the stuff we have to waste our time on sometimes... I'm very grateful for your help. Really, very efficient. And as for your Aston Martin, you should take me out on a bit of a joyride in it one day."

Jack didn't seem to take her suggestion seriously. He stood, smiling politely.

"My pleasure, Madam."

They had already stepped out of the little office when she turned around. "Oh... Jack... I almost forgot to ask something," she proclaimed. "Has Bronx taken any cars out of the pool since then?"

Jack hesitated. He seemed to be having some belated doubts about the legitimacy of her questions.

"Is that important? Do you really want me to look?"

"Yes—it is very important, Jack. This guy, Bronx—and this needs to stay between me and you, it is something I find very embarrassing—he keeps hassling me, trying to impress me with his cars. And I'm pretty sure that they all belong to the agency."

Jack nodded, once again sitting down at his computer, his fingers clacking on the keys. After just a few moments, he ended the session with a forceful tap of his right pinky.

"Bronx has not asked for another car since the one you have the printout for, however..."

"Yes?"

"We reserved a Lincoln Town Car for him at the Manhattan depot."

"New York? Alright, that does explain a number of things. Thank you very much, Jack. And if there's ever anything I can do for you, here's my office number."

The helpful service attendant took the small, official-looking card with a friendly, but impersonal smile, as was becoming of his rank and age.

PART II

27

Summer of 1997. The air outside shimmered in the 97-degree heat. The bug-proof conference room of the American embassy in Kenya had been pleasantly cool until a short while ago, when the air-conditioning suddenly failed.

Rick Bronx found the source of the malfunction. Someone always had to make things right, and Rick Bronx was one of those hardened people who clean up; who take care of messy business. Very messy business, if there was a need. In fact, that was a focal point of this very meeting, as the air-conditioning finally came back on with a rough clanging that settled into a monotonous hum.

He sipped at his cup of weak, cold coffee and listened to the droning sound that was addling his brain. His thoughts digressed to a time years back, to the recruitment office on a U.S. Navy cargo ship docked in the harbor of Aden. The same, mind-numbing drone...

"So you want to join the Navy Seals—aha," the burly, chalk-faced staff sergeant had said, his 'Aha' sounding like a testy chuckle.

"*Yessir!*"

"You realize that you are asking to be accepted into the absolute top fighting force in the world."

He beat a fist on his tank-like chest, as if to demonstrate the invincibility of his unit. Bronx was dead serious.

"It is the unit I most admire. I know a bit about weapons, I'm well-trained, and I thought..."

The man across from him wiped his answer away with the back of his hand. His little, dark brown eyes rested appraisingly on Rick Bronx's smooth, dark skin, then wandered up to the thick, pitch-black hair that you wouldn't find on any real American. He smoothed over the little curls behind his ears.

"Really. That's what you *thought.* Well, you need to be able to *obey orders,* not think. We don't need any wise guys around here. You're an Arab, kid."

He held Bronx's résumé between two fingers as if to prove his point.

"We're only interested in tough men, who are able to knuckle under and endure. Arabs are a bunch of gutless wonders, everyone knows that!"

"I am an American, sir. I grew up here. My father is the harbormaster. I speak Arabic. I thought...I mean, the Navy can use people with language skills, I thought."

"You don't say. Well, I'm here to tell you that we have nothing we want to talk to those people about. Get it? If they have something to say, let them learn how to speak English. The Navy's not for you. I'm Jewish—you think I made a career because I speak Hebrew?"

He chuckled to himself. Rick Bronx's sense of discomfort increased. His soft lips curled. He stood to leave.

"Try the Army. They'll take pretty much anything we have no use for over here."

Later, at the Nairobi embassy, the wiry officer with a crew cut sitting at the head of the table raised his voice ostentatiously—the picture of the staff sergeant's sneering grimace blurred before Rick Bronx's inner eye.

"The USS *Cole* is scheduled to dock in Aden for some time in October. It is carrying the latest generation of UAVs. That's unmanned aerial vehicles. Bronx?"

"*Yessir!*" The man who's name had been called slowly sat up from his hunched position. "I know what UAVs are, sir."

"Good. Effective immediately, you will be reporting to the station chief in Aden. You will be deployed to Yemen as soon as you have been briefed tomorrow morning."

Bronx nodded unenthusiastically. As the officer continued his briefing, his thoughts once again turned to the past...

28

...Rick Bronx had been an eleven-year-old boy by the name of Adil when President Kennedy had fallen victim to an assassin's bullets in Dallas. His parents' house, built of reddish volcanic rock, overlooked the old town of Aden, with its sprawling harbor complex. To the dismay of his meek-mannered mother, Amira, he preferred chasing stray cats in the shaded palm tree garden with his slingshot to practicing the piano, as she encouraged him to do. Mother came from the Pamir highlands, way up north, where headstrong people utter peculiar sounds. She had come to the Persian Gulf at a young age. Thanks to British Overseas Airways she found her way to the southern part of Yemen.

Whenever she had a stopover in Aden, the stewardess had felt herself drawn to Al-Burayqa, otherwise known as Little Aden, in the evenings. Large groups of lonely Englishmen and adventurous Americans would invariably be hanging out at the American bar. Men who worked around the large freight harbor, or who were with the Navy; adventurers who made rowdy passes competing for a few young women in their preppy uniforms.

Aden was Yemen's winter metropolis. Amira liked the town and its pleasant climate. And she promptly fell in love. The object of her affections was a bold, handsome man with a thin mustache. His tanned skin lent him the complexion of an Arabian Nights paladin. A man with sparkling eyes, thick hair, a beautiful mouth. One could only tell the American in him when he cursed like a cab driver from the Bronx, which is where he came from. Other than that, his customers praised him as being fast and reliable. A go-getting freight broker working for a global British corporation, he earned a good living before later joining the Schlumberger Concern, where he made a career as the person responsible for delivering oil production equipment to the entire Middle East. He had grown wealthy over the years.

Whether his name, as stated in all of his paperwork as well as on his social security card, was really Bronx—or whether it was just a moniker that had stuck... down here, nobody could have cared less.

It had been love at first sight. One year later, Amira gave birth to a son. The midwife had stepped out of the semi-darkness of the hallway, and whispered into the father's ear.

"Amiralla, I have a son," Bronx called to the gathered group, his chest swelled with fatherly pride.

"A son, a son!" the group echoed.

The men slapped him on the back; a few of his confidants emptied their shooting irons into the air, as was the custom on such occasions.

At first the father felt *Adil*, an Arabic name chosen by the boy's mother, was too feminine. But when she explained its meaning, *The Righteous,* he agreed.

Bronx made sure that Adil kept his American citizenship, visited English school, and learned to hit a baseball, while his mother spent many hours honing his language skills, and conveying to him the teachings of the holy Koran. Adil roughed around with the neighborhood kids, who were ready to accept him into their secret brotherhood for his beige complexion and light blue eyes alone.

As the war in Vietnam grew increasingly heated in 1968, Adil was fascinated by reports on American battles against the Vietcong. He admired the young, laid-back GIs, with their M113 armored personnel carriers. He marveled at photographs of the bulbous helicopters with their open sides, through which gunners fired heavy machine guns at the Vietcong hiding in the rice paddies. He yearned for nothing more than to be part of this force one day. Whenever he heard about American successes on the television news, he rejoiced, and fiercely hated the devious little men they called VCs for inflicting casualties on his heroes. Adil's father chafed at the White House politicians who would not grant the generals enough authority to win this war. The growing boy revered his father, and was shaped by his hostile stance toward the government. Above all, he felt the need to show them what he was made of one day; to prove that he could fight for America, in spite of the color of his skin, and the fact that he came from a part of the world that few people had even heard of.

"Adil," his mother said when he was fifteen, "our Arab people have been mastered by the West for too long. You must help us to master the West. Will you do that?"

29

When Rick Bronx left the Nairobi embassy building on that oppressively hot summer afternoon in 1997, he took serious account of the intense, deep-rooted hatred that he held for his employing agency, the CIA... for them, for Washington, and for the Jewish cabal that ran everything over there. Just like the arrogant, fat, bloated recruiting sergeant on that navy boat. The scorn that had wounded him so deeply had left its first mark on him right then and there. It was a sense of derision that was an insult to his mother, an Arab woman—and not just to her: to an entire, proud people.

When he was eighteen, he had experienced the ruthless and self-serving way in which American television corporations abandoned their soldiers in the jungles of Vietnam. Later, he came to know the country that granted him citizenship as amoral, covetous, and self-indulgent. The only things that counted were money, success, and power. They preached all kinds of virtue, but they had no true faith: how else could you explain the fact that they gave up the fight against Communism in Vietnam, shamelessly betraying their fifty-eight thousand fallen men?

Our Arab people have been mastered by the West for too long. You must help us to master the West. Will you do that?

The insults and arrogance would follow him into the United States Army.

Rick Bronx had driven (without paying attention, his brain steered him as if set on autopilot) through the dense Nairobi traffic and reached the small house that he shared with two embassy employees. He parked his dust-caked Chevy Suburban on the fenced part of the property, under the awning. A fire crackled in the pit on the terrace; evidently, someone intended to surprise him with a barbeque. He felt that a Jack Daniel's would be the best way to pass time until the guests arrived. Ice cubes clinked pleasantly in his ears. He was already salivating as he sank down in a basket chair, took a long, deep swallow, and stared into the flames. The pictures, which the officer-in-charge had chased away at the embassy, returned...

30

...His dad Frank had taken Adil to the States with him, and had made sure he got into the Army. *The military is the best preparation for life*, he always said. This simple bit of worldly wisdom fell on fertile ground as far as Adil was concerned. He was already fascinated by weaponry of all types. Back in Aden, he and his gang had crafted carbide charges, and an older English boy had horded a Kalashnikov AK-47, an Uzi, and a variety of pistols in his father's cellar, all of which he knew how to disassemble. This arsenal had mesmerized Adil. Together, the two would sneak off to a remote area of the beach where, covered by the noise of the surf, they used a Walther PPK to explode plastic bottles filled with gasoline.

Adil had procured small, illustrated HarperCollins volumes of tanks and combat aircraft, and his father had given him a book on wartime journalism from WWII to Vietnam. Adil looked forward to his basic training, kept in shape, and didn't doubt that he would be among the best when it came to handling weapons, explosives, and machinery. He fancied himself a Hollywood WWII hero, storming bunkers and smoking out the enemy. He couldn't wait to be one of them, to learn about new weapons—and he loved the sound of gunfire; the devastating force of a good explosion. He did not seem to know the meaning of the word *pain*. He rescued a screaming comrade from under a tilted Jeep with stoic calm, a tear on his head bleeding profusely all the while. This earned him the respectful nickname Advil. *Advil* for fast, strong pain relief! Then came the cold, hard letdown. They reassigned him to a paper-pushing post in Maryland. It was probably the biggest indignity that this country could have punished him with. A coffee-colored drill sergeant, who towered two feet above him, had borne down on him after close live-ammunition combat training one day:

"You know, they have a place for little guys like you in Fort Meade."

At first, Adil had not quite understood. Fort Meade was an enormous base on a sweeping terrain. Somewhere, it also housed the highly classified National Security Agency (NSA).

"You speak Arabic, Advil," the sergeant stated, as if that explained everything. When Adil continued to stand at attention, he added, "You don't fit in here anyway."

What he was referring to was, of course, the overwhelming majority of black troops in Adil's company. El Paso recruited mainly in the Southern states. And what he was saying was that Adil wasn't black enough—not like a black Muslim, or something. He was just some kind of a weird mix. The official explanation for his transfer was that the Armed Forces needed people with foreign language skills. Particularly Arabic. It didn't matter that he was superior to his comrades—physically as well as mentally.

"Hey, Advil, don't mind them," one of his buddies, and also one of the few white men around, tried to console him. "They think you're a security risk. Where are you from? Yemen? They think you're going to shoot us in the back if we ever have to defend the country against a horde of angry camel drivers."

They had rejected him a second time.

That same evening, he wrote his mother. The first three sentences that flowed from his pen did not take much thought to compose.

I am coming back—patriots are not valued here. I am coming home, where patriots are needed. They think that I am a security risk, and I will prove them right…

Before being shipped out to the NSA, he changed his name. The melodic, Arabic name that he had been given at birth had only harmed him. What he now proudly called himself could hardly have been more American-sounding: Rick Bronx.

31

Rick Bronx stared into the flames. Deep in the blaze, he saw the distant rock-strewn hillsides, the monstrous Soviet tank that was noisily rumbling toward him, its hatches firmly sealed. He lay on the stony ground, under the heavy body of a dead horse, pitifully helpless, as if trapped in a vise, waving his arms desperately. The tank that he immediately registered as a T-72 lowered its 120mm smoothbore cannon with the coaxial machinegun. Rick Bronx waited for the bang, the pain, the nothingness—the end, in this shitty valley at the back of nowhere.

The bang came. It was dreadful, deafening—the heat seared his black hair under the tight leather cap he wore. When he opened his eyes after the first shock, holding his droning head with both hands, he thought, stupefied, of the blissful prophecy of sixty-two voluptuous *houris* that would soon, if not imminently, be pleasing him—the martyr—in paradise.

"Move it, Amerikanski," said a strong voice that belonged to none other than the bearded Osama, whom he had, until then, taken to be a humble preacher.

The tank was ablaze. A soldier lurched from the turret, slipped, and hit the ground. Osama held a smoking antitank grenade launcher in one hand, while he tore at the reins of the dead horse that held Bronx pinned to the ground with the other. Two of his men rushed to his aid. Before the Soviet HIND attack helicopter had made it around the bend, all four of them had taken cover behind a large rock. Osama calmly helped a Mujahid position a Stinger missile launcher on his shoulder—and as the black thing appeared, glowering above them in the blazing sunlight like an enormous, evil insect, the missile fired. The Stingers had been delivered in 1986: Bronx had meticulously drilled young warriors on their use at a training camp near Jalalabad. Not in vain, as it turned out. The helicopter exploded in a massive fireball, burning debris raining to the ground.

"You saved my life," Bronx panted.

"Now you owe me one," said the bearded one with a grin.

They both lay on the ground, squinting up at the sky.

"Are we going to attack?" Ahmed, the Stinger operator, yelled.

"Retreat," Bronx gasped. Osama nodded.

The noises of battle died off as suddenly as they had surged. Not a single shot was to be heard. Only the sound of heavy motors drifted up from the valley below. A dozen men wearing the typical white pants, tight caps, and cotton *keffiyeh* wrapped loosely around their heads and necks, stood on the wreck of the downed HIND.

A sharp order caused them to jump down. Once the group had reached the summit, they saw a column of tanks turn in the valley. Nothing moved against the gray sky. Still, they needed to hurry. It would be less than an hour before the Soviets sent their fighter-bombers to search for pockets of resistance.

"I want to be a pilot," Ahmed said as they reached the Tora Bora cave complex after a long march, and gathered at the entrance beneath the cliffs.

Rick Bronx's full bottom lip pushed forward slightly as he skeptically assessed the young fighter, whose dark garments seemed to be virtually one with the black stone. Only his eyes glistened. It always seemed to Bronx that the men's clothes around here resembled tents.

They stepped into the dark corridor of the first cave.

"Stick to Mohammed," Bronx suggested, "he also wants to go to America, when everything is done here."

"I know. He is in contact with a group of brothers in America, who think like us. They are like Americans, without the ridiculous beard." Ahmed rubbed at his overgrown chin with a grin.

"You're only going to have a hard time there. I'd advise you to go to school, learn English for a year or two. Study something useful, like mechanics, or engineering... They have no respect for us Arabs over there."

Bronx tapped on his chest as he said this, as if wanting to include himself among the discriminated.

Ahmed nodded, as if he had made a mental note of everything he'd just been told. And that had been that. For now.

32

The black house servant approached, cleared his throat, and poked the flames. The pictures in Bronx's memory scattered in a hail of sparks. The voices he now heard in the house were coming closer. Bronx emptied his glass in a single, long gulp—he knew that it had been on that exact day, up in the Hindu Kush, when he vowed he'd do anything for the man who saved his life. Anything Osama might ask him to do.

They hid their weapons and munitions in caves near the training camp. Life in the compounds spoke to the young men's eagerness for action. They flocked from Saudi Arabia, Algeria, Uzbekistan—from everywhere. The Chechens and Tajiks usually came in groups of three, then there were Kashmiris, Yemenites, all mixed in with the Pashtun. They all grappled to become the best in the eyes of their instructors.

The instructors would wake the men before the break of day. Their first prayer was followed by a tough, half-hour physical training routine, before they set out to the mountains nearby. The objective was to teach them to move safely in the cold climate, through the rocky, rough terrain, while carrying weapons and a heavy load. Back at camp, their day continued with weapons training. Bronx instructed the religious warriors in the use of Kalashnikovs, RPG-7s, and surface-to-air missiles (SAMs). His policy was to drill them until they were ready to drop. The young men were eager to learn, impatient; but it was his job to teach them to be ready at all times, to be able to quickly disassemble and reassemble their weapons, often blindfolded or in the dead of night. The safe handling of all weapons preceded their use. He drummed into them all they needed to know about trajectories and maximum effective range, taught them the combat principle of 'fire and movement,' and how to set up an ambush.

The American weapons expert was known and respected. He was called, in casual, American style, by his first name: Rick.

During the eighties, a good 20,000 recruits came streaming to the camps from all parts of the world to fight the Soviets; and Bronx greatly contributed to their weapons and combat training, which gained him much respect among the Muslim leadership.

Five times a day, the men said *salah*, the ritual daily prayer; and after eating a salty stew for their evening meal, the recruits gathered for religious schooling. Any man wanting to fight as a Mujahid, in the name of God, had to understand the nature of God's will. The instructors indoctrinated the men with the law of Jihad. No one should shirk his duty to bring violence on the infidels. Most sat through the regimen in silence, while some ardent scholars desperately thirsted for spiritual preparation and wanted to do nothing less than fully fathom the rules of war as they were written in the Koran. Bronx let the religious teachers do their job and used this time to discuss mission planning with the leaders. The Soviets had 110,000 elite soldiers stationed in the country. They were doing all they could to destroy the training compounds from the air. Bronx prevailed in his insistence that most of the caves should not be used only as weapons and munitions caches, but that they should be developed to form integrated systems that provided room for accommodations, kitchens, and classrooms.

When a Soviet attack was expected, the men could move their camp within an hour. Bronx built a simple, yet effective defense system using the Stingers that had been provided by the CIA in 1986, via Pakistan's powerful secret service, the ISI. He applied the established fundamentals of ambush by picking positions that would force the Soviet attack helicopters to approach within firing distance of the surface-to-air missiles, thereby causing them to forfeit the range advantage of their 30mm chin-mount cannons.

Fridays, when the men came together for prayer and reflection during *jumu'ah*, the day of rest and communion, were a source of frustration for Bronx. Training ceased, and he was forced to ensure safety with the aid of just a few Western specialists while the faithful worshipped. The rules changed, however, after costly Soviet incursions caused Abdullah Azzam, the godfather of the Jihad and mentor to bin Laden, to issue the order that the Holy War would have precedence over prayer, even on Fridays.

Bronx, who, with time, had come to acquire the customs of the Mujahideen, had a keen eye for recognizing qualities of leadership in men. There were some who behaved pragmatically; who trimmed their beards and spoke little of the Koran. Bronx recognized them as the secular type, suited for assignments on religious holidays. His mission as a CIA agent was merging increasingly with his role as a Mujahid, fighting against the Soviets. His mother's exhortation—*Our Arab people have been mastered by the West for too long. You must help us to master the West. Will you do that?*—was the unimpeachable guideline that ruled his actions.

The reserved-acting Mohammed came to visit him in the canteen one evening. The caves were cold; it had been snowing outside for days without interruption. The men, wrapped in blankets, were clustered around a fire.

"I want to go to America, Rick," he began in a whisper.

Bronx did not reply.

"A few years maybe," said Mohammed, and slipped him a business card. "My father's business. They will always know where to find me."

Bronx looked into the dark eyes flickering in the light of the flames. He nodded, pocketing the address without reading it. He would remember Mohammed who, as a Saudi, would have no problems attaining a visa for the USA.

33

As the Russians began to withdraw their troops from Afghanistan in late February of 1989, bin Laden fell out with his friend and mentor, Abdullah Azzam. A factional dispute threatened to weaken the movement. Bronx did not hesitate for a moment in this critical hour—he knew where he stood. A while later, Azzam was killed outside the mosque in Peshawar, when unknown assassins detonated landmines as his vehicle approached. There were rumors that the British Secret Intelligence Service (SIS) had been behind it. Bronx remained in the background while bin Laden assumed leadership. Two days later, the new head of the mudjahideen called the CIA instructor to his field tent near Herat.

"You have accomplished great things, Rick," Osama praised, as he poured them tea. "Do you want to continue to follow me in the future? Consider your answer well. Think of the words of the prophet, 'even the way back is a way.'"

When Bronx was silent, Osama leaned back. His shoulder touched the barrel of the Kalashnikov leaning behind him.

"The Soviets are defeated; my fight is now against the secular Muslim countries."

Bronx did not falter for a second.

"The Arab people have been mastered by the West for far too long. I will help you to master the West."

"Are you ready to die for the cause?"

"I am ready to fight, Emir. I owe you one; have you forgotten?"

They looked at each other with earnest smiles. Both knew that they had formed a bond that would link them inseparably from now on.

And so Osama bin Laden, the new head of the Jihad, ruled the American, who had proven his loyalty in word and deed, his favored agent at the heart of America.

34

Having at first been taken by surprise by the developments in Afghanistan, the CIA could not have been happier about having a man like Bronx within their ranks. Bronx being perhaps their sole truly established expert, they stationed him first in Kabul, then Peshawar, and finally in Yemen. His Arab background, the fact that Arabic was his mother tongue, as well as his ability to speak Pashto—all of this made him an invaluable field agent in the Middle East. No one at Langley doubted his loyalty. Bronx was superior, solid, and reliable. His track record was utterly convincing. This being the case, not a soul would have thought to question his devotion to the United States of America.

"We must cause a bloodbath. Our goal must be to kill masses of people. I view suicide terrorism as an instrumental strategy," Osama lectured one evening. "The West has clichéd ideas about suicide killers. It is not some supposed rage or frustration, or envy of the fruits of the West that drives our enforcers. It is nothing more than an understanding of strategic necessity."

They sat on upholstered leather stools, eating chicken wings.

"What are you getting at?"

Bronx threw a fleshless bone over his shoulder.

"I want educated people; not oafish morons, paupers, or sick men suffering from depression. We must build an intelligent elite troupe over the coming decades. Their deployment will be based on two prerequisites—they must be prepared to kill, and willing to die for the cause."

"So, no wild-eyed fanatics or crazed executioners," Bronx concluded.

"Absolutely not. No. Quite the opposite—as far as true Jihad warriors are concerned, terrorism represents an entirely rational choice. In principle, they are educated, thoughtful, normal people. Socially adept, and inconspicuous."

Bronx nodded.

"Suicide attacks are shocking, bloody, and above all cost efficient."

"Exactly! Also foolproof and difficult to prevent. Our actions will create a feeling of paralysis and helplessness. Will you help me, Rickie? We will also liberate Yemen, the land that I owe my name to. You know your way around Aden, don't you Rick? And the large harbor?"

Bronx nodded again, puzzled. It had not really been a question, but a statement. He would only realize its implications years later.

For now, he grasped Osama's hand and pressed it firmly. Their intense eyes met, boring into one another. Then they grasped each other in a long, passionate embrace.

35

When his cell phone emitted that annoying buzzing tone on the midday of October 12, 2000, Steve Quinn somehow instinctively knew that something big had happened. At first it had been the screaming that had rudely awakened him from a restless sleep.

"Allah, Allah..." "Jihad..." "Allah is great..." "Laylat al-Qadr... The night of decree..." "Long live the prophet..."

At first Quinn thought it may be just another skirmish breaking out in the turbulent bazaar. But the words kept repeating. "Allahu Akbar!" Over and over.

Thank God the buzzing of his cell phone had turned to a forlorn ringing, and then fallen silent, before he had a chance to answer it. *Fine by me!*

Quinn pulled his shirt straight, shuffled listlessly into the bathroom, tired from the long night. He freshened his stubbly face with a few splashes of water. His Swatch wristwatch showed the twelfth, half-past-noon on this lethargic day, far from home, in this madhouse town of Peshawar—the last rest stop before his planned departure on an adventurous trek to Afghanistan.

His cell phone, lying on a cheap, round side table pockmarked with cigarette burns, began its second attempt. Quinn leaped to get it, if for no other reason than that he couldn't stand the damn ringtone and wanted to shut it up. It annoyed him no end that he had never managed to download a few bars of his favorite song from *The Entertainer* to replace it.

Grasping for a button, his index finger hit the gadget broadside, sending it careening against the solid casing of his digital camera, where it bounced off, then clattered across the floor and into the wall. As if to taunt him, the stupid ringing started up again immediately.

"Crap!" Quinn cussed, now down on all fours in an attempt to get hold of the nuisance. He grabbed it in his fist, as if it were a mouse or something. "Fucking piece of shit!" he thundered.

"Excuse me? Steve? When did you start answering your phone like that? It's very charming. I hope I'm not disturbing you?"

Even the lousy connection along the Afghani-Pakistani border couldn't disguise the unmistakable mixture of professional efficiency and sensual allure that was her smoky voice: Stephanie, the photo-editing assistant, was on the line from New York.

"Hey, Stephanie… no, no, you're never a disturbance, it's just…"

"Did you see the pictures?" she interrupted, her tone now so dramatic that Bill instantly lost all interest in flirting with her. *What the hell was going on?*

"Turn on CNN, Steve! They bombed one of our Navy destroyers," she burbled on, brightly. "The boss wants pictures. You have to head out to Aden."

Quinn pulled up the boxy black miniature television, turned it on, and waited for its flickering to evolve into an unsteady picture. Finally, he saw the black plumes of smoke that billowed up the aerial mast and enveloped the Star-Spangled Banner. His breath caught in his throat.

"I see it. That's just... *insane!*"

The elegant vessel stood in flames, a house-sized gash in the middle of its port side.

"That's the USS *Cole*, one of our most modern guided-missile destroyers, I mean, our Navy..."

The shaky pictures repeated themselves. Quinn listened with one ear to the reporter's choppy voice...

"Listen Stephanie, I'm heading for Afghanistan tomorrow, as planned. Please tell Frankie-boy that a detour to Aden won't be possible, so he'd better figure out..." He was interrupted by a deep voice.

"Steve? Frank here. Everything okay?" *The boss in person*. "Listen to me carefully—consider your trip postponed. You have to get to Aden. The USS *Cole* is our top story right now! Moored to a fueling dock, close to sinking! That's our highest priority!"

Quinn was only just able to keep himself from suddenly breaking wind, his voice was accordingly lame.

"What exactly happened?"

"As far as we know, terrorists entered the harbor basin in a dinghy loaded with explosives. They blew up the ship's hull. We need pictures—*your* pictures."

Quinn stared at the image reruns. The U.S. Navy was looking pretty wretched. Apparently, they had been taken completely by surprise, much like at Pearl Harbor!

"Okay, okay, fine. I'll call back, Frank, as soon as I have a connection—flight, I mean."

"Good, I'll be waiting. *On hot coals, my boy!*"

His boss in New York hung up the phone. Quinn sank heavily onto the side of the bed. *There went everything—down the damn drain again! Shit, shit, shit!* Those fucking terrorists had just screwed up all his plans. His trip had been prepared in great detail. They were to start out tomorrow because of good weather conditions. And now? His lovely photo safari to the Hindu Kush, Afghanistan's formidable mountain region, had simply gone up in smoke! It was enough to make a man sick.

Aden!? He'd been there before, knew the harbor, the hillside with its old military hospital, where he had barely escaped with his life... He shook off the thought, disgusted.

Suddenly, he really did feel acutely nauseous. He snatched a gin from the mini bar, downed it, practically panting. Shook himself like a wet dog. *Ahh, better already!*

In order to keep himself occupied, he checked battery and power on his camera. It was the cutting-edge of digital photography, worth about five trips, and property of the *New Yorker*. Shots rang out. The noise down on the bazaar paused. The dramatic events occurring in Yemen vibrated all the way up to Quinn's second-floor hotel room.

Later, they had announced the casualties: 17 American sailors killed, 39 wounded. Peshawar was in an uproar. Police and the Pakistani military contained the mob with fists and guns. Midnight had broken before peace set in, when the Arab news channel, Al Jazeera, broadcast an ominous message from Osama bin Laden, in which his Al Qaeda claimed responsibility for the bombing in Aden.

Quinn hated the long-faced, bearded, apathetic so-called prophet, with a passion. Without so much as blinking, the chief terrorist had gone on to say that the attack on the USS *Cole*, a symbol of American arrogance, would be just the first of a series of further, dreadful acts. This was immediately followed by a genteel, soft-spoken appeal to all religious Muslims to remain calm.

Quinn's dismal mood didn't improve much when Stephanie called back to cheerfully inform him that a five-thousand-dollar bonus had been made available to him effective immediately. Quinn's loyalty was never in question. The *New Yorker*'s editorial office staff knew that he would do exactly what they asked of him—in this case: drop everything and head for Aden by the first available flight. They were right, of course. And so Quinn predictably, if grudgingly, prepared to fill their expectations to a T. All the while, he could not know that it would be a whole seven months before he had another opportunity to set forth on his carefully mapped out photography expedition to the fascinating mountains of Afghanistan. Had he had even the slightest inkling of what would await him in the

Hindu Kush in the fateful month of May 2001, he would have finally and irrevocably turned his back on Peshawar on this very October day. He would have run as if there was a dragon breathing fire up his ass.

36

The day after the terrorist attack on the USS *Cole*, Leslie Palmer projected the very same picture of the cold-eyed, Kalashnikov-cradling, calmly preaching terror boss onto a large screen in her NIA office in Manhattan. Her eyes fixed to the image, she carefully scrutinized the motionless bearded man; she turned and zoomed, back and forth, in and out. She finally left the terrorist leader and his blank stare standing where he stood.

"*This asshole is an analytical enigma,*" she stated angrily, stepping toward the window, where she stood looking absently at the two massive, yet graceful, Twin Towers that seemed to be conspiring with each other, holding their heads together in the sky, high above where she stood.

She was endlessly fascinated by the naked, smooth contours of the slender, 110-story skyscrapers—in all of their glistening enormity, they seemed to be wanting to murmur a message to her. Only, she couldn't grasp what that message might be. Shaking her head, she returned to her PowerPoint console and wiped the despicable Arab away with the push of a button.

It was only much later that Leslie would realize that the signs had always been there. Of course—it had been staring right at her. It was just a matter of seeing it. The beard, that long swath of hair that covered his chin and neck—the axis that denoted flexibility. It was obvious why all of that was hidden by a load of hair. A whole lot of insecurity concealed by a matted mass of beard.

"By the beard of the prophet," Leslie exclaimed one day, "the man is completely desolate, afraid of enemies and rivals. He has buried himself at the back of nowhere, single-mindedly fixed on destruction, forever and all time!"

37

Back in the fall of 2000, the AQ, with its hairy caricature of a leader, had not yet attained the status of a serious adversary. At best a handful of concerned visionaries had ever discussed amongst themselves the possibility of a new Cold War between Islam and the West. Political leaders would never have listened to them anyhow. Unfortunately, AQ was not seen as an acute threat by practically anyone in the West, with the exception, perhaps, of a few members of counterterrorism units at the FBI and the British SIS. However, by and large, the security services saw the attacks on American troops and facilities overseas as something that was, fortunately, far from the home front: in Africa, or some other godforsaken place.

The noisy, successful surprise attack on the USS *Cole* would ring in a new era in Al Qaeda's fight against Western dominance on the Arab peninsula. But no one thought so far as to recognize the threat of terrorism becoming a dangerous global phenomenon.

Therefore, when photographer Steve Quinn disappeared without a trace in Afghanistan months later, there was at first little suspicion of any connection to the most extreme of all terrorist operations.

Meanwhile, in the USA, the director of the FBI's counterterrorism division was pretty much the only one who listened to Zawahiri's constant calls for terror attacks and saw in them an actual threat to American cities. But his urgings fell on deaf ears. The many branches of the American Secret Service were tangled and convoluted, and had countless offshoots; and all of them kept the crucial results of their inquiries to themselves for fear that someone might steal their thunder. Apart from the FBI, CIA, and highly clandestine National Security Agency (NSA), no less than 16 intelligence agencies were charged with gathering information. These included Army Intelligence DIA—the largest of them all—the intelligence agencies of the Navy, Air Force, National Guard, U.S. Immigration, Firearms, Tobacco and Alcohol (FTA), the Drug Enforcement Administration (DEA)... Separately, they gathered oceans of information—but they rarely communicated among themselves. And so the mosaic pieces gathered out of floods of information stemming from interceptions, wiretapping, and interrogations were never put together to show the picture that had always been there. This would later haunt the intelligence community. That they had failed to connect the dots.

It was thus no wonder that the explosive suspicions of an imminent attack expressed by Leslie Palmer's lover Ben Heller, highly specialized though he was in matters of hard and software, not to mention a number of intensely erotic sidelines, were damned to go unnoticed in the bureaucratic oblivion of the intelligence agencies.

On the other hand, this state of affairs proved extremely practical to a CIA man like Rick Bronx, who had no difficulty establishing a life of his own within the Secret Service jungle. Mutual monitoring and identity checks were only present in the dry theory of largely unread policy manuals. The fact that he was known and valued in intelligence circles also allowed him to be the perfect shadow.

38

About seven months after his hasty departure from Peshawar to Aden, Steve Quinn finally managed to return to the starting point of his journey. The last remnants of snow were melting under the increasingly bold rays of the sun in the northeastern reaches of Pakistan, in the foothills of the Waziristan mountains—the border region to Afghanistan. A dry wind blew from the highlands, and was not about to die down.

The Toyota Land Cruiser drove down the broad, bumpy gravel road that led through the pass at a relatively swift pace, whirling up a dust cloud in its wake that could be seen from afar. Steve Quinn sat on the worn, artificial leather of the passenger seat, his camera aimed through the open side window at the spectacular Hindu Kush backdrop, the endless, beige plains below, and the giant, looming silhouette of the Waziri range.

They had left Peshawar in the early hours, having purchased their provisions, water, and warm blankets at the old Qissa Khawani Bazaar, which consisted of a disorderly maze of narrow alleyways, ramshackle houses, and cave-like stores.

Abdulahi, a Pakistani from the barely controlled border region, hardly said a word during the drive. He spoke Pashto, the language of the Wazir, but when he occasionally wanted to point out to his passenger the sublime beauty of the landscape that was constantly renewed with every changing angle, he mostly did so with a silent motion of his hand. Steve Quinn kept his camera working, and was filled only with the thought that he was probably taking the most stunning pictures of his life.

They had reached the famed as well as infamous Khyber Pass after navigating hair-raising turns along steep precipices. As they now drove around dangerously slippery bends on the other side, Abdulahi seemed amused each time his passenger involuntarily tensed his legs as if wanting to hit the brakes.

For centuries, caravans had been tediously making their way across the long, difficult pass from Afghanistan, transporting supplies, food, and equipment to the "Piccadilly of Central Asia," as the Brits liked to call the Peshawar emporium during colonial times.

They passed heavily laden trucks, shabby, overburdened pickups came their way, men rested their horses from pulling their loads by the side of the road, and there was no doubt in Quinn's mind that not only rice and cotton were being pushed across this century-old route, but drugs and guns as well.

The barren, jagged landscape that characterized the Afghani-Pakistani border, known to be the stronghold of the Taliban, spread before them.

By the time they noticed a group of men in wide pants, long flowing shirts, and skew turbans, it was too late. Abdulahi yelled a curse, and applied the entire weight of his body to the brakes.

"Jihadis," he screamed, crunching the gear into reverse as the turbaned men rushed toward them, menacingly waving their Kalashnikovs in the air. Quinn still hadn't quite grasped the situation.

"What do they want, Abdu?"

Abdulahi emitted unintelligible sounds. His eyes wide with terror, he quickly backed into a passing point in order to turn. But masked men dressed in black, who had apparently been lying in ambush, were suddenly everywhere. They came from behind, ramming rifle butts into the sides of the car. Two tore open the driver's side door and hauled Abdulahi out. He tried in vain to explain himself in Pashto, the tribal language of the marauders. One of them, a man with flashing eyes who was a foot taller than the rest, silently grabbed the driver by the collar, hoisted him to the side of the road like a crane, and sent him tumbling down the steep slope of rubble with a forceful shove.

Quinn yelled in protest, frantically waving his passport, which only earned him a heavy fist in the face.

Everything unfolded with quick precision.

Early this morning, Quinn had tried calling his son in Brooklyn from the hotel, but he had not been able to reach him. It was still the dead of night in New York, so he had left a message on the answering machine...

The gunmen had tied his hands and were now jostling him harshly onto the bed of the truck. His thoughts raced. In these dramatic moments, he wondered whether this expertly executed kidnapping had targeted him by accident or by design. *Who knew about my travel plans?* He tried to order his chaotic thoughts. He remembered having told the British manager of his expedition while checking out of the hotel. The man had shown not the least bit of interest.

"Have a good trip then," was all he said.

Then Quinn's attention had been grabbed by a young Pakistani conspicuously roaming around his luggage in the lobby. He had been so irritated that he had completely forgotten to give his son more precise information about the next step of his journey.

As his kidnappers now sent the Toyota rumbling and careening further down the pass, it seemed to him as if he had seen one of them lurking outside the hotel as Abdulahi was loading the bulging bag that contained his camera gear. But these guys with their wrapped-up faces all looked the same. Still, he could have sworn that they'd been watching him. He cumbersomely twisted his body to steal a glance at the driver.

At that moment, something hard hit him in the back of the head—he instantly blacked out.

39

The bearded man leaning over him was not wearing one of the towel-like headdresses. His relaxed features were pleasantly tanned by the sun, his eyes had an intelligent spark to them. He spoke in a placid tone.

"You are an American spy."

Quinn blinked, pushing himself up on his elbows.

"Nonsense, I'm a journalist."

"Our information tells us otherwise. See for yourself." The bearded one held up a document for Quinn to see. Quinn's head hurt, he had no desire to look. His opposite motioned encouragingly with his bearded chin.

"Here, this is a list of all U.S. agents operating in Islamabad."

Quinn held his forehead, squinted. There was his name, underlined in red: *QUINN, Stephen (Steve).*

Leaning back, he countered, "I'm a photographer from New York. I have nothing to do with your issues!"

The leader shook his head with a sigh, strands of his long, black hair falling loosely.

"We know better than to believe you, Quinn. If you don't want to cooperate, I will make you talk."

He waved to the back. Two armed men appeared immediately, nodded in response to their leader's curt orders. They grabbed Quinn, who was struggling, kicking at whatever he could. They twisted his arms behind his back until he screamed in pain, shoved him before the leader. Breathing heavily, Quinn struggled for words:

"It's a mix up... sir... I... I'm not a spy."

"That's what they all say, don't they?" came the response in an English so well spoken that it might have been cultivated at Oxford.

They dragged him through low, dingy passageways. It was only now that Quinn realized, with a shudder, that they had to be far inside the mountain. The two warriors grinned maliciously at Quinn, whose forebodings worsened by the second. However, neither he, nor anyone with even the most gruesome imagination, could possibly have pictured anything close to what actually lay ahead.

40

"Where am I?" Quinn panted as they tied him naked to a wooden plank bed with a few lengths of rope. The arched ceiling above him was hewn out of sheer rock, two bare lightbulbs dangled from wires, casting a ghoulish light on the bearded faces. The men laughed wildly. There was a draft coming from somewhere. A door slammed, sending a clanging echo through the dungeon. Footsteps approached. The two Jihadis stepped respectfully aside.

"The Sheikh," whispered one.

It was the bearded, bareheaded one. He now wore a white robe that was delicately embroidered in gold. The figure behind him appeared, in every aspect, the polar opposite to his dignified bearing and educated demeanor. Black eyes were set deep in a glowering face; puffy lips emphasized a brutal expression, a scant beard fell on a black tunic, which covered an obviously muscular torso. The ominous, executioner-like character held a bag, which he placed carefully on the low, wooden table. He turned with slow dignity, smiling in cruel anticipation at Quinn's naked form. As he did so, he rubbed thick fingers over his moist lips. Then he turned, standing firmly upright, to look devotedly at the man they had called the Sheikh.

Quinn felt a cold shower rush down his spine. More footsteps rang down the vaulted corridor. A Taliban member entered, dumped Quinn's bulky travel bag unceremoniously to the ground, slammed the door behind himself. Once the echoes had ceased, the room was deathly silent.

The executioner reverently removed a case, a brown medicine bottle, and a thick wad of cotton from a black plastic bag. With the fingertips of one massive hand, he also extracted a scalpel, which he held, grunting, up to the light.

"You will talk now, Quinn," cautioned the Sheikh. "You will tell me who you are. Everything—your superior, your mission. *Everything.*"

Quinn struggled against his restraints, panting.

"Who are you? Where am I? I am a citizen of the United States. A photographer for the *New Yorker*, I am Steve Quinn, not a spy, damn it..."

He stopped, exhausted.

"You are being held by the Taliban," the Sheikh informed him. "That's all you need to know. If you talk—and I mean *really* talk, you will be treated well. Otherwise you will go to hell. You will experience worse pain than you could ever imagine and, believe me, you will die slowly. You are an infidel who wants to betray us. Admit it, American! Everything we do, we do in the name of Allah, to damn the infidel to eternity."

The Sheikh looked at Quinn to assess the effect of his words. Quinn shook his head desperately.

"I know nothing, I am..."

The Sheikh shut him up with a motion of his hand, and nodded to the torturer. One of the armed men held Quinn's head in a lock.

"You sing now, man!" he jeered.

No use trying to put up resistance. The executioner positioned the scalpel over the bridge of Quinn's nose and, with obvious pleasure, slowly cut the skin, just a millimeter deep, all the way down to the tip. Quinn's scream died to a groan as the man carefully dabbed at the wound with a burning liquid.

"Talk, and save yourself the senseless pain, Mister Quinn," the leader advised in his polished English.

"I can tell you're a rational man, sir, listen," Quinn begged of him. "I am innocent. I know that you are going to kill me. You kill all Americans. There is a fatwa to kill all Americans, whether I talk or not. But I am not a spy. I am a photographer, my son lives in Brooklyn, I work for..."

Quinn screamed piercingly as the torturer drew the knife straight across his chest. Blood welled from the cut.

"Oh... no, no... stop... please..."

Through clouded eyes he saw the shadowy face of the leader, contemptuously indifferent, as it leaned over him.

"Cry and whine and moan all you like, American. One last time—tell us what your mission is, what the CIA is planning against us, where the rockets of your womanizing weakling of a president are aimed, and I will show mercy..."

Quinn dribbled incomprehensible stuff, convulsively shook his head, pleaded with his eyes. His babbled words choked into a wailing scream as the sharp knife now sliced down the length of his chest to his stomach. The wound was deep enough for blood to squirt, and as the caustic tincture poured onto the severed, raw nerve endings, the infernal burning pain nearly drove Quinn out of his mind. The Sheikh, face void of expression, sat down on a leather stool and opened Quinn's bag.

"Listen to me, American! We are not a bunch of dumb camel drivers, as you arrogant fools seem to think. Our best people have visited your schools, or studied in England."

He paused for a moment, then continued in a droning voice.

"Steve Quinn, arrived in Islamabad from Aden, where he met with the chief of police and an American agent by the name of Carpenter, right?"

Quinn only groaned.

"Then the hotel in Peshawar, where you associated with the manager. Why this hotel? You tell me. The manager is a British undercover agent. You placed a call to New York. The number that the hotel reported to us is located in a building in Manhattan, in which the Secret Services occupies five stories."

"My... son... works there... for an engineering firm..." Quinn muttered.

"Don't deny it!" the Sheikh thundered. He gave a resigned sign.

The barbarian with the knife leaned over Quinn's spread legs, grabbed his swollen penis in his left hand. Quinn gurgled wildly, "I'll talk, I admit everything..."

The torturer made the cut. From the base, through the middle, and to the front. Blood pulsed forth. The man poured more disinfectant.

Quinn lay in a spasm, his eyes torn wide open, spit drooling out of his contorted mouth, his whole body shaking. Then merciful darkness enveloped him.

The leader turned away in disgust. He took the travel bag and stepped outside, followed by the two warriors. The torturer stared down on Quinn's body for a few moments, as if unable to decide what to do next. Then he reached under the many layers of his garments, took out a member that, even unaroused, was thick and long. He stepped up to the cot, legs apart, leaned his shaggy head back, then calmly pissed on the American's lifeless body with a long, disgusting, yellow stream.

41

Quinn was startled by the butcher's demonic face. His watery eyes saw the slobbering jaws of a dog, the crazed eyes of the torturer. A dull, babbling sound reached his consciousness from afar. Now the man took Quinn's penis into his hand, and cut it off with a glowing red pair of scissors. Quinn felt nothing. The rabid dog snapped at the severed appendage. Now they were all laughing, laughing, laughing, and the laughter echoed, it was the mocking laughter of a hundred devils, swinging their forks, and dancing on Quinn's lap. Fires burned within his body—the fires of hell.

Two stories further down in the subterranean complex, Sheik Bassan sank onto soft, green, embroidered cushions. He stretched one leg out on an artfully woven rug, and arranged a stack of magazines on his other, bent, knee.

Zawahiri, the operational chief of Al Queda, had made himself comfortable across from him, contemplatively stroking his long, thin, grayish-white beard.

"And, do we have our information?"

Bassan shook his head, no.

"The American isn't talking."

"Then let him go to hell!"

Bassan pointed carefully at the three *New Yorker* magazines he had found in Quinn's bag.

"Our information from Aden and Islamabad are not proof. They are just circumstantial evidence, Sidi. Quinn is probably a harmless photo-journalist—one of those naïve Americans that want to convert our country to hot dogs, jeans, and Coca Cola."

"What makes you say that, brother?"

The green tapestries covering the walls lent the room a cozy warmth. Bassan stretched his limbs.

"I studied his articles in these magazines. The *New Yorker* is a well-known publication that is read widely throughout the United States."

"So?" the other interjected. "Would that not be the perfect disguise for one of their agents?"

"It would," Bassan admitted. "But that's not the point."

The chief of operations raised his brows in surprise. He looked with interest at the issue that Bassan now extended toward him, opened to a woman's uncovered head against an ocean backdrop.

"Quinn probably had these magazines with him to be able to show his work," Bassan explained, stroking his index finger across the shiny cover. "He photographed the American woman in this one."

Zawahiri paged through the articles; he frowned as if he was missing some salacious nude shots of the pictured beauty.

"The pictures are excellent, but the article—I mean the story of this woman—could help our cause," Bassan insinuated.

The CO's eyes widened. He remained silent. He knew very well that Bassan had made nothing but useful suggestions so far.

A soft clinking interrupted the silence as a young Talibani came in carrying a pot of tea and cups, pausing respectfully. The men allowed the boy to pour as they continued to page through the journals.

The article that Bassan had referred to showed a smiling woman in various locations. Leaning against a terrace railing, walking across a Manhattan square with one of the Twin Towers in the background, in her office, holding a stack of books. An obviously older shot was taken on a sunny, green, California high school campus. The picture that appealed to Zawahiri the most had been taken by Quinn in the reddish ambiance of a darkened theater. In it, the woman wore long, white robes, and an elegantly wrapped headscarf. She seemed to be floating on air.

"The man takes good pictures," he muttered.

Bassan nodded, waiting.

"You think he'll be useful to us as a photographer?"

Bassan moved his shoulders in a noncommittal gesture.

"Possible, but I was thinking along other lines."

Bassan elaborated on his concept as the OP sipped at his cup and chewed on a thin piece of flatbread.

The woman had studied motion psychology, performed as an actress and dancer, and was now working for a Naval Intelligence department. "She specialized in the analysis of gestures and behaviors of statesmen, particularly those of countries that caused the USA difficulties…"

Zawahiri laughed out loud.

"Fidel Castro, the Iran, Saddam Hussein…"

"Exactly. The people in this woman's special department seek to pinpoint weaknesses and foibles that are expressed in body language, so that they can be deliberately used to their advantage."

"That's why we don't allow anyone to take our picture," the OP said with a grin, adding, with a now serious expression, "We must tell Osama to appear even more stoic and stiff on the videos we are planning."

"Good idea," Bassan praised. Zawahiri gruffly waved the comment aside.

"Continue, what else about this woman?"

"The article only hints at other things she does. It says that she is good at impersonating people and—listen here—that her government has employed her to play the double of the new First Lady."

"That's what the articles says?" the CO asked, skeptical.

"My own interpretation, Sidi, but if anyone knows, it will be Quinn. He conducted the interview, visited her, had dinner with her, maybe he even…"

A sharp glance from the CO was enough to silence Bassan, whose experiences with all aspects of free society always caught up with him, and disgusted him.

"The text only says that she has taken on an undisclosed assignment for the White House. Look at the picture, Sidi—do you notice anything?"

The CO shook his head disapprovingly.

"An uncovered woman's face is an insult to the Prophet."

"She is the spitting image of the wife of the American president who took office this year," Bassan said ambiguously.

"I don't know her face too well. What are you thinking, Bassan?"

Bassan took a careful sip of tea from the gold-rimmed cup, and cleared his throat.

"Quinn will tell us everything about this female, and then we will check with our cell in New York to determine whether she can be of use in the Great Plan."

For a moment, he doubted whether the man sitting across from him knew of the cell led by Sheikh Khalid at the heart of America, but he didn't ask. The principle was for every man to know no more than was necessary to fulfill his own, personal task.

"And say the information is useful—what would your plan be *then*, brother?"

Bassan's eyes sparkled enterprisingly as he leaned forward. He spoke for a long time, in a whisper so low that had anyone been trying to listen, they would not have understood a word.

Only once was a question audible in the room: "And you are certain, Bassan, that this—eh—First Lady regularly visits one of the Twin Towers?"

Bassan nodded emphatically.

"Exactly. Once a month, on a Tuesday. Even before she came to the White House, she went on secret visits to Manhattan regularly. Always to one of the big skyscrapers—those capitalist towers of worship."

It was now May of 2001 on the Western calendar. The new U.S. president had been in office for just five months. His wife's habits had, seemingly, not changed. Bassan wanted to get a clearer picture of what this meant. For a while, both men gazed silently ahead.

Then they spoke again, softly, quietly, occasionally motioning with their hands, bowing their heads, smiling. The tea had long gone cold when they looked at each other, their eyes bright.

"A good plan—no, a fantastic concept, my son," the CO praised enthusiastically, a tone of admiration in his voice. "I will speak to the council about it. Osama will decide. You will provide me with all the necessary details—get Bronx to confirm everything. Habits, times—we need layouts, everything! By the way, what is the name of this woman?"

Bassan answered promptly.

"Her name is Leslie Palmer."

They parted without much ado. An hour later, Bassan composed a carefully edited, encoded email. There was plenty of hard work left to be done. But a promising start had been made. *Bronx will not let me down*, he reflected as he sent the message on its way with a click of his fingertip. The date was May 25, 2001.

This Rick Bronx, Bassan knew, was the secret top AQ agent who worked under deep cover right at CIA headquarters in Langley. He would play a key role in the upcoming *Operation Great Plan*. If everything that Bassan was planning worked out... He leaned back, eyes closed. *Insha'Allah! Allah had written the book of life. Allah alone knew every word contained within it!*

42

When Quinn came to with a deep sigh, his hands felt different. His legs, too. He suddenly realized that he was no longer tied! Carefully he moved his arms, reached down with his hands. *The rabid dog from hell!* The terror that rose within him turned out to be unfounded. He took a deep breath. Everything was pretty much healthy and whole—well, at least it was still attached. Leaning up on his elbows, he looked down at himself.

His chest, his stomach, his pelvic area and everything down there, were rudimentarily covered with cotton and bandaging. Blood was seeping through.

Someone had placed his clothes on the stool, next to his bag.

A bottle of water now stood on the table that the torturer had used to spread out his instruments. Quinn sat up groaning, placed his feet on the floor, and carefully got up. Swaying, he grabbed for the bottle, drank greedily. Then he pulled on his shirt, and gingerly put on his pants, taking care not to move the bandages.

He had hardly completed this cumbersome and painful task, when the door opened to reveal the gloating grimace of the torturer's perverted, sadistic, unkempt bearded face. Quinn instinctively drew back. Clicking his tongue full of relish, the torturer pulled out his scalpel, made the primitive, yet unambiguous gesture of cutting off a penis, then roughly pushed him out into the narrow corridor.

"You have one last chance, Quinn. If you decide not to cooperate, I will leave you to him," said Bassan, in the green room, with frightening finality. With an impatient motion of his head, he signaled the torturer to leave. Quinn bit his lips. Shaking with anger and fear, he would love to have hurled himself at the throat of this seemingly civilized, disgusting bastard of an Arab. With all the contempt he could muster, he spat:

"Pigs, barbarian pigs. You twisted bastards, you..."

Bassan smiled in mock pity.

"We're just doing what your people taught us, you know."

Then he explained—about the *New Yorker,* Quinn's articles, the woman's portrait, and that he wanted to know everything about her. And he meant *everything*...

Quinn interrupted him angrily.

"I want a doctor, I need pain killers. And I smell like a Paris pissoir."

Bassan fixed him with a dangerously long gaze.

"Let's get something straight, Quinn. You will be asking no questions, and you will be making no requests or demands. You will remain a prisoner of Al Qaeda. If you meet my expectations, if—and only *if*—your information proves useful to us, we may be able to release you one day in exchange for ten of our people held at the Bagram Collection Point by the CIA. And in regards to your stench, thank you for your concern, but anyone dealing with Americans eventually gets used to it."

He gave a sign. A helper rushed in with a video camera, which he placed on an old trunk that looked like a skeleton might rise from it at any moment.

Bassan put in a tape, then commanded harshly.

"You will tell me about this woman, Leslie Palmer." He demonstratively raised a *New Yorker*, and continued coldly, "I want to hear everything. If I am satisfied, you will see a doctor and receive something to eat; if not, we will turn you into a corpse. Very painfully, and very slowly."

What Bassan had issued was not a suggestion, nor an order—it was a simple ultimatum. Talk or die. Quinn nodded weakly. What choice did he have, here, in this fortress, in the depths of the dismal Al Qaeda catacombs? With a shudder, he silently answered his own question: Your only alternative, old boy, is the rabid dog of hell!

43

Quinn began to talk.

"Leslie Palmer is a strategic research professor at the Naval War College. She is a certified motion analyst at the Ministry of Defense's laboratory for human assessment. She works at the World Trade Center, Manhattan, WTC 7, right next to the Twin Towers. Many intelligence agencies, including the CIA and NSA, have offices there on numerous floors. The Internal Revenue Service is in the same building. The Mayor of New York has his emergency nuclear shelter deep in the ground below its basement."

The tape was running. *Useful, yes, pretty useful,* thought Bassan and motioned the prisoner to continue speaking. Quinn went on with a sluggish voice.

"Alabama plays into it somehow. That's where Maxwell Air Force Base is located. Leslie Palmer spent some time working there before she moved to the East Coast."

Quinn examined Bassan's features, trying to tell if these pieces of geographical information meant anything to him.

"The Air Force runs a Counterproliferation Center on the base, their job is..."

Bassan interrupted him pompously.

"...to prevent the spreading of nuclear weapons to rogue states."

"More than that, as everyone knows," Quinn countered with ill-concealed satisfaction. "The U.S., as Leslie Palmer told me, neglected its enemies for a long time. As part of combat tactics, Army commanders learn that one of the ground rules is to know your enemy: his strengths, the weapons he has at his disposal, the way in which his troops are organized, and who commands them."

The Arab's face looked troubled, as if he could just see his picture up on the walls of every one of the American enemy's command posts.

"Go on!"

"However, politically speaking, the White House itself, but also the State Department, where foreign policy strategy is made, has completely failed to analyze and properly understand its opponents. Leslie was referring primarily to leaders of rogue states, such as North Korea, Libya, Syria, Iran, and terrorist groups like..." Quinn hesitated.

"Al Qaeda?"

"'Know your Enemy,' is the name of the scientific program, in which Leslie plays a key role. It deals with the ancient challenge of correctly assessing foreign leaders, and with making such analyses realistically useful."

Bassan bowed his head as if weighing the concept. The longer he listened, the more useful this fellow seemed.

"It's a tough job, trying to unlock the innermost human identity, to predict the behavior of complex, forbidding personalities whom we have no access to, and who, to make matters worse, have weapons of mass destruction," Quinn lectured haughtily. "The question remains why America, the land of opportunity, has seen itself unable to use the first-rate expertise of its scientists, and to close the gap."

Quinn took a breath, and tried to close off.

"Most of this is in my article."

Bassan put on a well-informed front.

"And I suppose they closed the gap in Alabama."

Quinn didn't bite.

"Palmer made a career in this field. She told me a number of things—unbelievable stuff."

A Talibani brought tea. The Arab put in a new tape.

"Keep talking, Quinn."

At about the same time, CO Zawahiri sat in his comfortably furnished commando post one story below, browsing the *New Yorker* interview.

...graduated from Taft University. She was fascinated by Reich's theory of 'body armoring,' and thus began her career in the analysis of gestures and motion, with a focus on people who made history. Hitler, for example...

...There is a lot to be read from the way a person walks, looks around the room, fiddles or plays about with something. At first glance, such unconscious movements may seem to be meaningless, even when we are talking about prominent heads of state...

...but they can offer compelling clues as to how the person in question might behave in a critical situation. They provide pertinent insights that allow us to decode and predict the behavior of the political leaders of this world. Their behavior is based on impulses and appetites that manifest physically...

Zawahiri clicked his tongue impatiently. He flipped to the interview.

Palmer: I process data from countless hours of television footage of interviews, speeches, and press conferences. My studies are longitudinal, reaching as far back as the available footage will allow. Of course, I also have access to the comprehensive Secret Service archives, in which tapes of all broadcasted television programs are stored.

Quinn: Can you give us an example?

Palmer: I once examined video footage of a man who appeared at an event in Northern Iraq. A number of experts believed that he was a double.

Quinn: A double for Saddam Hussein?

Palmer: Correct. In the laboratory, I examined the dictator's comportment over a span of a good twenty years. One rather unique habit soon stood out: the man snapped his fingers after rubbing his left eye.

Quinn: Isn't that pretty trivial?

Palmer: Not to me. This gesture confirmed that the man at the event was the real Hussein. His stress signal was to touch his finger to his eyelid. The sudden subsequent snapping of his fingers could reflect the same character trait that made him capable of actions such as the 1991 invasion of Kuwait.

Quinn: I know that you are not about to reveal your methods. Still—could you tell us a little about your approach?

Palmer: I can only be successful in what I do after I have studied details of my subject's comportment over an extended period, and pinpointed actual patterns of behavior. I studied Putin for a long time. The Russian president has a leaning toward undemocratic politics. He is difficult to read, and hyper vigilant.

Quinn: Do you also teach heads of state how to move?

Palmer: No. Most leaders already have a well-coordinated method of expression that allows them to adapt every move to handle high-pressure situations. Their attentive gaze, the posture of their spine, their motions—one can almost sense the buzz. Someone that capable of coordinating his or her expression can reach peak performance levels during public appearances. Ronald Reagan, Gorbachev, and Fidel Castro are true masters of this art.

Quinn: Sounds almost like an athletic performance.

Palmer: That's because it is. The control that politicians exert over their bodies can be compared to that of athletes who know exactly, which of their powerful muscles to bring into play at any given moment. They loosen up, focus on becoming one with their bodies, and then leap into action. Political leaders who know how to do it right can make the same kind of impressive impact. Those who aren't in complete control are tense—one can tell that they are ill at ease, and their countries can suffer accordingly.

Quinn: You are an actress.

Palmer (laughs): Actually, I was a dancer. Dancing is the epitome of body control. That is why actresses often make good dancers. You learn to express yourself through motion.

Quinn: It seems that you closely resemble the First Lady. Do you know one another?

Palmer: I met her once in Washington, but there's nothing to tell about our encounter.

Quinn: Come on—you probably analyzed the President for her, didn't you?

Palmer (laughs)*:* No, but I recently acted as her during a reception held for a group of Japanese businesswomen—really just for fun.

Zawahiri put down the magazine and stroked his long beard in contemplation.

Meanwhile, one story up, in the green room, Bassan was beginning to show signs of impatience. He stood and regarded a frame on the wall that held a silver curved dagger mounted against black satin—a gift from Yemen.

"Tell me about Palmer's White House assignment."

Quinn, who had given Palmer his word as a journalist, divulged the information with hesitation—and only after the sweat covered countenance of the rabid dog of hell had flashed across his mind's eye.

"She is supposed to act as a double in case of a threat to the White House. That's all I know."

The latter was made up—if not completely. Leslie had told him that she was practicing to play the role of the First Lady's double—that she was studying her fashion preferences, and analyzing her gestures. *I find that it comes to me naturally*, he remembered her saying. *I feel a connection with her.*

Bassan leaped without warning and, in one lightning-fast motion, ripped the bandage from Quinn's nose.

"*Everything!*" he snapped. "*Everything,* I said!"

Quinn gritted his teeth, held his throbbing nose, then wiped the oozing blood off with the back of his hand. The sudden, brutal gesture had broken his last inner strength to resist. Almost relieved, he told the Arab everything that Leslie Palmer had confided to him about her job for the White House.

44

Over the following nights, Quinn tossed restlessly on the hard cot in his narrow cell, plagued by confused dreams. Wild images invaded his mind: he saw himself floating weightlessly across a barren, stinking desert landscape—far below him lay the training camp in northern Yemen, where he had spent the night after completing an illustrated report about special police forces. Dark-skinned, naked figures waved to him. He stood before a green door with a golden knob. It opened, and he stepped into a courtyard with a fountain made of intricate mosaic tiles that was spouting red water—*blood!* And there the sweaty American, with his hard, nut-colored face and a thick cigar in the corner of his mouth, held court on a pile of thick carpets. He gaped at him, as veiled women danced seductively around him, the contours of their beautiful bodies showing tantalizingly through their scant white gowns. Oriental music filled the room. Then shots disrupted the eerie mood. The *New Yorker's* editor in chief could be heard outside, insisting that the camels needed to be saddled.

Suddenly, bodyguards appeared from nowhere and began shooting at him. He felt a stabbing pain throughout his entire body, screamed—and woke.

A grumpy guard opened Quinn's cell door, looked in, pointed to the bottle of water lying on the ground.

Quinn found his way back to reality. The absurd dream reminded him of the Arab-looking American from back then, when, after the dumb accident on that old Italian moped, he had—his arm bleeding—found the abandoned hospital not far from the training camp.

Don't treat him—shoot him, the American had commanded in the operating room.

Armed men had knocked him past the stacks of wood blazing in the yard with the butts of their guns. They had roughly ushered him behind a wall. Quinn's fate had been all but sealed, when soldiers suddenly arrived in a cloud of dust raised by their Jeeps, and stormed the yard with raised machine-guns. Military Police. They had been led by a narrow-faced officer with black hair who, heavy pistol in hand, had given curt orders without ever unduly raising his voice. He had aimed a single shot at the man who raised his Kalashnikov next to Quinn, killing him instantly.

It was only later that Quinn realized that he had probably disturbed a secret meeting. Who was the Arab-American man? What had those henchmen disguised as orderlies been doing in the long-closed hospital, before most of them had evaded arrest by fleeing? What had happened to the American? All Quinn knew was that, since the event, pictures of his stony, angrily flushed face, the hard lines of his mouth, his blue or gray eyes that stared at him without human emotion, had haunted his memory.

The longer he pondered his grotesque dream, the more he could have sworn that he had recognized that same face a month later, at Aden harbor. Quinn had practically run right into the American as he made his way back to town after shooting a series of pictures at the Navy base. The American, wearing a light gray suit with a markedly Western cut, had been in the company of an Arab man. His face had the rough texture of an orange peel, and he wore a crew cut. The look of surprise that flew across his face before he—almost instantaneously—regained composure, suggested to Quinn that he had been recognized.

When Quinn had noticed them following him, he had quickly put on a disappearing act by slipping into a bar and mixing in with the locals. The hefty innkeeper, who had a wide face and a mane of a black beard, was just showing him through the back exit as the Arab-American—now flanked by two muscular thugs—had entered the front, obviously looking for him.

Silky smooth skin brushed against Quinn, a pair of dark eyes in a veiled face dove into his questioning glance. "That is Rick, the American," the beautiful woman had whispered.

45

The Cave of Companions had received its name during the time when Rick Bronx was training the Jihadis fighting against Soviet occupiers in the use of weapons and explosives, and the young, highly respected billionaire Osama bin Laden had been pumping funds from his Saudi family empire into a bunker system in the Hindu Kush. Bin Laden had decided to finance projects that would serve the Holy War—the building of roads up in the mountains, the blasting of tunnels and caves, which would serve to protect the Afghani Mujahedeen from air raids. The colossal Bin Laden Brothers sent diggers, bulldozers and electric generators, cement mixers and steel to Afghanistan.

"This is where I treated our wounded," said Zawahiri with a yearning undertone in his voice, and pulled Bassan by the sleeve toward the bright light at the mouth of the cave. An inspection was taking place inside. About eighty Jihadis stood at attention in two ranks; their weapons shouldered, their eyes forward. Thus they waited for the inspector, who was slowly walking down the line.

"This cave was once the gathering place of our sworn leaders, and later, when the Russians invaded, our hospital," Zawahiri explained. They stepped onto the forecourt to the cave's entrance, and looked out on the countryside bathed in glaring sunlight.

"Sadly, we will have to abandon the Companions' Cave," Zawahiri lamented with a sigh. "Once the Great Plan is implemented, it will be raining bombs here."

Bassan leaned against an all-terrain vehicle that was white with dust and looked up at the ceiling of the entrance, which had been reinforced with concrete.

"How safe are we in Tora Bora?"

Zawahiri seemed not to be listening. His eyes had a strange, far-off gleam—as if he were looking directly into a future filled with wonderful promise. He suddenly snapped around.

"You know, brother, as a surgeon in the field, I always contemplated the possible outcomes before beginning an operation to amputate.

Success or failure. This amputation is going to be a success."

"Are you speaking in riddles?" Bassan asked.

Zawahiri shook his head, always the strategist.

"The Great Plan, my great plan, is simply fantastic."

His face practically glowed as he lectured on: "The operation is a massive, simultaneous attack on four strategic American targets. I like the way our people have camouflaged our mission: they refer to the buildings that we aim to destroy as faculties. Their aliases are ingenious. Nobody will be suspicious if fragments of our communications are intercepted and the talk is of universities, professors, and tuition fees. Nobody will imagine that the so-called college enrollment deadline could possibly represent our day of attack."

Bassan's voice sank to a whisper.

"Is it September 11?"

"That depends on Bronx. He is clarifying the final details. The pilots are ready."

Exalted battle cries and the rattle of guns could be heard from the cave as the soldiers performed their drill with the Kalashnikov.

"We will deliver four devastating blows all at once," Zawahiri said ever so quietly, as if he suspected the bunker walls of having ears. "The Twin Towers in New York—these symbols of capitalism, I think they are calling them the faculties of economics and law, then two targets in Washington: the Capitol, which houses their parliament, and the Pentagon."

"Why not the White House?" Bassan murmured.

"I have been told that the White House is difficult to approach by plane, but the Pentagon is not. These decisions will be left to the pilots."

"Providing everything works, brother," Bassan warned gently.

"Allahu Akbar, brother. Allah is great. The Great Plan was named for the greatness of Allah. One of our planes will reach its target—perhaps two. The shock will paralyze the Americans, the impact will be all surpassing. We will be as lightning out of a clear blue sky." Zawahiri heaved his fist through the air. "What the Japanese achieved in Pearl Harbor will pale in comparison to our daring deeds. We will make the Americans bite the dust, we will deliver a direct blow to their economy. The American myth will tumble."

"We are estimating five thousand dead," said Bassan.

"Good. The more, the better. The Americans will be torn apart by pain, anger, and grief. Then, brother, just when they all believe that the worst is over—just as they finally dare to breathe again—we will play the rest of our hand. Phase Two will be the final blow."

He placed both hands on Bassan's shoulders, looking deep into his eyes. "A great surprise!" he proclaimed dramatically. "Its implications even more terrible than the Great Plan! We will kill the President of the United States, the Commander in Chief of the Armed Forces. And his own wife will do the job. We will turn the First Lady into a suicide killer. *She* will deliver the coup de grâce that he deserves!"

Bassan stepped back, awed. He rubbed his beard, his eyes sparkling slyly.

"Brilliant, brother! Let us give this part of the plan a new codename—*Operation Cinderella!* Yes, that is fitting. As Cinderella stepped up from the ashes among which she was forced to sleep and made her way to the castle, she will step out of the ashes of the towers and conquer the White House..." He paused. For a moment, he seemed to be having doubts. "You believe that this can work? That we can actually make her do this?"

"Yes, I believe so," Zawahiri replied in a tone of complete conviction. "Look carefully at the plan, brother. She has no other choice. Either her own fate, or that of her brood."

"You mean her twin sons?" Bassan asked to make sure.

"Yes, exactly. Which mother could refuse to set out on that path, difficult as it may be? How could she possibly choose to sacrifice her sons in order to save the president? An idiot, to whom she has no ties. A stranger. Never in a million years, brother. No mother on this earth would abandon her own flesh and blood. No—she won't. And yes, brother, I am convinced that this will work."

"Bronx has served us well."

Zawahiri nodded almost imperceptibly, his eyes smoldering darkly.

"The magnitude of it all will be unimaginable. Just think, brother. The American will be broken on the ground. The myth of national security will be destroyed. Their national emblems will lie wasted. Already shot through the heart, he will now have to watch, as this president does not lead his country out of crisis, but instead is slain by his wife. By his own wedded spouse! It will be beyond belief! The shock will be deeper than ever. We will crush the myth of their Secret Services, *Allahu Akbar!*"

"They will eradicate us with nuclear weapons," Bassan weighed in.

"Perhaps. And perhaps not. First they would have to discover that the First Lady is a double trained and prepared by us. Apart from that, the world would never approve of a nuclear war."

"Much depends on Bronx."

"I know. He is the only man who can—eh—see this operation through to success. What should it be called again?"

"*Operation Cinderella,*" Bassan replied enthusiastically.

Zawahiri furrowed his brow.

"Why a Western name?"

"Because it is less conspicuous," Bassan replied without hesitation. "Their supercomputers have been programmed to filter everything that is sent through the ethers, or through fiber optic cables, and that enters their country, for certain key terms. If we choose a name from our language and they intercept it, then they will become alarmed and mobilize their Koran experts and language specialists. They will be vigilant and not rest until they have discovered what the Arab alias stands for."

Bassan paused, as if to take a breath, then lifted a meaningful finger, and raised his brows.

"But a Western name? Cinderella? The only thing that will make the Americans think of is their animated Disney movies... of pumpkin carriages that come for their storybook figure at midnight—absolutely harmless. No one will become suspicious!" Bassan gave a resounding laugh, but Zawahiri's expression remained earnest. "You could be right, but..."

Playing the devil's advocate, Bassan interrupted.

"Of course, Bronx could betray *Operation Cinderella.*"

"The possibility of betrayal is not what concerns me," Zawahiri retorted. "Bronx is completely loyal. A dependable loner with no soft spots."

"You mean he has no vulnerabilities—like a lover, an addiction, financial worries, an extravagant lifestyle…"

"Precisely. None of this is the case with him. He is firmly rooted within the American's center of power. Osama swears by him."

Bassan did not seem appeased.

"Do you know why Osama trusts him blindly?"

Zawahiri waved an outstretched arm across the untamed mountain panorama.

"They fought the Soviets side by side."

"We know that. Many did."

Zawahiri lowered his voice to a whisper.

"It was Bronx who liquidated Abdulah Azzam in Peshawar."

Bassans eyes grew wide in surprise and awe.

"*He* detonated the bomb that destroyed his car? That makes him an American hero."

"Certainly. More than that. It makes him their best man. Anyone who eliminates a terrorist on their FBI Most Wanted list is above suspicion all the way to the White House."

"I understand. But that is also why we must be circumspect," Bassan cautioned. "Bronx could unnecessarily expose himself with this mission. Until now, no one was concerned with his dealings, his manner of operating, the nature of his ties to us. That could change once the Great Plan has been carried out. And if anyone starts to question his loyalty… if he makes one wrong move… you know how these things usually end."

Zawahiri picked up a reddish stone and weighed it carefully in his slender hand.

"You believe that Bronx is a risk to us?" He dropped the stone. "You see, this stone could lie here for a hundred years, or it could be ground to dust tomorrow. That is also the nature of life. Insha'Allah, who knows whether fate will grind us to dust tomorrow?"

"Your words are fatalistic."

"Not in the case of Bronx," Zawahiri countered. "He will be careful.

If Osama wants, he can send him to his doom at any time by leaking information to the Americans. You understand? Nothing could be easier. Or, if the enemy holds Sheikh Khalid after the big blow, we could retain Bronx and use him as trading collateral. Bronx knows this, of course. But I believe that he genuinely supports our just cause. He hates his country, America."

Bassan spoke in a sharp tone that suggested he meant exactly the opposite of what he said next.

"Our military genius Khalid, with all of his bold plans, is sure to find great joy in Cinderella."

"Your ironic tone is obvious, Bassan. Have you spoken to him?"

"No, speaking to him would not be wise right now. But Bronx..."

"Bronx and Khalid are rivals, do not forget that..."

"Of course, Bronx meets with him regularly in New Jersey, where he lives. He frequently complains that Khalid will not tolerate any interference with matters of planning or implementation."

Zawahiri seemed to consider this carefully.

"If this is true, then Osama will need to intervene," he decided. "And as far as Bronx is concerned—we pay him more than enough. Perhaps you don't know this, but he is receiving ten million dollars for the Great Plan. American dollars."

Bassan's brows came close to meeting with his hairline.

"I can hardly believe that he should be worth that much to us."

"Not to worry," Zawahiri replied with a cunning smile. "It should appease you to know that we will be earning that money on their stock market, by investing in shares before the day of the Great Plan. Bronx knows how to handle it. He and Khalid agree upon this point, and Khalid will grant him access to his infrastructure to ensure that this facet of the plan succeeds. However, he may still become a liability once all of this is over. Khalid, too, that braggart. Then one or both may end as a martyr in the history of our war."

A Talibani approached and waited silently at a respectful distance. When Bassan encouraged him to speak, he reminded them that it was time to eat.

The men slowly walked the path back inside the large cave. Before they joined the other leaders, Bassan had one more question.

"And what will we tell the world?"

"You know, brother," said Zawahiri in a lecturing tone, "Osama is more interested in television images that speak for themselves than he is in making ideological statements."

46

Rick Bronx, dressed in jeans and a black, collarless cotton shirt, was sitting on the edge of the gray, speckled synthetic tabletop. One leg dangling comfortably, he gazed absently at the shelves overflowing with stacks of paper and magazines. Everything in the little study was gray—the carpet, the numerous pieces of office equipment, the lamp shade, the worn, swiveling office chair that Bronx kicked away angrily with his free leg. He ran his fingers through the gray hair of his temples and racked his brain, which felt just as gray, searching for possible loose ends in the Great Plan.

Sheikh Khalid was the head behind all campaign plans. Bronx had been forced, particularly in the preparatory phases, to communicate with the leader in New Jersey—a man who appeared both weak and worse for wear. These days he kept largely to his comrade in arms, Bassan. Connections to Khalid could prove to be treacherous. It was true that the chaotic man was seen as a dark genius by the underground, but he also had a propensity for boasting.

His soul cannot tell the sublime from the base and the crude. Bronx shook himself in disgust.

Khalid bragged that he had masterminded the attacks on the battle ships in the Straits of Gibraltar, and that he had implemented the 1993 truck bomb attack on the World Trade Center. His standing with Al Qaeda was solid; Bronx harbored no illusions in this respect. The Sheikh had the power. He was the final decision maker. He had only grudgingly agreed to Operation Cinderella in response to pressure from the leaders in the Hindu Kush.

Bronx had avoided contact with him wherever possible. Khalid was no blank page. As a member of an extremist movement, he was almost certainly under observation. Bassan, on the other hand, was a secure contact. As far as a select handful of informed individuals at the CIA were concerned, Bassan was a super double agent, recruited and led by Bronx, who had infiltrated the highest levels of Al Qaeda. He was proud of this ruse. Along with the killing of Osama's rival Abdulah Azzam in Peshawar, this had earned him an almost godlike reputation within the CIA.

Bronx nodded to himself in satisfaction. But he sensed that Operation Cinderella was not foolproof. There were too many unknown variables... The Palmer twins, at any rate, were still the strongest cards up his sleeve...

What could go wrong? He did not know much about the pilots—but then, he didn't really need to. Ahmed, the reserved Mujahid who had dragged him out from under a dead horse in the Hindu Kush, was now living in New Jersey, where he acted as a messenger for the Imam who had been chosen by the Sheikh to strengthen the heroic pilot martyrs in their will to die with promises of a happy hereafter in paradise. Should he send for Ahmed? He sighed inwardly—there was always more to be done, the job was never completed. He stared numbly at his damaged thumbnail.

True, he had found an elegant solution to the Howard Young problem, allowing him to intercept revealing information regarding key preparations that were taking place at various flight schools just in time. Khalid, that foul spawn of arrogance—never mind Sheikh this, and Allah that—really got to him. He had not deemed it necessary to acknowledge the courageous intervention with as much as a single word.

And the next difficulty was already apparent. Her name was not Leslie Palmer—he had her firmly in his grasp, thanks to her sons. The loose end went by the name of Steve Quinn, that damn reporter who had already escaped him twice. He could only hope that the turban-heads in Afghanistan had taken care of the situation, and had erased Quinn, who had—frankly—committed the unforgivable offense of embarrassing him, from the face of the planet.

Bronx was impatient for news. He chewed on the splintered nail until it tore, and a drop of blood welled from his fingertip. He wiped it off on his jeans, then walked, his face foreboding, to the barred window. The mighty Twin Towers gleamed dully in the evening sun—an emblem that no one could possibly imagine gone. He clicked his tongue, and his countenance cleared as he saw them swaying in his mind. He grinned to himself as he suddenly saw a red ball of fire, the setting sun over the Gulf of Aden…

…It had set lower than it stood right now, here, in Manhattan; it had been a day in October, the USS *Cole* had been docked in the harbor: a modern vessel equipped with cruise missiles. The briefing had taken place at the abandoned hospital on the northern hillside, on the main road that turned east and headed past the camp.

Bronx had determined that this would be a suitable place to meet. The hospital was situated on a plateau that allowed a clear view of the street all the way down to the village. The orderlies gathered around the wooden table in the run-down operating room knew far less about First Aid and lifesaving measures than they did about explosives and killing.

Bronx had stood at the head of the table and unfolded a map of the harbor.

The bearded commando chief leaned forward. Another brooded over pictures of the Navy destroyer.

The door to the operating room was shut. A red light outside signaled that entry was forbidden.

Bronx was in good spirits. The hospital had been closed for months. He had approached the health care administration as a supposed investor, and announced intentions of renovating the abandoned complex and establishing a treatment center.

The man who ripped open the door and stumbled in, covered in blood, had no knowledge of any of this. He swayed toward the dumbfounded gathering, leaned, groaning, against the table, and motioned to a gaping wound on his arm.

This just took the cake! Would these ignorant idiots never learn how to establish an effective watch? Practically steaming with rage, Bronx had crumpled up the map, and hastily swept the pictures from the table.

"What the hell do you want?" he roared at the new arrival. Without waiting for a reply, he commanded sharply: "Get rid of him!" He clarified his order by running his hand across his neck in an unmistakable cutting motion.

But Quinn had escaped—and had seen his face . . . Bronx cursed inwardly each time he revisited the embarrassing scene at the abandoned hospital in Yemen. And he did so now. An unintelligible stream of profanities hissed from between his teeth, unheard, as he angrily stepped to the fax machine. Nothing! Still no news!

But wait! He had almost overlooked a piece of paper that had slid from the paper tray and down onto the carpet. He picked it up and read. A crooked smile spread across his lips. "Operation Cinderella!" he murmured to himself, before feeding the paper into the teeth of the shredder. As the metal jaws gnashed, he started fingering keys on his burgundy-colored cell phone. Holding the receiving end to his ear, he grabbed for the bottle of whiskey that served to prevent the light-blue bound volumes of *Foreign Affairs* from slipping off the shelf.

The number that Bronx had activated rang in the White House. Seconds later, the Secret Service agent whose phone he had called answered with a cautious sounding "Hello?"

"I need an escort," said Bronx, skipping the pleasantries. He held the phone to his ear with his shoulder as he screwed open the bottle cap.

"Where?"

"Same place as last time, same time, four o'clock."

A few *Foreign Affairs* volumes slipped and slapped onto the carpet.

"Okay," the man answered. Bronx cut the connection.

The conversation had lasted less than ten seconds. His coded message had let his secret contact at the White House know that Bronx required information on the First Lady's agenda—*escort*—and that their meeting would be set for the fourth day of the week—*four o'clock*—at the place that was designated for Thursdays.

Unable to locate a glass in the mess on his shelves, Bronx raised the bottle directly to his parched lips without further ado. He took two large, gulping swallows. Grunting with satisfaction, the world instantly appeared in a better light. Flooded by a sense of energy and courage, he shot his right fist toward the ceiling.

"*Cinderella!*" he shouted.

47

One day, having just placed a plate of salty stew on his table, the guard on duty lingered indecisively. Quinn looked up in surprise. It was Salim, a young Talibani with a scar that ran from his ear almost down to the corner of his mouth—the one who treated him the most cordially. He now wore an expression that suggested he had something to say.

"What is it, Salim?" Quinn said encouragingly.

The young Afghan looked around uncertainly before he whispered "Do you not pray?"

Getting a quick hold on himself, Quinn put his spoon down with a smile.

"In America, we go to church to pray on *Sunday*."

"We pray to Allah five times a day. That is better."

Quinn poked at the pulpy mass of beans and lamb, and mumbled, "I know." But he had a feeling that Salim wanted to discuss more than religion. He looked up. "Do you have a girlfriend, Salim?"

Salim fumbled with his belt, nodding. A light had appeared in his eyes.

"What's your girl's name?" Quinn asked in a quiet, conspiratorial voice.

Again, an uncertain glance.

"Natalia."

Salim raised a finger to his lips.

"Russian?" asked Quinn, in the tones of an accomplice.

"Psht!" Salim slapped his entire hand over his mouth in fright.

"Don't worry, Salim," Quinn reassured him.

He was still trying to think of his next question, when the young

Talibani suddenly kneeled before him as if he were about to say a prayer, placing one hand on Quinn's sleeve.

"Natalia is in Kabul. I am not allowed to see her. She is..."

"Not Muslim?"

Salim nodded with tightly pressed lips before suddenly breaking out in a broad smile. "She is so beautiful," and in the same breath, "what is your wife's name?"

Quinn's face clouded. Slowly, he shook his head. Salim stared, aghast.

"Dead?"

Quinn corrected him with a smile, "No, no, we are divorced," adding crudely, "I don't suppose there are any women around here?"

Salim motioned vertically with his index finger. "There are chambers for the houris. In a locked area. Only the leaders are allowed to enter it."

Footsteps approached. Salim sprang to his feet, once again pressed his finger to his lips, then assumed his guard posture and marched stiffly outside.

From then on, the ice was broken. Over the following days and weeks, when Salim was on duty, they would talk whenever they had the opportunity. Quinn spoke of New York, of America, of the things that people ate and drank. "We are a mixed society. The people of our country are white, black, Asian, Latino, Muslim, Jewish, and those who don't believe in anything but the almighty dollar," Quinn chatted one day. In response, Salim confessed that he wanted nothing more than to ride through America with Natalia by his side, in a big, luxurious car, see Niagara Falls and all of the big canyons in the West.

Quinn, on the other hand, learned much from Salim about the fortress. It appeared to be a cleverly thought-out system of caves and tunnels. There were at least one hundred subterranean chambers that, Quinn estimated, could house a minimum of five hundred men. Salim reported that he basically knew his way around the area to which he was assigned, but that he would never dare to stray into the labyrinth of side corridors.

"But you have to know how to get out, if there's ever a fire, for instance," Quinn suggested one morning as Salim demonstrated, scissors in hand, how to trim his now ragged beard Taliban-style.

Salim straightened.

"We each have an assigned exit route. There are over fifty of them altogether."

Later, Quinn received permission to start taking his meals in a dining chamber. Over time, his excursions there and to his interrogations in the green room allowed him to develop a sense of direction—albeit a limited one. Still, he had no idea, which corridor might lead to one of the exits—and, of course, he couldn't just come right out and ask Salim.

"If I ever got out of here," Quinn laughed, as if telling some sort of utopian joke, "if I were free, then I could take you and Natalia to America with me. Would you like that? What do you say, Salim?"

The young Jihadi looked at him with eyes big as saucers. He opened his mouth, but no sound came out. Then he shook his head, his face blushing brightly, and stepped, backwards, out of the cell, as if the American had just proposed some depraved sexual act.

Quinn knew that the bait had been successfully laid.

PART III

48

September 11, 2001.

Sarah Crawford, First Lady of the United States of America, stepped out of the black Cadillac. *Anything but sovereign and dignified*, Bronx, who watched her over the pages of a boating magazine, noted wryly. She moved hastily, like someone who had been caught by the rain and wanted to reach shelter as quickly as possible. Two Secret Service agents followed close behind. Just before she disappeared into the five-story lobby, behind the imposing glass front of the mighty South Tower, she managed an absent wave, as if she had just suddenly remembered that a handful of her husband's voters might be waiting for a wave from her somewhere outside.

Building superintendent Tommy Fisher stood just inside of the revolving doors, legs apart in a firm stance, wearing an earpiece, and flanked by two bodyguards who were also wired. Fisher's eyes strayed to the approaching legs of the president's wife, which were slender and straight, with knees only just covered by a tailored skirt. He signaled with one hand, whereupon his people opened the smaller side door.

As Sarah entered the high-ceilinged, marble paneled lobby, she nervously touched her fingers to her hair, which played attractively around her high cheekbones, pausing for a moment. She wore a two-piece costume with fine lilac stripes, and a pink blouse. She quickly straightened her jacket, and headed toward the elevators. She had exited the sedan and entered the building so briskly that most of the pedestrians milling around this morning had not even noticed her arrival. This suited her just fine. Anything but a commotion! This was the second time she visited New York within a short period—a fact that caused her some anxiety, as the moment of inevitable radio, press, and television exposure drew closer. A part of it all would be the sensationalized question of what the First Lady from the Deep South, who had always been made out to be socially reticent, if not downright shy, was doing in—of all places—the financial district.

A group gathered at one of the coffee stands on the plaza seemed not to have noticed the flash celebrity appearance either. It was a bunch of tourists from Iowa, who had flocked to the Rockefeller Center at the break of day and stood in line to see the taping of NBC's *Today* show. Now they waited for the opening of the observation deck on the WTC South Tower.

"Welcome, Madam," Fisher offered with an inviting gesture toward the short red carpet that led across the marble floor and to an elevator off to the left of the long row of public elevators.

The now world-famous woman smiled politely, held her hand out briefly, and continued.

The people arriving at the towers through the other entrances at this hour were all employees of the businesses housed within the buildings, whose bosses arrived in the underground parking structures in sedans and took the elevators from there directly to the upper stories. Curious glances were cast at the red carpet; the woman was recognized as one of the many VIPs who visited the trade center daily. The two very diversely built bodyguards did not go unnoticed; nor did a few New York police officers outside, in their short-sleeved, blue shirts, and their heavy belts, from which their service weapons and various unshapely police implements were suspended.

It was pure coincidence that Tommy Fisher turned in time to see Leslie Palmer, who arrived a little later, as she stepped up to the elevator next to the one with the red carpet. She turned slightly aside as she waited, then looked up and straight into the manager's eyes.

Fisher started—that face! Had the First Lady come straight back down? Was she on her way out already? No, he said to himself. That wasn't possible time-wise. He shook his head and fixed his eyes on her figure. The similarity was striking. He had to ask the woman what her name was. As the building super, he had every right to do so. But before he was able to break out of his state of surprise, Leslie had already lowered her eyes, entered the elevator, and vanished behind the closing doors. The last thing that held Fisher's attention were her legs. Slender and elegant, they carried a shapely pair of hips. He was rarely mistaken when it came to a woman's legs.

In the express elevator, First Lady Sarah Crawford looked down at the red tips of her pointy shoes. It was the first time that Sarah had seen the large, broad-shouldered Secret Service agent among her personal guards. His name had slipped her mind. Next to him, Julia seemed positively dainty. Her stature and light blond hair, cut in a short military style, put her in perfect contrast to the black giant. Sarah met Julia's warm eyes. They exchanged a smile, then both looked up at the display, which was counting the stories in bright, yellow numerals.

As they reached 62, the male guard gave a discreet cough and crowded closer to the door, which opened noiselessly. The agent took two large steps into the broad corridor, stood on the gray carpet, and snapped his head to either side, looking for any suspicious signs. Then he gave Julia the 'all-clear' with a nod of his head.

A messenger wearing an earpiece and a turned-around baseball cap stared studiously at the ground as he chewed his gum; a corpulent black woman with white earrings carried an envelope along the hall with a slow, bouncing gait—other than that, there was no one in sight. The First Lady and her escorts neared a broad mahogany door at the end of the corridor. Looking over her dark blond head, the large black man read the name *Bradley Burk Moseley* spelled out in silver letters. He spoke quietly into the small transmitter that he held hidden in his enormous paw.

The heavy meticulously polished exotic wood door swung open—Jerry Moseley Jr. stepped forward to welcome the small group. The handsome man with a full head of thick, silver hair wore a black pin-stripe suit. His elegantly tanned face lit up in a brilliant smile. He greeted the First Lady politely, with a small bow of his head, then ushered her toward the office, the doors of which stood open, with a charming flourish of his hand.

He barely gave the two Secret Service agents a glance. For all the attention he afforded them, they might have been part of the cleaning crew who made their rounds through the legal offices at nine to remove coffee cups, crumpled balls of paper, takeout leftovers, and any other traces of billable nighttime activity left by young, ambitious attorneys.

At forty-five, Jerry Moseley Jr. was somewhere around the middle of the age range of the partners that composed the large, renowned law firm. However, the earnings he generated from legal fees put him well within the top league of sought-after trial attorneys.

"Welcome, Madam. May I ask how your journey was? How is the president?" The Secret Service agents heard the man, who seemed pretty damned arrogant to them in his overpriced suit, wheedling with exaggerated politeness. He may have treated them as if they were non-existent, but this did not interfere with their attention to detail for even a second. They quickly and efficiently inspected the outer office and reception desk, Moseley's office, and the conference room. Julia canvassed the ladies room. Then, as always, and usually on a Tuesday, she assumed her routine position in the corridor. The heavy-set black man spoke into his miniature transmitter, his alert eyes constantly scanning the surroundings. Raising the palm of his hand to his lips, as if to politely cover a cough, he spoke quietly, "Cincinnati on the sixty-second floor, time: zero-eight-thirty-five hours."

The announcement was routine. The report would travel first to the receiver in the back of the First Lady's Cadillac. There the signal would be amplified before being transmitted to the next closest antenna used exclusively by the secret service from where it would be sent directly via satellite to the White House Secret Service headquarters. As far as the man with the coffee-colored complexion knew, the nearest antenna was located on a high-rise on 69th Street. The agent's cheeks billowed rhythmically as he worked on his gum.

"Jerry, at last!"

In the office, alone with Moseley, the First Lady threw her arms around his neck, and kissed him gently on the lips. He held her in a tight embrace.

"Sarah, you know that I love you!"

49

When Leslie Palmer got onto the express elevator on her way up to the 56th floor in the South Tower, she had two quick calls to make. The first was to Bronx, whom she had not seen downstairs. Hadn't he said eight-thirty out front? Or was she mistaken...

"Hello," the gravely voice responded.

"Bronx," said Leslie into the screaming-red phone that she hated almost as much as she did Bronx himself. "I'm going to be there half an hour later than planned, okay? I have an appointment."

"No, damn it! Where are you?" he demanded, his voice edgy. He suddenly sounded somehow worried. *Hmm, what have we here... that's a new twist!*

"Up in the South Tower. I'll be back down at about quarter past nine. Could you perhaps wait for me for a change?"

For a few seconds she heard nothing but static. The intensity of the torrent of words that ensued nearly threw her back against the wall. "Leslie, damn it, you had better listen to me. I have to see you *now*, understand? You will come straight down here, and you will do so immediately, do you hear me? I want..."

"Go fuck yourself," she interrupted him heatedly, "I believe I just told you—I have an appointment," and hit the end-call key. She was met by stunned glances from the other elevator occupants. A young man in a dark business suit and a blindingly white shirt grinned at her and nodded. "You tell him, Madam!"

As she stepped off on the floor that housed Steinberg & Friedman she placed another brief call to Shelley in the office, leaving a message on his voicemail to inform him of her meeting in the South Tower, and that she would be there until well after nine. "Please tell the boss to start the budget meeting without me," she ended the message, and entered the reception area, which was stylishly decorated with original English furniture.

"Oh, Ms. Palmer, I'm so sorry." The reception assistant, who was dressed in an elegant, rust-colored costume, rushed toward her, blushing.

"I left a message for you at your office. I really am sorry, but Mister Steinberg was unable to leave at midnight as scheduled. He was delayed in California due to problems with the technical clearance of his plane," she said, looking very guilty—as if she had been the personal cause of the cancelled appointment. Leslie smiled, unconcerned.

"Please—it's no problem. Really."

"Have you heard? Apparently something bad has happened over in the other tower."

Leslie shook her head uncomprehendingly. "No, when?"

She couldn't say that she was all-too-sorry about the appointment with Spike not working out. Shrugging, she turned to leave, but was stopped by the receptionist's attention-grabbing gestures.

"Just now—about ten minutes ago."

Leslie automatically checked her watch. Almost nine.

"Mr. Steinberg wants me to give you the papers for the apartment, if you would like to take a seat for a moment." She motioned invitingly toward the red Chester visitor's sofa. "May I offer you a cup of coffee?"

"Thank you, yes please. No milk, no sugar."

Leslie sat on the firmly upholstered leather cushion, but stood up again immediately and walked to the window that afforded a breathtaking view of the southern tip of Manhattan Island. The Statue of Liberty seemed to be waving a greeting through the light, early-morning mist. In the distance, the Verrazano Narrows suspension bridge cast its great, elegant arch over to the New York Bay. Her cell phone buzzed. She checked the display. It was Bronx—five minutes to nine. She brusquely disconnected the call. *The bastard can kiss my ass! No, scratch that,* she smiled to herself, amused, *that would be way too disgusting!*

50

Up on the 62nd floor, Jerry Moseley Jr. was wasting no time. With great charm, he led Sarah Crawford through the library filled with thick, leather-bound law volumes, and to a door that opened to a rising spiral staircase. They ascended and stepped through a heavy, soundproof door into a corner room that never failed to take Sarah's breath away. The smoky glass that reached from ceiling to floor on two sides transfigured the stunning view of the Hudson River, up past Manhattan and over to Central Park, and—to the west—across the majestic river and all the way to the New Jersey Shore. Sarah sat on the edge of the broad bed with a blissful sigh. The captivating view, the secrecy of their clandestine meeting, and the eager anticipation of Jerry's caress, sent little tidal waves of arousal through her body.

A light bang sounded from the kitchen alcove in the rear part of the tasteful love-nest, causing Sarah to utter a happy "Ooh!"—Jerry arrived with two delicate flutes filled with Champagne.

"To you, darling!"

"To us, sweetheart!"

She took a small sip, stood, and stepped to the corner between the windows, where an elegant golf bag made of light leather stood.

"Why is it that the television is always on whenever I come here?" she asked, amused. The little set flickered on a sideboard near the window. Raising her eyes from it, she was looking directly at the North Tower, which reached straight into the crystal clear sky in all of its majesty, and which stood so close that she could see the shadowy silhouettes of people behind its windows.

"It's practical," Jerry replied. "You can see the outside temperature, the stock market ticker." He stuck a cigarette into the corner of his mouth. "If anything worth knowing about happens in the world, I'm immediately informed. But I'll turn it off for you." He put the gold-plated lighter back in his pocket and searched for the remote as Sarah ran her hand over the titanium head of one of the clubs that jutted out of the elegant leather bag. "Please don't smoke, Jerry!"

"That's a *Lady,*" he said, holding the cigarette between his fingers. "I got it just for you. It has a nice, flexible shaft."

He stepped up to demonstrate the new club. Suddenly the building trembled. The First Lady started.

"What was that?"

The deafening noise of the explosion hit her body like a giant fist. She screamed and stumbled back against the edge of the bed.

"My God, Jerry, what . . . ?"

The glass panes shuddered with a loud rattle as they were hit by a hurricane force gust of wind. The entire South Tower structure shook and quivered and quaked, as if it were about to come apart at its joints at any moment.

Down below, the Pleasure Cruise Riders had set out under the clear blue sky on this balmy autumn day. They had begun their tranquil ride along West Broadway, and were now headed south. Nassim was just calling out directions, "We'll take the Brooklyn Bridge, then ride down to . . ." He stopped and turned his head toward the sound of a roaring howl. It was a low-flying jet. "Holy crap! What the hell is that?! *Hey*!" The blood ran cold in his veins.

Then the others saw it, too—a silver passenger aircraft flying at low altitude, and . . . into the tower. Right into it. Straight as an arrow . . . The red fireball of the explosion, the smoke!

"Christ! Can you *believe* it—someone just flew into the fucking World Trade Center!"

They revved their engines, and rode up the sidewalk for half a block to gain a clearer view.

People ran toward them, screaming.

"Come, let's go back to Fulton Street. If we stay behind the hotel there, we won't be in the way." A fire engine screamed past them, its sirens blaring at a nerve-shattering volume. Dull explosions rolled through the concrete canyons.

They pulled up the curve on the east side of the street, staring in disbelief at the smoke-filled sky.

Ronnie had pulled up, maneuvered his Suzuki in front of the group, revved so hard a few times that the bright shriek of his engine filled the air before he shut it down. He dismounted, placed his helmet on top of his sky-blue gas tank, fumbled with his mustache, held a video camera up in one hand. His bald head was glistening with beads of sweat.

"I got all of it . . . Unbelievable! Look at this!"

He almost got caught on the handlebar as he hastily lowered the kickstand before rushing over to his buddies.

"Hey, I just had a great shot of your formation when I heard the noise... the jet engines... it was like being at an airport... So I turned my camera toward it... Look... It's all here!" He gasped for breath.

Ronnie was the group's technology freak, and now they descended on him like a bunch of locusts. Everyone wanted to see the pictures.

"It's a passenger plane."

"Probably a Boeing 767," Ronnie said knowingly. All of their comments came tumbling out in a rush, they speculated back and forth, resorted to 'who knows' whenever there was a lull in ideas, kept watching as Ronnie hit REPLAY over and over, kept looking up from the screen at the smoking North Tower.

"I have to get closer," Nassim screamed over the noise of his roaring engine. "Let's get over to Fulton Street! Maybe we can help!" The doctor's appeal finally woke them from their stony state of shock.

Sarah Crawford stared across at the North Tower, her face pale. Glaring red and toxic yellow flames hissed from the façade. At eye level, she saw white trails of smoke pouring out of burst windows like fountains. Suddenly, as she watched, a gruesome, impenetrably black mass of greasy murk began coming out of the entire width of at least five stories simultaneously. Sarah slapped both hands to her face.

"My God! Something has exploded in the North Tower!"

Moseley stared across at the inferno of fire and flame over there as if his complete being had gone numb. Entire pieces of the building were now coming loose with sickening, cracking sounds, and plunging from the tower in a wide arch.

"For heaven's sake, Jerry, do something! Call the fire department!"

The digital clock on the television screen read 08:46.

Moseley hastily hacked a bunch of numbers on the keypad of his cell phone, spoke excitedly once he had a connection, his head bowed. Sarah didn't catch a word; the brutal noise of explosions filled the room. Desperate, she held on to the golf bag. Another blast shook the room—soot and dust began to gather on the glass of the window walls.

"Jerry!" the First Lady screamed, fumbling her way toward the door. "I want to get out of here! Something terrible has happened. There—what are they saying on TV?"

Moseley forced his eyes away from the smoking North Tower and onto the television screen.

"An accident. Insane!"

A television announcer with a grim expression moved his lips. The volume was on mute.

Sarah cowered next to the golf bag, her head lowered as if she expected a rainfall of debris to shower down on her at any moment..

The telephone buzzed poisonously. Moseley pushed the speaker button: "No disturbances, I said…"

"Sir! This is Julia Arnold, Secret Service, please come downstairs with Ms. Crawford immediately. Do you understand?"

"Yes, will do. Ms. Crawford is fine."

"I'm frightened, Jerry. I want to get out of here!"

Moseley was somewhat calmer.

"Come on now, darling, let's not panic!"

He wrapped his strong arms around her upper body, kissed her forehead. "First we need to know what actually happened." He turned the sound up on the television set.

Sarah shook her head. She felt as if she were stuck in a deathtrap. For the first time in her life, she was experiencing what it meant to be afraid of heights. At this moment, the North Tower appeared on the screen from a different angle. A massive hole gaped where some of the higher stories had been. Thick, black smoke billowed out of the terrible breach in a sickening flow.

"At eight forty-five a small plane flew into the North Tower," Sarah heard the TV announcer say. She could hardly believe what he was waffling on about. She had spent countless hours in the air learning how to fly. She found it perfectly unimaginable that a pilot could become this disoriented in the early morning and under almost perfect weather conditions.

"Jerry, the pilot couldn't have flown into one of the highest buildings on earth in these clear weather conditions unless he was stone-cold drunk—unless the plane had a technical problem. No, that's also unlikely."

"Why?"

Moseley stood next to the TV, holding his cell phone to his ear.

"Around here your flight path is lovely and straight, right along the river—you don't have to turn, as you do on the other side over the East River, where you have to avoid the La Guardia no-fly zone."

"The hole is enormous," he noted. "But the tower will hold."

"What makes you so sure?"

"The towers were built to resist the impact of an airplane crash," Jerry said knowingly. "During the war—I'm sure you've heard this story—a B-25 Army bomber crashed into the Empire State Building in the fog. The thing is still standing to this day."

"Jerry, there's no fog today," Sarah retorted with absurdly compelling logic. "Who are you calling? Jerry, look!" She stretched out her arm. "My God! The man standing by the window. Can you see him? *No!"*

Jerry looked, aghast, at a figure outlined against the sooty black, torn façade of the North Tower, which, at this very moment, was detaching itself from a shattered window, one leg bent, plummeting to the earth as if in slow motion.

"My God," Jerry panted, "that... is... complete insanity!"

The eminent trial lawyer had been reduced to a stammer.

"I need something!"

He ran to the refrigerator, grabbed the vodka bottle, tore off the cap, and began gulping it down as if it was water.

Sarah had shouldered the golf bag, and was already waiting by the door. "Come on, Jerry!"

She spun toward the sound of a loud knock on the door. When Jerry opened it, he found the blond Secret Service agent standing before him. She pushed past him, discreetly taking in the layout of the room, and the bed.

"Madam, is everything alright? Please come downstairs with me!"

The tone of voice, the deadly earnest expression on the face of this highly skilled professional, strongly suggested that she was not going to take 'no' for an answer.

51

Six stories down, a nauseating apprehension was beginning to catch up with Leslie Palmer. *Something terrible had happened in the North Tower! Might it have had something to do with the dull bang that she had heard as she stepped out of the elevator?* Uncertain, she walked across the small outer office and to the window, then back again. A babble of voices could now be heard in the otherwise quiet offices of Steinberg & Friedman. *She really didn't need that apartment paperwork right away. It wasn't as if it wouldn't be here tomorrow, or whenever.* She checked her digital watch: 09:00. *She should just make an exit. Bronx was sure to be stewing down on the plaza.* Leslie returned to the front desk—the rust-colored lady was nowhere to be seen. As she passed the counter, she peered into the large office. The office's employees where packed like a bunch of grapes beneath the television set that was suspended from the ceiling.

A young, slender female employee shot around the corner, almost right into her. Her eyes, framed by remarkably long lashes, were wide with the apparent effect of adrenaline.

"Have you heard? The tower's on fire!"

"Where?" Leslie was drawn back into the outer office.

A nasty feeling at the pit of her stomach, she circled the low tabletop with the dark-green leather insert, where the rust-colored lady had been just about to serve her coffee, and looked out the broad window at what appeared to be nothing but a pleasant, peaceful morning. *Completely quiet. No smoke to be seen.*

In recent days, her thoughts had constantly returned to the same topic. Even now, she found herself going there. Set on revenge, she kept ruminating on her difficult plan, imagining the airport in Dushanbe—the green, luscious landscape all around, just like she had seen in the glossy magazine that she had picked up. She tried to picture Bronx's mother. How would she be able to get close enough to the woman?

The commotion that was growing behind her back, the increasingly loud voices, the nameless sense of urgency gnawing at her subconscious, would not allow her to remain at Steinberg & Friedman for much longer.

Deep in thought, she cast a final, distant glance across the Hudson River estuary and over to Staten Island, saw the tiny sailboats leaning against the wind, the white, foamy wake left by a motorboat, then—suddenly—the plane.

A giant passenger plane!

It was turning in closer at low altitude. Damn it—was she dreaming?

She screamed.

"It's flying much too low!"

Now its massive fuselage was darkening the sky. Leslie saw everything in perfect clarity—the engines, the cockpit windows shining in the morning sun—she could even read the inscription—*United.*

Before she could begin to wrap her mind around this aberrant reality, it came—the massively devastating force of the impact. Higher up in the tower. The building rocked, the window burst. Later, Leslie would be unable to say what exactly she had felt during those first moments. It was only once she found herself running down the stairs two steps at a time that she understood what she was doing. She was fleeing. An airplane had smashed into the tower. Her mind knew only one thing, and that was—*out,* she had to get out! Not the elevator. She counted steps, counted floors; people scurried past her in a blur, voices everywhere, screams . . . one single, endless scream . . .

It was quite an incredible coincidence that the two women, unknowingly linked by a mysterious fate, should be so close during these dramatic minutes—Sarah on the 62nd and Leslie on the 56th floor of the South Tower—and yet have no idea.

The First Lady had been privy to an exquisite view of the city, all the way up to the distant George Washington Bridge, when the first plane, American Airlines flight 11, coming from over Central Park and West Broadway, had crashed into the North Tower at 08:46. On the other side of the South Tower, Leslie Palmer had caught talk that an accident had occurred in the North Tower, of which she had no view. She had been contemplatively looking out in the other direction, over the southern tip of Manhattan and across to the wide New York Bay, when—to her utter horror—she had seen the second plane right before her very eyes, United

Airlines flight 175, curving toward the tower that she stood in. She had briefly lost sight of it overhead only as it rammed its way into the floors above her at 09:03…

52

The sound of agitated talking echoed from the offices downstairs. Sarah now heard a clear announcement over the speaker system.

"Jerry, keep everyone calm and tell them to remain at their desks," called a disembodied voice. She looked at her watch. It was nine.

"Jerry, come *on*. What are you waiting for?" She tightened the strap of the golf bag on her shoulder, mincing down the spiral staircase behind Secret Service Agent Julia Arnold.

Jerry Moseley Jr. stared steadfastly at the screen, at the gloomy, smoking floors. Who worked there? The fires were around the 90th floors. The ravages were unimaginable. He gave himself a jolt.

"Move, dammit!"

It was difficult to put a sequence to the events unfolding. It was as if the end had come—a true *Armageddon!* The violent explosion that had shaken the tasteful Bradley Burk Moseley offices shortly after nine on this beautiful, cloudless autumn day, knocking everyone to the ground with a dull, thundering blow, seemed to be continuing in an ongoing rampage somewhere overhead.

The world would later learn that at 09:03 terrorists had used the scheduled passenger flight UA 175 as a missile that they landed between the 78th and 82nd floors of the South Tower, which crumbled a scant hour later at 09:59, within a matter of approximately ten seconds. It was only at 10:28 that the North Tower, which had been hit first, also collapsed in on itself in a free fall.

Pieces of ceiling, plaster, and dirt littered the luxuriously carpeted floor of Bradley Burk Moseley on the 62nd floor. Smoldering ends of exposed wires hung down. A caustic smell had unfolded almost instantly. The windows were unnaturally darkened by smoke and dust.

"Oh, my God," groaned Sarah, who looked as if she had turned into a pillar of salt.

Moseley tore her from her paralyzed state by her arm, screaming at her.

"Follow me!"

They plunged toward the corridor, where they made it to the elevators. Moseley beat wildly at the down button, shook the first elevator door, then the second. "Damn it!" he hissed. Then a sharp, barking voice cut into him like a knife to the back of his neck.

"Freeze, man! Don't *move*!"

It was the giant, black Secret Service agent, screaming at him with full force, his face a grimace of intensity. Sarah spun around.

"We will remain here until help arrives. Nobody moves!" the agent bellowed through the crashing, breaking sounds, his heavy index finger tapping importantly on his miniature walkie-talkie.

Moseley ignored him, kept the elevator button pressed as he maltreated the doors with a series of kicks. The few express elevators that ordinarily stopped on the 62nd floor seemed to be out of order. The First Lady pleaded with her lover.

"Jerry, I beg you, do what they say!"

She turned to the security agent.

"Where is Frank?"

Moseley stopped his useless attack on the elevator doors.

"No, Madam, out, *now*!" he commanded, suddenly taking on a highly formal tone. He grabbed her roughly around the hips, pushed and shoved her in a run toward the furthest elevator, where an emergency exit led to the stairs. Moseley panted and coughed.

"Who the hell is Frank?"

The Secret Service agent was hot on their heels. Weapon drawn, he heaved Moseley roughly by the shoulder, tearing him around.

"Sir, you will stand *still*. You will not touch the First Lady!"

Men in white shirts and ties tore through the stairwell, screaming and gesturing frantically.

"To the roof, to the roof! They told us to go to the roof!"

The president's wife seemed to draw hope.

"Jerry, did you hear? We have to go to the roof!"

Moseley had no intention of doing anything of the sort.

"What we have to do, Madam, is get out of here. Down and out!"

"There's a fire down there," a woman screamed as she passed them, her eyes vacant in terror. "Nobody can get through!"

"Sir!"

The agent again! This time he grabbed Moseley's arm in a vise. A faint ringing announced the arrival of an elevator. Moseley eyed the door like a wild animal.

"We are responsible for her security!" the agent hollered. Turning to the First Lady, he ordered, "Follow us, Madam."

The powerful swing hit the massive black man squarely in the solar plexus, taking him completely by surprise. He bowed, laboriously raised a baffled face. Moseley was in a state of pure rage. This time he landed a well-aimed hook straight to the guard's chin. The man swayed back, momentarily losing his balance. The arm with which he held the weapon waved ineffectively through the air. Moseley saw his only chance—grabbing Sarah brutally by the arm and tearing her along with him, he raced toward the elevator. Its doors were opening slowly. Inside, over a dozen people huddled in fright. Some stared at Jerry with open animosity. Someone screamed "Get *in*, damn it!"

"Stop. Freeze!"

The command came from the female agent with the short, blond GI cut. She was crouched down and aiming her pistol with both hands. The shot from the 9mm automatic came at the same time as the powerful shove that Moseley used to push Sarah into the elevator. The bullet hit the doorframe. Moseley lay on the elevator floor, with Sarah buried beneath him. "Ouch, crap!" he croaked as his jaw made heavy contact with a golf club. *That lousy fucking golf bag! Why the hell was she carrying that piece of shit around with her at a time like this?*

"Julia fired," Sarah panted, "I can't believe it!"

People were screaming and cursing, but none of that mattered now. The elevator lurched into motion—the only functioning elevator in the entire South Tower that was still running downward glided sluggishly to the depths below. People were holding their breaths, staring as if hypnotized at the flickering display that showed the descending floors.

"Who the hell is Frank?" Moseley whispered once more.

"Frank *Sureman*, my personal guard, who always escorts me up. Just not today, of all days... Frank is the best."

A powerful wave of heat crushed through the elevator. A woman screamed.

"We're burning!"

The lift ground to a stop, then immediately lurched back on its downward path.

Somebody was quietly counting the floors in a warbling, monotonous voice. It sounded like a prayer.

"Fifteen... *God, please help*... twelve. For heaven's *sake*... eight, six."

A deafening screeching of metal caused everyone to shriek. The elevator caught with a crashing, crunching noise on something on the side of the shaft. Then another screeching noise, even higher pitched this time. The cabin came to a chafing halt.

"Where are we? We have to get out. You over there, do something!"

The demand, voiced by an older gentleman with a broken lens in his glasses, was aimed at Moseley, who was shielding the First Lady with his back.

"We're on the 4th. We have to get out. Someone has to climb up there and open the ceiling hatch."

The man with the broken glasses, who had made the suggestion, was brandishing his hands upward.

Three young men in light blue overalls set about trying to heave the doors open with their bare hands. At first they managed about three inches; a woman's purse was used to keep the gap from closing again. Then many hands pitched in, the doors opened wider and wider. A gap revealing a space and the concrete post that supported the floor above it appeared at eye-level, right in front of Moseley. White smoke streamed in, the cabin swayed, there was a dark rumbling sound from above—the light went out. A young woman broke down, sobbing.

"This is the end!"

Moseley held the First Lady tightly, looked up to the only way out. It was hopeless. The terrible crashing and banging sounded as if the building above them were about to collapse at any second. His voice was a single, clear command.

"Come, now!"

He hooked one elbow over the edge, pulled himself up laboriously, and crawled out. Harsh smoke burned at his eyes and throat—coughing, he reached down, groping for Sarah, grasped the golf bag, yanked and tore at the strap, lifted her with it. Finally, he was able to grab hold of her hand. Pulling her up was a slow job; she seemed to appear a centimeter at a time. Suddenly the elevator moved. Another scream.

"We're falling!"

Now Sarah was screaming. Moseley pulled her up and over the edge with the last of his strength. *Her feet—damn it!*

"Pull your legs up," he hollered, throwing his body to the side with a violent yank. Sarah fell on top of him. The elevator had jammed again after just a short drop. The saving gap through which Moseley had rescued Sarah was now no more than a few inches wide. The people inside were trapped, with no hope. Sarah had lost her shoes, one foot was bleeding. The bag of golf clubs was still hanging off her. Moseley was breathing so hard that his lungs were threatening to burst.

"We got lucky, darling."

"No! We are lost."

Moseley began to fashion a makeshift bandage for the wound on her foot with his handkerchief, trying all the while to keep her focused on practical questions.

"Is it broken? Can you stand on it? Try it!"

"It's okay. What now?"

A crashing sound thundered into the tight, claustrophobic space that had once been the 4th story hallway. Debris and splinters of glass rained down on them, everything went black, everything collapsed. Glass flew about as if they were being hit by a tornado, hard pieces of something bashed against arms that were trying to protect a head, shoulders, chest... Moseley bellowed like a wounded animal.

"The elevator! The elevator collapsed!" He pulled himself together, yelled, "Out of here! The stairs!"

Another deafening explosion—it seemed incredibly close. The air turned black around them, choking them. Moseley reached for Sarah, she caught up to him, limping. He felt a break in the wall—a door! He threw itself against it, and it gave. Now they found themselves standing on a staircase landing. The stairwell was filled with black smoke, but the steps were sturdy, and so was the railing. They began to descend as fast as they possibly could. A ray of light reached them from below. Firemen in heavy gear trudged up the stairs. The one in front lifted his protective mask.

"Are there still people up there?"

Moseley motioned his free hand in a gesture of denial. Another thundering wave of sound rolled down the stairwell—an explosion from above. The stairs swayed. A fluorescent lamp burst, sending off a hail of sparks. Sarah screamed and bumped against Moseley, who almost lost his balance. He saw a woman in the ghostly, flickering light. She was African American. She sat on the ground, her legs outstretched, her hands clasping her belly. Was she pregnant? Moseley yelled at her.

"Come on! Get up!"

The woman stared at him apathetically. Moseley simply left her sitting there, turned his attention to encouraging Sarah.

"Darling, we've almost made it!"

Things were lighter on the 3rd floor. People were dashing into the stairwell.

"The elevators are broken. We have to get out!"

A man met them with outstretched arms. His skin hung in long shreds from his arms right down to his fingertips. *Both of his arms!* Then Sarah saw the face, of which pieces were missing. The man just kept asking, "What happened? What happened?"

"There's a fire, we're going to burn, we've been buried alive!"

A black woman clung to Sarah's arm. The First Lady tore herself loose.

A measured voice pronounced, almost unctuously, "The generators have exploded. Calm down, people. Calm down!"

"We're almost outside," Moseley wheezed. "Just a few more steps, and we'll be down in the lobby. If only the tower holds up!"

The Secret Service agent on the 62nd floor sent out one last message at 09:52. It came across in clipped fragments. "We have lost Cincinnati... buried... oh, God... everything is destroyed... it's the end."

Moseley looked around for Sarah. She was following close behind, barefoot, still carrying that ludicrous golf bag, clutching it to her chest like a giant, unshapely infant. Moseley saw her eyes, saw her twist her face to shriek. Then he saw what she saw—a massive crater opened, a white wall of dust shot up. Sarah threw herself at him, grasped convulsively at his upper body, and then the ground, the stairs, the entire stairwell, disappeared from under them. Their two bodies plummeted, the golf bag wedged between fell... everything fell... the entire earth descended into an abyss...

53

Finally—it seemed as if it had taken her an eternity—Leslie Palmer found herself standing in the mighty entrance hall, which had once boasted high windows that tapered into elegant pointed arches like Gothic architecture. A man was screaming and waving his arms frantically, "The elevators... The elevators are on fire!"

The glass had been obliterated, the beautiful marble tiles torn from the walls, large pieces of concrete lay strewn all over the place. Leslie searched her way from the rubble-littered chaos into the open.

A NYFD woman stood outside in a broad stance. She clasped a walkie-talkie in front of her brown, sooty, sweat-covered face. "Vacate the area. The tower is coming down. Did you tell them that the tower is coming down? *Yes,* it is in the process of collapsing!"

Looking up with pinched eyes, Leslie saw flames licking up on what was the 92nd floor of the North Tower. Pieces of rubble were breaking away from a giant smoldering hole and falling into nothingness.

Bronx raced across the plaza to his Explorer, which he had parked next to the church. Not far from him, Leslie looked up against the sky, saw the spire begin to collapse, then come down. She ran—ran for her life.

She bolted across the square that had, until maybe an hour or so ago, been a popular meeting place for New Yorkers and tourists. It was now littered with twisted, sharp, smoking pieces of debris. She ran with everything she had left, her eyes on the Millennium Hilton diagonally across the way. The dark, solid square of a building promised security. She avoided an ambulance, ran over to the street along which crowds of people were fleeing in panic to who knew where.

Shards of glass everywhere—choking, disgusting, black dust. A tourist with a dirty backpack limped along ahead of her, firefighters wearing black protective gear and carrying long, narrow oxygen tanks, rushed by. She had to make it across Fulton Street. A body... *a corpse!* lay on the ground, its head turned at an unnatural angle, its eyes staring blindly. Screams. Leslie struggled for air. A common cry echoed everywhere... "*Out!* Gotta get out of this hell..."

54

Falling seemed to go on forever. They would shatter, lie buried by the rubble, be crushed and broken. Instinctively, Moseley reached for the railing, waiting for the moment of impact. Sarah held on tight, even when a mass of something descended upon them. It was not stone, nor metal, but bodies. She smelled and felt their flesh. For a moment she thought she recognized the crazed whites that she had seen in the eyes of the pregnant woman in the stairwell.

Darkness, nothing but darkness, broken only by bright yellow rings, was the last thing that Jerry Moseley Jr. saw before his eyes. And Sarah...

...Sarah felt a blunt blow to her chest that left her winded. Crashing, roaring, bursting all around. A landslide, the hissing of water, showering sparks. From way up above, she saw herself lying in a massive rubble landscape, on the soft skin of a snowy white lamb. She felt nothing anymore. This, then, was death! She felt light as a feather.

You are looking at your own, pitiful body, your soul lives on. Free of pain, it allows the thread of life to unravel, it exhales. Don't give up, Sarah, your soul is drifting, but you are alive!

But the darkness, the smoke, the misery was stronger. The pictures dimmed in her mind. The First Lady was beyond suffering.

Rick Bronx, sitting in his Explorer next to the church, received a choppy-voiced message from his contact: "FLOTUS is down. Cinderella made it out." Then the connection was lost.

Bronx's calculations had panned out. Operation Cinderella had gone according to plan. He started the Explorer. Time to get out of the danger zone. Cinderella had, fittingly, stepped from the ashes, and was now the new FLOTUS. The First Lady of the United States.

55

Rain. *No*—pieces of debris were falling from the sky. Leslie flinched, then dared a glance up to the North Tower. Dreadful, dark clouds of smoke rose into the morning sky; white puffs, like cotton clouds, poured from the windows. The picture was horrifying and unbelievable, all at once.

A patrol car stood stuck in the rubble, almost unrecognizable under a cover of dust and dirt. She tripped, fell, pulled herself up, looked around in desperation. Her forehead hurt, her knee burned. She made herself go on, swaying forward toward the police car. Everything was covered in disgusting, dark gray dust—her hair, her skin. Explosions shattered the air, quaked through her body, sirens howled, firefighters dragged in equipment, someone was yelling orders.

"The whole damn thing is going to come down any moment," Leslie heard someone say as she felt a searing pain in her back. She stumbled, but had stopped feeling before she fell, face first, into a pile of rubble…

Nassim sat stiffly on his Honda. The motor was running. He turned nervously at the handles. The other bikes scattered with a loud roar, his crew making unmistakable signs for him to follow them. He let his engine howl, jerked forward, turned around again to look at the burning towers. Large building pieces were now coming down in a virtually constant bombardment. A piece of stray metal or concrete could fall on him any moment. He had to get going; follow the others.

Then he saw the woman. Her blond head was bobbing in the artificial dusk of the descending smoke as she ran, racing over the rubble like a hounded animal—and fell. Nassim flinched inwardly.

"The woman! Christ! She caught a bulls-eye—did you guys see?" he yelled. But his friends had already fled.

Without so much as a thought, Nassim dashed toward her on his brand new bike, swerving around obstacles, got almost to where she lay. Something hit his helmet.

"Get up, girl!" he yelled out into the commotion. She remained where she was, lying there as if broken and dead. A jagged, small scrap hit the front of his machine with a loud bang, shattering the headlight. Nassim fought to keep his balance, reflexively opened the throttle, bumped rudely onto the pavement, over debris, metal, plaster, and all of the other terrible stuff that was lying around, falling, grazing him—whipped on by a rush of adrenaline, he noticed none of it.

Fortunately, Nassim had spent a good deal of time at the Bogey Dump on Long Island, teaching his friends how to ride off-road. Motocross represented the highest level of control that one could achieve on a bike—it involved suspended flight, rough landings, skidding around obstacles, being able to hit the upward inclines just right, and—above all—maintaining balance on steep downward slopes.

The woman was bleeding, her face pressed to the ground. She had a gaping shoulder wound. He tore a rough strip from his black shirt, wrapped it around her shoulder and axilla, strategically placing the knot so that it would help to stem the blood flow.

What now? Was there no soul here to help? Where were the damn paramedics?

"Come on, lady! Up!"

He grabbed her by the hips, lifted her with all his strength and managed to place her lifeless body onto his bike. He saw no option other than to drape her, face down, across the bulbous red tank.

The screaming and the din raging around him carried on relentlessly.

His eyes burning, he looked for a way out. The picture perfect, cloudless morning, the clear, blue sky that seemed to favor Manhattan, had turned to night.

The Apocalypse had come to the middle of Manhattan Island!

As he rode off, pieces of junk were coming down on either side of him. It was only with great difficulty that he managed to keep the motorbike on course in the rising mounds of dust and detritus, rounding past bodies lying motionless, as he hunched protectively over the woman. He finally reached a clear stretch of street. Again, there was a particularly loud crash behind him. A gray cloud of dust rushed forward, like a wave, breaking over him, tearing at his lungs. He ducked down further, managing to reach the pier.

South Street Seaport said the green board on the lamppost. The proud old Brooklyn Bridge, half enveloped in the evil smoke, reached elegantly across the East River. Masses of people stood at the wrought iron railing on the other side, staring over.

Nassim rode to the edge of the wooden deck at the waterside and stopped, exhausted. His leg hurt like hell.

Huh! Slowly, carefully, he lowered the woman onto the wooden planks. She stirred, he spoke to her, she was breathing. Thank God!

He heaved a sigh of relief when she opened her eyes. He could see an ambulance on the other side of the street. Where was the driver?

Nassim left the Honda standing, limped over to the red and white rescue vehicle, half-dragging the woman with him. *Harlem Hospital,* he read. *May not be my hospital, but it is my ambulance,* he decided.

It was only now that he had the chance to get a good look at her face. A beautiful face that leaned against his shoulder, triggering a vague memory, as if he had seen her somewhere before.

The ambulance driver was kneeling down in the gutter and throwing up. Unbelievable. He was puking his guts out. His formerly light-blue uniform was cloaked in a sticky layer of dust and grime. Without hesitating, Nassim packed his impromptu patient onto the empty passenger side of the bench up front. Then he checked the cabin in the rearview mirror.

It was empty, the back door hanging open. Nassim put a seatbelt around his trauma victim. "Just try to stay calm!" he said, pressing his flat hand onto the painful area of his bum leg.

Where had his buddies gone? He was still carrying his full-face helmet with its integrated walkie-talkie. He hit the send button. There was only the crackling noise of static. No network. *Nothing!* His hand found the box in his pants pocket. He had just swallowed a small handful of pills when a bunch of people appeared from the dust and crowded around the open door. Anxious voices called out, "We are injured! Take us with you! Doctor? Are you a doctor? Help me!"

A man covered in blood fell lengthwise into the back, onto the metal ambulance floor. Others just got in. It was chaotic!

Nassim went around and threw the door shut. He grabbed a girl who was sitting on the curb, sobbing, her foot completely twisted. He lifted her up into the driver's cab, next to himself and the woman. He activated the siren and brutally hit the gas.

He saw nothing but a gray wall of smoke and dust in his rearview mirror. He did not notice a black Explorer, its headlights beaming eerily, appearing from the man-made darkness behind him.

He leaned over the steering wheel and breathed deeply. *War in Manhattan. Who would do such a thing—who was behind all of this?*

"I'm bringing you to the ER at my hospital on 33rd Street," Nassim yelled back through the barred hatch, as he yanked the improvised bandage on his patient's shoulder straight.

"No worries, we'll get you fixed. Where are you from?"

"Why do you ask?" she asked half-heartedly.

He looked at her intensely, once again. He could not rid himself of a nagging feeling that he should somehow know this woman.

"Are you a celebrity—famous or something?"

Traffic obediently made way for the fast approaching ambulance, with its flashing lights and wailing sirens. Nassim floored the gas pedal.

"Hold on!"

The vehicle suddenly skidded with screeching tires as he was forced to hit the brakes. A young woman wearing extremely high heels and a tight skirt was traipsing, cool as you please, over the crosswalk. She may as well have been walking on a haute couture catwalk in Paris—she certainly didn't give a crap about the ambulance.

"Fucking *bitch*," Nassim hollered, opening the window.

"Baby, you're not *nearly* hot enough to be holding up traffic with that slow-assed waddle of yours!"

He stepped back on the gas, yelling through the loud whine of the engine, "Can you believe it? Bunch of crazy-assed people in this city!"

As he turned onto 33rd Street and the ambulance bay came into sight, he saw that the woman was holding the hand of the injured girl. Nassim would not relent.

"Really, your face looks familiar. Am I nuts, or *what*?"

With the hint of a smile Leslie touched her aching shoulder.

"How about *Desperate Housewives*?"

56

CIA Agent Bronx had roughly turned the wrong way up Church Street, his windscreen wipers working heavily. At first he couldn't make out much in the chaos, but then he oriented himself by noting landmarks that he had memorized as a precaution as he had stood outside of the coffee shop earlier. He hazily registered two things: Secret Service agents were running to their vehicles. One of them was whacked to the ground by something. He did not get back up. And further on, he saw the motorbike rider turning into a side street, with Cinderella dangling like a life-sized doll across his tank. It was a bizarre sight. He started following them, his mouth set in a tense line.

The ambulance stopped in front of the ER with screeching tires. The siren died down, while the lights continued flashing unabated, signaling the seriousness of the emergency. Half a dozen EMTs and nurses in scrubs rushed up, rolling stretchers.

"X-ray," Nassim ordered one of the trauma nurses. "This woman has priority, then the bleeder lying in the back, then the girl up front with the ankle injury." The preliminary triage instructions were professional and brief. Routine. NYU Medical Center saw thousands of gunshot wounds (GSWs), skull and facial fractures, and seriously wounded motor vehicle accident (MVA) victims. All of that was just in an ordinary day's work.

They strapped Leslie down to one of the stretchers and pushed her inside at a slow run. Nassim jogged along, his hand on the side rail.

"It won't take long," he said, casting a worried look over his shoulder. Leslie looked straight into his eyes.

"Who are you?"

"Nassim. I'm a doctor here."

"*Nassim?*"

She found his face curiously attractive, with all of its grooves and furrows. Noisy engines and the clipped sound of a howling siren disturbed the efficient hum of the emergency department. Heavy SUVs raced into the driveway. The doors opened, and men wearing black suits and dark glasses ran inside.

Bronx watched the action as he pulled in behind the Secret Service convoy. He quietly parked his car in a spot reserved for physicians. Then he walked calmly inside, one hand on the 9mm that sat in a holster beneath his jacket.

"Go. Move it—into the elevator!" Nassim commanded sharply.

The three Secret Service men arrived seconds too late. The doors to the broad employee elevator closed right before their noses. Two ran, as if conditioned, straight for the stairs. The other waited, watched the elevator display, and cursed as he tried to get his radio set to work.

"Everything's blocked!"

"Damn it—who the hell *are* you?" Nassim barked at his patient. "A couple of extraordinarily ugly people seem to be chasing you. Do you happen to know who they are?"

Leslie silently shook her head. Her eyes had a pleading look, a mute cry for help. If there was one thing that Nassim had always had a soft spot for, it was the pleading eyes of an attractive woman—although the soft spot was usually selective. Here and now, he was a surgeon first and foremost.

"To Surgery!"

When the elevator stopped, Nassim pushed the button for a higher floor. This ploy bought them only a short-lived advantage.

A few minutes later, Bronx put on his imposing public appearance.

Leslie Palmer lay on a stretcher on the surgical floor, surrounded by wildly gesturing Secret Service agents. One aimed his pistol at the young doctor, who stepped back against the wall, his hands in the air.

Nassim remained remarkably calm. Even with the muzzle of the gun directed at him, he tried to get rid of the uninvited visitors, who were making a dramatic show of their badges.

"I am a doctor, and this woman is critically injured. Go to hell."

At this moment, Bronx stepped up, stuck his badge in the faces of the baffled Secret Service men, and proclaimed with a stentorian voice that made him sound as if he were New York's Chief of Police in person, "Sir, this patient is the First Lady of the United States. Step back."

The men in black stared blankly at the badge with the bronze depiction of Nathan Hale within the round CIA insignia. A broad-shouldered agent with messy hair was the first to catch his bearings.

"We know that, of course, sir. What are *you* doing here?"

"Special Agent Bronx, CIA. Arrest this Arab immediately. We've had an eye on him for quite a while now. He tried to kidnap the First Lady. A terrorist. He's one of the damn bastards who just attacked our city."

"This is a hospital. Get lost," Nassim attempted. To his own surprise, he was completely thrown. *Where is hospital security? Why has no one informed the Chief of Surgeons?* The EMTs had disappeared into thin air. *No witnesses!* The place was completely dead. Nassim pushed an instrument tray closer, and leaned over his patient. As his hand searched for the scalpel, he suddenly knew where he had seen her face before. What should he do? Unnoticed, he placed the instrument in his pocket, where he kept it grasped with his hand. He straightened up.

One of the men, who made a levelheaded impression on Nassim, had been silent so far. Now he raised an imperious hand.

"Let the doctor do his job," he commanded. "She needs to be treated—her shoulder is bleeding!"

Nassim leaned over her once again. He mumbled to her as he

inspected the wound, "You're fine, Madam. Nothing broken. Why don't you do me a favor and say something to these Rambos!"

The same man raised his somehow calming voice again.

"Is she fit for transport?"

Nassim nodded. "But first this woman needs a prophylactic tetanus shot."

His opinion seemed to be of no interest.

"*We'll* take care of that," said the group's spokesperson.

They had made up their minds. They believed the CIA agent. As far as they were concerned, Nassim was a terrorist in the guise of a doctor. *Guilty until proven innocent!* shot through his head as he, rebelliously, reached to rip the receiver from the wall-mounted telephone—and one of the Secret Service agents twisted his arm behind his back with lightning speed. The cuffs clicked, and he heard an apparently heart-felt "Terrorist pig!" before he was pushed aside. Nassim summoned a sudden burst of strength that allowed him to spin around, temporarily throwing the two agents holding him off balance. He saw the CIA man bending over the First Lady. He had to grin in spite of his predicament. *A celebrity! You could certainly say that again!*

57

Bronx took advantage of the shuffle he had started around the doctor to give Leslie a few last instructions.

"Pay close attention now, Leslie," he whispered, "The situation we discussed is at hand. Now you have to go the distance. What is your name? Tell me!"

As he asked the question, he squeezed her upper arm with an iron grip, so tightly that her eyes were distraught with pain as she looked up at him.

"Sarah Crawford, First Lady of the United States," she said.

"Good," Bronx commended her. He glanced over to the agents who had circled the doctor and were restraining him.

"You have yet to be put to the test," Bronx hissed through clenched teeth, barely moving his lips. "If you fold, your boys will be dead and gone within hours."

Callous as he was, Leslie's look nevertheless went through him like a poisonous dagger. Her eyes were so deathly cold that he involuntarily took a step back.

"What's going on here?" the seemingly reasonable Secret Service agent asked behind Bronx with a cutting edge to his voice.

"The First Lady would like a fresh set of clothes," Bronx answered calmly. He pulled himself up to his full height and eyed the agent from head to toe.

"Who are you, if I may ask?"

"Frank Sureman, Secret Service. Personal Guard to the First Lady."

"Do you happen to have ID on you?"

Sureman stoically produced his badge.

"Madam knows me."

Bronx appeared to check the proffered source of verification carefully.

"Good," he decided, "you will bring the First Lady to safety."

Nodding, Agent Sureman got down on one knee next to the stretcher. His voice was genuinely concerned.

"My God, ma'am, what happened to you? Have you been treated well?"

Leslie looked away, closed her eyes.

"We have a small problem here," said Sureman, standing up. "We have to keep her somewhere until we can arrange for transport. Do you have access to clothes? A secure room where she can recover?"

The Secret Service had access to a few rooms in the Mayor's nuclear shelter, from which they could manage operations in Manhattan. It also contained a medical aid center, but the WTC 7 building under which it was located was situated right next to the towers, in the middle of the danger zone. So that was out of the question.

"Did you hear what I said?" Sureman urged.

Bronx nodded contemplatively a few times.

"Why not? Yes, we have a safe house in Brooklyn. The roads there are clear as far as I'm aware. You will simply follow me—I'll take the First Lady and lead the way."

Leslie propped herself up on her elbows.

"Excellent. Then I won't have to lie around here any longer."

Her voice suggested that she was not going to tolerate dissent. She swung her legs off the side of the stretcher and stood.

"Agent Bronx will come along with us, Madam," Sureman hurried to assure her. He motioned toward the end of the hall with his chin, as a sign that it was time to leave.

A warm breeze blew across the square outside. As Leslie took a seat in the back of Bronx's Explorer, as Sureman had instructed her to do, she glanced over the roof of the flat structure that housed the hospital reception area, and across to the buildings that lined the southern tip of Manhattan. She searched the skyline for the familiar silhouette of the Twin Towers—those proud landmarks of contemporary Manhattan—in vain. The colossal towers had vanished from the face of the earth. Leslie felt her stomach sharply contract. Her heart, however, was beating somewhat more calmly than it had been.

Seconds later, Bronx pulled sharply out of the parking space, turned onto the street, and continued up toward the FDR Drive. He activated the red and white flashing lights. Two Secret Service vehicles followed close behind.

"Where are we going?"

The loud noise of the engine almost drowned her words.

"To a safe house," Bronx yelled over his shoulder, "then to Washington."

"Where is Sarah Crawford?"

"Dead. Buried under the South Tower. Forget her. You made it out. Having barely escaped with your life, you will return to the White House, still in a state of shock. That is the role you will play. Your trial has begun!"

The newborn Sarah Crawford didn't bat an eye. Suddenly, she felt as she usually did shortly before going on stage—excited, inwardly tense.

And then she channeled her first riposte, delivered with a casually mocking attitude, just as one would expect of a lady of her station.

"I'm sure you meant to say *trial by fire!*"

58

The safe house turned out to be a waterfront building with a flaking red exterior, about five stories high, and isolated from the other buildings. A fence of thick, tall iron bars was interrupted by a massive gate, which opened automatically as the Explorer's reinforced bumper approached.

Public Storage, Leslie read, on a bright yellow sign.

The SUV drove smoothly into the underground parking structure.

"A safe house," Rick Bronx repeated a little later, as they entered a dreary, gray room with a utilitarian office desk at its center. He opened a small refrigerator, sent a couple of ice cubes clinking into a broad glass, handing it to Leslie.

"I don't drink whiskey," she declined, and walked over to the window.

The picture was woeful. Clouds of smoke hovered darkly over the city. She still could not believe that the towers were missing from the Financial District. In the dark gray haze she could make out her building, with the offices of the Navy Intelligence Agency. It was at this moment that the realization hit her full force. Suddenly wheezing, she let herself fall back on the brown, badly worn sofa. She pointed to the whiskey glass.

"Fine. Give it to me!"

She was Sarah Crawford, First Lady, which essentially meant that Leslie Palmer no longer existed. *Of course!* Ms. Palmer would never again return to her office, nor to her apartment. Craig and Alex would think that... it was terrible. *Ben!* And then her father's funeral. This afternoon! Leslie Palmer, victim of a terrorist attack! Fighting for breath, she knocked back the drink that Bronx handed her with a scrutinizing look on his rough-hewn face.

Leslie didn't get any further in painting her picture of the unthinkable.

A large flat screen flickered to life and instantly commanded every ounce of her attention. Disbelieving, she stared at two young faces upon which a remote camera was now zooming in.

"Craig, Alex!" she screeched, jumping up abruptly, the glass falling from her hand.

"Who are you? What are you doing with my boys?"

A black mountain of a man with a narrow brow entered.

"You have seventy-two hours to complete your mission, Leslie," Bronx spoke into the tense silence. His expression was ice cold. Leslie wanted to go for his throat, to get her hands around it, like she had on the plaza, but the heavy hand of the enormous black man pulled her back.

"The clock is running, and the water is rising...Take a good look, Leslie."

She stared numbly at her twin sons. They were huddled in a flat boat—a kind of framed platform, it seemed, that floated on the water like a pontoon.

"The room is hermetically sealed. The water level is slowly rising according to precise calculations. Allow me to show you exactly what is going to happen. Don't worry, this is—for now—just a simulation."

Bronx casually pressed a button.

Leslie squirmed against the black man's iron grip. The pontoon with the two cartoon figures representing her sons rose slowly but surely toward the ceiling, as the clock on the edge of the screen counted down. Now it had reached the top, water entered the boat; the two digital figures desperately waved their arms as the water reached their necks. They battled for air, their extended heads banging up against the hard ceiling—then the room had filled. The virtual figures went limp. Bronx switched off the tape.

Leslie suddenly and unexpectedly—albeit futilely—beat and kicked with all of her limbs.

"I will drown your sons, just as I demonstrated, unless you do exactly as I tell you during the next seventy-two hours."

"You, you are..."

"You have precisely seventy-two hours. That is exactly the amount of time that it will take for the water to reach the ceiling."

Bronx gave the black man a wave. The man let go of her, and left the room without saying a word. As soon as he had left, Bronx began detailing what he wanted from her. *Monstrous!* Leslie sat paralyzed, staring at the screen. The camera was now, once again, showing Alex and Craig *live* in this terrible water-filled death trap. Bronx's voice reached her from far away.

"...you will receive detailed instructions as you need them. If you contact the police or the FBI, I will know about it. Your time is running out. You alone hold the fate of your sons in your hands."

Leslie got up, ran to the screen, beat her fists against it, screamed the names of her sons. She finally sank to her knees.

Bronx handed her a glass of water containing a tranquilizer.

She drank obediently, almost gratefully. *Right now, they're still alive!*

A while later, Secret Service Agent Sureman came upon a seemingly calm First Lady sitting in the lobby, wearing an ill-fitting, gray costume. "The president has been advised, Madam. Your transportation back to the White House has been arranged," he informed her efficiently.

Advised? She felt a strange urge to laugh. *This is pure insanity!* Then Bronx stepped into her line of vision, sticking his thumb up in that dumb, tired gesture. He came closer, leaned over and whispered to her.

"Be brave. Everything will end well!"

'Thumbs-up' people are all about making things look good, the sentence reared up in Leslie's memory. *They just love to poke around for something positive in even the biggest pile of shit. Their thumb is like a substitute hard-on, a personal anal probe. 'Thumbs-up' people are false, because they are anally fixated, and...* These thoughts felt good. Bronx was simply an asshole. A dry, puckered-up asshole. She would deal with him. She had to find a way. Bronx had a weak spot, and he had no idea that she was aware of it. He would be terrified of losing the one thing that meant anything to him in his whole fucking life...

"Three of our best people died in the course of duty," Sureman said to Bronx, his mouth a terse line. "Her escort was killed in the South Tower."

Hours later, on her way to Washington, Leslie alias First Lady Sarah Crawford became very clear on one thing: *This is not about America. This is only about saving Alex and Craig. Nothing else mattered.* She would do it. Whatever it was that Bronx wanted her to do. In seventy-two hours, it would all be over. Before she eventually drifted off to sleep, she saw that peculiarly beautiful, furrowed face leaning over her. Her lips opened slightly, as she waited for him to come closer. What was his name again? *Nassim!* It sounded like the name of an exotic flower.

59

Half an hour had passed since the Secret Service agents had safely escorted the First Lady from the hospital.

Two ill-tempered, visibly exhausted New York City cops trudged in, dusting off their uniforms. They looked at the suspect with open antagonism. Their faces, covered in light-colored dust, looked like primitive masks in the stark hospital lighting, and the spark in their eyes signified nothing but pure anger. One was compulsively opening and closing his fist, much like a predatory cat flexing its claws. Nassim's complexion could be described as tan—perhaps a touch lighter than beige—and the striking lines on his face lent him a stroke of beauty resembling that of a young Yemenite, or Lawrence of Arabia. An FBI agent by the name of Tom Lazio, a workhorse wearing a wrinkled suit and loose tie, read Nassim his Miranda rights from a small, laminated card, which he held up like one might a little powder mirror. *Obviously not the sharpest crayon in the box, if he can't remember that much!* Nassim smirked quietly to himself.

Then the two cops were already pushing him roughly into the elevator. Once the door closed, the twitchy one—who was presently in no particular mood to observe the constitution—kneed him swiftly in the groin.

"You want war, you fucking Ayrab? Well, now you've got yourself one!"

The other elbowed Nassim in the head as he bent over in pain. In front of the entrance, they shoved the dazed and staggering man into an unmarked van. Nassim took a rough fall onto the metal bench in the back.

"We're bringing in a suspected terrorist, do you copy? Shit, no network—everything's down." The cop on the passenger seat tossed the piece of equipment into the compartment. He stared grimly at the traffic blocking the street ahead of them.

Nassim heard the driver curse. They were moving only yards at a time. The lights and sirens only proved effective once they had reached the broader avenue. Now the van was making up for lost time. The cop on the passenger side was drumming his fist on the radio set in frustration. It rewarded him with an ongoing crackle. Then it happened. Nassim had just managed to sit up to look out front through the wired partition, in order to get a sense of where they were taking him.

An NYFD ladder truck swerved onto the avenue at high speed—honking, flashing, and skidding. Nassim ducked and instinctively held his cuffed arms protectively over his head. The police van screeched, shouts could be heard from the front, then a terrible collision. The truck belonging to Ladder Company 4 had caught the prisoner transport head on. There seemed to be no end to the screaming of metal, to the crashing and banging around him. Finally, everything was still. Was he even alive? Nassim carefully moved his shoulders, then his arms, his feet. The force of the collision had catapulted him into the partition that separated the driver and passenger from the transport cabin. On the other side of the partition, which was now beneath him, he saw a hand, then a bloody face. The driver. He realized that the van had been turned on its nose. He pressed against the metal grid, yelling at the man, "Give me the keys to the cuffs!"

The officer opened a dim pair of eyes.

"The keys, man! I'm a doctor. I'll get you out."

The van smelled dangerously of gas.

The cop stirred, laboriously raising his hand. It took awhile and a great deal of effort, but Nassim was finally able to reach the small, flat key. He hastily unlocked the handcuffs and pocketed them. When he looked down again, the policeman's eyes were rigid.

Nassim climbed from the wreck, jumped onto the street, and felt a stabbing pain in his thigh. The scalpel! He was in the process of carefully removing it from his pocket, when a voice caused him to freeze.

"Don't move! You can forget about making a run for it!"

A short officer with frizzy black hair came toward him swinging his set of handcuffs.

Nassim didn't take long to think. "Your fellow officer is still alive," he called in a commanding voice. "Get over here, what are you waiting for—I'm a doctor, I need your assistance!"

He brandished the scalpel, clamped it between his teeth. He must have offered a ghastly sight, not to mention that his eyes were boring through the cop with a fear-inspiring stare so effective that the latter completely forgot that he was supposed to be in charge. Meek as a lamb, he crouched down to help with the supposedly injured man.

It was probably the rage boiling up inside him that allowed Nassim to act coldly, and with no qualms. The cop had barely made it to his knees when Nassim grabbed him brutally by the wrist. In the same second, the cuffs locked—once, twice, on the man's wrist, and on the twisted window frame of the wrecked van.

With two expert flicks of the scalpel, Nassim severed the officer's leather uniform belt, pulled off the weapon holster with the heavy SIG Sauer. Next the police radio. That was pretty much all he needed. He looked around, then calmly got up. No one was paying the least bit of attention to the loudly protesting, handcuffed cop—his screams were drowned by the noise all around. Most people were staring south—where the Twin Towers had stood as a symbol for American economic sovereignty, and where now there was only a pitiful, smoldering void. They all stood in the shadow of this truly monstrous crime—Nassim, too. And this is what allowed him to escape, relieved, behind the ladder truck, jumping elegantly across a puddle of oil that was spreading from underneath it to the gutter.

60

The sight of the White House always overwhelmed her. This time was no exception. The center of power was now open to Leslie. If she played her cards right, she was now effectively First Lady of the U.S.A.! She was flooded by a mass of exciting, yet conflicting, emotions. Not one, but three lives were dangling by the thin thread of her ability as an actress. She was genuinely shocked to note an inner glow. *What an amazing challenge!*

The massive black iron gates opened automatically, the soldiers of the Marine Guard gave a dashing salute. A young woman was already standing in front of the entrance. Her matronly, ramrod posture and starched pantsuit uniform perfectly complemented her professional countenance. The Secret Service agent rushed up to the vehicle, her dark, oval face shone with a lively expression that clearly showed that she was ready for duty.

"That's Rita. She's new," her driver informed her, just as the door swung open.

"Good afternoon, Madam. Where may I escort you to? The red room?"

Leslie would get used to not having to open doors for herself. *Red, green, blue room?* An uneasy feeling spread at the pit of her stomach. She hesitated. What should she answer? She remembered absolutely nothing. The carefully studied layout would just not come to her. Her thoughts whirled in her head like a swarm of disoriented locusts.

"The kitchen, please," she said, getting a hold on herself. "That's supposed to be a woman's place, isn't it?" A hint of humor tinged her business-like tone. The Secret Service woman dared a short, faint smile. *Not exactly what you'd call thundering applause—I have some work to do on my dialog!*

The White House kitchen was in no way inferior to that of a five-star hotel. Particularly not when it came to its perfect cleanliness, for which the head chef would have vouched for with his grandmother's life, had he been asked to do so.

A large, polished stove with gold handles dominated the almost clinical-looking facility, which catered to hundreds daily—always with meticulous regard to the preferences and religious customs of its multinational guests. The man who was responsible for the smooth and timely execution of all requests and quirks, 24/7, stepped from his office next to the air-conditioned kitchen. He greeted them in a friendly manner, with a little bow.

"Welcome back, Madam. How are you?"

Shitty, thought the former Leslie.

"Good, excellent. And you, Chef?"

Chef de Cuisine Mosiman was taken aback for a short second. His broad chest, dressed in a perfectly bleached and starched uniform jacket, deflated almost imperceptibly. The First Lady had never called him *Chef*. Not that he was unhappy with it. Not at all.

"Very well, Madam. Thank you for asking. I hope we get those swine." He balled his fists against an imaginary bunch of terrorists. "May I prepare something for you? The usual, perhaps? Some nice grilled vegetables?"

"You can keep the usual, Chef. I could eat a horse right now. What I would really like is a decent steak."

"Right away, Madam. Ten minutes, max. We'll have it brought up."

Leslie leaned casually against the sideboard, picked an olive from a bowl standing next to a basket of bread.

"I'll wait right here," she announced, chewing. "I wouldn't mind looking over your shoulder for a bit. That way you can serve me my meal personally, Chef."

Mosiman smiled impishly. He quite liked this new tone. The woman had just gone through a whole lot in New York, but she was certainly acting pretty cool.

As he handled the pan, olive oil, and spices, he cast a furtive glance in her direction—a glance that perhaps lingered a heartbeat longer than was proper.

"Stop staring!" Leslie admonished him firmly. "You're making me twitchy."

"Sorry, Madam, I really am, Madam, I've been a bundle of nerves today, with everything that..."

He began to, almost violently, whisk something in a glass bowl, rather obviously trying to hide the shaking of his hands. She laughed her light laugh, ran her fingers through her thick hair.

"Oh, come. You can say it! I look like hell, right?"

Mosiman paused in the middle of his attack of sappiness and admitted, meekly, "Well, when I looked at you, I thought for a moment..."

"Thought what? I want to know! I'm not going to bite you."

"Well, Madam, I was just thinking, we had that look-alike visit recently, and she came to the kitchen on her tour. Just for a few moments. You remember? Your double?"

He looked up, befuddled, as she stepped up to him and boyishly poked at his chest with a pointy finger.

"You're not going to tell me you didn't *recognize* me, are you?"

Mosiman shrank back, a look of consternation on his face. He began to protest so wildly with his hands, that the whisk got away from him and fell, with a soft clatter, onto the snow-white tile floor. The former Leslie burst into resounding laughter.

"No, no, quite the opposite," Mosiman protested vehemently, his face now bright red. "I was just thinking to myself, no, I thought, the First Lady is unmistakable. Nobody, no double, could ever take her place. That impersonator was nothing but a cheap replica, if I may say so."

"Absolutely, a horrible person," Leslie agreed with a smile. "Watch your pan, Chef!" she said, pointing meaningfully toward the stove, where hot grease was splashing from the skillet in all directions.

Mosiman wiped his hands on his apron, and deftly threw a piece of meat in the large, flat pan, announcing proudly, "Filet Mignon from a first grade Texas ranch, well hung."

"Medium, please, Chef!" the First Lady interjected.

"Absolutely, Madam. A salad to go with that?"

"Yes, and fries, please."

She dunked a piece of freshly baked baguette in olive oil.

This was new, too. The First Lady had never had much of a liking for French fries or olives. But Mosiman had been around long enough not to bother himself too much over trivial details. Once the filet was à point, as the First Lady wished, he arranged her meal on a plate, and followed her lightly upstairs, tray in hand. The large table in the private dining room had already been set by the housekeeper.

"You're from Switzerland, aren't you, Chef?" Leslie inquired as he placed her plate on the immaculate white tablecloth. Even as she scrupulously displayed the body language that she had learned from her careful observations of the First Lady, the sharp teeth of revenge turned relentlessly in the clockwork of her mind.

"Yes, Madam."

"Do you happen to know a place by the name of Gestaad?"

"*Gstaad?* Yes, certainly, Madam—it is a luxurious mountain spa resort. I once worked in Montreux, about half an hour's drive from Gstaad."

The newly crowned First Lady sat.

"Do you happen to have any acquaintances there?"

He shook his head.

"No, Madam, apart from a few kitchen chefs, whom I know mostly by name."

"Good. Thank you, Chef."

"*Bon appetit,* Madam. Please allow me to say what a great joy and honor it is to have you back with us."

The First Lady produced a quick, suitably flattered smile.

"Thank you very much. You're a true gentleman, Chef."

Which sent Mosiman on his way, blushing brightly, and giving three short bows as he backed out the door.

61

Rosa Falhony was an elegant, dynamic middle-aged woman with straight black hair. Her sparkling eyes, and almost blindingly white teeth stood out in her dark face when she laughed, which she did often, probably aware of the fact that she drew everyone's attention to her fire-red lips when she did. Rosa had a Latin, high-energy temperament, which made her indispensable in her position as assistant to the First Lady.

"I understand completely why you would want to seek counseling in New York, Madam," she was telling Leslie that same evening, adding, "New York is vibrant, it is the essence of life, but still..." She fleetingly touched her hand to her lips in a gesture of fright.

"Look Rosa, I have been advised to return to the scene of the catastrophe in order to come to terms with my traumatic experience there. If I just stay here in Washington, I am in danger of nourishing grievances against everything that has to do with New York. That is why I have been told that it would be best to attend therapy there."

Rosa was a practical woman. "I worked in the Big Apple for a few years, Madam. On Duane Street, not far from City Hall. My boss was an attorney who represented the dockworkers' union. I tell you, Madam, New York is a good city. Its scars will heal. So, which of these shrinks look good to you?"

She spread out a list of illustrious names.

"Rosa, listen, you are a pearl. What I want, dear, is a therapist with a back door."

Her assistant looked at her blankly. *Didn't everybody have one?* Leslie smiled back with the same sophisticated smile that she had learned to use when delivering Noel Coward witticisms on holiday theater stages.

"I would like you to find me a nice little practice between Park and Fifth—somewhere between 66th and 70th Street. That's a safe, pretty discreet neighborhood. What I'm saying is that it would make me happy if it had a backyard exit."

Rosa nodded and smiled to herself in understanding.

"I do not wish this therapy issue to be known, Rosa. It is imperative that you observe strict discretion. I absolutely do not want to find myself faced with a horde of reporters as I leave the therapist's office. That is why I need a second exit—alright, dear?"

She looked Rosa directly in the eyes to see if the woman with the intelligent face was hiding a reaction. It was quite possible that Rosa might suspect that Leslie needed the back exit for other useful purposes—she had the air of a courtesan, and was almost certainly not easily deceived.

"Is there a problem with that?" Leslie added, scrutinizing her.

"No, not at all. To the contrary—your precautions are very wise, ma'am. I will make a few calls, and then I will present you with a new selection."

Relieved, Leslie nodded. She dismissed Rosa with a few friendly words, in the sure knowledge that she represented an ally. *If a smart woman like this accepts me and my voice in this part,* she contemplated, *well, then... then... how did they put it in the theater? It ain't over until the fat lady's sung.*

62

Sarah Crawford alias Leslie Palmer was seated at an elegantly shaped antique desk, staring at the white telephone. Should she? She looked up, then stood and stepped over to the large window overlooking Pennsylvania Avenue. It was dusk, and somewhere out there was the carefree life that should have been hers, had Bronx not maneuvered her into this impossible situation. The fact was that she was truly afraid. She felt a twisting sickness in her stomach that heralded a panic attack. She took a deep breath, and released it slowly. Afraid of being exposed—by the president, his children, the housekeeper. Now that she thought of it, hadn't the secretary eyed her rather strangely when she thought she wasn't looking? No, it really wasn't the fear of being caught. The real dread lay elsewhere. If she messed up, if she made one wrong move, then Bronx would take terrible revenge on her sons. She had to go with the dreadful, but lesser evil. She had to complete her mission. She would prepare herself exceedingly well in order to make sure she did not blunder. Her presence of mind had rarely failed her so far. She would succeed—she owed that much to Craig and Alexander. Even here, alone, she was the perfect method actress. The First Lady sat back down, lifted the receiver, and searched for the button that would give her an outside line.

"Yes, Madam, can I help you?"

Startled, Leslie abruptly hung up—and immediately wanted to kick herself. *Why would you want to dial yourself, you stupid heifer?*

When the pleasant voice answered a second time, Leslie assumed a natural, benevolent yet authoritative, tone.

"Please put me through to the Texas Attorney General."

"Of course, Madam, we will call you right back."

"Thank you."

She was wound tighter than a spring as she sat there, waiting.

Outside, down there on the pavement, she recognized the man pacing up and down, carrying his protest sign. He had been steadfastly demonstrating for male emancipation for years. "Husbands, get out of the kitchen!" his slogan read.

Jennifer had spent a year in an unhappy relationship with a guy like that, who felt completely entitled to be catered to like royalty. A macho man whose tiny brain only had room for football, motorbikes, and sex. *Motorbikes... Jennifer...* I somehow have to manage to contact her. And the young doctor who had rescued her on his motorbike... What was his name again? He walked with a limp... Na... Na... *Narim*?

The telephone buzzed quietly.

"Your call, Madam. The Attorney General in Austin."

"Thank you." She waited. A deep voice appeared on the other end of the line. "Greg Dexter speaking, to what do I owe this honor, ma'am?"

Leslie quickly came to the point. "I need your help, sir. I had a motor vehicle accident in Midland—on November 6, 1973. Do you know anything about the incident?"

The line was still for a moment. The Attorney General, seated in his office on 15th Street in Austin, pinched his lips. Of course he was familiar with the tragedy that had taken place in the rural wasteland close to the First Lady's hometown. But, until today, she had always refused to talk about it. The precise circumstances had remained her secret.

"Yes, I do remember something happening. A lot of time has passed since then. I recall—around the beginning of the year—you visited the house in Midland where the president spent his childhood. That was a really nice gesture, Madam, and we sure do appreciate it."

"Well, when duty calls, I have to answer, don't I?" she responded casually. "Listen, Greg, I need the court transcripts of the case, the accident report, the entire file. You understand, I am—*er*—I trust that our conversation will remain confidential...?"

"Of course, ma'am," the Attorney General hastily replied.

"You see, I'm working on my biography, and I wish to reprocess this chapter. I was only seventeen years old at the time. I need the documents as quickly as possible. Would tomorrow evening work?"

Attorney General Dexter's astonishment was audible in his rather long silence. Leslie stared breathlessly at the number on the display: 1512 463 2111.

"Yes, Madam. I think that can be arranged. I will immediately contact the central archive and send out a special courier. I suppose this all has to do with the terrorist attack, somehow. How are you? Janet would love to inform you on that project of hers the next time you come down and visit us."

Janet? His wife? Project?

"Absolutely, of course—my best regards. How is she getting along with that? It's a madhouse around here right now, but around Christmas time, perhaps. Will you be staying in Austin, Greg, or are you going..."

"No, I think I'm going to be right here, putting in overtime," he said, responding to her unfinished sentence. "There are some pending arrests. We are following every trace. We'll be celebrating at home—just the family and the grandchildren. Janet doesn't feel up to traveling to Maine right now."

"I understand. Well, thank you for everything, and take care," Leslie said with courteous warmth. "And enjoy those grandkids, hear."

Phew! She put her elbows on the mahogany tabletop and cradled her head in both hands. *A madhouse. If that isn't the truth, then I don't know what is! On the other hand, it is kind of exciting to perform; to be back on the stage, in the limelight—even more so because all of it is invisible!*

63

Leslie shuffled grudgingly into the bathroom. She seriously searched her face in the broad mirror, as if she were seeing herself for the very first time.

Her thick hair was parted to the right, where it fell luxuriantly across her cheek. On the left, its waves covered most of her ear, the delicate gold earring on her lobe only just peeking through. She carefully plucked at her hairstyle, arranging it so that it would resemble that of her role model as closely as possible. *Everything immaculate and First-Lady-like*, she reassured herself, breathing deeply. But her heart would not stop pounding in her chest.

Then her eyes fixed on the hairbrush that was lying on the gray marble dressing table. A few fine, hairs had tangled in its natural bristles. Leslie grasped the elegantly worked wooden handle, and raised the brush toward her head. In mid-motion, she flinched. Slowly she put her hand back down again. She stared at the bristly thing as if it were some kind of spiky insect. She felt suddenly nauseous—and she knew the reason instantly. Being in the First Lady's most private sphere was getting to her. The woman she was impersonating was dead; buried under the rubble of the collapsed towers, and she had just marched into the most intimate realms of her life—her *mausoleum!* It felt like some curse must await her here—she just didn't know what it was yet. Leslie abruptly shrank back, like a voyeur, caught. She couldn't touch another thing.

However, practicality did not take long to win over her scruples. What was the First Lady's scent? Husbands knew the intimate scent of their wives. Surely, the president would be no exception. Now curious, she opened the cabinet, taking in the collection of bottles, tubes, and jars—color enhancing shampoo, night cream, moonstone, mauve and lilac-colored eye shadow—a wonderful complement to her brown eyes, Chanel No 5. Nothing extraordinary. A door fell shut somewhere. Leslie quickly closed the cabinet door and hurried into the bedroom on the tips of her toes.

At first glance, the clothing she found in the closet was anything but lavish—a bit petty bourgeois, if the truth be told. But upon closer inspection, she had to marvel at some of the exquisite materials and exclusive designs that she found hanging amid dull-colored skirts and boring brown ensembles. The First Lady seemed to have preferred pastels. Apparently she had been in the process of updating her style, Leslie noted, producing a little whistling sound. She pulled a satin Jil Sander top off its hanger, held it speculatively over her breasts. Same size, she estimated, continuing to rummage the rack. The hippest Los Angeles labels and chic blouses—all were very stylish and urban in mood. Not to mention that they were just waiting to be worn.

Inquisitive, she pulled open the other closet door. She wondered at the barely worn power outfits—just right for a woman of influence, she smiled to herself. Classic lines, elegant, with perhaps a hint of 80's retro. A refined business look. She pulled out a black jacket and began to change into it. It had a really sophisticated cut, she decided once she had done up the buttons on the Yves St. Laurent piece, clicking her tongue in approval as she regarded herself in the mirror. "Just the right size," she informed her image, smiling coquettishly, then went on to rummage among jeans and jackets with shoulder pads.

She would try those on later! She turned to the drawers. Underwear... conservative JC Penny things, good Walford hosiery—*aha*—here we had some pretty sexy Missoni, then Basics by American Apparel. *Buy American!* She was just preparing to move on to the countless shoes, arranged like so many birds on a wire, when there was a knock at the door.

It was Keisha, a black secretary wearing large, brown horn-rimmed glasses. Her hair was up in a bun. She wore a gray suit with a pink shirt, which was a bit strained with trying to contain her ample bosom.

"How are you, Madam?" she asked unobtrusively. "Do you have time to go over your appointments, or would you like me to come back later?"

Leslie reached theatrically for her forehead.

"No, Keisha, that'll be fine. What do we have?"

"Your foundation, Madam. The Chairman of the Program to Promote Literacy..."

Keisha paused, as if expecting a display of enthusiasm.

Leslie just looked at her, eyebrows raised in question.

"Well, Mr. Portman, the chairman," Keisha continued deliberately, "you aren't always on the same page, but he was inquiring whether you..."

"Whether I what?" the First Lady interrupted her with a well-feigned mixture of annoyance and impatience, which she still had handy in her repertoire from her performances in a couple of Neil Simon plays.

Keisha didn't exactly crack up laughing, but she did, at least, nod and smile.

"I understand, Madam. He wanted to know whether you would be willing to hold the lecture at the Library of Congress?"

Leslie frowned.

"When? Why?"

Now Keisha was looking over the edge of her glasses and, for the first time, she did clearly seem a bit baffled.

"We already set the date. The chairman would like to move the venue to the library."

Leslie sighed and, once again, grasped her forehead. "Keisha, I'm still totally overwhelmed. Could we not cancel? I am really completely shattered—these headaches I've been having, ever since..."

"I understand, Madam. I will ask the chairman. Over two hundred people have already confirmed that they plan to attend."

The First Lady acted distracted.

"What was the topic, again?"

"Reading. To encourage reading. It was about the significance of books in building character in American children."

"Okay, of course," Leslie exclaimed, relieved. "At the Library of Congress!"

Keisha stood.

"We can talk about your other commitments tomorrow. There's no rush."

The First Lady let the secretary go. But before she had shut the door behind herself, Leslie called out, "Wait, Keisha. I've changed my mind. We won't cancel. Tomorrow is fine. Library of Congress."

The secretary nodded affably. Before gently closing the door, a smile spread across her round face, and she confessed, humbly, "I like it when you call me Keisha, ma'am."

Leslie raised her strong shoulders, felt the adrenaline rushing to her limbs. *The Library of Congress? Ha—I can pull that off!* Time for a reality check. She posed in front of the mirror. *And so the pathetic vanity of a common actress raises its moribund head. . . !*

64

The president had not yet returned to the White House for security reasons—a fortuitous circumstance, as far as Leslie was concerned, since it allowed her to immerse herself in her role without too much pressure to perform. Rosa Falhony was proving to be a valuable support. When Leslie informed her that, in the wake of the dreadful events in New York, she would like to make some changes instead of continuing with her usual routine as if nothing had happened, Rosa expressed her approval by smiling brightly and nodding enthusiastically, instead of putting on a worried frown.

"Madam, you know that I am always here for you," she ensured her. Leslie thought she had even seen a little wink. "By the way, you *have* already changed something."

Leslie had looked at her, perplexed.

"I think that it is very nice that you started calling me by my first name."

Leslie had breathed a sigh of relief, as if a weight had fallen from her shoulders. She raised her arms as if to say *"but of course!"* Then she had asked for a new laptop. She had written a note for Rosa with precise specifications as to the capabilities that she needed the Mac to have. She had also listed all of the software that she wanted installed. She was amazed to find that the slender, silver machine had been delivered, and ready for her to use, just a few hours later.

Much to her surprise, her password still gave her access to the internal system at Navy Intelligence. Security could well have suspended her. She considered that she might possibly be denied data access at any time, since Leslie Palmer had to be, at this point, officially considered missing. And so she hurried to copy all-important work that she had saved, and to download the central data she needed. She was most interested in classified reports on Tajikistan, and a picture showing a determined face, which she had not had time to examine more closely. She now thought that she remembered a name that might go with it.

Tense and filled with anticipation, she opened the program, found the photograph, and maximized it to its full size. The face was looking out from behind a group of men wearing wide, colorful robes. She zoomed in on it, and examined it carefully. There was no doubt in her mind. It was him. The man shown somewhere on the Arabian Peninsula was Steve Quinn, the press photographer that had taken her pictures for a multi-page interview less than a year ago.

Steve Quinn. I must speak to him.

She searched the drawing room to see whether the *New Yorker* with her Steve Quinn interview might by chance be lying around somewhere, then the Treaty Room, where the president usually put his feet up on the desk during meetings—nothing there either. Dusk was slowly turning to night over Pennsylvania Avenue and the meticulously cared for lawn in front of the White House.

Satellite pictures of a mountainous region were spread out on the table. Leslie was scrutinizing them, looking for anything that might prove useful. She had completely lost all sense of her surroundings.

A shy knock on the door startled her. Rosa stuck her head around the corner. She was wearing her shiny black hair in waves today.

"Madam, didn't you hear the bell?"

Once again, Leslie fabricated that slightly absent smile, which she would easily be able to incorporate in the First Lady's mannerisms, and use it as what was referred to as a *crutch* by actors. The world would interpret the smile as that of a brave woman who had been through the hell of the World Trade Center disaster—and excuse or ignore every circumstance around it.

"I may have," she said airily. "And?"

"The president has arrived. He would like to take dinner at half past six. In the drawing room, ma'am."

Leslie felt a blossoming panic. She had been completely submerged in her research. She practically gasped for air.

"My husband! What a godsend. Good Lord, Rosa, how do I look? What should I wear?"

She looked down at herself in dismay. *Darn it—aren't I much thinner than... than... Sarah? What if the president notices? I can attribute three or four pounds to stress—but what if he...*

"Black is always wonderful on you," Rosa announced, expertly eying her tight ensemble. "It makes you look as slender as Nicole Kidman."

65

The new cell phone that Rosa had brought Leslie rang four bars of one of Chopin's Mazurkas. She hastily picked up. "Hello?"

It was the voice of the president. She hardly heard a word. At some point she said, "I'm not feeling too well," breathed something about suffering from headaches, in a carefully distracted tone. "I keep feeling dizzy. I'll see the doctor tomorrow." It was the strangest conversation she had ever had. She breathed deeply once it was over: so that was that! Not her big, trial by fire entrance—but at least a little vocal audition, right?

Minutes later he stood before her. Her husband, a real man's man! The President of the United States! Silently, he wrapped her in his arms, holding her tightly.

"Honey, I'm so happy that you got through it all!" he whispered in her ear. "How you feeling, hon?"

How was she feeling? Like someone had stuck her in a freezer! Her body had instantly stiffened at his embrace. She was shaking, darkness enveloped her, strong arms were pushing her forward—toward the scaffold, the executioner, who was laughing cruelly, his evil grimace was that of CIA Agent Bronx. He held an axe over her two boys, who stood and stared at her, their hands tied. Their eyes pierced through her like daggers. Alex moved his lips, "It's your fault that we have to die," Leslie read.

"Everything's going to be just fine, hon," she heard the world famous voice say. Leslie opened her eyes. A pin of the flag on a collar—the Stars and Stripes—moved backward, a face came into view, followed by a very manly scent. The president was leaning over her with a look of concern on his face, stroking her cheek.

"It's alright," he said, consolingly, as he cast a sideward glance at his watch.

Leslie came to. She was lying on the deep chaise lounge made of soft, brown leather, remnants of dizziness still wafting through her head. Her eyes fell on a framed photograph of a group of men on a fishing cutter. Slowly she regained her sense of orientation, caught a hold of herself. She leaned up on her elbows.

"You have to rest—don't think about it anymore," she heard the president say. "How are you feeling now?"

She shuddered in fear; surely her entire ruse would go up in smoke in a few seconds. The man kneeled before her, resting a hand on her shoulder.

"Are you up to having something to eat, hon? Maybe some fennel soup?"

Fennel soup, Leslie repeated to herself, then jerked back into her role, almost as if she had been given the cue for her appearance.

"I'm sorry, I get faint so easily. I see the whole thing repeating itself in my mind. It's terrible, you know?"

She squeezed his hand tightly with both of hers.

"Well, that's only natural, sweetie. You had an awful experience. You have to take it easy. Unfortunately, I won't have time to eat. There's an emergency session that I have to get to. Rosa will take care of you." He got up. "I have to put a call through to Rudy. The conference with our commanders begins in fifteen minutes. We'll get them, that I can guarantee you."

He planted a gentle kiss on her cheek with softly pursed lips, and headed for the door. Already at the threshold, he called back over his shoulder, "By the way, I think it would be a good idea to invite Mom, she can look after you for a bit. And the children also want to come. We'll talk about it, alright?"

The door closed. Leslie breathed.

Her laptop rested in sleep mode on the desk, its screen black. She randomly pressed a key and instantly found herself back in the real world.

Later, Leslie couldn't have said whether her fainting spell had been acted or real. But she could clearly still see those terrible pictures of the executioner before her eyes. They served as a sobering reminder of why, and for whom, she was playing this dangerous double role.

Clever and cunning, brave and daring: those were the attributes that she would have to live and breathe, without fail—and without scruples—from now on! Whatever happened, her boys would one day be proud of their mom. This is what Leslie silently swore to herself as the president ended his conversation with the New York Mayor two stories below, got up with a satisfied smile on his face, and took a few steps over to the bathroom. There he gazed skeptically into the mirror for a while, then tried on a quick series of determined facial expressions. It was important that he appear resolute and dynamic when he addressed the commanders in a few minutes. Throughout their globally scattered command posts, they had to have a clear image of a purposeful and tenacious commander-in-chief. He had to deliver an infectious message, carried by a sense of presidential level-headedness and a strong fighting spirit.

He was in his element. This terrible crisis had, in a sense, been just what he needed. It was a blessing in disguise! Yes, the Lord sometimes moved in mysterious ways, His wonders to perform. The country needed him now. He felt that the moment was smiling upon him and his presidency. Perish the thought of his opponent sitting in the Oval Office right now, not knowing what to do for all of his weak-spiritedness. He looked at his image with overt pride and satisfaction, then clapped his loosely balled right fist against his chest. To anyone passing, he might have looked like someone trying to suppress a belch.

"I won the elections. Now I will gather my strength to lift this nation in this time of infamy. I will exact revenge. I will prove to the world that I am the right man, chosen to command in this critical era for a reason. A president that is willing to mobilize his forces, and to destroy these bomb-throwing, camel-riding fanatics—around the globe, everywhere."

He felt good. The delivery of patriotic speeches was his strong suit. That's not something they taught you at school. You had to be blessed with it!

Sarah will be fine, he thought in passing, *she's tough*. He thought it was a great idea to invite his mom over for a visit. What he was less happy about, was that dad wanted to come along, and of course he wanted do discuss matters. *To hell with that. Dad had his time, now it's my turn!* Mom, of course, was a saint. She had offered to take care of the First Lady. When she was around to care for her daughter-in-law like a mother hen, to support her in everything she did—she would probably even invite her to come and relax at the ranch down South—yes, then he would have the necessary time and space to dedicate himself completely to the nation's well-being.

During these tumultuous days, he really did not want to be distracted by the needs of his wife—particularly since she hadn't exactly been very warm toward him lately. She had also decided to go into therapy, which he approved of—*who knows what the results of that might be, hopefully a bit more enthusiasm in*... Well. He didn't know what kind of treatment she was thinking of undergoing. Rosa would make all of the necessary arrangements. And if the children also came to visit—which was to be expected around Thanksgiving at the latest—her state of mind would surely be back to normal in no time. All in all, particularly in view of the turbulent circumstances, the prognosis for house and home—and perhaps even his bedroom—was pretty damn peachy!

As he walked to participate in the apex of the video conference with a slight bounce to his step, his thoughts strayed freely from Sarah to another woman—one who didn't only agree with his goals, but who let him know in no uncertain terms how much she appreciated his work, and who supported him wholeheartedly in his intentions to assert himself as a world leader.

66

In the Secret Service office, Bill Baker waited for the presidential video conference with the commanders of the Armed Forces to come to a close.

"They're done," Agent Sureman informed him after half an hour, which Baker had used to rearrange the delicate questions in his mind, ruminate on possible objections, and practice the speech in his head.

Sir, we are under the impression that she has changed. May I speak frankly? What I mean is that we have gathered observations, and we have come to believe that the shock of recent events has possibly affected the First Lady...

In the Oval Office, the president shook his hand with the world's most demonstrative power grip.

"Five minutes, Bill. Shoot!"

Bill Baker, deputy director of the FBI, harbored no illusions when it came to his mission. What husband liked to hear from strangers that his wife was cultivating strange contacts behind his back? That she was possibly even having an affair? Bill presented the FBI's concerns cautiously.

The president raised his head in surprise, examined the man across from him, squinted at his watch.

"What are you saying?" he asked abruptly. "What are you getting at?"

Baker stood still, cleared his throat, his arms loosely by his side. He had a handsome face, with a strong, straight nose, bright, grayish-green eyes, and a high forehead. The president, however, had an impregnable disdain for police officers and intelligence gatherers who lurked around in their raincoats and floppy hats, shamelessly sounding out members of his cabinet, and always finding reasons to shadow even him, the Commander-in-Chief of the Armed Forces. And now this! Targeting the First Lady! Anger boiled up inside of him. Fortunately Baker's posture was upright and respectful, which softened his mood somewhat, since he had a special fondness for dashing soldiers, and felt most comfortable around the fighting forces. Baker's deep, calm voice came through to him as if from a great distance.

"She may be destabilized, sir, she may have lost her bearings, and we are—of course—concerned."

"Listen, Baker, your boss didn't inform me that he was going to be sending around some ass to tell me that my wife is cheating on me, out of her mind, or anything else that you bozos think you may have discovered. I want you to know one thing, and remember it well: I will not tolerate anyone badmouthing my wife." His cheeks were flushed in anger, his fingers drummed on the leather inset of the desktop. "Tell me, Baker, what the hell is your problem, anyway?"

Baker pulled himself together with some effort.

"If you will pardon me, sir, but the First Lady has been very active lately. There have been regular trips to New York. And we have been having difficulties checking all of her contacts."

The president huffed, "You don't mean to tell me that you think she's some kind of security risk. My wife—a danger to the nation? That is the most ridiculous thing that I have ever heard." His laugh was something between a derisive snort and his typical, odd snicker. "If you ask me, Baker, you're the one who's lost his marbles. My wife was right in the middle of 9/11. She probably had the shock of her life. Speaking of which—where were *you* when the towers came down, heh, *where?*"

He peered at Baker obliquely. The poor man only just had time to pull the corners of his mouth up to mimic a friendly face. He dearly wanted to respond that at least he hadn't spent a long time sitting speechless with a dumb-assed look on his face in some Florida classroom, like the President of the United States, for instance. Instead, Baker responded as politely as possible, "Pretty close to the Pentagon, sir. The jet crashed into the building right in front of my eyes." He displayed a gap of about an inch between his thumb and index finger. "About this close, sir."

The president stared at him blankly.

"Really? Well, fine then. Fine. That makes you a real hero, Bill. And the Lord knows we need heroes—now more than ever. Okay, let's get to the point. What exactly do you want?"

"Well, sir, with all due respect, have you noticed anything particular about your wife recently?"

"I don't believe that I even want to think about it, Baker. She's been forgetting to feed Barney—no wonder the little critter growls at her all the time."

Again that staccato cackle.

"I'll tell you what... I'll let you know if she runs off with the Chief of Staff. Heh heh. So you tell me—why did the director send you?"

"Because of the First Lady, sir. We believe that you, Mr. President, are perhaps not adequately informed on the First Lady's contacts."

The president abruptly got up from his chair. He was in no mood to submit himself to this line of cryptic questioning. Now he really was getting pissed.

"Now you listen to me good, Baker. I really would have thought that the FBI had enough problems to deal with after the terrorist attack on our country, but apparently I was wrong. Either you really have nothing better to do, or you haven't realized that we've got a war on our hands. You can tell the director from me that it's his job to bring me the heads of those goddamned bastards on a silver platter, instead of spying on the First Lady. By the way, my Secret Service people always know who my wife is meeting, as well as when and where."

Baker pressed his lips together and nodded his understanding. The president now continued in a somewhat more subdued tone. "Okay, Bill, what I'm saying is this: don't you worry yourself about my wife. The First Lady has been through a lot. I would be the first one to notice if anything was wrong. I mean *really* wrong. Understand?"

The deputy director of the FBI nodded his assent emphatically, following up with a loud and clear "*Yessir!*" He allowed his hand to be shaken, did an about-turn on his heel with military precision, and marched out briskly, leaving the president standing at his desk with that striking rascally smirk on his world-famous face, which had done a good deal toward reeling in the female vote.

Those FBI people all think they're J. Edgar Hoover, that old queer. The commander in chief of all U.S. fighting forces sat down. He casually swung his cowboy style indoor boots onto the desk, crossed his arms behind his head, and leaned back. The president had a certain glint in his eye, and his smirk had gone from rascally to roguish.

Nuh-uh, people, don't even think of bothering me with that kind of bullshit, he said neatly to himself. *I've been riding around in this rodeo way to long to take that crap!*

67

It was ten o'clock when the president stepped into the apartment upstairs to lie down for a few minutes before he had to join the briefing session in the basement, which would almost certainly go on until long after midnight. The rage that he had worked himself into during his meeting with the FBI man had dissipated. But the embarrassing fact that his wife had given the FBI cause to seek clarification was galling him. He was accordingly snippish as he ordered one of his beloved baby hamburgers, and was seriously contemplating whether he should get a massage from the charming Filipina woman up in the gym. But his thoughts wandered. Baker had roused his suspicions with his insinuations. The thought that his wife could embarrass him in some way was niggling at his mind. Perhaps all of this was nothing but a misunderstanding. Where had she been? He gulped down his last bite, dabbed his mouth with the napkin, and got up from the elegant, small mahogany dining table.

Sarah was probably no longer in her study in the East Wing, he decided. Then he noticed that there was light in the back rooms. As he walked past the desk, he noticed pieces of paper that had been torn from a yellow legal pad. He paused and picked one up. It was full of notes. He felt for the others, held them up under the light of the reading lamp, concentrating on the handwriting itself. He wondered who might have written these. A gentle voice cajoled in his ear.

"Hello, darling. Can I get you a drink?"

She stood behind him, scantily dressed. Her appealing, lithe curves stood out under a silky, lace-trimmed slip. He started, as if she had just woken him up.

She gazed at him, a dreamy look in her eyes.

"Hi, hon. A drink?" he asked sheepishly. *What was she up to?* "Sure. But Jim can take care of that."

He was about to ring for the butler, but Leslie was already scooping the ice at the bar. She brought him a crystal glass containing gold, shimmering liquid, with a smile on her lips—lips that seemed somehow fuller to him. "It seems to me that the Commander-in-Chief could use a bit of fortification from the weaker sex."

He took the drink, surprised.

"I like your new style," he grinned. At the back of his mind, an unpleasant, nagging thought was poking at him like a nasty splinter.

When Leslie didn't respond, he said with a boyish smile, "You've changed somehow—in a good way. I like it."

"Love is the greatest refreshment in life," she answered deftly. "Picasso said that, by the way."

"Oh, really? When did you start liking *him*?"

He took his glass and started walking leisurely toward the bedroom.

"Just the quote—not the paintings."

Leslie felt uncomfortable. She had the feeling that she was standing on a slippery slope. She had to find her way back to safe ground. But the president's chatty tone was calming her for now.

"You know what, honey? A guy from the FBI was here today and, can you imagine, they're worried about you down there? It was just about the silliest thing I've ever heard."

"Why?" she called after him, into the bedroom.

"I think they want you to be a good little housewife instead of gallivanting around," he droned in reply, then returned wearing nothing but a bright white terry-cloth towel tied around his waist.

Leslie swallowed. She tried to read his face. *Is he annoyed?* It seemed to her that he was not quite present. She could see that he was preoccupied with something. *What is going on in his mind?*

"Don't you think we should relax a bit?" she cleverly changed the topic, nipping at the Champagne flute that she had brought herself from the bar.

He raised his eyes. They had a look of surprise to them, but there were also the beginnings of a mischievous glint, as if her gallant suggestion had sparked a little fire in him. He placed his empty glass resolutely on her desk.

"Unfortunately I don't have time to chat, Madam, duty calls. Who wrote all that, by the way?"

She followed his stern gaze and outstretched arm to the pieces of notepaper with her scribbling, and acted clueless.

"Wrote what?"

Instead of answering, he snatched at the notes, the sudden motion making the towel come undone from his hips and fall to the ground. Unconcerned, he turned to face her, and stretched the papers out to her with a questioning look in his eyes.

Leslie heroically forced her gaze to the stupid notes, instead of following an urge to eyeball the hopefully more interesting view that the president was so openly putting on display. Leslie tried desperately to focus on the handful of paper as she felt herself completely losing her cool. A hot blush was spreading across her cheeks. She felt like a teenager attempting her first kiss. The president seemed oblivious. He made his displeasure evident with a dark grumble and a deeply furrowed brow.

"You're not even going to look at it?" he complained.

"Of course, of course! Those are the notes for my speech."

"That's not what I meant, silly woman," the President of the United States grouched. He pushed the papers at her with a dark expression on his face. He turned on his heel and headed for the bathroom.

Leslie stared flabbergasted at his plump behind, as she tried feverishly to figure out what mistake she could possibly have just made. Absently, she put the pages back on the desk.

"Where is Barney?" he yelled from under the shower. "Has he been fed?"

"I hate that damn mutt," Leslie hissed to herself.

It was only now that she began to feel the excitement coursing down her spine and into her pelvis. She took a large swallow of Champagne. Pictures of Ben awoke in her mind, and she saw him embracing her, pressing her down on the large bed. She hastily patted her figure, and carefully approached the open bedroom door. She paused. *What was he talking about with the FBI? Something was going on.* She wanted to catch his eye, stroke his neck and back, calm him down.

She was just in time. The president had put on a pair of navy-blue boxer shorts and was busy slipping his well-built body into a red silk gown with a blue collar and cuffs. He began to apply snow-white dabs of shaving cream to his face. Along with the red and blue of his attire, he looked to Leslie like some kind of American flag on two feet, or perhaps like Uncle Sam on his day off.

She leaned coquettishly in the doorway, looking covetously at him. Excited by her close presence to the most powerful man on earth, who had just stood before her without a thread of clothing on his body, she felt magnetically drawn to him. *Power corrupts*, she thought to herself. *It also has a way of making you incredibly horny.*

"Those shorts are very sexy," she tried to chat up her supposed husband.

He grumbled stubbornly, as if to say that the mood was gone and not to be redeemed.

"What's the meeting about tonight, darling?" she purred like a cat, reaching around and gently stroking his chest with both palms from behind. "I'll be waiting for you." Light as a feather, she slid both of her hands across his nipples.

His face began to take on a boyish air again. A smile appeared around his lips. He liked it when her hands, a woman's hands, caressed his body. Especially his nipples. Which was totally new as far as Sarah was concerned. *I wonder where she got that from? Has she been watching porn without me knowing it?* In spite of the unusual tickling sensation, he was longing impatiently for her to get her hands down on his rump.

Secretly, he really did feel that his wife had somehow changed. On one hand, she had this shyness about her—she had just gone every shade of red, as if he were a complete stranger to her. But then there was also that lascivious look, followed by gentle touching. He pressed his backside against her thighs. *Maybe my being strict with her turned her on... maybe that therapy was good for something!* Frankly, he didn't really believe the latter.

"It's about Afghanistan, hon," he said, in answer to her question. "We're going to get that bastard."

Leslie responded to his opening up to her by slipping a hand under the band of his boxer shorts. He kept talking, although he was perhaps a bit more relaxed.

"You know, sweetie, I think we should attack Afghanistan. Our people out there, the whole world, they're all waiting for us to do something. And we have no plan of action. It's unbelievable! Can you imagine? The Pentagon, with all of its hundreds of generals, is not prepared. Rumsy is just beside himself with anger. Tenson is way ahead of us with his CIA."

"Afghanistan is a huge country," Leslie commented carefully. But the mightiest man on earth was deep in thought.

"There's a detailed section of a map on my desk in the Treaty Room. Get it for me please," he commanded and slipped away from her caresses. He pulled his right cheek taught with his left hand, and began pulling the SuperMach3 razor across it in slow, even strokes.

It was a topographical map riddled with various military symbols. In spite of a concentrated effort, Leslie was not able to orient herself. She called satellite pictures to mind, looked for a familiar relief, speculated over geographical contours. In vain. It was one of those military maps of engagement on an oversized scale that focused in detail on a border, a city, or a river. Tora Bora was the only geographic landmark that was labeled and made any kind of sense to her in light of the research she had done. She knew that the Taliban had their hiding places within this outcrop. Someone had sketched a skull and crossbones on the map. From it, hand-drawn lines led to two points marked by letters.

The president looked toward the door with a raised chin and a turned-down mouth, as Leslie returned waving the map in her hand.

"Did *you* draw that terrible skull on here?"

"*That?* Rumsy did that. You know what he's like. He wants to launch a nucueler... I mean nuclear attack. Three thousand dead in New York, *thirty* thousand dead in Afghanistan. That's what he said. What do you think?"

"Just a moment. At these points here? The Tora Bora caves? Nuclear weapons in Afghanistan? Has he lost his *mind*?"

She shot her hand up to her mouth, as if wishing she could take back her words.

He put the razor down on the glass shelf, patted the remnants of shaving cream off with the towel, splashed some aftershave on his cheeks—then, as if having a delayed reaction, he looked at her sharply.

"Exactly! That's exactly what I said to him. Hey, hon, you really know what you're talking about! Tora Bora. You know that means *Happy Widow*. In three days they'll have to rename it to *Howling Widow*. Because by then we will have pulverized all of those assholes."

"I think Tora Bora means *Old Widow*."

He measured her with a surprised look.

"You don't say—well, whatever it is, it's going to be fun smoking them out of there."

She stepped up to him, re-did his shirt, which he had buttoned wrong.

He pocketed the map, stroked Leslie in much the same way that he stroked Barney after he'd scolded him—putting her off until later. He hurried into the hall, then turned back one more time.

"When are you giving your speech?" He waved the yellow notes. "I want to work on this!"

Leslie held up her arms, uncomprehendingly.

"Tomorrow, darling, you know that. The speech is finished. You don't have to worry about it."

He pulled the door closed behind him, his face marked by an expression of confusion. He only just had time to put on a smile before the gap closed and it clicked shut.

Leslie felt her way over to the bedroom, where she sank into a chair, and pressed her hands to her temples.

She had been suddenly gripped by one of those melancholy moods that occasionally paralyzed her being and provided fertile ground for eruptions of self-doubt. The skull and crossbones flashed before her inner eye. Her fate seemed sealed, the end near. A catastrophe was closing in.

She had behaved like an idiot, letting her emotions guide her, letting her lust take over. *He's seen through me now. What have those people from the FBI been whispering in his ear?*

She already saw herself on the dock, thrown out of the house in disgrace. Their boys had a mother who had failed miserably when she was responsible for saving their young lives—when the only important thing was to remain cool and intelligent in all of her actions, when her aim had to be to get ice-cold control over everyone at the White House, to pass her mission with flying colors. *No, I am the worst kind of failure, in every sense of the word. And tomorrow... tomorrow, at the Library of Congress, my disgrace will be complete.*

She lay down on the bed with a sigh, longing to cuddle up to Ben, with his warm body, and the steady motion of his breathing... and somehow she slept. Her dreams were not beset by any frightening visions—it was as if her subconscious respected that she was already living a terrible nightmare.

68

The next day, Rosa delivered her carefully researched results for a psychiatric consult in New York City, as requested. She donned her glasses and pointed to the sheet that she had prepared.

"This woman here is supposed to be the best in her field. She has stellar references from various university professors. She has published many respected articles on her treatment methods for panic and anxiety syndromes in peer-reviewed journals. Her offices are on the corner of 79th Street and Fifth Avenue. There is no back door—however, there is a connection to the neighboring building, so that..."

"What else do you have?" Leslie interrupted. Seventy-ninth Street was too far up for her purposes.

"Jonathan Betason. Who, by the way, has a deep, vibrating voice that almost bowled me over, 69th Street between Madison and Fifth. You know what he said? He told me he needed a back door himself, and that he would be happy to receive the First Lady. He is a veteran of the National Guard, and he claims that he is very adept at shielding celebrity clients. He seemed great."

"Good. I like the sound of this... Betason, Rosa. Arrange an appointment for me."

"Consider it done, ma'am." Rosa flashed a set of pearly whites between the fire-red oval of her talkative lips. "Doctor Betason will take you any time on short notice. He says that it will be his honor. Just what we need. How does today sound, three o'clock?"

Leslie brooded over how she could manage to fit in everything that she needed to get done in New York. "Three o'clock is perfect," she decided. "I'll make it to my lecture at the Library of Congress by eight, right?"

She asked herself whether the excitement that was flooding her at this moment was showing on her face—but Rosa had turned her back. She was already calling the doctor's office. The day was set.

69

"Well, darling—I must say, you look very well to me," the president said lightly, and stuck an examining nose into the wine jug. "California Merlot, I would say," he analyzed knowingly. A smoked filet of salmon and a few lemon wedges had been set out as an attractive starter to a midday meal. Leslie cut a few slices, laid a piece of black bread on his plate.

"That's an Italian Amarone, darling."

She took the glass to her lips, took a sip.

"Why should I not be well?"

"You still have to ask?" the president said, with all the indignation he could muster and chew on a piece of salmon at the same time. "After everything that you've been through? You look younger—really young, sweetie. I meant what I said as a compliment!" He tasted the wine, swayed his head. "In wino veritas!"

Leslie chuckled.

"I think that's *vino*, not *wino*. And what do you mean by that?"

He waved her comment jovially aside.

"Vino, wino, whatever—it's just a saying. I'm happy that you're enjoying a good glass of wine again. You wanted to stop—alcohol stops the body from burning fat, you always said."

Leslie felt a knot in her throat. The president was inspecting her with slightly narrowed eyes, as if he had just unmasked her. But instead of realizing her fears, he smiled a very charming smile, and simply said, "You are beautiful, honey, really beautiful."

She deliberately did not reply, knowing that wives accepted the compliments of their husbands as a matter of course, without further ado. *Better change the topic!*

"My doctor explained to me on the phone that people can react to terrible emotional trauma in two ways," she looked at him with interest as he buttered his slice of black bread and topped it with a slice of salmon.

"You mean your shrink?"

"Exactly, Betason. Some, he explained, are paralyzed after a bad shock. They internalize everything, and have a hard time coming to terms with fate. People that fall within this category tend to stay bitter, and don't benefit much from therapy."

"And the other kind?" the president wanted to know, as a young waitress wearing a bright white uniform served a platter of Ravioli al Limone.

"One of our chef's specialties," she announced with half-hearted curtsy. The First Lady responded to the awkward courteousness with a polite, somewhat dismissive smile. The girl made a clumsy retreat, backing away sideways.

"The other kind thrives, because people in this category interpret their experience of narrowly having escaped death as a sign," Leslie lectured, dramatically emphasizing the bit about death. "They are happy to be alive. They see their narrow escape as a kind of second chance dealt to them by fate."

The president chewed on a piece of pasta, nodding his acknowledgment.

"Tastes good. And what category do you fall into?"

"You still have to ask?" she teased, laughingly. "According to Doctor Betason, I am among the two percent of people who transform traumatic experiences into a new zest for life. *Voilà!*"

"*Voilà?* Isn't that frog-speak?" the Commander-in-Chief of all of the United States Armed Forces asked in a suggestively drawn-out drawl. "Is the guy teaching you French now?"

"The traumatic event releases a great deal of new vitality," Leslie added pointedly. "Do you understand?" She sent him a dark, seductive look from under demurely lowered lashes. *Real Desperate Housewives stuff.* The president wiped his mouth with a glaringly white napkin.

"Did the doctor really say that?"

She puckered her lips slightly.

"Well, yes, something like that. At least that's how I interpreted what he said. Aren't you happy that I'm part of the two percent who grow and blossom as a result of tragedy?"

In jest, she sat up, thrust her chest out and swayed her shoulders boldly in mock pride. Her breasts strained against the material of her rose-colored blouse, capturing his covetous gaze.

"Sure, sure, absolutely. I'm very happy—just surprised, is all. You almost seem, to me, like you were reborn as a different woman. This Betastrahl . . . your doctor . . ."

"*Betason,*" she corrected him cheerfully.

". . . is he one of those sonny boys who likes to play hanky-panky with his female patients?"

"*Mister President!*" she protested reproachfully, and then continued on, her good spirits in no way dampened, "Fear not, sir. My libido is, however, fully intact."

As if to prove her point, she leaned back lasciviously and began to slide her bare foot along the inside of his thigh.

She sensed that he knew what she wanted, but he slithered away, sounding suddenly indignant.

"How is your foot, by the way? Have you made an appointment?"

"My foot? What's supposed to be wrong with my *foot*?" she burst out, and immediately wanted to bite her tongue. Hard.

"The shock seems to be messing with your memory," he laughed, obviously very amused. "The operation on your heel..."

"Oh, that! Yes, of course!" Sweating proverbial bullets, she casually raised one hand. "I'm not sure yet. Maybe physiotherapy will take care of it. Let's just see."

The discreet hum of the phone saved the situation. The president tossed his napkin on the table, stood up rapidly.

"That'll be Tenson." He picked up the receiver, said only a short *okay*, gave her a business-like wave, and headed for the door. Watching the man on television, his stiff, broad-legged gait had always left her cold. But here, from up close, she found him sexy against her will and better judgment. *Power corrupts...* she quoted to herself.

"...briefing..." she heard, and then he was gone.

She breathed a glad-I-managed-to-pull-that-one-off sigh. It was noon. Downstairs, a limousine was waiting to take her to Andrews Air Force Base, where a jet stood at the ready. And how did the rest of that nice little saying go?

...and absolute power corrupts absolutely! Shuddering, she noted that she would not mind being corrupted a bit by the most powerful man on earth. No. She wouldn't mind at all.

70

Psychiatrist Dr. Jonathan Betason greeted the First Lady in a bright waiting room littered with magazines, gallantly ushering her into what he humorously and pragmatically referred to as his *headlock* room.

Secret Service Agent Frank Sureman insisted on setting up his post in the waiting room while his partner, Rita, checked all three treatment rooms, and the bathroom, informed herself on the building layout and rear exit—which the doctor denied having—and finally assumed her post outside in the car.

Rosa had whispered to the First Lady that she should stick to Agent Sureman. Leslie had wanted to know what she meant.

"Your security guard. There is a bunch of new people in the Secret Service since 9/11. You know what I mean," she had said with a conspiratorial glance. "The White House is a bigger rumor mill than a hairdressing convention. Frank is old school. No one will ever get a word out of him. Take him with you when you go to New York—or anywhere else, for that matter."

Frank Sureman was a good 5 foot 10, had dark brown skin, an athletic body, and a pleasant swagger when he walked. His shaven head shone in competition with his bright, hazel eyes. A thin mustache ran past the corners of his mouth, where it turned into a short, black beard that was shaven to a neat point. Leslie might have thought she was looking straight at Gordon from Spin City, were it not for the bulge under his left shoulder, where his 9mm Glock Police Special sat casually in its holster. All in all, Sureman seemed very present, tough, and professional, but was still pleasant to be around.

Doctor Betason was a stocky Jewish gentleman somewhere in his mid-fifties. The thick salt and pepper hair that fell in strands over his lofty brow lent his head a heroic dimension—but his clean-shaven, ruddy face was benevolent, Leslie noted, and his gentle eyes inspired trust. He didn't offer Leslie the classic black leather couch, but instead motioned an invitation for her to take a seat on a swivel chair—also black leather—in front of his desk.

Leslie gazed at the framed pictures of diplomas that hung on the wall, then she looked searchingly into his eyes, which sparkled adventurously behind his glasses.

"You see," he said, without sitting down, "this door here leads to my garage, where I park my old Mercedes."

Leslie looked perplexed—she didn't see a door.

Smiling, Betason manipulated a piece of the bookshelf. A knob appeared, and he pushed the disguised door open with his broad shoulder. Leslie peered through the crack into the dark hallway.

"The garage is in the backyard, which exits onto 68th Street. Very practical. I can quietly disappear without the patients who are waiting out front noticing that I'm not here when I'm here." He gave a big belly laugh.

To Betason's surprise, Leslie got up, stepped briskly through the secret door, then down the hallway, to inspect the garage. A sleek Corvette was parked next to the veteran Mercedes, and a motorbike stood squeezed in the back. A small window in the garage door allowed a good view of the yard, from which a narrow concrete driveway led out onto the cross street.

Leslie pursed her lips, nodded like a connoisseur, and returned to the office, where she lay on the couch without further ado, even though the psychiatrist had not prompted her in any way to do so. Betason pulled up a chair, unperturbed, and sat on it backward, his short legs circling the backrest.

"Your assistant informed me of your situation. You were fortunate enough to escape…"

"Oh, let's not get into that," Leslie interrupted him animatedly. "Only one thing is of any importance here, doctor—and that is that no one learns of my visit to you. The fact that the First Lady was almost killed by a terrorist act is to remain a national secret. Furthermore, doctor, I need a two-hour session. All that you will be asked to do is to let me into your office, and to let me out again through the same door once my time is up."

The doctor nodded thoughtfully, as if he sensed that a plot of giant proportions was afoot, in which he was to play a central role.

"I understand. I will give you a key to the back door downstairs, for when you come back." He dug around in his pocket and produced a bunch of keys, which he placed on the table. Leslie was honestly impressed by Dr. Betason's quick and casually practical compliance.

"Then we're clear on our agreement?"

"I'm probably getting myself into trouble, but my instinct tells me that you know what you're doing. You can count on me. Apart from that, do you need any kind of professional counsel?" His broad grin was infectious.

Leslie smiled conspiratorially, "I hate our dog."

"*Barney*? The entire nation knows him."

"He growls at me as if I were a stranger," Leslie said, compulsively playing with fire.

"The Demon of the Pit Syndrome," Doctor Betason explained calmly. "Cerberus guarded the gate to Hades, as you probably know. Let's say that you went through limbo on September 11. A hail of debris, screaming, fire and death all around. An enormous emotional trauma. And a particular incident within this experience remains fixed in your mind. Can you think of such an incident in your case?"

She shook her head.

"No matter. The dog that is bothering you could be a symbolic Cerberus. A person, an object. At any rate. Post-traumatic repercussions are complex. There's no need to worry. I can't stand pesky mutts either, and there's nothing amiss with me except that I could do with more of what most healthy men of my age need every once in a while."

His smile was so disarmingly charming, that she lowered her eyes. Which certainly didn't mean that she was playing into the innuendo. She was, after all, the First Lady—and, as such, it was her duty to maintain the honor of the White House. But she made a mental note of the unreserved comment just made by this presumptuous, but nevertheless apparently very capable psychiatrist.

"By the way, just a routine question—are you taking any medications?" he asked, looking at her intensely over the edge of his glasses.

She stole a glance at her watch, got up and took the key that the doctor had removed from his keychain for her. She hesitated for a moment. "Medications?" she repeated. "Well, okay, yes, I take testosterone."

"Aha." He eyed her with new interest. "Had you been losing interest in sex?" he wanted to know as he scribbled a note on his pad.

Leslie smiled a graciously tolerant smile, as befit a woman of her status.

"No, certainly not, Dr. Betason. My sexual appetite has always been healthy. I have been taking testosterone for a long time. To answer the question I'm sure you are about to ask—my father advised me to take it. I'm sure he knew what he was talking about. Do you take anything of that nature?"

Doctor Betason furrowed his brow—his lips moved as if searching for a fitting response.

"I see," Leslie noted with a smile. "In other words, yes."

"Testosterone is the fuel of love," Betason said, somewhat piqued, trying to save face. "The sexual centers of the male brain are approximately twice as large as corresponding structures in the female brain. Men literally have more sex on the brain than women do. Many women believe that testosterone is an exclusively male hormone. This is a widely held error. If a woman's testosterone levels sink below a certain level, she will completely lose interest in the sexual act. Her libido will waste away. Your Dad, you said, told you...?"

"Yes, he had the foresight to educate me on the matter. I'll see you later, then," she nodded at him, moving toward the secret door. "And please don't forget to get some coffee to Frank, my security agent. He takes it with milk, no sugar."

Dr. Betason remained at his desk for a few minutes after the secret door had closed behind the First Lady. Finally, he looked over at the small, discreetly hidden clock on his wall, got up, walked the few steps over to the couch, stretched out on it, and closed his eyes. A faint smile lingered on his cultivated, urban features for quite a while after he had dozed off.

71

Leslie leaned against the silver-gray Corvette in the garage, soaking up the musty, oil-soaked air like balm. The sports car was open; a box of Cuban cigars lay on the passenger seat. Leslie felt a sensual flood streaming through her body. She could not have said whether the red leather of the bucket seats, or her testosterone confession or her imminent expedition provoked it. Her hands were steady as she pulled the wig from her purse. A quick look around revealed that there was no one in sight. There was no sound of approaching footsteps; the only thing to be heard in the isolated garage was the dull noise of traffic.

Quickly she pulled on the wig, adjusted it. A completely different woman looked back at her from the Corvette's rearview mirror. Satisfied, she applied a set of fake eyelashes, and dark rouge, rubbed her lips against each other, and was ready to set out. Before exiting onto the bright backyard, she removed her jacket and donned a pair of fashionable, tinted D&G sunglasses.

She unsuspectingly hastened around the corner onto 68th Street, where she suddenly found herself with a scream frozen in her throat. An ugly, jagged piece of piping flew past her, grazing her shoulder and almost bowling her off her feet. Two startled faces looked at her from under light blue protective helmets.

"Can't you watch what you're doing?" she scolded. The workers stammered an apology, a third, on the telephone company truck, whistled admiringly through his teeth as if Madonna had personally appeared before him.

I probably look like a vamp! Not even Sureman would recognize me if he turned up here now!

The M66 bus, on which she had traveled to the West Side so often, droned past her. Everything seemed so familiar to her now, that she would dearly have loved to just walk away from this whole pile of shit. Why was she doing all of this? She cast her eyes up toward the light blue, clear sky—it held no answer.

It took Leslie only ten minutes to walk to Third Avenue, where five lanes of lunchtime traffic roared toward her. She crossed over further down at 67th Street, and found herself at the newsstand just moments later.

High piles of the *Post* and *Times* lay adjacent to each other, weighed down by metal bars. Leslie scanned the headlines, looked around thoroughly and inconspicuously, then entered the store. Out of awkwardness, she bought a pack of dental gum as she dialed the number. Ben immediately responded. His voice sounded like home.

72

The freshly crowned First Lady, now Leslie Palmer once again, allowed herself to fall, exhausted, on the couch of Ben's book, magazine, and jumble strewn bachelor pad. Ben had tidied up—or whatever he called tidying up. A bunch of red roses welcomed her from a too-small crystal vase on the grand piano, which took up a third of the room. The Champagne on the drawing room table was as much a harbinger of his unmistakable intentions, as was the masculine aftershave that wafted around her beguilingly as he sat down next to her. The high-tech cinema display screen showed the news on mute. Evidently they were talking about new airport security measures.

Ben kissed her softly behind the ear, just next to her hairline—that very erogenous spot of skin with the first fine wisps of hair. It seemed that he found a new, intoxicating way to turn her on each and every time.

But she tore her attention back, winding herself out of his embrace.

"Ben, we can't—not today. We have to have a serious talk. I'm up to my neck in trouble. It's tearing me apart inside. I can hardly bear it."

She stood and walked to the other end of the room.

"Nobody can know that I was here. Nobody! You have to promise me. Nothing that is spoken here leaves this room—*nothing,* okay? This has to do with my secret mission. Unfortunately I can't talk about it. We haven't met, you haven't seen me. Is that clear?"

Ben had grasped the gravity of the situation—his head bowed, he went to put the bottle of Champagne back in the refrigerator. When he returned, he was looking as serious as his face would ever allow.

"Leslie, I only hope that you're not seeing ghosts. Is this about that CIA guy? About the emails? Maybe you should keep yourself out of all of that, whatever it…"

"Shut up, stop, *for Christ's sake!* You have no idea, not a damn clue, about what is going on, believe me."

"Fine, I'm stupid, I'm ignorant. All I know is that I don't know what you're up to. So, what's the plan?"

"I have to know who Bronx is exchanging emails with. Do you remember?" She spoke in an urgent, pleading tone. "You told me that your amazing program could trace that email traffic back to its origins. Right?"

Ben nodded uncomfortably.

"I don't have time. Get me that information. I have to know who is in contact with him, his bank, his account number. You can do that, can't you?"

"That's all, is it? You're sure you don't need his shoe-size as well?"

Ben turned away, shaking his head.

"You'll manage, Ben. You can do this. I need you." She embraced him from behind, rubbing his six-pack abs, his muscular thighs.

He turned abruptly.

"You're playing with fire, baby. This is risky—it's criminal to be more precise!"

She stepped back, staring at him.

"You're chickening out on me! Criminal, you say? And what about the *mess* I'm in?"

Ben raised his hands to shoulder height in an appeasing gesture.

"Okay, okay! I'll try, I'd do anything for you, you know that. But be careful. They'll be watching you. What do you think this whole deal is about—what's the big danger?"

She shifted her shoulders, undecided. He looked at her lowered head, pulled her toward him. She practically melted into him.

"That's what we have to find out, Ben. That's exactly the thing. I don't have much more time right now. Send the information to my email account at ONI."

"The building is no longer standing. It collapsed after the towers—there's nothing left but rubble."

"My email is still functioning. I have to go now. You know I don't want to."

"Let's look at things from another angle. What if you go to the FBI. They could run a covert investigation."

She slowly shook her head.

"I've gone over all the angles, Ben. If this were just about me, then yes—I wouldn't hesitate to do that. But there's more on the line... So much more."

After a while, she spoke in a more composed tone into the gloomy silence that had spread between them.

"This whole thing is killing me inside. Please, help me, will you?"

She stopped, and covered her face with her hands. Seeing this, Ben seemed to gather his pride.

"Fine, then it'll just have to be you and me alone against the powerful, and the highest ranks of the Secret Service."

"No," Leslie countered, feeling a renewed sense of courage. "We won't be completely on our own. I still have allies who will be able to help me. People who know their way around the spying game."

She didn't want to reveal any more than this. *Only give out as much information as absolutely necessary*—that had to be her principle. Even when it came to Ben.

"So, what do we do now?"

He sounded a bit sorry for himself.

"I have to run, Ben. I'm sorry. I have an important meeting I have to get to." She said, kissed him passionately on the lips, then raced into the bathroom to hastily touch up her disguise.

Ben suddenly appeared grinning in the doorway, casually swinging a revolver. His pose was straight out of an old Bogart and Cagney movie—even his speech was perfect.

"Don't forget your *piece,* doll."

"You're a sweetheart, *Bogey!*" She pocketed the weapon with a smile. "By the way, is everything okay in my apartment?"

They had reached the hall downstairs. "Leslie, you remember..." he said. She stood and turned to him. "Those coded messages about the faculties of economy, medicine... an enrollment deadline?"

She nodded, her eyes growing large.

"I... I've been wanting to tell you this for a long time..." he began to stammer.

"I sent those things to the FBI, and..."

"And? Who else?"

"Well, the FBI's deputy chief of counterterrorism..."

She interrupted him.

"Get to the point, Ben—damn it, I have to go!"

"He called me back and thanked me. They received messages from the NSA, and..."

"And? What did they have to say?"

"They wanted to know if I had any other information. Of course I said I didn't."

"Are you sure?"

"I swear. You can depend on me."

"Man, I really do hope so." She had begun speaking ominously slowly. "And who all else did you contact?"

"Well, I thought, the CIA..."

"*Shit*, Ben, you sent that stuff over to the fucking *CIA*? Who the hell did you address it to!"

She looked at him, stunned. He looked back, just as appalled. She had never used language that foul around him before. Outside, a tenant was sticking a key into the lock of the front door. Ben composed himself a bit.

"Come!"

They stepped outside. He raised an apologetic hand to his chest.

"I addressed it to the Director of the CIA. He'd be able to put things in motion, I told myself... None of them got back to me though."

"I hope this doesn't end in a catastrophe," she moaned, "I can't believe it."

"We were on the right track, baby," he whispered, almost begging.

They kissed demurely out on the sidewalk, brushed cheeks with each other on both sides, old Hollywood style. Finally, Ben planted one more emotional kiss on the beautiful curve of her lips. Standing on the stairs outside his apartment building, he watched as she got into a cab at the corner.

She didn't turn around to look at him, not even through the back window of the taxi.

Whatever lies behind me, stays there. There's only one way to go now—and that's forward! She closed her eyes. Just as those people probably had before they leaped to their deaths from the burning Twin Towers.

73

The television stations had sent out their second-tier people. CBS nighttime editor Bob Marks was lounging in a chair that he had placed beneath a painting of some cultural icon in the lecture hall with the vaulted wooden hallway. He adjusted his headset.

"Can you hear me?"

The cameraman gave him a thumbs-up in lieu of answering.

"First get a wide shot of the audience, then zoom in on her as she begins to speak. There are two senators front and left—get a close-up of them when the audience applauds."

"Sure thing," the cameraman answered. But Bob knew all too well that nothing was ever completely sure. Surprises were always possible—like when the president mispronounced something, or suddenly decided to make an unforeseen announcement, or just sat there—silent and help-less—as he had in that Florida classroom, in front of that bunch of kids, when someone had whispered to him about the attacks on the World Trade Center. Such moments called for a good reporter to be on his toes. The very respectable First Lady, on the other hand—Mrs. Well-Behaved Schoolmistress / Prissy Librarian—was really not very newsworthy. Her appearances usually didn't make prime time.

The director of the library had begun his introductory speech, which he emphasized with dramatically expansive arm movements.

"Ladies and Gentlemen, we are proud to welcome this wonderful, dynamic guest in our midst today. Allow me to present to you—the First Lady of the United States."

There was a surge of applause. The president's wife walked onto the stage with measured steps, her head slightly lowered, her elbows pressed against her sides in a typical posture, as if she needed to keep her dress from somehow slipping out of place, her loosely held hands raised to the level of her chest.

Bob whispered into the mike, "The dress, do you have her dress?"

Her appearance was very preppy, almost a little tarted up. She wore her hair in a chic, obviously new style that was better suited to downtown

Manhattan as far as Bob could make out. He caught himself reflecting stupidly that downtown Manhattan was anything other than chic at this point.

"Ladies and Gentlemen—I am particularly honored and pleased that I have been invited to address this wonderful audience today..."

Bob turned his head, sending his yawn toward the anonymous wall, then began rummaging around for the lecture notes, which resulted in a distinct crinkling noise. This got him a dirty look from an old, spectacled lady, who fit the image of a strict village schoolmarm.

"...our nation, we all are faced with a daunting test of our faith, and in this hour of need our thoughts go out to the family members who have lost their loved ones in this terrible, treacherous attack..."

"The audience!" Bob hissed into the mike. The camera turned to focus on earnest faces, pausing on an older couple wiping tears from their eyes.

"Well done," Bob praised. He raised his eyes from the small monitor at his feet.

"...In spite of the pain, in spite of the shock—and I would add: in spite of the anger—that we find ourselves almost overwhelmed by, our task is to remain level-headed now and in the difficult days to come..."

Bob's face turned to a concentrated frown as he searched for this part of the speech in the notes. It was not to be found.

"...We owe it to our children, I have two that I am concerned about myself, and to the youth of our nation to be good role-models, and to set an example of composure during this time of crisis..."

"She's ad-libbing," Bob advised, as the First Lady turned her head slightly to the left, so that she seemed to be looking straight at him. The open collar of her shimmering, reddish-violet blouse complimented the graceful line of her neck as she continued. "The media needs to be attentive, careful in its investigations, and truthful in its reporting. Its responsibility to all of us is significant. Our great American author, Mark Twain, who lived from 1835 to 1910, was a great observer of human nature. He once said. 'Get your facts straight first, and then you can distort them as much as you please...'"

There was a wave of laughter from the audience, in which one could hear a distinct note of irony.

"Watch it Bob, she's talking to you," the cameraman joked. But Bob felt a slight stab to his insides. What was she trying to say?

"In spite of the terrible tragedy that has shaken us, that has frightened us deeply, Ladies and Gentlemen, we cannot allow ourselves to throw the bathwater out with the baby. We must ask ourselves why it is that our nation has been made the victim of such a catastrophe. Perhaps we should recall the famous adage, that it is easy to forget where one has buried the peace pipe, but all too easy to remember where one has buried the hatchet."

Very composed, she reached for her glass, calmly took a sip of water, and looked around with a smile.

Throw the bathwater out with the baby... "Hey, did you get that lapse? It should be the other way around. *Throw the baby out with the bathwater*, which means to overreact. Looks like her old man's rubbing off on her," Bob sneered quietly. He glanced furtively over at the bespectacled woman, as if fearing a look of punishment from her.

The cameraman had captured the two senators, and their furrowed brows.

"Mark Twain, the reading of whom my foundation encourages, was of the unfortunately correct opinion that education is the adult world's organized defense against youth. I believe that children should read in order to form their own beliefs and opinions, and I call upon you to celebrate their freedom of thought, even if it seems like a sinister proposition to you."

Bob shook his head in wonder. The woman was just saying whatever popped into her mind—not at all following what was scripted.

"Allow me to quote Mark Twain one more time: 'The difference between the right word and the almost right word is the difference between lightning and a lightning bug.' So, what is right, and what is not? Often that, which appears to be correct, is false—and conversely, what seems false may later prove to be true. Every human being is a moon with a dark side, which is kept carefully hidden from everyone else. Reading is an education in freedom, and in critical analysis. Sometimes, when I hear our politicians giving their speeches, I ask myself—have they lost 'the right words'? Ladies and Gentlemen, we owe it to our children to set the intellectual bar high. I have been told that I have a lunar face."

A laugh relieved the latent discomfort that had spread through the room. The camera showed the audience.

"Perhaps. But what is my dark side?"

She paused. Only when complete silence had replaced the scattered mutterings of the crowd did she continue.

"My dark side is an accident that I had when I was seventeen years old. It was 1973, November 6, in my hometown of Midland, in West Texas."

"Hey, this is sensational, zoom in as far as you can!" Bob whispered excitedly. This time his indignant neighbor's angry stare caught him like a poisoned arrow.

"I kept the story a secret for a long time, but in light of the tragedy that befell us all on September 11, my little personal drama seems very dim. The time has come to talk about it."

A whisper passed through the audience, heads turned to one another as if to seek in each other's faces confirmation of what they couldn't believe they just heard.

"Michael, a friend of mine from college, and I had been drinking that night. It had been one of those countless, wild parties, where we also smoked grass sometimes..."

More whispering and muttering.

"I took the wheel of the car, and we drove outside of town looking for an isolated spot. We were kids, who thought they knew everything. I was driving fast, way too fast, without any concern. We were chatting, joking around...and exchanging kisses. Then, suddenly, there was a bend in the road. It was late; the light of the moon was dim. Suddenly we saw the glaring headlights of a truck heading toward us. This monster of a vehicle just appeared out of nowhere as I followed the curve, aiming straight at me. I tore at the steering wheel, but I wasn't quite fast enough. The truck hit the back of the car. I'll never forget the sound of the screeching metal before we went over the embankment. Our car rolled over a couple of times. The engine was still running when it finally came to a stop. There was an eerie crackling sound, a smell of gas. I have no recollection of how I managed to get out. Michael was nowhere to be seen. I called, and I screamed. I scrambled back up to the road. A bus came by after what seemed like ages. They later found Michael's body under the car. He was dead."

She looked around the audience. Not a sound. You could have heard a pin drop.

The camera was closely focused on the First Lady's face.

"Man! Well this sure is news! Holy crap!" Bob panted and wondered how fast they would be able to broadcast this footage. Four other stations had their crews in the room. He read in the faces of his colleagues that they were having the exact same thoughts. The race for the scoop, for the breaking headline news, was on.

The First Lady now spoke more softly, and even more urgently.

"I was to blame for his death. I could have avoided the accident. If I had been paying attention, Michael would still be alive today."

In a stronger voice, her head held high, she now asked the members of her audience, who were staring up at her as if dazed:

"Where are *your* dark sides, Ladies and Gentlemen? Do we want to be bright bolts of lightning, or nondescript lightning bugs when we try to reach our children? My two children, dear audience members, are like most children in this country—full of hope, and ready to achieve something special in their lives. They believe in truthfulness. Let us support their belief that their opportunities are endless. God bless America, God bless our children! Thank you."

The applause wouldn't stop. The people seated in the front row rose, the senators hesitantly following suit. The director marched up on stage bearing a grandiose bouquet of flowers. His words of thanks to the speaker were drowned out by the deafening acclaim. The First Lady smiled graciously, holding her head characteristically bowed, slightly to one side.

She really does have a lunar face, Bob thought, before he ran out to the television van. If everything went well, then the First Lady's sensational speech would make it on the ten o'clock news.

74

Admiration spoke from Rosa's dark eyes as she brought in the newspapers early the next morning. Leslie had been beset by doubts the entire night—had it been wise to attract attention with her speech? But the television commentary before midnight, and then the morning talk shows, all showed the First Lady in a flattering light. Leslie sank onto the chaise lounge with the *Washington Post* under her arm, but then immediately let the paper slide to the floor and closed her eyes. *I have to act. Time is running out. Do something. Yes—but what, and how?*

She stood abruptly, started pacing the room. Her plan was gaining shape, but she felt she had to clear her mind. She walked up to the top floor, where a treadmill in the gym promised to quench her craving for physical activity. Once upstairs, she opened the first door, and stopped short. Instead of a row of top of the line fitness machinery, she was looking at a comfortable sofa in a dimly lit room with pink wallpaper, and thick drapes covering its only window.

She was inexplicably overcome by hot, unbridled desire. An almost audible static of carnal lust led her to sink onto the sofa, her legs slightly spread. Her protocol frock did not allow her to properly feel her fingers, but even the pressure that she was able to exert through the material made her shiver. *If only Ben were here! Could I at least call him?*

Seeing a chrome Kleenex dispenser on the little glass table, she pulled out a tissue. A small, pink cell phone slid out from behind the box. There it lay, as if forgotten. She grasped for it and pressed the call button to see the last number dialed. Accidentally, really wanting to turn it off, she pressed the same button again, and found herself connected. Frantically she tried to stop the process, but then she already heard the sound of a pleasantly deep male voice:

"Sweet thing? Are you looking for me?"

She startled.

"What?"

"Is it time for your whip?"

She finally managed to disconnect, but it was too late. The call had been placed, and someone had answered. *Whip? Sweet thing. Am I nuts?*

Never mind, girlfriend! She rose, determined. She would not have noticed the wallpaper-covered door, had there not been a big, lazy fly crawling around close to its margins. As Leslie looked more closely, her heart started to pound. A secret door?! She walked up to it, pushed against the wall—and it swung open. Her eyes widened. A hazy light automatically came on to reveal a lush, red boudoir. A love nest! A broad bed, a mirror, a half-open door to a bathroom, towels…

And all of a sudden, a slender man stood before her.

"Did you call for me, sweet thing?"

Leslie stared at him, speechless. *How dare he! How had this impudent person even managed to get in here?*

He smiled and came closer. Very close. He smelled manly. His hand felt for her hand and—it was beyond belief—pressed it to his groin, where she could feel a bulge, its hardness. She recoiled, shocked.

He raised his eyebrows in obvious surprise. Leslie finally realized what was going on. She smiled and said coolly, "Not now."

She shook her head firmly.

"No, not now." Gathering her wits, she quickly raised her hand to her forehead, feigning one of her notorious, all-powerful migraines.

Did the First Lady have a lover? Right in the middle of the White House? Who on earth is this guy?

"I—*em*—I have to get back," she stammered, stumbled out into the hall, ran down the stairs. Finally back in the living room, she threw herself, exhausted, into an armchair.

She stared at the pink cell phone, still clasped tightly in her hot hand, in disbelief. She checked the list of called numbers. The name Ted lit up on the display. *Ted?*

At this moment, the regular phone buzzed. She crept toward it with a sense of disquiet, lifted the receiver.

"Will you accept a call, Madam?"

It was the operator with the New York accent.

"Who is it?"

"Your daughter, ma'am. She tried the direct line earlier, but you were busy."

Leslie's thoughts were racing. *Which of the twin girls was calling? What direct number?*

"Madam?"

"Thank you." Leslie pressed the button and said a cautious, "Hello?"

"Who the hell are you? And what the hell are you doing in my home?" an agitated voice reverberated in her ear, piercing through her heart like a knife. She had lost her ability to speak. She stared at the handset as if she expected a grotesque ghost to fly from it and into her face at any moment. She had just heard *her own voice.* Speaking to her as if from a grave. Leslie's mind spun. Where was her quick thinking now that she needed it? How could she be speaking to a dead person? Why had she pretended to be her daughter? She stood frozen, understanding nothing, feeling nothing but dread.

"Hello? It's me! Your favorite daughter. Gotcha, ha ha!" said the same voice, now in a conciliatory tone. "Lighten up! It was just a little joke for the tape. You know the switchboard is always recording."

A joke for the tape? Switchboard is recording? Why was she pretending to be her daughter? That voice could never pass for that of a twenty-year-old... Leslie, who suddenly realized that she was speaking to no other than First Lady Sarah Crawford, tried hard to play along, stammered the name of one of the president's daughters. She couldn't think of anything else to do.

"We need to talk."

She sat and heaved out a breath of air that swept like a hurricane across her desk. She pulled herself together.

"Okay, when? Where are... Where are you? Why don't you come by?"

"Can't," the voice responded. "I'm on Wilson Boulevard in Arlington. We can meet at *Victoria's Secret.* In an hour?"

"Who else is... Are you alone?"

"Yes, I am. Something else—can you bring me your wool sweater, the lilac Missoni, you know the one. Can you do that?"

Leslie began to see clearly. The woman—First Lady Sarah

Crawford!—was speaking in veiled messages. *The switchboard is always recording. Missoni sweater*... She was trying to tell her something. *But what?*

"Okay, darling," Leslie said in a composed voice—hell-bent on dealing with the situation, whatever that might be. "I can arrange that. See you later, okay?"

The voice on the other end sounded unconcerned.

"Fine, there aren't any sparrows on the rooftops over her. *See you!*"

No sparrows on the rooftops? Sparrows whistled things from rooftops. I get it. Now she had everything back under control. *No one is to know about our meeting. Simple as that!*

Like her subject, Sarah, Leslie valued an impeccable sense of style. Even under the worst kind of stress, she would not be caught without at least a light application of make-up. She hurried into the bathroom, put berry red lipstick on her lips, dabbed beige base on her cheeks, selected a moonstone color for her eyelids. All the while, she was racking her brain. How was it even possible that the First Lady was alive? How had the woman survived? *What had stopped her from not just walking into the White House and kicking the imposter to the curb? Does the president know that she's alive? No sparrows on the roof. The First Lady had signaled discretion. But what if this was a trap?*

Leslie suddenly felt a sense of panic, she raced for the wardrobe, pulling aside jackets and jeans—and there it was, the Missoni wool pullover. She slipped on a pair of designer jeans, stuffed the pullover into a paper bag she found, hurried to the phone and ordered a limousine.

Her doubts began to flare up again. What if she failed because the First Lady exposed her. What then? Mission Impossible. Her boys would have to pay the price. Bronx would kill them just as certainly as he had murdered her father in cold blood. Should she inform Bronx? One thing was sure—she had to keep the First Lady from talking. Leslie Palmer could not afford to be exposed. But what should she do? Shut her up? She'd need a weapon for that. She paced the room, undecided. Then she reached a decision—the First Lady had to appear to be dead. To kill a corpse would be the lesser of two evils.

She ran back to the dresser, pulled open random drawers, rummaged under blouses, and finally found her little colt with the mother-of-pearl grip. It still had six rounds in its barrel. She was placing it in her purse, under the pullover, when the telephone buzzed in the living room—the limousine was waiting for her downstairs.

75

Leslie felt as though she was sitting on pins and needles in the roomy passenger cabin of the spacious Ford. She was still contemplating whether to let Bronx in on the latest developments. She finally dismissed the notion as unnecessary. As if to deposit the final straw on the camel's back, her cell phone buzzed aggressively. *Bronx!*

"I have to speak to you."

Wonderful. Apparently, he also possessed the gift of telepathy.

"I'm out. Come to Arlington Shopping Mall," she instructed him rudely.

"When?"

"Right now," she snapped, described a meeting place, and hung up. She thought it might not be a bad idea to have Bronx near by after all, just in case she needed help. In addition, she wanted to meet him on her home ground... *right in the middle of a bunch of hot garters, slips, and push-up bras... let him just squirm in discomfort, screwed up-worm that he is!*

Leslie walked up and down in front of the window, with its tempting display of scantily clad mannequins. Through the glass, her eyes fell on the back of a woman rummaging around in a pile of colorful slips on a discount table. *That could be the First Lady*, she thought, just as a hand tapped her on the shoulder.

Bronx grinned at her stupidly. It was going to be a short meeting. The bane of her existence did not, however, have any intentions of following her into the candy-pink lingerie store, remaining stubbornly planted on the sidewalk. "The president will be attending a reception at the Plaza Hotel in

Manhattan. You will accompany him. This coming Sunday," he whispered.

Plaza, New York?

"What am I supposed to do there?" Leslie whispered back, even though she knew the answer and was using the exchange only to discreetly scan the surroundings. It was obvious—Bronx had his henchmen with him. She had easily spotted Leon, that hulk of a man whose head looked like his mother had dropped him on it once too often. The slant-eyed one had to be around somewhere, too. So she had to be twice—no, three times as circumspect.

"The president will be addressing a group of business people. His aim is to crank up investments in spite of what happened at the World Trade Center. As I said: you will accompany him. It seems you will be participating in a discussion panel, or something of the sort, organized by *Executive Woman*."

"Where?"

"Plaza Hotel. Corner of Central Park South and Fifth. The day of reckoning."

"*Reckoning?* I thought this was about investments."

Instead of answering, Bronx reached under his leather jacket and produced a white purse.

"Take this. You need to keep it with you at all times."

Leslie stared at the white Fendi.

"What am I supposed to do with it?"

He stood before her in a broad-legged stance, pressed the purse to her chest.

"This bag here is my reassurance, dear Leslie. It will be our sign of recognition. By carrying it, you will be signaling me that you are in the process of carrying out your mission. Is that clear?"

She looked into his cold, blue eyes.

"If I do not see you carrying this purse when you enter the Plaza Hotel with the president, then I will conclude that you have backed out, and are disobeying orders. Then it will all be over for your boys. Have I made myself perfectly clear?"

Leslie caught her breath. Mechanically stroking over the fine leather of the purse, she felt a bulge. She was surprised at how firm her voice sounded.

"What is in here?"

He opened it, and held it under her nose. Leslie saw the blood-red cloth. It felt greasy to her when she reached in and touched it. She also felt the hard object that was wrapped inside of it.

Bronx still had her fixed with a penetrating stare.

"The weapon. Ready to fire."

He stepped up to her, whispered a sentence in her ear that seemed to reflect in her cold and bloodless face.

"With the revolver," he now said in a conversational volume. "Six bullets. You will receive further information. Stay in touch."

He gave her a small, hard push.

"My reassurance!" he repeated before he turned briskly.

Plaza Hotel. Manhattan. An assassination!

Her blood felt as if it had turned to ice. She swayed sideways slightly, held on to the window frame. When she looked up, Bronx was gone.

Although her inner turmoil showed little sign of abating, she eventually at least felt steady enough to walk. She slid the strap of the bag over her shoulder, hurried through the broad glass door into the pink *Victoria's Secret* boutique, then stepped up behind the woman who was still busy having fun with the discounted slips and suspender belts.

"Are you looking for a Missoni sweater?" she asked quietly.

The face that turned toward her twitched in bewilderment, looking quite as if it were contemplating the vision of a ghost.

"Oh, excuse me—I mistook you for someone else," Leslie stammered. She looked around further. A dark, woolen cap was moving around in a little grove of negligee stands.

Leslie cut across the store in that direction. But the cap had disappeared.

"Are you looking for a Missoni?"

Leslie spun around—and found herself looking into her own face. No, it was not the reflection of a mirror image. It was *her*—Sarah

Crawford, the First Lady—smiling as easily as if she were standing on the manicured lawn of the Rose Garden behind the White House.

"We can talk here."

Leslie found herself overcome by shock and alarm.

"I don't believe so!"

She grabbed her look-alike by the arm.

"Come!"

Slit-eyed Chenny, who was sauntering past the cash registers with a hat pulled down low over his forehead, definitely wasn't blending in. *The ass that sat on my dining room table!*

"Out! The other door!"

It had started to drizzle outside. The women ran toward the Ford.

"Rick Bronx, a CIA agent, is behind all of this," Leslie panted.

Agent Sureman tore open the door as they piled into the back. Speaking quietly into his phone, Sureman started the engine. Leslie's breath was coming in bursts.

"We're safe here. Where do we go now?"

"To the harbor."

"Fine. Nobody would recognize you," Leslie whispered. "You look like Michael Jackson."

The women laughed. Leslie leaned over to the driver. *What was he waiting for?*

"Frank…" The sentence stuck in her throat.

The ensuing bang was terrible. Glass shattered. Sureman slumped down in his seat. Up ahead, Leslie saw a black vehicle. It pulled away from the curb, its beefy front-end heading straight toward them.

The real First Lady groped for the door handle, a wild scream issuing from her throat. "We need to get out!" she groaned.

"No!"

Leslie grabbed the closed umbrella, leaned over the back of the seat, and pressed down on the gas pedal with the metal tip, simultaneously ripping the gear into reverse. The massive Ford shot back. There was a grinding of metal as they grazed a parked car, then they were swaying toward the intersection. Cars honked frantically. A bus screeched to a halt. The heavy sedan swerved sideways and crashed into a hotdog stand on the corner. Customers and pedestrians scattered.

Leslie let out a deep, raspy breath, and surveyed the chaos. The bus, which was standing sideways, barring the intersection, was shielding them.

She dashed to the driver's side door, pulled it open, and froze—a black, bloody hole gaped in the middle of Sureman's forehead. His eyes were wide. *What should she do?*

"Help me!"

In a concerted effort, the women pulled the corpse from behind the steering wheel, out onto the street. Sureman's leather jacket fell open. Leslie immediately noted the bulge in his inside pocket. Reflexively, she reached inside and pulled out papers and an ID badge. She pushed them at the First Lady.

"Here, take this, and get back in!" she commanded sharply, threw herself behind the wheel, shifted into drive, and was already swerving back onto the street before the back door slammed shut.

"Stop right now! We have to go to the police! This is insane!" the First Lady screamed from the back.

"I need you to shut your trap right now. The people who are after us are very, very *mean*. If you value your life, then you will let me drive." Leslie felt a fresh rush of adrenaline. She grew coldly calm, her hand found its way straight to the button that activated the official vehicle's emergency lights.

"Look around back there and see if you can find a gun," she called to the back.

"What?"

"Behind the back rest, in the rear, a weapon. Move it! There has to be a flap there or something."

"Who are these people? We have to inform the president. Why would anyone want to kill me when I'm completely incognito?"

"Do me a favor and ask me something I know. We don't have much time to waste." Her next words came out in a shout, "*We have to stop them!*"

"We can't do that on our own. The FBI..."

"Forget the FBI, Bronx has informants everywhere."

"I have no idea what you're talking about. What are we going to do now?"

"First of all, we don't lose our heads. What's down at the harbor?"

"Water, among other things," Sarah said meaningfully.

"A boat is a bad idea. They'll be on our tail before the engine runs warm."

The First Lady had evidently pulled herself together.

"I don't recall saying anything about a boat."

Traffic parted in front of them as if swept aside by a giant hand. Leslie looked over her shoulder, confused.

"No boat? What are you suggesting we do—*swim*?"

"Take the second street to your left, then follow the river past the harbor."

Leslie threw her a stunned look.

The first lady ripped off her dark glasses, followed by the fashionable woolen cap. Next, she pulled the wig from her head with her free hand. She squeezed lithely through the gap between the seats, and slid onto the passenger seat. She held a heavy pistol in her hand.

Leslie cast a sideways glance at the weapon.

"Good! A 9mm SIG Sauer."

"Listen you, whatever your name is, where we're going now *I'm* the First Lady of the United States. So just stay cool."

She explained quickly what lay ahead. Leslie saw the gray car in her rearview mirror. It was following them at a steady distance. Their pursuers would wait until they had left the houses behind them, then they would close the gap and open fire. She nervously pressed her hand on the purse in her lap, feeling for the hard steel of the gun.

"Okay, right! I'm Leslie. Leslie Palmer. At the beginning of the year..."

"Ah, I'm beginning to get it!" The First Lady looked conspiratorially over at Leslie, as she donned the woolen cap and sunglasses. The transformation was perfect. In a few minutes they had agreed on a plan of action. Leslie could still clearly see the brutal hole in Sureman's head.

"Maybe the shot was meant for *you,*" she said, not taking her eyes off the wide rearview mirror.

"Who knows." Sarah Crawford seemed unimpressed. "Maybe the shooter wanted to prevent us from talking to each other."

"Or they wanted to stop the car and then bump both of us off."

This was as far as they got in their speculations. The row of houses had come to an end. An isolated field stretched ahead. The street ended in the dense, colorful autumn foliage of a group of trees up ahead. A quick glance in the rearview mirror confirmed Leslie's fears. Their pursuers were closing in behind them.

The dirty, gray car started to pass them, crowded them dangerously, matching their speed and staying level with them. Leslie saw a blur of white teeth in a broad, dark face. A muzzle appeared through the open side window. "Watch out!" she screamed.

She floored the accelerator, the car shot forward. Both vehicles were now hurtling toward the bend nose to nose.

"Up there, turn left!" her dignitary passenger squealed.

Leslie hit the brakes abruptly, yanked at the wheel, caught the other car on the tail as she turned, sending it swerving across the embankment. Leslie managed to right the Ford just in time. Their tires screeched to a stop in front of a massive double gate. A sign warned. No Entry. Government Property. She jammed both hands on the horn.

A Navy SEAL in full gear stepped out of the low building and opened the first gate to the double system. Leslie took a deep breath.

"Oh, man, that was close!"

Then everything seemed to unwind in slow motion. The First Lady fixed her hair, Leslie pulled the woolen cap down further. Through the dark tinted glasses, she watched as the real First Lady calmly got out, walked the few steps over to the reception desk.

"Hi, Sergeant," she greeted, "how are you today?" as she alternated both index fingers on the electronic fingerprint reading device.

"Thank you, Madam, excellent—everything is under control," the sergeant answered, grinning politely as he checked the results of the scan. "Drive safely!"

The second gate slid open.

As they rolled onto the grounds, Leslie took a look back. Everything seemed perfectly fine. The sergeant was just notifying the hangar chief that *FLOTUS* had made a sudden, unannounced arrival.

The women hurried with echoing footsteps through the high-ceilinged, gloomy airplane hangar. On the other side, they stepped out into the glaring light that reflected off the water.

A small, metal staircase led down onto a gray pontoon, to which a floatplane was tied. *MARINE TWO* Leslie read the official looking lettering under the painted seal of the President of the United States. *E pluribus unum,* it said above the grim looking head of the bald eagle, clutching thirteen arrows in one talon and an olive branch in the other. *They might as well have gone ahead and made it arrows on both sides!*

The hangar chief hurried up to them, having pulled on an orange jacket in mid-run. His face looked as if he had just been disturbed in the middle of an intense making-out session. The First Lady stopped him with a cool motion of her hand.

"No need to hurry, Tom," she called, climbing on board. "We'll call you if we need you."

Leslie marveled at the white, spacious fuselage with its high tail. It sat beneath a broad, massive wing that stretched across the aircraft's back, its engines located under either side. Two sturdy floating devices carried the plane, which appeared elegant in spite of its immense weight. Two ropes held the imposing fixed-wing aircraft tied to the pontoon.

"Wow! Room to stretch!" Leslie called, impressed, as she climbed through the door, tossing the stupid Fendi purse onto a seat. Everything simply reeked of luxury—the beige carpet, the mahogany siding, the blue leather. On an impulse, she sent her shoes flying across the floor. She suddenly felt like an optimistic teenager again!

76

"And you can really fly this monster?" Leslie asked in amazement.

The First Lady had already taken the pilot's seat and was going over the checklist. Occasionally she muttered something inaudible, pressing buttons on the flight management system.

"I'm from Texas. Women do a whole bunch of things where I come from. They ride in rodeos, shoot... I'm checking the power on the aggregate... Here goes the left engine."

She pressed a button and looked up at the wing, where an airscrew now began to rotate. The sophisticated engine sputtered to life under its shiny titanium paneling. It quickly settled into a constant drone.

"We're fully equipped. Weather radar, LORAN, and GPS navigation systems," she explained, repeating the procedure with the right engine as the man with the orange jacket emerged from the hangar at a jog. The fuselage vibrated mildly.

"I'm testing the engines."

Leslie was getting extremely antsy. She was certain that a bunch of Navy SEALs would be storming the aircraft at any moment! As if to confirm her trepidations, a siren started to howl. Yellow lights flashed from somewhere.

The First Lady jacked the engine up to 2500 revs per minute.

"Now!" she shouted into the noise. "Untie the ropes!"

Leslie jumped down the boarding stairs onto the pontoon and deftly loosened the first rope. The hangar chief suddenly appeared next to her.

He called into his walkie-talkie, and then yelled something at her, which she didn't understand. Leslie's woolen cap threatened to come off her head. She pulled it down with both hands, ran to where the other rope was fastened, and yanked it from its thick, black post. She raced back to the stairs, quickly began to clamber up them. A hand grabbed her arm. The man was dressed in a military uniform—he was shaking his head, yelling, "Security! The flight plan. We need a flight plan!"

Leslie felt for the red button to activate the closing mechanism on the door. She found it as the plane was already beginning to move. Leslie threw herself into the cabin. The door locked audibly just as she was sitting back up.

"No need to worry," the First Lady said with a grin. "The dear boy won't be coming with us."

She pushed the throttle forward. The big, white bird glided—slowly at first, then with a surprising increase in speed—across the glistening water, then took majestically to the air.

77

Leslie felt light as a feather. Was it the fact that they had left the ground beneath them? The knot at the pit of her stomach had disappeared into thin air the moment the aircraft door had closed behind them.

"You were saying something about having no time to lose? Allow me to introduce myself, by the way—I'm Sarah."

Leslie nodded, but remained silent for a while. The events that had occurred over the previous hours had shaken her to her core. Only when she looked up and read the obvious question in the First Lady's eyes, did she begin to speak in short sentences. She began by telling her about Craig and Alex.

Sarah Crawford did not interrupt her. She could hardly believe what she was hearing from her look-alike.

"He is holding them hostage. They will die once the ultimatum expires on Sunday," Leslie finished in a tense tone.

"That's unbelievable! Where is this torture chamber that he is keeping them in?"

Leslie desperately shrugged her shoulders.

"I have no idea, Sarah. Maybe in Brooklyn. Yes, probably. But I only saw the boys via a live camera feed."

"Are you married?"

Leslie looked at her uncomprehendingly.

"I mean, do you have someone to help you?"

"Ben. I have Ben. But I can't pull him into this thing. Otherwise he'll be dead, too. What are we going to do in New York? Do you have a plan?"

"I know somebody in Manhattan. We'll see!"

Leslie was less than convinced. She had to regain control of the situation. *This cold-blooded extortion! This bastard is going to see some payback. I'm going to finish him!*

"An eye for an eye," she said out loud.

"I beg your pardon?"

Sarah looked over at her.

"My plan. *E pluribus unum.*"

Sarah remained straight-faced.

"I don't know any Latin."

"It means 'all for one,' or to have a common goal. That's what this is about. My goal is set."

It took Leslie a good half hour to carefully explain her plan. The constant sound of the humming engines had a calming effect.

"So you want to fly to Dushanbe?" Sarah asked with more than a hint of admiration in her voice.

Leslie nodded. She felt incredibly relieved. She would finally be able to do something. Her voice was full of conviction.

"It will work. I know it will."

The dual engine Twin Otter droned evenly along the Atlantic coastline. Leslie looked at the view below.

"I'm dead in this game. My sons think I'm dead and buried. It's dreadful!" She sighed. "How else am I going to rise up from all of this? What else can I do? My existence has been officially erased. That's what's so awful. And I'm stuck with this Bronx, who won't leave me be—everything has been arranged down to the last detail. If I make the slightest mistake, he will slaughter Alex and Craig."

"We're flying into Kennedy, by the way," Sarah informed her matter-of-factly.

Leslie laughed out loud.

"Nice joke. Why don't we take a bit of a spin over Manhattan first!"

The First Lady didn't bat an eye.

"Air traffic is severely restricted and is being closely recorded. The Air Force is monitoring every movement right now."

"Exactly."

Leslie looked out at the sky, obviously worried. It looked as though she expected an interceptor to come whistling out of the ether at any second.

As if to taunt her, the radio began to crackle. A voice reported weather conditions, cloud formations, wind force and direction…

"Who is that?"

"Kennedy International with an automatic weather report. By the way, we have a strong tail wind. It's going to get a bit bumpy."

Leslie looked at her, dumbfounded.

"We're really headed for New York? That'll only end in disaster. You have to change course!"

The First Lady shook her head and addressed her microphone. "Foxtrot Lima Oscar Tango Uniform."

Air traffic control responded. Leslie couldn't understand a word.

"Of course we won't be landing at Kennedy. We're heading for Rockaway—an old Navy airbase. It's between the Atlantic and Jamaica Bay. A really desolate area. The Coast Guard still runs a little station there. I know those boys. We'll be undisturbed there. We can work out what we're going to do next once we land."

"But…"

"Don't worry. You're aboard a government aircraft. My own little state secret. Air traffic control has already identified my transponder signal—*FLOTUS*."

Leslie shook her head in frustration.

"Wonderful! Now the whole damn world will know where we're heading."

The First Lady was rather enjoying the situation. She turned the frequency dial.

"Foxtrot Lima Oscar Tango Uniform…"

Turning to Leslie, she said, "Marine Two with FLOTUS on board has first priority! It's no different to Air Force One carrying the president.

ATC is bound by policy to keep the flight plan and everything having to do with it strictly classified. Calm down. There won't be any leaks."

Leslie was in no way appeased.

"Trust me, the agencies are always listening in on everything from two or three different angles simultaneously. Bronx will be informed before we get our feet back on solid ground, and I'll be screwed. You are putting my boys lives at risk!"

The First Lady negated this with a shake of her head.

"The regulations are strict. Just settle down. I've done this plenty of times before—Jerry would sometimes meet me there."

The latter sounded so wistful that Leslie instinctively reached over and softly squeezed Sarah's arm—but she let go again almost instantly.

This really isn't about Jerry Whoever or Whatever, dearest Sarah. This is about Alex and Craig. This—First Lady—is about us!

78

In the noticeably empty departure lounge of Reagan National Airport in Washington, D.C. Rick Bronx pressed his lips together angrily, then grumbled querulously into his cell phone. At the other end, someone cleared his throat, then described the base from which Marine Two had just taken off. Bronx was not at all pleased with what his contact had just told him. His men had lost the seaplane!

"She was flying along the coast. We don't have a signal there."

"How long will it take her to reach New York?"

"The machine is a DHC-6 Twin Otter, with two powerful turbo prop engines. In this tail wind, I reckon it should take her about 90 minutes."

She'll turn up again, it's not like she has a choice, Bronx decided. *She has to land at some point.* His flight—US Airways 2178 to New York—was called. Bronx strolled over to the gate, searching for the number he had saved for the New York Air Traffic Control Center. He took a seat in the first row of the plane, smiled encouragingly at the earnest-looking stewardess, and put the phone to his ear.

"Susan? Rick here... No, I'm on my way to La Guardia. Listen, this is about a flight—a Twin Otter... the flight ID? No. Tell me, where do planes like that land in the New York area? Okay, call me back. What? Really? Are you on the market again?" He laughed. "I didn't know. We'll get together some time, but get that information for me. It's important, *sweetheart.*"

Waiting for takeoff somewhat impatiently, he deposited his cell in his breast pocket. *A total waste of time, this flying business,* he muttered to himself, pulled the cell out again and re-entered the speed dial number for Frank Sureman. The monotonous ringing vibrated in his ear—*zrrrr zrrrr zrrrr*... endlessly...

"We're going to take off now, sir," the stewardess said with a smile and a discreet gesture toward Bronx's telephone.

He shook his head in annoyance, leaned back and closed his eyes. What was Palmer up to? He thought of her offspring. Those sonny boys sitting in the empty hull of that boat. The water level had to be close to 50 percent... *Whatever the Palmer woman's intentions were, she could not escape him. His plan was seamless and dead certain! The boys' fate was dangling over their heads like a naked sword suspended by a horse's hair... yes, like that corrupt Greek character's sword, that... eh? Whatever... the point was that it would fall, that very sharp blade... if she didn't toe the line, that Navy bitch. Damocles... yes, that was the old Greek's name... didn't want to get that danger was lurking everywhere... the Palmer woman had better be aware of it every single minute... that silky thin...*

His mouth pulled to a malicious grimace, he nodded off, even before the plane had thundered down the runway. Mother Amira appeared to him—her lovely countenance unafraid as she walked beneath a sharp, blazing sword. Now she was leaning over him, embracing him devoutly, as he stared up over her shoulder at the threatening weapon...

79

Leslie eventually settled down, but couldn't keep herself from scanning the horizon for possible fighter planes, which were, apparently, patrolling the sky over the East Coast in order to intercept any unauthorized air traffic.

But their journey went without a hitch. Over the wide beaches of the Carolinas, Leslie grew chatty.

"Sarah, why didn't you return to the White House?"

"Why should I have? I had ceased to exist. Grotesque, isn't it? I survive the worst catastrophe of all time, only to discover that I have been severed from my identity. Someone else just cheerfully marched into the White House and assumed my place as the First Lady! A pretty big shock, wouldn't you agree? It took a while for Jerry and me to digest this unbelievable turn of events."

"You've known Jerry for a long time?"

"An old flame. You obviously know about my youthful trauma stemming from that accident in Midland. Brilliant, Leslie, really—that was a true star performance." Leslie couldn't help but notice a cynical undertone. Sarah switched the Otter to autopilot and leaned back.

"My companion, who died in that car accident back then, had an older brother. He was the love of my life, but he decided to follow a bitchy blond bimbo to New York. *Lawyer.* No children. They divorced pretty quick. Then, one day, I accidentally bumped into my high school sweetheart at a baseball game in Atlanta. We were forced to recognize that our attraction to one another was—even after all the time that had passed, or perhaps because of it—undiminished. I had to make a difficult decision, you understand. Had I said 'no' to Jerry, it would have ended up killing me. My marriage didn't offer me what Jerry did. He taught me how to fly—it was so amazingly romantic. Our secret meetings were breathtakingly exciting. Then came the damned day that ruined everything."

"Did he...?"

"Yes, and no. It was a miracle that we both lived. We crawled out of the rubble—it was the dead of night. In spite of all of our misfortune, we were lucky. We had been lying in a massive pocket, with concrete, smoke, and stench above and all around us. There was this dreadful, lead-gray dust everywhere. It was unbelievable—my golf clubs . . . the dead firefighter, *anyway,* when we crawled out of the rubble we looked like we had just landed from Mars. Unrecognizable, shrunken, gray, our clothes in tatters. We waited for the ambulance—my joints were aching, I had a lot of scrapes and bruises, but no broken bones. Jerry wasn't doing as well. He took my hand and said, "Come, we're leaving."

Leslie was hanging on to her every word.

"Where to?"

"That's what I asked him, too. He just pulled me away from the aid station by the arm. Nobody tried to stop us. We made it to the yacht harbor not far from Ground Zero. His boat was docked there. It was so peaceful. Two cabins, a kitchen—we just stayed on board."

"Then you called the president?"

Sarah shook her head. "Of course I thought of calling him right away. He had to know that I was alive. But my cell phone was broken, and Jerry had left his behind, upstairs. Then . . . it's funny, you know . . . the fact that Jerry and I had survived suddenly seemed like a gift from God. At any rate, we didn't just want to go back to our old daily lives right away."

"Wow. So that's what the two of you decided?"

"Again: yes and no. Jerry had internal injuries. The fall. A torn liver, or something like that. I had to drive him to a hospital. And there . . ."

She stopped, bowed her head. Marine Two droned on, securely on course.

"He died. Shortly after they admitted him."

Leslie reflexively put her hand to her mouth.

"Oh, my God! How terrible!"

A gust of wind rattled the plane; they hit an air pocket and dropped a bit. Sarah Crawford adjusted their altitude. The dreadful images reappeared clearly before her mind's eye. . . .

Sarah had no idea how long she had been unconscious after their fall into the depths beneath the South Tower. She awoke to the feeling of a constant dripping on her leg. When she reached for it, still very dazed, she found it to be sticky and viscous. *Blood!* She startled, her eyes flew open. She was looking up at a black concrete slab, which was suspended above her at an angle, like a harmless marquee. It was black as night, with only a few, dim rays breaking through some cracks off to the side. The body next to her moved. *Jerry!*

They called and screamed until their voices gave out. There was no reply. Then they discovered the crack through which the scant light was shining. Jerry began to systematically examine their tight, narrow dungeon using the flame of his lighter.

He thought that they had collapsed into the underground parking level with the staircase, and that the roofs of cars, or boilers, had broken their fall. *Or corpses, Sarah thought. It was dreadful. Wasn't that the smell of gas?*

"Oil, Jerry, there's oil dripping down here," as the beam of a flashlight lit up. "He's dead. Crushed," Jerry panted. And now Sarah could see him holding his side, like someone trying to contain a stabbing pain.

"A policeman. I've taken his water bottle. There's a firefighter right next to him—also dead. Here's his pick."

But the tool did nothing to help them. The rubble around the hole was too massive and hard, and Jerry didn't have enough room to swing the pickaxe properly.

It was hopeless. No voices, no search parties—nothing.

"The policeman has to have a radio on him," Sarah said hopefully. But they couldn't find one on his dead body. Then Jerry had an idea, the gravity of their situation evidently having sparked his resourcefulness.

He told Sarah to catch the dripping oil in the aluminum bottle. It seemed to take forever. Drip, drip, drip... Meanwhile, Jerry had managed to undo the strap and remove the oxygen container and the breathing apparatus tubing from the dead firefighter's back. When she asked him what he was planning to do, he groaned painfully, "Building a bomb. Help me."

They heaved the oxygen tank over to the hole. Then Jerry wedged the aluminum bottle into the gap in the concrete. Sarah used the golf bag and the body of a dead woman, who had presumably softened her fall, to build a makeshift protective barrier. Jerry pushed the breathing apparatus tubing into the opening of the bottle. The next steps had to happen at lightning speed: he opened the oxygen valve and laboriously crept back.

Using the golf bag for support, he aimed the cop's weapon, which he grasped in both hands, at the aluminum bottle. Sarah directed the flashlight beam over the Glock Police Special and at the target. Jerry concentrated hard on aligning the rear and front sight. He held his breath, then carefully and deliberately pulled the trigger with his index finger. They felt an atrocious bang, no, an infernal thunder, on their faces, then a wave of heat singed at their hair. Debris and rubble rained down. Sarah was convinced that the concrete slab that had been covering them would now come crashing down and finally end up burying them alive.

As soon as the biting smoke cleared, they found that the gap was no longer there. Apparently the improvised explosion had done the opposite of what they intended, and had hermetically sealed everything off. Still, they didn't give up. They hacked frantically at the loose stone with the pick and the golf clubs—and they succeeded. The rubble that blocked the would-be exit after the blast came loose. They beat, clenched, and scratched as if possessed. Finally the hole had grown large enough, and they were out... covered with cuts and bruises, but out in the open! They were alive...

...the gusts of wind had let up, and the plane had stopped rattling. Sarah entered their new altitude into the automatic pilot system, sat back, and said in a passionate voice:

"We stuck together, we loved each other on that tiny boat—it was as if the twenty years that separated us from our youth had never passed. I secretly went to his apartment on the Upper East Side to fetch some things. Well, that's when we became aware that another First Lady had taken my place. Believe me, girlfriend, that really rattled my cage. It's impossible to even describe what I went through. It was a shock on top of the one I was already suffering. Then, when Jerry died... what was I supposed to do? I was completely on my own. It was the sensational speech that you gave at the Library of Congress that finally prompted me to secretly contact you. I felt that I heard a message in what you said, and I had an idea who you might be. But, more than anything, I wanted to find out what treachery was behind all of this. I wanted to know who would have the audacity to steal my home and my life, you understand?"

"Had I been you, I would have immediately alerted the president."

"I thought of it, and I was a hair's breadth from doing exactly that. But something held me back."

"What?"

"Well, it was strange. I almost believed that you were me, myself. Nobody questioned your little ruse. And I asked myself, why? My husband, at least, should have realized that you were an imposter."

"We never had sex," Leslie reassured her, and suddenly had to laugh at her own serious demeanor. Sarah readily joined in.

"That doesn't surprise me. The two of us haven't done it with each other in ages. We grew apart. It really started before the presidential campaign a year ago. He was all over this San Francisco representative. He even wanted her on the ticket as the vice president. Then he had the hots for that African American security advisor. She played the piano and God knows what else for him. Maybe she *blows* well, too—I know, that's a callous thing to say, but please try to put yourself in my place. Our marriage was nothing but a farce—maintained for the sake of our children and, of course..."

"The president's marriage has to remain intact."

"Right, our image was perfect." Sarah reached into the purse, as if she had just had a sudden thought. She handed Leslie a wad of paper.

"Here—your documents. From Sureman's pocket."

"Thank you!"

Leslie took the bundle. The first thing she felt between her fingers was the hard leather of an ID badge. *United States Secret Service* was engraved on the golden, star-shaped plaque. Beneath it Frank Sureman, and his picture. A light blue certificate issued by the James J. Rowling Training Center (JJRTC) confirmed that Frank Sureman had completed a course in cryptography... Then a torn-out newspaper article on the First Lady's speech at the Library of Congress. There was a brownish piece of paper. Leslie unfolded it last and groaned dully.

"Oh, dear God."

"What?"

The skull and crossbones? Rumsy did that. We're going to pulverize all of those assholes. Happy Widow...

"This... map clipping... here," Leslie began, haltingly, "it's the plan."

"What plan?"

"Tora Bora. The president asked me to fetch it from the Treaty Room and bring it to him. The skull and crossbones, see?"

"A secret document," Sarah noted expertly after a short inspection. "The classification is noted on the bottom left-hand corner. The code signifies that it is strictly classified."

"Strictly classified? That's what I thought. I believe that it shows planned targets. This here, Sarah... is pure dynamite!"

"You think Sureman was a double agent? Whatever the case may be, one thing is sure as hell, Leslie. This document was not meant for Sureman's eyes. His level of clearance wasn't high enough. And it certainly wasn't meant for his jacket pocket. What do you reckon?"

"Yes," Leslie said, hardly audible. All at once, everything seemed so obvious. *At the hospital, before the drive, at the safe-house... Sureman had always conferred with Bronx. Hadn't they constantly stuck their heads together?*

"He was spying for someone. He was probably in cahoots with Bronx from the CIA. Just imagine. A mole at the White House, in the Secret Service! Through him, Bronx would have known about all of the president's appointments, would have been informed on all planned security measures, every step that the First Lady ever made."

They were silent, each following their own thoughts for a few dozen heartbeats. But what could they possibly do? Did they have a shred of evidence against Bronx—anything sturdy?

"Time out," the pilot said finally. Then, "Hey, Leslie, could you get me a soda from the galley? It's party time, child. Time to let loose!"

The women broke into liberating laughter. Leslie wriggled out of the co-pilot's seat. She had put on her best Noel Coward face.

"Well, count me in, *child*—any bottle will do, as long as there's no *message* in it."

80

The Otter was now flying along the coastline at 15,000 feet. They could see the fine, jagged white line, where the waves were breaking on the sunlit, grayish-brown sand below. Leslie brought out a tray of hot dogs and Coke. "The kitchen has absolutely everything," she said, impressed, as she found her way back to her seat. Sarah smiled wistfully.

"Jerry loved hot dogs more than anything else."

Leslie bit into her sausage, then said randomly, and bluntly, "You know, I've been feeling incredibly horny lately."

Sarah laughed and adjusted her mouthpiece. "How old is your lover?"

"Ben? Don't ask. We were at a restaurant recently, and this woman indignantly burst out 'For God's sake, she's about twenty years older than her boyfriend.' In a sense, I was quite flattered, because I'm actually almost thirty years older than he is. Ben is a force to be reckoned with. Being with him knocks me off my feet—he gives me two orgasms a night. It's always fresh. Every time with him is like the first."

"Do your children know?"

"I think so. The boys don't say much, but I believe they think it's cool. Jennifer, on the other hand, would find the thought of me having a young lover disgusting, I'm sure. But who cares. And you?"

"Why do you ask?"

"I slept in your bed. I looked around."

"My sexual energy is part of who I am. It's got nothing at all to do with age. It's simply human. Frankly, sex with myself was the only kind of sex I had for a long time."

Leslie nodded silently. The humming of the engines roused her curiosity. She remembered the pink cell phone.

"And then Ted fell into your lap," she said casually.

Sarah threw her an alarmed look. "You didn't...?"

Leslie shook her head, laughing.

"Look, I had practically no other choice," the First Lady contemplated. "I had a certain role that was expected of me at the White House. I hosted parties, all of those receptions, a ton of acquaintances... But sex? Sex was a faint dream that I remembered only vaguely. But I was damned if I was just going to just sit around the house and mope."

"So, you got something going with Ted?"

"Sure. The most amazing things can happen out of the blue, if you let them. I want to be passionate—to consciously live out my inner being."

"And the president? How do you manage to handle two men?"

"Three. Jerry was the love of my life." She sighed so loudly that Leslie's ear was filled with a crackling rush.

"Well, you're pretty darn hot—I can only admire that. Doesn't the fact that you're committing adultery bother you?"

"My husband is far too busy. When he does want me, it's a nightmare. I'll be in bed, half asleep, and he'll come back from some briefing... then I'll feel that hand creeping over. He wouldn't even know how to spell foreplay. Give her a kiss and then you can go ahead and stick it in, is what he thinks. *Mission accomplished.*"

Leslie doubled over with laughter.

"Sex is supposed to be a joy. Ted and I are one steaming number in bed, I can tell you that much. It's not cheating as much as it is taking a well-deserved break from something way too dreary."

Leslie was still shaking with mirth. She felt an inner connection to this woman. Was it coincidence or fate that they looked so much alike? "You know," she agreed, "many people just can't accept that we could still be sexually active at our age. Why would I be feeling this kind of desire, if my body couldn't handle it anymore?"

"Sure," Sarah burst out, now laughing as well. "I need sex like I need food and air. It's probably a reaction to my conservative upbringing. I was always faithful to one guy."

"I still am! I find it makes me strong," Leslie countered, her face glowing at the thought of Ben. "It's like we're in our own little world, and nothing else matters to us."

Sarah was really warming to the topic.

"The thing with Ted... Well, our eyes kept meeting. You know you can feel it when somebody really wants you. So I came up with an excuse to have him sent to me. I was shaking with nerves. *What on earth had I done?* Then he came sauntering through the door—a tall, handsome man. He just walked straight up to me, pressed his body against mine... Getting into bed with him, that feeling, it couldn't be compared to anything else. My body had been dead, and it came alive."

"And?"

"And nothing. I can talk dirty with Ted, I can explore the kinky stuff, he keeps me young. Jerry—well—Jerry has, I mean had, style. He stimulates me—it's a whole other intellectual plane. And as a lover, he is... *was* fantastic. But now let's talk about you and... Ben?"

"What can I say? He makes me come longer and more intensely than I did twenty years ago. Have you ever had a real extended orgasm?"

"Listen, you," the First Lady of the United States giggled, "let's just say I've been around the block a coupla times."

Leslie rolled her eyes like a teenager.

"I'm so much less inhibited, and so much more imaginative, than I ever was—we laugh a lot. Everything is playful. There's always more foreplay to our foreplay—there's never any after play, because it's never really over."

"... who are you telling, you monster! That's exactly how things were for Jerry and me. And then he also had all of those other attributes that turn me on."

"Money, I presume."

"Sure, plenty of money, but something much better than that: he knew how to tell a story, his punch lines always made me laugh, the scope of his knowledge was baffling, and whenever he had that thoughtful expression on his face, it was so sexy... oh... Leslie..."

Foxtrot, Lima, Tango... the radio interrupted their sensual chat. Sarah confirmed the announcement, then turned back to Leslie.

"My friends call me Franny!"

"I like that, Franny. Does your husband also call you Franny?"

"Him? He calls me Lorry—like I was his mare, or a truck or something. Terrible. Franny comes from the Italian 'Franella.' Do you know what that means?" She smiled mischievously. "Franella is the pretty indecent vernacular for 'flirt'! The really heavy variety!"

Leslie slapped her thigh. "Perfect... Flirt's your middle name. You're wicked!"

Sarah pointed down.

"Those two old trucks there—in the water, next to the dilapidated hangars? I'm going to make a water landing farther up the bay.

"It looks pretty dismal," said Leslie, her eyes wide open with surprise. Sarah had completely snapped back to her role as chief pilot again.

"Is your seatbelt buckled? The National Weather Service uses aircraft like this to fly across the Everglades, to monitor water depth coupling. These planes are perfectly suited to searching rivers, or jumping from pond to pond, and so forth.

Leslie laughed at the idea.

"Talk about jumping a bit on the side in style! Where did your escapades take you to?"

"The Florida Keys, Texas, down to the Gulf. Having a floatplane allowed me to have everything I wanted—freedom, adventure, the ability to break away." She sighed again.

"There's nothing like being able to just fly away," Leslie smiled. "The public never got wind of your capers, am I right?"

"No, like I said—it was a secret between me and Jerry. Just imagine, everywhere we went, they thought we were with the National Weather Service."

And she gave a broad, warm laugh such as the nation had never heard or seen. A laugh that washed over Leslie like a summer breeze from the Deep South. An all-American laugh, born and bred in a country that would never be the same again.

81

The deep blue bay lay beneath them. A silver ribbon drew out toward the estuary, where the waves of the Atlantic were throwing white crests. Sarah guided the Otter into a curve, then lowered the seaplane's nose. They approached the water's surface in a steady descent. Leslie pulled the woolen cap over her mass of hair, adjusted the sunglasses. A swarm of gray birds startled and scattered, the plane's pontoons sliced through the surface, spraying glittering tails of water.

Men dressed in overalls came running out the hangar as the First Lady turned toward the wharf. With precise hand signals one directed Sarah toward an underwater rail lift. Once the engines died down, the winding mechanism screeched into action and began hoisting the airplane across the ramp and onto a yellow circle marked on the concrete square. First Lady Sarah opened the door waving and smiling. The ladies exited onto dry land, eliciting secretly admiring glances of the ground crew.

Leslie recognized the emblem of the Coast Guard on the landing team's uniforms.

"Welcome to Rockaway," a man wearing dress shoes and a captain's uniform greeted respectfully before enquiring whether their flight had been pleasant, and whether a return trip was planned. Sarah exchanged a few words with him, as if she were talking to an old acquaintance, then stepped toward a freshly washed, shining green Jeep Cherokee, where Leslie was already waiting.

The First Lady took the wheel. "We're taking Flatbush Avenue to the Long Island Expressway," she informed Leslie as she steered the large Jeep across the dirt road and onto the street.

"That will take us to Queensborough Bridge. It's about twenty miles to Manhattan. We should be able to make it in half an hour."

Leslie looked back at the hangar, and the plane.

"I wouldn't have believed that you could do something like that. Does anyone know about your trips to New York?"

"My husband, actually," Sarah said with a grin. "He and one of his staff guys believe that I go to the city to raise charity funds. New York is where the money is. You know my foundation, I believe."

She laughed jauntily.

"Then you landed here on September 11, to meet Jerry at the WTC?"

She nodded.

"We wanted to play an early round of golf at his Country Club."

"And who flew back?"

"Who do you think?"

Leslie shrugged. "Well, *someone* had to fly the plane back to where it came from."

"My flight instructor accompanied me to New York that day. It was a good opportunity to get in a bit of flight training. Then he brought a plane that happens to bear the name Marine Two back to where it belongs."

"Excuse me," Leslie laughed.

"Just don't forget your role. You piloted that plane to New York today. And this is a matter of life and death."

"I know, Sarah, and that is why I will be heading to Dushanbe before the day is over." This announcement earned her a look of surprise. The First Lady picked up the thread.

"His mother lives in Dushanbe, doesn't she?" she asked. Leslie nodded absently. She was mentally rehearsing the next few hours in her mind. When a helicopter flew in low across the street, she jerked back to the present.

"I have to be at the Plaza Hotel on Sunday at noon—not a minute later."

"*The Plaza Hotel?* What on earth would we be doing at that posh joint?" the First Lady asked irritably.

Leslie screamed.

"Watch out!"

The scary-looking roadblock on Flatbush Avenue consisted of a full dozen wildly flashing patrol cars. Two SWAT helicopters hovered above them with a high-pitched rumble.

A man wearing sunglasses stood broad-legged in the middle of the road, the tail of his jacket flapping in the wind.

"What the hell is this?"

Sarah applied the brakes, allowing the Jeep to come to a stop. The well-built man stepped up to the driver's side window.

"Bill Baker, FBI," he announced with a sharp salute. "*Good afternoon.*"

Sarah reacted angrily.

"What's going on here?"

"This is a CTU," Baker explained. "It's a troupe composed of FBI, CIA, and NYPD. We are checking airport access roads. We were informed of the shootout in Washington. We have a few questions if we may?"

"That can wait, sir. We have an appointment."

Bill Baker nodded understandingly, adding immediately, "Your husband, the president, would like to speak to you." He waved to the back. A woman stepped out of the group and approached holding a walkie-talkie to one ear, and firmly pressing her free hand to the other to keep out the noise. She wore a black police jacket. The dark blue uniform cap couldn't quite contain her raven hair.

"My God, that's Jennifer!" Leslie whispered.

"Jennifer?"

Leslie pulled the cap further down over her forehead.

"My *daughter.*"

"Okay, Mr. Baker, pass it to me."

The hefty walkie-talkie passed from the woman, to Baker, to the First Lady.

"Hi, buddy," Sarah called into the device, turning to Leslie with a mischievous smile.

A deep voice responded, "Darling, *what* have you been up to? Is everything alright?" A dog could be heard barking in the background.

"I'm fine, everything's fine. No problem. Is that Barney with you? Where are you?"

He kept on at her. Leslie caught only bits and pieces of what he was saying.

"... Dinner tonight... Stay away from that damn city, darling..."

Sarah covered the walkie-talkie with her hand. "Leslie, this is perfect!" she whispered.

Then she spoke to the president again.

"I'll see you then, I'm glad you're close. Call me on my cell... I had it switched off, okay? See you later, *sweetie.*"

"*What's* perfect? What's going on?" Leslie whispered. She sneaked a glance at Jennifer, who was just putting a stick of gum in her mouth.

"I'm taking back over. That's what's perfect—don't you think? Now you'll have no trouble going back to Manhattan, and to... well, you know."

As she said the latter, Sarah cocked her head conspiratorially at Jennifer.

The familiar tone warmed Leslie's heart once again. She placed her hand on Sarah's shoulder. "We'll stick together."

The First Lady saluted, grinning like an accomplice.

"Through thick and thin!"

She started to get out. *The reassurance!* Leslie grasped her arm tightly.

"Wait, don't forget your bag! Here."

The First Lady looked confused, but took the white Fendi bag and clasped it under her arm.

"Is there something I should know about this?"

Leslie gave a short nod. The FBI agent turned to look at them. She lowered her voice.

"Just take it. I'll explain it to you later. You have to carry it wherever you go! It's important. *Crucial!*"

"Okay, don't worry. It's my bag."

Sarah made herself get out. She said something to Bill Baker, who motioned to Jennifer. After a short exchange, Jennifer briskly walked toward the Cherokee. Leslie froze. She stared rigidly forward.

"I'll be your driver," the uniformed woman informed her, sitting down in the driver's seat. She looked at Leslie askance. "My name is Jennifer."

Leslie's profile, partially hidden under the woolen cap, remained mask-like. *What a monumental role to play! So Brechtian—the good mother duping her own daughter to save the lives of her sons.* And still, it all seemed suddenly very simple—she would maintain the attitude and inflection that she had brought to her portrayal of the First Lady. She gave the destination address in a cool, almost derisive tone.

"Third Avenue and 72nd Street. And step on it, if you could!"

82

As Bill Baker later gave the command to disperse the roadblock on Flatbush Avenue, tossing his FBI jacket onto the back seat of his Chevy Blazer, Ken Cooper approached with a long, thin cigar dangling from the corner of his mouth. He clapped a heavy hand on his colleague's shoulder.

"You wanted to talk to me about something, Bill? Wanna get in?"

They got into the front of the vehicle. Ken kept on smoking. Bill kept the motor running in neutral to fuel the air-conditioning.

"It's about her," Baker began, motioning with his chin in the direction where the First Lady's car had just disappeared.

"I recently made myself look like an idiot in front of POTUS. I mean, I asked him about his wife, and whether she might be..."

"Having an affair?" Cooper interrupted.

"Not exactly, but something like that—*anyway*, the meeting was a disaster."

"But, knowing you, you were on the money? Right?"

Baker nodded thoughtfully.

"It's just a niggling gut feeling that something isn't right with her. What would you do if you were in my shoes?"

Cooper shrugged, as was to be expected.

"Do you have any evidence?"

"Well—there was that speech of hers. At some point she said... listen closely, '*In spite of the terrible tragedy that has shaken us, that has frightened us deeply, we cannot allow ourselves to throw the bathwater out with the baby.*' Notice something?"

"Sure, it's supposed to be *'throw the baby out with the bathwater,'* not the other way round."

"Exactly. What was she trying to say by twisting that phrase? She is well educated. She wouldn't just quote something like that wrong."

"She might." Cooper was not entirely convinced.

"She also said in her speech—wait," Baker looked at his notebook, "there, she said *'Often that, which appears to be correct, is false—and conversely, what seems false may later prove to be true.'* What did she mean when she said that?"

"It's just another one of those banal statements that's supposed to sound really meaningful," Cooper responded, disinterested.

Baker was not to be deterred.

"A platitude? I don't think so. And then there's the fact that she suddenly outs herself as the guilty party in the teenage accident that killed her boyfriend. She tells a breathless audience about swerving to avoid a truck that was racing toward her... but our old FBI files say that she ran a stop sign and hit her boyfriend's car head on. If she was going to drag that skeleton out of the closet, why would she bother to change everything around?"

Ken seemed to be ruminating on this question. He took a drag on his cigar, and blew a billow of smoke up at the beige trimmed ceiling of the car.

"No idea," he had to admit. "Fine, and what do you plan on doing next?"

Bill Baker looked over at Cooper with a glint in his eye. The corners of his mouth twitched mischievously.

"Let's say somebody wanted to put a bit of pressure on the First Lady, for whatever reason, right?"

"Okay," Cooper nodded.

"What would that someone need if he wanted to do something to her somewhere—always assuming that that was his plan? What would he need?"

Cooper deftly maneuvered the butt over to the other side of his mouth with his tongue.

"Well, he would have to know what's on her agenda, her meetings and so on. Is *that* what you're getting at?"

"You nailed it, Mister. Bingo!"

"I still don't understand what you're trying to say." Cooper looked pointedly at the face of his flat Chrono Swatch.

Baker put on a triumphant smile.

"I had a few fictitious events added to her agenda. For instance, the presidential couple is meant to be attending a business power luncheon at the Plaza Hotel this coming Sunday, then..."

Cooper pursed his lips disparagingly.

"That's where Bill Clinton liked to hang out and meet showbiz beauties. Our current president would never set foot in that place."

"That's true—but perhaps our certain somebody wouldn't know that. Or he might think that everything has changed because of 9/11, which would be true."

"Okay, fine. I'll bite. So you think your Mister X is going to try and get to the First Lady at the *Plaza*?"

This time, Baker did the shrugging.

"I honestly have no idea *what* could happen. But I did order the usual security. And every call to and from the White House is being monitored."

Cooper didn't seem exactly thrilled. But, as some would say, they had been through some 'stuff' together in their time.

"What can I do to help you, Bill?"

"Keep a lookout, and tell me personally if you notice anything."

Cooper turned to Baker. The name *Bronx* lay heavy on his tongue. He was burning to mention the mysterious death of CBP Agent Howard Young. But he only just held back. Baker sensed that there was something not being said.

"What?"

"Sure," Cooper said evasively. "I'll keep my eyes open."

"And your sphincter closed," said Baker with a grin, which sent the two buddies laughing so hard that it got their old battle scars itching. Cooper was still going over his mental notes—Bronx was a real counterterrorism hero these days. The accomplished Afghanistan field agent had defused one of the most prominent heads of the movement over in Peshawar—Azzam Abdullah. Even though the successful hit was years back, his status within the CIA had been untouchable ever since. *And what interest could he possibly have in the harmless First Lady, anyhow?*

"Alright," Baker drawled. He opened the sunroof and all of the windows, which Cooper correctly interpreted as a more than a subtle hint.

"I'll keep you posted, Billy boy," he said in a manner that was just as collegial as it was non-binding. "*See you later, alligator!*"

He gave his pal a friendly punch on his muscular arm, and got out with a grin on his face. Wearing an even broader grin, Baker took his cue in this timeworn brotherly ritual, and readily shot back the world famous Bill Haley and the Comets response:

"In a while, crocodile!"

83

The door to her apartment was ajar. Leslie took a few tentative steps into the hallway. "Hello? Is anyone there?"

A light was on in the living room. A paper cup lay on its side on the table, next to the greasy remains of a pizza.

She waved Jennifer in, her eyes searching for the computer that contained the data on Tajikistan.

She saw the running shoes first, then legs, then the blood. She screamed sharply. Jennifer rushed in.

"Dear God! Who is that?"

The man lay in a pool of blood that had soaked into the carpet. His throat had been cut from ear to ear. A dreadful sight!

"Ben! Oh, Ben. God, no!"

Jennifer pulled the radio out of her bag.

"No, stop! Don't!"

Leslie tore the woolen cap from her head, the glasses flew from her face.

"Jennifer, it's *me!*"

Jennifer was at a loss for words.

"For heaven's sake, Mom—*you?*"

Leslie got a bottle of cognac from the closet, set two thick, short glasses on the table, and allowed herself to fall into a chair. As if in a trance, she reached over and pulled one up for Jennifer, too.

"Here!" Leslie handed her a glass that was nearly filled to the brim. She emptied her own in a single shot, and groaned.

Then she started talking, not leaving out a single detail. Time seemed to be standing still. Jennifer listened, her mouth agape. Occasionally, she sipped at her cognac.

"And now they've killed Ben," Leslie finished, and walked into the bedroom where she found her computer, which she remembered having hidden beneath the bedspread.

"Why did they kill Ben? What did he know that would have made it worth killing him?"

Leslie opened the laptop on the table as Jennifer looked around.

"Maybe this is it—look here. Ben sent this email on the evening of September 10."

Jennifer leaned over and read out loud:

Howdy, sweetie, the faculties represent buildings. What are the emblems of the city? The Twin Towers. Enrollment deadline September 11. You think something might be going down tomorrow? I love you, Ben."

They sat together in shocked silence.

"Mom, I have to call the cops," Jennifer decided.

"You know, Jenny, Ben was everything to me. He was gentle, intelligent. He showed me that I could be more imaginative than I ever was. We laughed a lot. Everything was fun. He was just amazing. He was worth his weight in gold."

"Mmm, tell me, this Rick Bronx, what are your plans with him?"

Leslie in no way wanted to burden Jennifer with her plans. She began carefully.

"I analyzed his body language. He shows signs of a relatively rare syndrome. We call it a true Oedipal latency. It is an extraordinarily close, intimate fixation on his own mother."

"And you can tell that just by looking at him?"

"A maternal fixation is related to sexuality. The son wants to return to where he came from. *Inter faeces et urinam nascimur.* That is what draws him.

"He wants to return to the womb?"

"His mother is holy to him. She is his religion. He will let nothing touch her. These are profoundly intimate sentiments—more intimate than the most fanatic Muslims harbor for their prophet."

"Pretty obscene."

"But useful."

Jennifer looked at her mother questioningly.

"What do you mean by that? You know that I'm here for you."

"Then find out where he's keeping Craig and Alex, please. That's all I ask."

"You said it was a house on the waterfront. A warehouse, maybe?"

"No... Wait, yes!" Leslie suddenly saw the bright sign in front of her eyes. "*Public Storage* it said," she burst out, relieved.

"At least that's something to go on. There are a number of those. Good disguise."

Jennifer jotted down a quick note.

Leslie packed the bare necessities into a carry-on bag—her laptop, phone, credit cards, passport. She didn't need much more than that. She weighed her Navy Intelligence Service Badge contemplatively, and finally pocketed that also.

"I'll take the car. I'll see you the day after tomorrow, Jenny." They kissed. Jennifer handed her the card with her direct extension. "You don't want to let me in on your plan?"

Leslie raised her hands beseechingly.

"Trust me, darling. All in good time."

She left without another word. *Would she ever see Jennifer again?*

Plagued by heavy thoughts, she got into the car and stuck the key in the ignition. The passenger door opened suddenly, and Rick Bronx slid in beside her. Here was her prompt physical proof of how dangerous the man was. She had recoiled instinctively, her hand reaching over to the side pocket of the door, where she felt the 9mm that Sarah had put there. *Good girl, Sarah!*

"How are you?" Bronx whispered menacingly, eyeing his victim intensely. "I thought I might find you here."

"So, what do you want, Bronx, a medal?"

"Your mission, Leslie!"

"Shoot, but watch your foot."

"The water is rising. Your sons love you, you know."

"To the point, *dar*ling!" she spat.

"City Hall, Sunday. The president will be there to honor the cops, the firefighters, the mayor. You will..."

"The *Plaza* isn't the same thing as City Hall, in case you hadn't noticed..."

"There has been a change in plan. You will accompany the president to City Hall."

"Alright, if you say so. I'll be there. And how are we supposed to pull this off, you genius conspirator?"

Her question was no less than a venomous hiss.

"The president is scheduled to appear on an outdoor stage, in front of City Hall. You will do it in front of everyone, with the television cameras running, as soon as the ceremony begins. Do not hesitate! You will use the revolver. You will calmly aim at the president, and you will empty the barrel into his body."

Leslie acted theatrically calm.

"Really? Not into the air? Fine, Bronx, you can depend on me. I was once the prompter for 'The Final Curtain,' where Booth shoots Lincoln. I know all about Reagan and Hinkley. Kennedy, Ruby, Oswald... anything else?"

Her sarcasm rolled right off of Bronx's back. He didn't bat an eye.

"Sorry about the boys, dearie. They are merely our guarantee that you will do what we want."

Leslie felt a strange rush of excitement. She knew that this was it—this was war. *Now I'm right in the thick of it. So this is how it feels!*

"The water is on the rise, Ms. Palmer. I can only stop it once you have done everything that you are supposed to do. Is that clear?"

Leslie gave him a saucy wink.

"You don't say. You know what, Bronx? You are an unscrupulous pig. And you're damn stupid to boot. *Get out now!"*

The 9mm glistened dully in her hand. The resounding metallic noise of the safety being released made Bronx shrink back. He raised his hands defensively.

"Alright, alright. I'm going already. Just you think of that water level."

"Yeah, right, the water level," Leslie hollered. "I almost forgot." Bronx carefully backed out of the car. Leslie raised the weapon further. "Just *you* be careful that I don't make *you* drown—in your own blood!"

The CIA agent stumbled, regained his balance, and ducked off. The wail of sirens approached. That would probably be the police that Jennifer had called. Leslie drove off abruptly, steering the Cherokee toward Kennedy International. On the other side of the Triborough Bridge she activated her blue flashing lights and easily made up for lost time.

She left the car on the Terminal 4 driveway, stuffing her 9mm in her hand luggage. Then she purchased her ticket and headed for the security check.

Safety measures had been hiked up massively. She recognized a senior CBP officer.

"Sir—Leslie Palmer." She produced her ID badge. "Navy Intelligence, sir. Would you please discreetly escort me to the plane?"

The large, youthful-looking man peered skeptically over the rim of his glasses. She showed him her ticket to Munich.

He raised his walkie-talkie without addressing her directly, shielding it with his hand. After a while, Leslie heard "*Check*. Her name is Leslie Palmer, Navy."

It took a while. Leslie looked around and noticed the changes in the airport. There were long cues in front of the hand luggage checks. Army soldiers patrolled the building with machine guns. The walkie-talkie crackled.

"They want your security code," the border patrol officer said, raising his eyebrows apologetically.

"Odessa," Leslie answered immediately. Her city of birth.

The man reported back to headquarters, then he flashed a friendly smile. "Everything checked out. Come with me please."

He led her through a passage to the electric cart storage area. Together they drove one of the noiseless vehicles down long passageways and side corridors that Leslie had never seen. They eventually arrived at the Lufthansa 404 boarding gate.

"Have a good flight," said her escort. "And please excuse the questions. Damned terrorists!"

"No problem. That's exactly why I'm traveling."

Leslie produced her most charming smile. After all, he had just channeled her past security, right along with her hand luggage containing the 9mm.

"Good luck!"

He continued to smile and wave as she left. She rewarded him by raising her hand one more time. *Luck? Thanks, young man, I could certainly use some of that!*

84

In the nose of the refurbished 747, Leslie was shown to a window seat in business class. She closed her eyes as the plane gained altitude.

Spike... she had to call him, if only to thank him. She pulled the in-seat phone from its beige plastic cradle and dialed the number. He answered immediately.

"Hi, Spike. I'm in the air right now... Where to? Munich."

"Did you get my text message?"

"That's why I'm calling. To make sure. You're sending your machine to pick me up in Munich?"

"You know, my pilots might as well get a bit of flight practice in. As it is, they do nothing but hang around most of the time."

"What are you doing in Zurich?"

"Business. I'm negotiating the takeover of a Grand Hotel. So I thought to myself, if I can't see you, I could at least send you my jet."

"You're incredible. You could come along, you know."

"Tajikistan? I wouldn't mind, now that you mention it. I've been there before. But I can't right now, unfortunately."

"Pity."

"Listen, Leslie, I'm going to give you my pilot's cell number, in case you miss each other at the gate, or something."

"Okay." *What did he mean—'or something'?*

Leslie listened and wrote. On a whim, she asked, "And how long will you be staying in Zurich?"

"Oh, these old farts need another couple of days to make sure that due diligence is done. Apart from that, I have to say this town could grow on a person."

"Spike, what would I do without you? What's the time over there?... *What!* Oh Lord, I'm sorry!"

She said goodbye and replaced the receiver.

"The menu," said a friendly steward.

"Thank you. Wake me up for breakfast, please."

"With pleasure. May I make you comfortable?"

"What? Oh."

They smiled at each other as he put her seat in the sleeping position with a few expert motions.

Her thoughts drifted aimlessly before she dozed off. The look in Craig and Alex's eyes as they sat trapped in that dreadful prison burned in her soul. She was crystal clear on her objective. She saw Rick Bronx wiggling and wailing as he went under in the trap that he had set for her sons... her boys carrying her... happily toasting to a new friendship with the First Lady. *Champagne?* The picture bothered her somehow—was there something she should be thinking of? She shook off the nagging feeling, focusing on what lay ahead. *Dushanbe.* She imagined a derelict airport that dated back to old Soviet times, Nick Negroponte, the defense attaché, awaiting her with his woolen scarf in the rundown arrivals hall. Was he still driving that old Range Rover, with which he had turned up to the bilateral intelligence conference in the English town of Cheltenham, constantly chewing on his pipe, whether it was lit or not?

A fleeting smile crossed her face as she thought of him, then she saw Ben. *Oh Ben! That pulling sensation between her legs!* She turned on her stomach as best she could, and thought of the long, wooden table in the newsroom, of Ben's gentle caress. If only he were lying next to her, here and now, if she could only feel the touch of his hands! *Yes, the way that only you... ooh. Be... don't stop...* the long, strong muscles of Leslie's thighs squeezed rhythmically and tightly... *Ben, Ben, yes, like that, don't stop... now...*

By the time the steward arrived with the water she had asked for, the striking woman was already fast asleep. He glanced admiringly at her beautiful, satisfied features, before he carefully maneuvered the bottle onto the empty seat next to her.

85

The two Hotchkiss engines on the Spike Corporation's private jet hummed evenly. Leslie sat in the co-pilot's seat, looking out onto the breathtaking panorama that spread before them all the way to the distant horizon.

"The Bosporus and the Dardanelles," the captain, who had intercepted her even before she had left the finger dock in Munich, oriented her. The second in charge handed a bottle of water over her shoulder. "We'll begin descent in an hour," he stated.

At around the same time in New York, Rick Bronx was growing increasingly irate as he listened to Ahmed's report. It was past midnight. Rain was beating down hard on the broad windows of the house on the Brooklyn waterfront.

"In other words: you've *lost* her. Well done!"

"She didn't check in at the regular counter at JFK," the voice on the other end justified itself. "She disappeared with an airport official. We had to lay low. They look at Arabs like pestilent rats these days."

"Fucking asshole!"

Bronx angrily slammed down the receiver. His blunt gaze was fixed on the broad monitor. The display showed that the water level had reached 60 percent. What were those idiots doing? Fucking *calisthenics?* And so they were! Alex and Craig had locked their fingers and were stretching their arms. *They have balls, I'll give them that much,* he admitted grudgingly.

An email from Afghanistan had also somewhat soothed his nasty mood. The CIA agent answered by transferring the grid square coordinates of a pre-defined area on a map. It was a seemingly harmless message that designated a cruise missile goal in the Tora Bora cave complex. Bronx didn't doubt the strategic nature of the target. It was probably a command bunker. What annoyed him was the distribution of the message within the CIA. It was primarily addressed to the CIA Chief of Operations. Rick, Chief of the Middle East Desk though he was, only warranted a somewhat belated copy of the message—so his hands were tied. No doubt the email with its target definitions had already made its way to CENTCOM in Florida.

He thought for a moment, then reached for his cell phone and entered a text message. "Telegram could arrive at the Red Rock Hotel at any moment."

Bronx hit *send.*

A cell phone lying on top of a copy of the *New Yorker* buzzed at the Tora Bora command bunker. Once, twice.

Steve Quinn was alone in the green room. He walked to the door, looked out into the empty vaulted corridor. Then he crept back to the table on tiptoe, and quickly pressed the menu button. The message lit up on the screen. Quinn was just busy reading it when he heard distant footsteps. He pressed the *back* button and looked at the sender ID: Rick. *Rick? Search the contact list...* He quickly entered R, Rick Bronx. *Bingo!* The first digits of the number were 1-971... U.S.A.

By the time Zawahiri entered, Quinn was lounging back lazily on a pile of pillows. He kept on repeating the number to himself, until he could have recited it in his sleep.

Suddenly the caves were filled with a frantic mood of departure. Just half an hour after Zawahiri had also noticed the message on his phone, a column of all-terrain vehicles was making its way down the steep mountain road.

At NSA headquarters in Fort Meade, where Rick Bronx had—ironically—enjoyed his training as an intelligence agent, a mainframe computer spat out the catchphrase *red rock*. The intercepted text message remained where it lay on a pile of similar-looking printed messages. It was only the next morning that a female soldier from the intelligence department delivered the note to her superior with a semi-cute flourish.

86

Nick Negroponte was not waiting in the arrivals hall at Dushanbe Airport. He was, right along with his light brown patterned woolen scarf and his legendary pipe, waiting at the bottom of the airplane stairs with a broad smile on his face. His blond hair was blowing in the wind. Leslie stepped down and gave him a hug.

"Nick, I'm so glad you're here!" She looked around. "Beautiful, wild, but also at the end of the earth."

"If you're referring to *me,* I won't object," he grinned, grabbed her hand luggage and walked ahead toward a white helicopter.

"I thought about your message. We'll make this short and sweet. You said that you wanted to fly back this evening. *Unfortunately.*"

He gently put his arm around her.

"I have no choice, Nick. Where are we going? I reserved a room at the Sovesto."

"You didn't need to. We'll pick the woman up—and off we'll go!"

She looked at him admiringly.

"There's nothing like a bit of military tactics!" she complimented.

"A rescue plane?" she asked the helicopter pilot, who greeted her.

"Registered in Switzerland," came the melodious response from the dashing pilot, in perfect English.

"They fly for the Aga Khan. He insists on having only Swiss pilots," Nick offered by way of an explanation. "If you look on the tail fin, you will see a diagonal red stripe on green. The Ismaeli flag. But the aircraft are, without exception, registered in neutral Switzerland, so that they are able to fly to all neighboring countries."

"The Aga Khan?"

She marveled at the helicopter—a brand-new Agusta AB139. Nick nodded affirmatively. The pilot added, "His Excellence finances aid programs in the Pamir highlands."

"Spike does real estate deals with him," the jet pilot, who had followed them, added. Leslie got to the point.

"Listen, Nick. I have a problem with the CIA."

He laughed.

"Well, you wouldn't be the only one."

"Really. No, I mean it..." She pulled him aside. "If the local CIA contact gets wind of this Amira thing..."

"Don't worry, Leslie."

"They're a bunch of air-heads," the Swiss pilot, who had heard bits of their conversation, interjected.

Nick hastily explained, "His boss, the Aga Khan, is also very invested in providing security for the country. Border patrols, war against drug trafficking. We're talking about significant amounts of money. Those CIA buffoons searched his downtown offices."

"Why?"

"Because they honestly believed that he was financing terrorist organizations. Just imagine! I tell you, I had a lot of appeasing to do. The station chief isn't on my wavelength. I'm not at all opposed to pulling one over on that idiot. By the way, he's currently attending a conference in Almati."

"And him?" She pointed to the helicopter pilot.

"Hans flies. He sees and hears nothing. He's smart, and he's neutral—right?"

The man being spoken about smiled, flattered.

"For two hundred years! By the way, the Aga sends his regards!"

"He what? How does he know me?"

"Apparently there aren't many Palmers who are rascals and happen to be enrolled in the same exclusive Swiss boarding school as his sons, where they are studying hard to become part of the world's elite. He had background checks run on them as a matter of routine."

Leslie's features darkened.

"I let Hans in on what you told me," Nick said quickly.

The pilot had a worried look on his face.

"Did I say something stupid? I'm sorry."

"No, Craig and Alex, my twins, are in trouble. It's very bad. I can't talk about it. But that's the reason I'm here. This Amira has to be in New York tomorrow. Believe me! Please relay to his Excellence how deeply I appreciate his help."

A troubled silence settled over them for a while.

"So, let's get to it!" Nick yelled into the racket of a veering jet.

87

Nick had a simple plan. He informed Leslie on the daily routine of the 'target'—as he called Rick Bronx's mother, Amira.

"She bicycles over to the Hotel Sovesto around noon and drinks a cup of tea in the lobby. Usually she meets a CIA representative there. After that, she rides to the post office, and from there she makes her way home. About two kilometers. She often stops at the store on her way. Usually to buy cat food."

"Does she live in an apartment block?"

"No, she's bought herself a small dacha on the edge of town. She lives there with her animals." He looked at his watch. "We'll wait inside the house. Leave the rest up to me."

Hans had scouted out a landing place. The Agusta helicopter set down gently on a field. They jumped off, waited for the propellers to die down.

They were able to approach the house from behind, hidden from the view of the street—which seemed ideal to Leslie.

The door that led out onto the backyard had a cat trap. Nick stuck his hand in and undid the latch. They found themselves in the kitchen.

Leslie marched briskly to the living room. A stack of envelopes lay in a flat, woven basket on the sideboard.

She found the letter. It was the same one that she had seen in Bronx's car—it had the same typo in the sender's address: *Braodway.*

She opened it, "*. . . something big is going to happen within the next few days. The entire world will be paralyzed. We will conquer the West, just like you always told me we must. I have made preparations. You will be proud of me. I have included a check, as always. Do not breathe a word to a single soul. It is best you burn this letter—just remove the check before you do! I am your eternally loving and adoring son, Adil.*

Adil? Probably a pet name, Leslie thought to herself, continuing her search. An amber box stood on a small chess table in the corner. Jewelry? She opened the lid with the key that was hidden beneath it. And, indeed, a pair of golden earrings sparkled at her, also a heap of gold coins, and beneath them—she had almost overlooked it—golden letters . . . a passport! Amira's passport! Leslie grabbed the dark blue booklet, sending the coins clinking and—*Bingo!*—a U.S. green card came to light. Leslie was just taking a closer look at the document when the sound of an engine swelled outside and abruptly died after a few moments. A car door slammed, then a second.

She hastily stuffed the letter and the documents into the pocket of her jeans and stepped away from the window. Nick entered the room holding his finger up to his lips.

"Some guy drove her home. He's coming in with her." He rubbed his fists. Leslie positioned herself by the living room door. "Should I call Hans?" she whispered.

Nick shook his head and skulked out into the hall.

A key turned in the lock. The sound of jovial voices. The driver had taken the bicycle down from the car roof and was following Amira into the house. The hallway was poorly lit. Grunting lecherously, the man dug his fingers into her well rounded behind. "Mmmm, yeeesss," the woman muttered, taking a step over toward the light switch.

At this moment, a cat magically took flight and landed right on the man's head. The animal hissed, and then shot off. The man was bleeding from where he had been scratched in the face, but he was anything but dumb. A full-blooded Tajik was not to be caught off guard that easily, as Nick found to his dismay when he swung a frying pan at the man's skull. The Tajik easily ducked the blow and had the American by the throat before he knew it. He strangled Nick with an iron grasp, uttering vile curses all the while. Amira, who had since recovered from her initial fright, quickly grabbed a kitchen knife. There she stood, waiting for the right moment to plunge the deciding thrust into Nick's back.

It all happened in a matter of seconds.

Leslie had no choice. She pulled her SIG Sauer, firmly gripped the angular barrel, jumped up and slugged the Tajik, who was still working on Nick's throat, on the shoulder, which was protected only by nothing more than a checkered shirt. The gun made solid and precise contact with that sensitive spot on the collarbone, right around where the carotid artery ascends. The man, who had just gone through a quick succession of lust, horniness, and being on the winning end of a good old brawl, now slumped moaning onto the cold, hard floor.

Amira didn't get the chance to plunge or do anything else.

Nick used a well-aimed chop with the side of his hand to knock the knife cleanly out of her fist, then turned her arm rudely behind her back, and pressed her down on the kitchen table. Leslie held the open first-aid kit out to Nick. His voice was a single, high-pitched command.

"The syringe!"

Leslie had already practiced handling it in the helicopter. But her hand was shaking. Then it happened. The woman lunged forward with her head and bit into the back of her hand.

Leslie screamed, and cursed. The syringe lay broken on the ground.

"Take the kit, and run to the helicopter," Nick bellowed.

Nick got a good fistful of Amira's hair, pulled back her head, and brutally whacked it on the hard tabletop. Her body went limp.

Nick saw the curtain tie, tore it down, and bound Amira's hands behind her back. A few cats crept up, meowing. A dog barked. Nick emptied the bag of dry food into their bowl. Then he heaved the lifeless woman onto his shoulders with a grunt, holding her by an arm and a leg, like one would a dead deer.

Before he stepped outside, he surveyed his surroundings. Not a soul in sight. He carefully crossed the yard, then fell into a laborious jog, which finally brought him, panting, to the helicopter. The blades were already turning.

Hans pulled the woman up, and fell back into the pilot seat. Nick closed the hatch. The aircraft took off effortlessly and gracefully. Nick was still catching his breath, but with a happy grin on his face.

"Things rarely go according to plan."

Amira still looked elegant, in spite of her battered shape. She wore an ankle-length green satin dress, with a generous, Bedouin-style décolleté, an embroidered belt with an artful cloth rosebud discreetly emphasizing her paunch, a proud sign of affluence. A black, transparent designer veil bearing the golden initials of Yves Saint Laurent barely covered a pale face with heavy, dark brows. A row of thin, ornate gold bracelets jingled on one arm, while a fancy gold watch with a wristband decorated with black gems adorned the other.

Leslie handed Nick the first-aid kit. This time they met with no resistance as they injected the woman with the tranquilizer.

"You'd better get straight back on your plane," Hans recommended as he circled the airfield. "The faster you leave the country, the better."

He landed on the side of the jet that put him out of the direct line of view of the control tower. They switched to the other aircraft. Even if someone in the tower had made the effort to take a closer look at the scene, they would hardly have noted anything out of the ordinary. An onlooker would have observed two men helping a frail woman out of a known rescue helicopter bearing the red and white flag on its tail over to the jet—a purely routine humanitarian aid service.

The Spike Corporation jet received permission for takeoff just minutes later. It roared into the darkening sky over Tajikistan.

88

It was still broad daylight in Washington. Bill Baker rubbed his eyes, massaged his chin, and looked out of the window onto the familiar, boring vista of brown housing façades, reflecting windows, and treetops. He realized that he was facing a dilemma. His eyes, used to expertly scanning the distance, making out clear horizons, were not seeing anything in particular—only the patch of clear blue sky that his limited field of vision over Pennsylvania Avenue allowed.

This particular shade of blue reminded him wistfully, for an instant, of the island on which he was working on building his sailboat—which looked like it would never get finished. 9/11 had pushed a vacation on Turks & Caicos, and the completion of his project, into the unforeseeable distance.

As so often before in his career, he was forced to accept the strange phenomenon that sometimes a wrong decision can lead to the right result. And so Baker had learned over time that it served him to promptly and pragmatically change course, rather than trying to prove the validity of an initial assumption at all costs, even if it was—analytically speaking—compelling. This only made one lose sight of the big picture—and with that came the risk of missing a slew of opportunities that might arise from the new situation at hand.

The path that had led him to seek out the president in the Oval Office that night had, from this viewpoint, almost certainly been the wrong one to go down. He still cringed whenever he remembered the awkwardly initiated, and overall plain embarrassing, conversation. How could he have been so idiotically naïve as to think that the man in the White House would immediately be on board with the nebulous suppositions that some subordinate was hatching in regards to the First Lady; that he would trustingly give him carte blanche to spy on his now no longer sacrosanct spouse... Baker shuddered, disgusted by his own stupidity.

Of course, he owed this disgrace to no one other than the director himself—and Baker was not amenable to just taking that up the ass. No, siree! There were limits to his loyalty.

On the other hand, it had been precisely that humiliating scene in the Oval Office that had spurred him on. He had been focusing his mental energies on the First Lady ever since. Unsuccessfully at first... that is, until he confided in his old buddy Ken Cooper, whose reaction had been disappointingly unenthusiastic—until yesterday, when he had landed a surprise on him by deciding to tell him, after all, about the aerial sightings that his little high-tech toys had picked up. Howard Young and Rick Bronx! An express courier had slapped the police files on the Young murder case on Baker's desk just a short while later. He had dug into it with a vengeance that very same evening, without, however, making much headway. There was one single lead, thin as a silk thread, that he still wanted to follow up on. He eagerly awaited a call back from CBP headquarters, which was only a few blocks down on 1300 Pennsylvania Avenue.

Of course, there was also the admittedly interesting suspicion that Mossad agent Avi Leumi had thickly hinted at in his strictly confidential memo. Pretty conflicting stuff, it seemed to Baker.

Had Bronx really been at the scene of the crime in Bennet Park? A CIA vehicle had been there, certainly. But who had driven it? Had Young already been dead by the time the CIA man arrived, had Bronx stumbled on a corpse? There was no proof that Bronx had anything to do with the actual murder. It was all circumstantial evidence, which had about as much of a chance of being taken seriously—considering Bronx's legendary status within the CIA—as any of the countless impudent jokes made about the President of the U.S.A. A CIA agent could have any number of reasons for operating under cover in the line of duty—whether that meant driving somewhere, or keeping a death secret. Only the CIA itself had the authority to run a thorough check on one of its own. He, Baker, certainly didn't.

He eyed the memo morosely. The Mossad had discovered that Bronx was apparently heading an operation in New York. How else could he explain that the CIA agent had moved into a Brooklyn apartment and was meeting this woman—Leslie Palmer. But on the other hand, that was exactly the point. She was with Navy Intelligence. Why *shouldn't* Bronx be meeting with her?

The Mossad agent had been intermittently shadowing Palmer up until the day of 9/11 without uncovering anything of interest, other than the fact that she frequented the home of a young lover. Sure, sex provided grounds for suspicion, particularly since this Ben Heller was working on sophisticated spy software.

But what did Bronx have to do with any of this? Bill Baker had reached a dead end. *Maybe it was time to admit that he was on the wrong track!*

But something kept nagging at him. There had been that incredible statement made by Martin Wagner, the department director at Navy Intelligence, who had—according to the Mossad—discovered a number of oddities, namely that Leslie Palmer had been in the South Tower shortly before nine o'clock on that fateful day. A colleague by the name of Shelley had been able to substantiate that. Since then, she had been listed as missing. A victim of 9/11. Only, according to Wagner, someone had logged onto the secure Navy Intelligence server using Palmer's password combination after 9/11. Two or three times. Whoever had done so, had downloaded classified information that only people with a certain level of security clearance had access to. Palmer, for instance.

Was she still alive? If she had gone underground, what reason did she have? And how does someone like Bronx fit into the picture? Baker had a gut feeling—*the Palmer woman is the key figure here!*

Bill Baker wanted to avoid putting his size 14 in his mouth again. If Palmer, who did after all work for Navy Intelligence, was also working for the CIA, then an over-eager move on Baker's part could end in disaster. Blowing her cover might not only cause a major scandal—a prospect that anyone in the intelligence community looked forward to just about as eagerly as Count Dracula would being stranded in a field of garlic at high noon—but it could also be seen as obstruction of justice and result in a shameful conviction. *I'm keeping my fingers off this one! Let the CIA clean up their own damn mess.*

The buzzing of the phone interrupted his complex, catch-22 deliberations.

"Mister Baker? Gwen Gates here, Customs and Border Protection. You wanted to talk to me about Howard's…about the Howard Young murder case?"

A pleasant voice that immediately sharpened his senses.

"Yes, Bill here, thank you for returning my call, Gwen. You were Howard's secretary?"

"No, we're actually a secretarial pool over here..."

"Yes, I know..."

"Well, I recently—I mean, before this terrible...I took care of a few things for him."

"Did you know him well, Gwen?"

"No, only, I did notice that he preferred me over the others. I was the new kid on the block and we're both into...I mean we both liked Macs, and then we also discovered that we like roller-blading—that did create a kind of a bond, but not..."

"Not a more intimate relationship, you wanted to say?"

She laughed quietly.

"Exactly. We did develop a good friendship quickly. But no sex, sir!"

The FBI deputy imagined a blond, curvaceous Gwendolyn with a broad smile on her red lips, and bright white teeth, and rued that he neither belonged to the sworn Mac community, nor had he ever been able to skate.

"Mmm," he said, in a noncommittal tone. "So, Gwen, on the day of his murder, did you see Howard?"

Her voice grew darker.

"Yes, sir. He had a meeting outside the office, and he had left this envelope lying on his desk. Well—it was under a newspaper, to be more precise. But the yellow color caught my eye."

"Yellow?"

"Yes—one of those dark yellow manila envelopes"

"What did you do?"

"I looked inside. I immediately noticed the tab. It was light green—the color used by our intelligence department."

"And then?"

"Well...em...do you have time? Would you like me to explain it to you over a cup of coffee."

Bill Baker's quick thinking skills tended not to extend to matters regarding the female sex. Such was the case now. *Coffee? Since when did a Deputy Director of the FBI have time for stuff like that!*

"Please, what did you do next?" he asked, businesslike—which promptly extinguished the refreshingly frivolous undertone in Ms. Gates' voice.

"I copied the documents and filed them. I think that Howard didn't know that files that are taken outside of the agency have to be signed out and copied. That's what people like me are responsible for."

"Aha! And did you tell Mr. Young about this? Did he say where he was going with the dossier?"

"Unfortunately I didn't see him again."

The line fell silent for a moment. Baker thought he might have heard the young woman blow her nose.

"So he had no idea that you had seen these documents and saved him from committing a policy error?"

"No," she said, her voice now more firm. "I had work to do elsewhere, and Howard was gone by the time I returned. Do you want the dossier?"

Baker caught his breath. *Why didn't I think of that? Coffee? Sure. She was probably pretty, this Gwen.*

When he didn't answer straight away, she said, "I'll have it sent over. It won't take long."

Baker started stammering.

"Good… er… well, and we'll keep in touch."

"You should probably speak to my boss," she said in a professional tone. Apparently, the nice young lady was through with him. *Well, so much for that!*

A good half hour later, a big, white puffy cloud drew in front of the sun shining over Pennsylvania Avenue in Washington, D.C. The shadow that the delicate model sailboat had cast from the table where it stood and onto the CBP intelligence report began to pale. The Arab names noted on the paper seemed, on the other hand, all the more striking. In fact, they practically seemed to be jumping out at him. Baker carefully read through them one more time, checked them against the current 9/11 database, got up and used a secure landline to call his longstanding, good friend—the only person in the Washington beehive that he could currently trust with absolutely anything, and protocol be damned.

"These are the names of the terrorists who hijacked American Airlines flight 11 and the Boeing 767 that crashed into the South Tower. Howard smuggled this information out and brought it with him to his meeting in the forest in Maryland."

"That's crazy—that means that he was on the edge of uncovering the whole thing," said Ken Cooper. "He entrusted Bronx with the information—but why him?"

"Don't know—let's say it *was* Bronx that he met, and Bronx killed Howard Young when he got a load of what the CBP agent had dug up . . . then . . ."

Baker practically felt the force with which this piece of information hit Cooper at the other end of the line. He was quick to add fuel to the fire.

". . . then Bronx would have been involved in the planning of 9/11. Your agency, Ken. The CIA!"

"Suicide pilots did it."

"I know, Ken. The question is, what are we going to do with this information?"

"Assuming your suspicion is correct," said Cooper, in a calm, analytical tone, "that would make Bronx a double agent for Al Qaeda. Still, we're left without proof."

Baker had fished around in murky waters often enough to know when he had a bite.

"There is one more trail that I haven't followed up on yet."

"Come on. Let the cat out of the bag!"

"A hacker sent us information shortly before 9/11, which turned out to be extremely relevant—not to say explosive—in hindsight. He intercepted a bunch of emails. We could find out whose system he was hacking into. That might help us along."

Cooper was nearly bursting with impatience.

"Name? Do you have a name?"

"Ben Heller. He sent us the data via FedEx—probably to protect himself. I have his address. And—get *this*, Ken . . . !"

In spite of the fact that his curiosity was damn near killing him, Ken opted to respond with a pointed silence as Baker kept shoveling.

"Because of the precise data he sent us, we were able to determine which computer he was doing his hacking from. It belongs to a certain Leslie Palmer, Navy Intelligence."

"Interesting... Palmer..."

"I would agree," Baker said, reaching a decision for himself at that very second. Cooper's tone had conveyed to Baker that they were now, finally, singing from the same hymn sheet.

"Great, listen, Bill, we should meet. Tomorrow in Manhattan, around ten? I have to be in New York anyway. Would you believe that it's harder to put together an agency-spanning CTU than it is to get the president to attend a dinner with Fidel Castro? Unbelievable—like kids in a sandbox. I'll see you tomorrow!"

Baker was about to hang up, when Cooper's voice rang in his ear again.

"Bill? I believe we're going to let the Mossad handle this. Avi Leumi seems to have some unfinished history with this Bronx. Suits me, is all I can say. It'll be the other way around for a change. Let *them* get their fingers burned."

He laughed, then severed the connection.

Bill Baker wasn't having any of it. He issued an urgent APB on Leslie Palmer within the hour. Let her explain why she had done a disappearing act, what she was doing on the Navy Intelligence server, why she had given a notorious hacker access to her platform and allowed him to execute precarious data exchange operations, and what her meetings with Bronx were about. Baker was convinced he was doing the right thing. *To hell with his trepidations about blowing a CIA agent's gig... Those sneaky Langley cover-up artists weren't his problem...*

Finally, Baker released a sigh of utter contentment, which had been brewing in him like a fart after a vat full of beans.

The very next morning, every police and border patrol station throughout the nation would be able to admire the FBI all points bulletin on their computer screens—right along with the picture of the suspicious

Ms. Palmer! No one was going to pull the wool over this old hound's eyes! *God damn it, Gwendolyn Gates, with the roll that I'm on, you'd have been boasting to your grandkids about that coffee break you had with me!*

89

"Spike, we have a problem."

There was silence in the ethers.

"Spike, I have to get this woman to America urgently," Leslie insisted, irately. "She needs specialized medical attention."

Still no answer.

"Spike, this is serious. I, we, won't be able to make it on a scheduled flight. Spike, can you fly us there, can your pilots... Spike... I..."

"Leslie. I don't believe a word of what you're saying," she finally heard his calm voice. "There are a whole bunch of specialists in Europe who are excellent in their fields. Zurich has a particularly strong reputation when it comes to cutting-edge medicine. But you sound desperate—truly desperate. I don't really care about your reasons. Does it have anything to do with 9/11? Doesn't matter. I feel your need. Hand me the pilot."

"He wants to speak to you," Leslie stammered to the captain, gesturing at the headphones.

"Sir, this is your pilot, hello?"

He listened, glanced over at Leslie a few times. Nodded.

"Fine, I'll tell her. Good night, sir. Over."

They stopped for fuel in Düsseldorf. It was long after midnight before they took off for Teterboro Airport in New Jersey.

As the co-pilot was serving Leslie Palmer a dry vodka martini with an extraordinarily fat caper floating inside of it on the spanking new private luxury jet, as the lights of the English Channel shone up at them through the clear night, an old golden grandfather clock in the second-floor White House living room—which had beaten time for Lincoln himself—chimed ten high tones.

"You've also grown to be a lot more serious. You used to be such a fun person to be around," Sarah Crawford, First Lady of the United States, began hesitantly, as she poked her fork around in her pie. "You shouldn't always take your work home with you. No wonder you're exhausted."

The chef on duty on the second story had also prepared a simple dinner of soup, vegetable tureen, and filet of red snapper in the private dining room next door.

The president slowly chewed on a piece of bread, but remained silent. Sarah struck a conciliatory tone.

"Do you want to watch the baseball game together?"

"Are the Mets already playing again? The bodies of our 9/11 heroes and martyrs have barely been buried..."

"I take it they want to send the message that life goes on," his wife said with an encouraging smile.

"Mmm. I really don't feel like it. Game's almost over anyway. Have you made plans for the girls' birthday yet?"

He looked at her inquisitively as he said this. He had made a point to keep November 15 strictly open—now he was waiting to see what her reaction would be.

"Why do you ask? It's a bit early to be worrying about that."

"November will be here before you know it. There's going to be a lot going on. Putin will be visiting Washington, Chirac will be visiting Ground Zero. The Blairs, wait, yes, we can invite them to the ranch—or, better yet—Putin. He loves to go shooting—ex-military man. What do you think?"

"Hey, I'm not your advisor—I'm your wife. And what about *my* birthday? We could do something alone for a change—go hiking, maybe. By the way, I'm firing the head patisserie chef."

"Why?" he asked, confounded. "Don't you like his birthday cakes?" He laughed artificially and thought of Bill Baker, who had put the bee in his bonnet about there being something odd about Sarah lately. *Was she starting to lose it? Firing people?*

"No, no. I just don't like his French attitude. He's constantly complaining about his salary and... he's just plain arrogant."

"Aha, and you *have*, of course, considered that my mother is coming. And that she swears by him."

"I fail to see the connection. Don't tell me she's planning to be here on my birthday, like last year. That's all I need. Anyway—it's my decision, not hers. And that's that!"

She dabbed the corners of her mouth with the white napkin, her face showing clear signs of annoyance.

Memory like an elephant for family arguments, he reflected, slightly peeved. "I just mean, in your condition, you know what we spoke about."

What did they speak about, the First Lady wondered.

"Yes, I know. Well that was a few days ago," she answered shortly. "I'm fine. I don't need anyone to hold my hand." She pushed her plate away and stood up. "I'm going to take a shower. Come along if you want!"

She said the latter with a certain hint of suggestion, which went right over the president's head. Baker was right, he thought. She *has* changed. He was just thinking of asking her about that therapy of hers, but she had already disappeared into the large bedroom. Did she want to share a bed with him again? The thought made him feel somehow queasy.

He shuffled off to the Treaty Room, looked listlessly at the pile of folders on his desk. He really didn't feel like serving the nation, so he irresolutely turned to the living room, where he sank into a comfortable wingchair in front of the television. A news broadcast was monotonously flickering across the enormous flat screen. He closed his eyes and dozed off almost immediately.

He awoke with a start to the sight of her standing before him stark naked. Her broad hips, shapely legs and strong thighs—so familiar. *What the hell had Bill Baker meant?* She stroked her flat hand across her stomach, which showed a faint Cesarean scar.

"Do you even remember what I look like?" she asked seductively, turned pertly on her heel, and sashayed back toward the bedroom.

"The results of your blood tests are back," she called from the bathroom.

"I got them," he answered, amazed that she even remembered. "Ideal blood pressure, cholesterol's back to normal."

He got up, deciding to call Baker in the morning. The man was seeing ghosts. Definitely heading down the wrong path. His wife was completely normal—her same old self. *Old*? That was a bit mean! He caught himself doing her an injustice, tiptoeing back to the conjugal bedroom. The telephone buzzed—the secretary of defense.

"Found anything, Ron? And how's your dearest?" the president asked, sitting down on the edge of the bed. One foot played with a beige silk slipper—lifting it, rotating it, then letting it drop again. He watched the First Lady through the wide-open bathroom door—his battle-tried wife and partner. Still completely naked, Sarah was preparing herself for a mating ritual with the mightiest man on earth—and that included Putin and Osama.

"Great, great," droned the secretary of defense. "I just wanted to let you know that we may have found the bastard."

"Finally some good news. Anything else?"

"Yes. The CIA has target coordinates."

"Why is it always the CIA, Ron?"

The mightiest husband on earth pushed his right big toe into the left slipper, lifting it gingerly. In the bathroom, Sarah had cleverly positioned herself in front of the pink marble sink, so that only about a third of her, admittedly, now somewhat matronly hips could be seen through the door.

"We're close, Mister President. The carrier groups have the classified target info. All we need is your order, and we'll bomb the crap out of them!"

He lost the slipper. *Fuck!*

"You've always been a man with a sunny disposition and full of positive predictions, Ron. Where are our ships?"

The president, now angling for the lost slipper with both feet, had a hard time hearing what the secretary was saying.

Meanwhile, the First Lady had started to reveal a little more of her—in spite of its increasing volume—still shapely ass, managing to perform a clever little pivot that showed her bushy pubic hair, still dark blond if somewhat paled with age, to full advantage.

"Good. I know, Ron. Come by for breakfast. I want you to fill me in on all the details."

The president's voice had now taken on an iron edge of authority, which was—truth be told—partially meant to impress Sarah, who had now walked into the spacious, pink-tiled shower stall without bothering to close the milky glass partition door behind her. Now she was turning at the faucets, giving little routine squeals because the water was either too hot or too cold. Finally, she found a temperature that suited her, began spreading soap all over herself. The mating ritual of the nation's First Couple would now usually call for him to join her.

"Dick has called for a midnight briefing," the secretary of defense's voice sounded dimly into the couple's bedroom, followed by a roar that sounded like waves crashing onto the cloud-covered beach of Oman. "I'll come by beforehand. Maybe we'll see each other in the Situation Room. I just spoke to the commander of the 8th carrier fleet."

The president gave himself a jolt. Whether it was because he really didn't want this conversation to end, or whether it was because Sarah had now turned to give him a full frontal view, he could not have said. Apparently not aware of the effect that the sight of her was having, she reached between her still firm thighs and began lathering her bush so boisterously that it sent bits of foam flying around her.

"Damn it," the president hissed, buttoning his trousers back up. "Okay. Ron, I'll call you right back."

Gruffly kicking the unruly slippers aside, the president got up. He was already on his way to the Treaty Room as he fastened his belt.

"Where are you, darling?" he heard his wife beckoning him. "Are you coming?" But he was already in the hallway and backing toward the elevator.

"Later, honey, give me ten minutes," he called, leaving her to her fate. In his heart of hearts, he was quite relieved.

"Yessir!" a loud, clear military response issued from the handset that he had put on speaker.

As he was on his way down in the elevator, Sarah was placing her cell on the nightstand and wondering what Leslie Palmer might be doing right now. Then she fetched the vibrator out of the bathroom closet with a sigh, and placed the fetchingly shaped thing next to the phone. *I wonder what's going to be thrumming first tonight?* she contemplated, amused, but stopped herself from providing an answer to her own question right away. She dreamily stroked the plump head of the vibrator with her right hand, as her left slid, already somewhat absently, down her freshly showered thighs, which smelled appealingly of lavender... but she couldn't quite get in the mood. She lay down and pulled the light down bedspread over her breasts and looked, now seriously bored, up to the stark white ceiling...

...and remembered the white purse. She blinked over toward the dressing room, where the precious piece had probably been tossed heedlessly onto the floor. But she was too comfortable to check right now.

Just a few hours later—the sun had already reached its zenith over Afghanistan—twenty-one Tomahawk cruise missiles, equipped with bunker-busting payloads, were fired from the USS *Gonzales* and hit the Tora Bora cave system with a terrible force, reducing the sophisticated hidden labyrinth to a pile of rubble. Half the mountain came thundering down into the valley—but the heads that the Tomahawks had been sent to split had long escaped somewhere into the safety of the wide countryside.

Zawahiri, Bassan, and their honored leader, Osama, were already a long way off by this time, well on their way to the safe HQ B, ninety kilometers southeast. The Saudis had coolly calculated that it would be best to take photojournalist Quinn with them to their new headquarters. Not that their bearded leader felt any kind of empathy for the American—far from it. But on the grand bargaining scale, when prisoners were to be traded, a Yankee like Quinn could be worth his weight in gold...

90

Leslie Palmer sat alone in the brand-new airplane. The *Gulfstream* was a thing of beauty—its interior composed completely of mahogany, leather, and crystal. She leaned back comfortably in the broad, multifunctional seat and put her legs up on the cushion opposite, holding the directions on how to use the in-seat telephone in her hand. Paul Engl, the second officer, had placed a gin and tonic on the immaculately polished exotic wood side table, and announced their approximate time of arrival in Teterboro. Leslie gazed out into the night sky through the cabin window—not a star in sight, only darkness, even where she imagined there should be land beneath them. Only the position light shone its even, reassuring beam into the black heavens somewhere over northwestern Europe.

Teterboro, inaugurated around 1919 by Walter C. Teter, was the oldest airport in the New York vicinity, where it presently served general aviation—which meant chiefly private and corporate aircraft. According to Paul, Spike had registered his *Gulfstream* in Bermuda, that attractive little Atlantic island southeast of New York. And so the racy machine waited at her hangar in Teterboro, always prepared to go on any mission demanded of her.

On this flight, the kidnapped Amira had been bound to a stretcher in the rear, so that Leslie had a perfect view of her hostage whenever she sat up. The steward was currently spreading a blanket over the woman with a less than enthusiastic look on his face. He was not exactly gentle as he adjusted the pillow under her head.

Leslie raised the glass to her lips with one hand, took a small sip, then carefully dialed the number on the keys of the delicate handset with her index finger. She heard a buzz three times.

"Hello?"

"Sarah! It's me, Leslie!"

"Oh, hi! How wonderful of you to call. Everything go well?"

Leslie explained succinctly—she did not want to remain on the line too long. She tried to give a precise situation report, added information on flight number and ETA, then she lowered her voice.

"Did you take all that down?... Good. I need you to listen, Sarah. It's about this Amira. I need your help. I can't afford to have any difficulties entering the country, you understand?... Okay, I'm giving you her passport data. Ready?"

Leslie put her gin glass on the open document to keep it in place.

"Her name is Amira al Raisi, the green card is issued to the same name, I'll spell..."

"She has a green card?"

"Yes—I presume that it is valid indefinitely. Her husband was an American citizen. She also has a passport that was issued in Dushanbe on... wait..."

After she had double-checked by going over details and repeating them, Sarah said, "Don't worry, Leslie, I will have someone from Customs and Border Protection pick you up. Who's doing the handling for the machine?"

"*Handling?*"

"The clearance."

The co-pilot stood in the galley, where he was busy bustling around with a tray. She waved him over.

"Tomorrow at noon, Sarah, is our appointment still solid?"

"It looks like we will be going to Manhattan to attend Medal Day at City Hall..."

"Just a second, Sarah."

Leslie whispered the clearance question into Paul Engl's ear as he leaned across the table to serve the smoked salmon plate.

"Jet Aviation," he answered, and discreetly withdrew.

"Leslie? I heard. How are you getting into the city?"

"Listen, Sarah, City Hall Plaza you said... wasn't *Medal Day* in summer?"

"I have no idea, it's, wait... ah... a memorial service. My husband is scheduled to hold a memorial speech. Was there something else you wanted to tell me?"

Leslie's heart stopped for a few fractions of a second. She had a hard time breathing. *City Hall. Was she really to appear there and commit such an infamous act?*

"Leslie, is everything alright?"

"Excuse me? What do you mean...?"

The white Fendi purse! The sign that Bronx expected to see. Leslie debated feverishly whether or not she should warn Sarah that she absolutely had to wear it.

"Sarah, I . . . em . . . have to follow my path," she said flatly, not answering her question.

"What is your plan—do you need help?"

Leslie sat upright; peering over to Amira she said quietly, "No . . . or rather, yes: I need you to keep this to yourself. The Secret Service, the police, none of them can know about my sons. The whole thing has to stay strictly between us . . ."

"Don't worry. Call me if you need me—I have a lot of pull, and I can get things moving for you. Together, we make a darn powerful team."

Leslie ended the conversation with a sigh.

A weight had fallen from her shoulders. The last thing she needed was for the Secret Service or the police to appear on the scene . . . She calculated the timing. The ultimatum expired tomorrow at noon. She was determined to complete the job. *City Hall!* She would not disappoint her sons. Never in a million years. She would rather die than to abandon them! *Bronx would be stunned at what Leslie Palmer was capable of.*

She chewed on her salmon, and was completely *d'accord* with the Canadian steward, who had reappeared, when he opined that wild garlic ravioli and the *scaloppini al limone* served *en suite* would be very nicely rounded off by a California merlot.

After she had finished her *mousse au chocolat*, she was pleased that junior district attorney Chuck Browne answered his phone immediately, almost as if he'd been waiting for her call.

"Leslie Palmer here, do you remember me?"

The line was silent for seconds. *Was he going to hang up on her?*

"*Palmer* . . ." she pressed, "I'm calling from a plane . . ."

"Of course, yes, the circumstances of our meeting were unfortunately very sad. Is there something I can do for you. I just got in the door." *The night was still young in Manhattan.*

"You were wearing a leather jacket, that night at my father's house, it said something . . . Pleasure . . . and something else . . . do you ride a motorcycle?"

"Yes, why?"

"Do you know a doctor by the name of Nassim? He works at..."

"I know him well. He's a fellow club member. The one with the damaged leg. He's one of the Pleasure Cruise Riders."

Leslie's wine almost went down the wrong way, she was suddenly so excited. She took a quick swallow of water, and a deep breath.

"I want to... could you get him to call me...?"

Chuck Browne cleared his throat. But Leslie was faster.

"No, better yet," she said, "it is imperative that I see him, tomorrow morning..."

She could have kicked herself as she heard herself indiscriminately spewing out her request. The junior district attorney immediately picked up on the urgency in her voice.

"Where will you be landing, Ms. Palmer? If you want, I can pick you up—with flashing lights, if necessary. I'm still a junior district attorney, after all." She could almost see the grin on his face. "And I'll get Nassim out of bed for you. What would you like me to tell him?"

"Just tell him that I'm the woman he saved on his Honda on 9/11. He'll get it... And one more thing, Chuck..." The idea had come to her out of the blue.

"Yes?"

"A big car... Could you arrange that? And as many people as possible on motorbikes, your Pleasure Riders...?" She held her breath, as if she were waiting for a barrage of critical questions. But Chuck Browne kept it short and sweet.

"You've got it!"

Completely relieved, Leslie gave him the exact details concerning the arrival of Mr. Steinberg's *Gulfstream* VA-SPK in Teterboro.

A short while later the steward accompanied her to the sleeping cabin and handed her a lilac bathrobe with Spike's initials on it. The hot water beating down on her at 30,000 feet altitude made her body tingle so powerfully that it had her alternately trembling and catching her breath. She felt a strange thrill welling up inside of her. An unbelievable chain of events was about to unfold over the next few hours—and the result would be either triumphant or devastating. She was aroused, almost painfully alive. She had never before felt such a rampant sexual lust in response to stress—it was almost as if it were her last chance at attaining the height of pleasure.

She dried herself off, threw the robe around her shoulders, and lay down on the bed. After she had dimmed the lights, she began to touch herself. Gently, then harder, pictures of passion before her eyes... *Ben*... and when she thought of him, heard his words echoing in her mind, felt his embrace, her arousal grew sweeter and more urgent—her hands were everywhere—and it was as if a volcano erupted within her. A small, sharp cry, and then she lay there, whimpering, her knees pulled up tight—like a baby. She almost put her thumb in her mouth, and had already fallen asleep before she could remember that she had wanted to call Jennifer, that she had no chance, that... any of it... never... again...

91

It was a glowering sky over Afghanistan that saved photojournalist Steve Quinn's maltreated skin and tired soul. The column of vehicles, which had been laboriously winding its way along the mountain road, had been caught in a heavy storm that had sent hurricane force winds sweeping across the nasty plains at the end of the canyon. The vehicles threatened to be swallowed by sand. The column chief commanded that they stop, and all hands were suddenly needed. Gusts of wind ripped tarpaulin covers off and carried them into the distance. Barely recognizable hooded figures braced their weight against the horrific storm. Pieces of baggage and boxes of ammunition could be whipped away at any moment.

Quinn had made the riverbed out through a crack in the tarp before the thick, dark, treacherous storm front had obliterated everything from view.

A few huts, or what was left of them, offered uncertain cover. The trucks maneuvered arduously between the bullet-riddled, burned ruins. *A ghost town. There must have been a battle over a bridge somewhere near here,* Quinn thought.

Salim suddenly appeared next to him, clinging onto the loading bridge. "The ford is down there!" he screamed.

"What about it?" Quinn yelled back.

"March halt! Secure the loads! There, that rope, grab it!"

They struggled. Suddenly Salim had disappeared from sight. Quinn lost his footing as he angled for a gas canister. *Or had he deliberately let go?* The storm grabbed him, tumbled him over hard, rough ground. Quinn tried to stand, waving his arms in a vain attempt to balance himself. Gusts of wind followed one upon the next. His wide robe caught the wind like a billowing sail. All at once, Quinn lost sight of everything. There were no trucks, no black walls, and no slanted silhouettes of figures battling the elements. He allowed the wind to carry him, stumbled, got back up, and suddenly found himself kneeling on wet gravel. Water. *The river. The ford.* He fought to regain enough balance, then cowered under the cover of a slab of rock.

He had lost all sense of direction long ago. *Back? But where to. This river was good news. Water flows downward, toward the ocean. So follow the water! As quickly as you can!* Leaning against the rock, he squinted to both sides. The current was quite weak. Then Quinn decided to change his mind. He would walk against it. If they were going to look for him, it would certainly be downstream.

Slowly, his posture bent, he prowled up the side of the rocky riverbed. He seemed to have made the right decision. The wind had the good grace to blow from behind, driving him forward...

He trudged into the night, always uphill, wading, climbing, scraping the skin on his hands and knees, feeling blindly for a hold, and on he went. Hours had passed. Of course they had taken his watch a long time ago. He finally lay down, exhausted. So here he was—next to a large boulder, on a piece of even ground, the water rushing below him. *Lost and alone.*

Deathly tired.

When he woke, he found himself staring down half a dozen muzzles. The men looking down at him wore the traditional Jihadi garb—wide pants, long woolen jackets, leather caps, boots. The bearded faces did not look friendly. One kicked him roughly, and asked in Arabic who he was.

Taliban! Was he ever going to catch a break?

He said nothing. What good would it have done at this point? The men stuck their heads together and mumbled. The glances they shot him were anything but promising.

"Get him on the truck. Give him water," one of them suddenly ordered, sounding remarkably like a New York cop.

Quinn sat up, surprised. "I'm American," he sputtered, "I'm fleeing…"

The men eyed him suspiciously, their weapons at the ready. Their eyes took in his long beard, the gray robe, the wide jacket.

"Where are you from?"

"Steve Quinn, photojournalist with the *New Yorker*, I got away. You have to alarm headquarters immediately."

"What the hell are you talking about, man?"

The fact that these wild warriors were actually a U.S. Special Forces unit could only be told when they opened their mouths. They led him to a sand-colored Swiss military all terrain vehicle with a long loading bridge. The leader of the special unit was Major Brad Freelander. He studied a laminated map.

"We have to check out what you've just told us, sir. Where along the river did you say the convoy had to halt?"

Quinn shook his head. He didn't have the foggiest idea where they had started from, or which route they had taken down to the river. "They had me in the back of a dark truck until the storm broke loose."

One of the soldiers checked a GPS apparatus.

"Pass the information on via your satellite phone, Major," Quinn insisted. "The traitor's name is Bronx. An American. I saw his text message with my own two eyes."

"And you want me to convey that? What did the message say?"

"It was a veiled tip-off that the cave system was about to be attacked."

"Mmm, an American—are you sure?"

The major obviously bristled at the thought of a traitor on his side of the fence. Quinn nodded. He was getting impatient.

"Of course. And now please bring me to a secure location as quickly as possible. I have to get back to New York."

The two soldiers sitting on the bench, shoveling canned meat with metal spoons, grinned through their bona fide Taliban beards. "New York. Wouldn't mind that right now myself…" one said.

"Listen," the major decided, "we have *procedures* that we have to follow. You have to be brought to the base for debriefing. Army intelligence defense specialists from the DIA will check every word of your story. That's not our job. We're interested in targets, understand? If you could at least tell us approximately where this vehicle column got stuck? How long did it take you to walk up the river from there?"

Quinn shrugged in resignation. The major exhaled sounded like a whistling safety valve.

"No idea, huh? *Very strange indeed!"*

Frustrated, he threw the map down on the seat.

Quinn skeptically peered out from under the tarp and up at the forbidding, black sky.

"This is no weather to fly in, Major. Your Air Force can't do a damn thing right now. But your phone could get you all the way through to Washington. Why aren't you doing something?"

"Operating procedures, sir. We have a battle mission. The SatPhone is strictly reserved for aerial deployment—for target definitions, not for friendly chats. Sorry."

"But this constitutes an extraordinary circumstance, Major," Quinn persisted, desperately. "This Bronx is conveying the coordinates of our targets to the terrorists…"

"What you're telling me there seems very fishy to me, man. But, like I said, the Army intelligence guys will know what to do with you once we get you to base. We'll have enough on our plates just getting you there alive. Believe me."

He gathered his men—hunched over a map, they planned their course of action. A few minutes later an all terrain vehicle was rumbling back onto the dirt track. It was quickly lost from sight in the pale blue-gray of the lowlands that had just been washed clean by the storm.

92

Rick Bronx's sour face told the men who had gathered in the room for an urgent briefing not to expect good news. The boss stared silently at them, with dark, heavy eyes, as if he could not quite decide what best to do with them. Because the steel blinds of the secret base disguised as Public Storage on the waterfront hermetically sealed out the day, the only light came from neon strip lamps, which lent the faces of the subordinates a pale and fearful distorted sheen.

Sheikh Khalid had positioned himself in the corner, like a general about to inspect his troops—only that his power of command was really the sole aspect he shared with any given military leader. Khalid was bound to a wheelchair—his gaunt legs under a long, worn horse blanket made him seem debilitated. New York cops had made him a cripple years ago, in a shootout, he claimed. Bronx was inclined to believe half of his story at most. And maybe none of it. They had robbed a bank in Queens one winter morning. A completely befuddled clerk, whom they got hold of at the back entrance, was forced to hand over the keys. They had plundered the safe, pistol-whipped the sorry bastard. Everything would have gone fine had Khalid's masked accomplices with their bags full of cash not run into a DHL courier who happened to be parked next door, in front of the coffee shop. The guy in the brown uniform had sounded the alarm. Sitting behind the wheel of the getaway car, Khalid had blown through a roadblock, launched over a ramp, flown through the air in a high arc, then landed on the subway tracks, which he managed to rattle across to get back onto the avenue. Just then, a trigger-happy cop had opened fire on him at the cross street... The bullets had hit him in the back, Khalid said, instantly paralyzing his legs. In spite of this, he had still managed...and so on...at any rate, after the robbery (if, indeed, it had ever taken place) Sheikh Khalid had managed to escape with his sidekicks as well as the loot...

The longer Bronx contemplated the characters in the room before him, the less he understood of the world and its workings. Just days ago, on September 11, these naïve and amiable Arabs had accomplished a deed that addressed the entire world, which was unsurpassed in its braveness and grandiosity. The fate of the entire globe had been on the line. The Great Plan could not fail at any cost...And still...Bronx stared at Ahmed, the Stinger shooter—a harmless-looking guy. Just like all the others, really, with their friendly, everyday faces. Not a bunch of leathernecks, or highly trained and rehearsed commandos...And this joke of a tattered figure in his wheelchair wants to have led this operative super-coup? The thought of it was a downright insult to him. He, Bronx, had been the drillmaster, the troubleshooter, the one to smooth out the rough edges, identify areas of weakness, keep the men going...motivate them, like today...

They had set about it like a bunch of amateurs. Bronx shook his head. Only Allah Himself could have guided them over all of the obstacles, and through all of the stupid mistakes that they had made. There was the guy in Florida, for instance, who had got himself arrested for violating immigration regulations. Then one of the eleven AA hijackers had been stopped by the traffic cops, not once, but *three* times for speeding. And nothing had happened to them! The men had displayed all kinds of conspicuous behavior—they had messed around with women, boasted in a bar that they were pilots. Bronx had been forced to intervene. He had called together all of the logisticians and the caretakers, just like he had today, in this dreary room. But what good had any of it done? None.

In Boston, the group had come from so far away that they were only just able to reach the flight that they were planning to hijack at a fast jog. How could he possibly understand this type of behavior? These jokers didn't fit his image of a well-trained elite troupe that remained under the radar, carefully calculated their schedules, knew how to change their appearances, avoided running red lights, had worked out a viable plan B...Not by a long shot.

...Bronx had come up with his own explanation. The martyrs had taken into account that they might not make that flight in Boston, or that they might be stopped by police in Florida and placed under arrest, because they secretly hoped that Allah would allow an obstacle to get in their way, thus exempting them from having to go through with their dreadful mission. *They didn't want to die!* That's what it was, thought Bronx—it must have been. And when they did reach the planes after all, they must have seen it as a sign that they really had been chosen to sacrifice themselves...

Bronx cleared his throat. He would just have to deal with whomever they gave him—even now, during the final phases of Operation Cinderella. He couldn't shake a stubborn, yet nondescript feeling of impending doom, a sense that something was afoot that he hadn't thought to plan for. What the hell could it be? Ah—probably just the normal white adrenaline rush before the grand performance!

"Men. This is a military operation. I want to make clear the importance of keeping our focus on the crucial purpose of our mission at all times. The West has had us under its thumb for too long—now our time has come to rule the West."

He had to get them fired up.

"Our mission is the only thing that counts—nothing else! Consider well what is at stake. Up to this point, everything has gone according to plan—almost too easily. Difficulties usually come unexpected and unannounced. We have to change our values. I am not fighting for a religious cause, but for the cause of *justice*, and my sights are set entirely on accomplishing this mission. The enemy is everywhere, and since 9/11, he has been roused. He is still disorganized, but as unpredictable as a wounded predator."

Sheikh Khalid gave a rattling cough, as if he wanted to interject.

"So be on guard. I am not ecstatic about the thousands of deaths, but war demands victims. That is its way."

"War demands victims," the Sheikh called. "That is good!"

Bronx pointed his finger at him, amused.

"I expect iron discipline—more than that, I expect each and every one of you to be prepared to kill, and willing to die. Ahmed?"

"Yes, brother?"

"You have become complacent, just like the others. Remember this: Allah is not leading this operation. I am. Rick Bronx. And if any man here makes even the slightest mistake, I will kill him with my own hands."

He pulled his pistol, made a loading gesture, and waved the muzzle in front of their faces.

Khalid grumbled approval and wheeled around to face the men with astonishing dexterity.

The threat had been effective. The room was so still, that one could have heard a rat breathe.

"What will you do with the boys, Bronx?" Sheikh Khalid suddenly croaked. Before Bronx could answer, Khalid spastically waved him over, commanding him to put his ear to his mouth with dramatic gestures.

The group of men finally exhaled in relief.

Bronx leaned forward, pinching his nose with his hand, as if he feared that the stench of the Sheikh whispering in his ear might well knock him out.

"You, Bronx, will kill them both!"

93

Craig and Alexander Palmer, trapped in their dark, windowless dungeon, which was now two-thirds full of water, were feverishly working on a plan.

They had immediately noticed the man in the black uniform in the arrivals hall, after landing on Swissair flight 100. He stood behind the barred gate along with a row of chauffeurs, who were all lifting their signs in the air in order to attract the attention of their clients, who were streaming in with searching looks on their faces. Craig was first to notice the sign: C & A PALMER it read, in blue ink, on the limousine service's board. They went up to the uniformed man and introduced themselves. The driver was friendly, in a gruff kind of way.

"Hi, I'm Johnny. *Welcome to New York!* Your mom sends her best. I'll be taking you to her apartment on 72nd Street. The car's outside in the garage."

He took Alex's trolley case without waiting for a response. They followed the man guilelessly—after all, Mom always sent a car to pick them up at the airport. It was completely normal.

They found the limousine after a short walk through the bleak parking structure hallways. It stood in the basement, polished to perfection, next to a large van with tinted windows. Johnny clicked open the trunk with his key fob as he approached, and was helpful in stowing away their luggage. Then he officiously opened the door with a polite, inviting gesture—as any New Yorker worth his or her salt would expect of a driver.

Then everything went very quickly. The kidnappers had the element of surprise on their side. Two men suddenly appeared. Their attack was decisive, and intimidating, crushing any seedling of resistance before it had a chance to emerge. They caught Alex and Craig in a stranglehold, simultaneously kneeing them brutally in the lower back. This sent both of the surprised victims neatly into the cargo space of the van. The side door slammed shut. The men kneeled on the boys' backs, pressing their faces hard onto the rough mat on the floor, twisting their arms behind their backs. They forced handcuffs on them, and—the van was already making its way toward the exit—gagged them with brown tape, which they wrapped multiple times around their heads. They were fast, professional.

Their jail had to have been a boathouse at one point. Before the water level had started to rise, they had been able to make out the landing stage, as well as the iron gate that neatly sealed off the room and evidently opened onto the water. *East River, Hudson? Long Island Sound?* Alex studied the gate's mechanism. It could be pulled up vertically. Where were the controls located? On the other side, an iron ladder attached to the wall led from the only door up by the ceiling down to the stage.

A bare bulb shielded by a wire grating shed stark light into the miserable room. Next to it hung a hoisting device that had obviously not been used for a long time. It consisted of two horizontal, rusty iron carriers, which could be lowered via a steel rope that ran over two pulleys that were attached to the ceiling. Long loops of strong material had once been used to pull a boat ashore by its hull. They were now covered in algae. Alex discovered a thick pipe on the wall facing the landing stage, about three feet above the paved ground. It was the water inlet.

The kidnappers had marooned their victims on a flat, white yacht tender, which was tied to the iron ladder with a strong rope. The dinghy's fiberglass hull measured about eleven feet in length, and the interior of the torpedo shaped craft was about three feet wide. The seat and the cockpit had been removed, so that the boys had just enough room to stretch out next to each other. A few woolen blankets constituted the only comfort that the stripped rigid-hull dinghy had to offer.

The entrance to the guardroom was located at the top of the ladder. The door opened with a metallic creak twice a day and one of the guards would motion them to ascend. This meant that they were allowed to climb the ladder and eat in the windowless room. Craig remembered the guardroom's technical equipment: a video camera console with a surveillance monitor, a number of switches, and a loudspeaker system, which allowed their captors to speak to them in the *water tank* as they called their prison. There was a wash trough in the other corner of the room, a metal table with a microwave on it, a bunk bed with two naked cots. A toilet and basin were located behind another door, which did not reach to the floor. Three dirty, bundled neon strips shone a depressingly dull light from the ceiling.

There seemed to be no need for more than two guards to watch over them. Craig had noticed that usually only one of them was up there at a time—and he was pretty sure that no one was there at all during the early morning hours. The only time that both of them were there was when they brought them something to eat—usually the thin one with the slanted eyes and the fat black sleazeball with the nasty face

"We have to prepare everything down to the last detail, we can't leave anything to chance," Craig whispered as he got up and held a blanket by two corners, spreading it wide as if he were going to fold it. He started rapping loudly, on and on... "We'll string you up by the nuts—and crack 'em like it's Christmas, we'll string you up by the nuts—and make you sing like bitches. We'll string you..."

Alex quickly stripped off his pants and shirt and slid over the round edge of the dingy into the water. He took a deep breath, then dove down. The camera, suspended in its waterproof cover on the ceiling, pivoted back and fort to compensate for a narrow field of vision—but it could not capture the diver behind Craig's woolen blanket.

The strong halogen light shimmered on the surface of the landing stage, which was already a good six feet under water. Alex found the button that probably controlled the iron door. He pressed it—but nothing moved. The lever for the hoisting mechanism did nothing either. None of the electric switches, even the waterproofed ones, seemed to be active. Alex came up behind the protective hull of the boat, carefully took another deep breath. He gave Craig a sign and went under again.

This time he examined the water inlet. Alex approximated the diameter of the pipe by comparing it to his lower arm, looking in vain for some kind of mechanism to stop the flow. His lungs were pounding, aching, as he turned toward the side of the stage where he could resurface next to the dinghy unseen, gasping for air. As he did so, a black shape caught his eye—there was something shadowlike stuck near the bottom of the iron door. He used his legs to powerfully launch himself off the wall, and reached the area with a few strong strokes. Alex's lungs were ready to burst, but the lifeguard diving training he had completed at Lake Geneva now helped him to hold his own.

He felt for the black thing, took hold of it, tore it loose—an angular object that had been lying there, covered by a coating of algae. Seconds later he resurfaced, hungrily gasping for air. The boys kept completely still for a few moments, squinting up to the guardroom door. Nothing. Craig shook out another blanket, held it up like a curtain, then began to fold it meticulously—like a recruit waiting for his sergeant to show up for inspection. Alex lay on the planks, exhausted, his entire body shaking. He did the best he could to dry himself off with the blanket, then put his clothes back on.

The boys inspected the find that Alex had salvaged—it was a massive iron angle with screw holes and filed down edges that were almost as sharp as blades. It's arms, which stood at 90 degrees from each other, were almost two feet long. Craig cleaned off the algae, wiped the narrow edge appraisingly with his thumb, whistled through his teeth, and made sure the tool—or should he say weapon?—was well hidden beneath the blankets. Their plan was slowly but surely beginning to take shape.

"We'll string you up by the nuts..." The grim chanting of vile tirades boosted their morale. *Never say die!*

"We're going to get out of here, Alex!" Craig whispered to his brother. "You can bet your ass on it!" He couldn't wait to pay this bunch of thugs back for what they had done to him at Paul Mercier's chalet.

That evening, as they climbed the ladder back down to the boat after they had eaten, Alex managed with all his might to push a metal spoon that he had secretly flattened beneath the joint of the doorframe. The guards were acting on the careless side—they seemed quite sure of themselves. Slit-eyes heedlessly slammed the door shut in mid-conversation with fatso—although he was forced to give it another hefty yank when the latch didn't click into place right away.

Just as Alex had hoped, a gap had appeared between the iron door and the concrete joint of the frame, where the spoon was now jammed. The twins grinned at each other. Alex didn't need to say a word, Craig knew exactly what was on his mind... *Yes, dear brother—there's nothing like achieving big things with little means*... they writhed with silent, suppressed laughter.

94

You, Bronx, will kill them both! The Sheikh's words reverberated in his mind. Bronx rose, took a deep breath, looked up sternly.

"Leon!" he barked with a commanding gesture.

The fat black man with the misshapen head jerked.

"Boss?"

"Once Cinderella has done her job, the boys have to go." It was an order, and it was given with no sign of emotion.

He lowered his angular face and bequeathed the pair with an icy look from under his bushy brows before finishing what he had to say. "I will tell you when it's time, then you'll take care of the two mama's boys. And you will leave no trace, understood?"

The black man gloated, the corners of his mouth twitching.

"Sure, boss. No worries. The meat grinder's been oiled." And with a stupid grin, he added, "Fish food, boss."

"Good. All know their job. *Stand down!*"

He hollered the latter at them, menacingly raising his gun. The two of them started, then fled from the room as if the devil were on their tails.

Bronx stared at the Sheikh's hunched figure—the shabby, long beard, the beautifully worked leather cap on his large, bald head. Looking at his distinctive features, Bronx saw one thing—an iron will. The lively set of his mouth, his sparkling eyes, all seemed indicative of a wild determination to make up for all of the old man's physical inadequacies. To anyone with a sense for such things, Khalid's firm voice, which was now sinking dangerously low, emphasized his brutal resolve. He was not a man to be doubted or underestimated.

"The ultimatum is tomorrow at twelve, Bronx. For you, too. The plan must be carried out. If it fails to succeed, it will be on *your* head. What do you plan to do if the woman doesn't shoot him?"

Bronx had always relied on his lively imagination. Whatever he could see in his mind's eye had always seemed attainable to him. And what he saw was the hand of the First Lady, as it reached into the purse, pulled the revolver out... He gave himself a jolt.

"She *will* shoot, Sheikh. But if anything should go wrong, I have rigged her purse."

The Sheikh leaned so far forward in such excitement that Bronx almost dared to hope that he might keel over, right onto that grotesque, bulbous, red hooknose.

"What the devil does a woman's purse have to do with all of this?"

"It's a masterpiece of destructive technology, Khalid. Lightning will strike and kill everything even close to the president. The detonator is set for 12:30 in the afternoon. If Cinderella has not done her job by then, the bag will do the rest, you understand?"

Khalid turned his nose up, pursed his lips in an ugly manner. An unmistakable sign that he did not approve of the plan—as indeed he did not approve of any plan that he had not thought up himself. Bronx went on to explain once more the entire sequence of events. Then they discussed security, debated evacuation measures, which would be necessary in order to eliminate trace evidence once Operation Cinderella had drawn to a close—on Sunday, less than 26 hours away!

95

Craig and Alex waited until the early morning hours. At about three, Craig climbed the rungs of the stairs and banged his fist against the door as if he were desperate to go to the bathroom. The noise would have woken the most moronic guard from even the most comatose sleep, had one been in the room. They held their breath, listened. There were no footsteps. But even after minutes had passed, Craig was relieved to note that there was still no sign of life. No cracking doors. Nothing but silence.

Finally, as planned, Alex maneuvered the tender under the hoisting mechanism. He used the angle iron to get ahold of the algae covered material loop. It was a precarious undertaking. The dinghy swayed dangerously, and Alex had a hard time keeping a steady balance. The loop, once he had finally captured it, got away from him again, because his movements pushed the boat across the water. Whenever he finally managed to grab the loop and bring it over the camera to cover the lens, the stupid thing would always end up slipping off again. What had seemed like a relatively simple thing was turning out to be extremely tricky—not to say impossible—chiefly because the smooth encasement offered no place to attach the fabric.

Time was running out. Craig decided that it would be senseless to keep experimenting. They had to hurry! If their luck ran out, one of their damnable wardens might show up, or—an idea that made Craig even more nervous—there could be another surveillance monitor somewhere in the building.

What the two boys did next was nothing short of an acrobatic masterpiece. Alex climbed on top of Craig's shoulders—which was not too difficult, thanks to the iron ladder. Then he braced his arms against the ceiling and began walking his hands away from the wall. The dinghy's buoyancy allowed them to remain relatively stable as long as Alex exerted enough pressure with his arms, but the trick to the whole balancing act was that they had to remain absolutely vertical. If they lost their center even slightly, the tender would glide out from under them, and they would both end up in the water.

They worked their way toward the camera encasement a centimeter at a time. Alex held his breath as Craig fought to maintain their equilibrium by skillfully balancing them with his strong thighs. But the entire undertaking was about as steady as a house of cards. One wrong move and *bam*—that would be it!

Sheikh Khalid had long since had his two bodyguards escort him to an inconspicuous gray delivery truck with a wheelchair ramp in the underground parking garage. In the briefing room in the northern part of the building, Bronx turned to his other side and pulled the blanket over his head. He wasn't exactly comfortable on the couch, starting from a troubled sleep about every half hour. He saw unnaturally glowing faces. Leslie Palmer, her hair ablaze, a bearded man waving from a cave, old man Palmer stretched out on the floor with blood seeping through his white mane of hair—or was it Howard Young, with an axe stuck in his split skull? Two girls swayed on a boat, one waving a red bundle... the red documents... Charles Palmer's notes from the bedroom drawer... and now two strong young men were swimming closer, lifting themselves over the edge of the boat... Bronx came wide-awake, threw the blanket back, and practically jumped up. *The Palmer boys!* He searched for the light switch, then opened the refrigerator and took out a bottle of water. He grabbed a box of Aspirin from the shelf, poured a heap of pills into his hollow hand, tossed them all back at once, drank greedily...

"Give me the blanket," Alex panted. He was just a few inches away from the camera now. Craig had pushed a torn piece of the woolen blanket under his belt. He reached for it ever so carefully, balancing his own body and his brother's weight unsteadily with his other arm. As he held the blanket up, he was horrified to feel the tender drifting. "Hurry up!" he yelled, but Alex's hasty forward movement only worsened the situation.

"Have you got it?" he called. "I, I..."

The boat seemed to be drifting away from under his feet—slowly at first. Craig's attempts to stop it were in vain. Then the inevitable happened—he swayed and fell, the tender sloshed away and banged against the wall. Where was Alex? When Craig resurfaced, he looked up and saw him. The little devil was dangling off the ceiling, holding onto the encasement for dear life and floundering with his legs. What was he doing? Craig reached for the boat. Then he saw that Alex had managed to cover the camera. The piece of blanket was wrapped around it, blocking them from sight. A terrific feat—even Christo would have been proud...Alex let himself drop.

"The angle," he panted, as his head popped out of the water. "We don't have any time to lose."

They tied the boat to the ladder. Alex climbed up to the bottom edge of the door holding the iron angle. Craig breathlessly held himself at the ready right behind his brother...

96

Grunting, Bronx turned to the blank, black monitor screen that was connected to the boathouse camera. *Boathouse,* he croaked into the silence. *Drowning chamber! How high was the water now? And what time was it, anyway? If only he had a couple of sharks that he could let loose on them in the end. Fish food! Ah well, we'll see...*

Sitting alone in the dingy technology room in front of the little surveillance monitor, he was slowly but surely beginning to lose his cool. Nothing seemed to be working! He let loose a stream of obscenities. The blank screen was getting him riled up—the damn thing was dead as a doornail. No picture of the boys nearing their doom to tickle his sadistic fancy. Or was his agitation due to the fact that some drippy, sentimental sense of compassion had perfidiously burrowed its way under his skin? *You, Bronx, will kill them both.* Who did that arrogant cripple think he was, messing with his business? His pride was telling him that he might want to sabotage Khalid's order, just let the boys go once everything was done.

This internal uncertainty was pissing him off even more. He hammered on the top of the monitor with his fists, hacked at the keyboard in random frustration. To no avail. *Those idiots had turned the camera off. Where were those limp dicks anyway, damn it?*

Discontented, he dragged his tired bones to the door and yelled into the hall.

"Ahmed... *Fuu-uuck it!*"

In the water dungeon, Alex Palmer forced the angle into the gap left in the door by the tablespoon. He slammed it in with all his might, driving it home. The part of the iron that he had managed to jam in was now protruding from the door at a 90-degree angle. Craig checked its hold by yanking down on it with both hands. He gave Alex a nod—this was it. Supported by his brother, Alex climbed up to the top rung of the ladder, turned slightly and fixed his eyes on the iron angle.

Their plan would only work if they managed to exert a maximum amount of leverage on the metal door leaf. Alex was convinced they could do it.

"Ready," he panted.

"One, two, three, *GO*!" Craig yelled.

Alex jumped off the rung and squarely onto the protruding arm of the angle. His entire body weight, greatly increased by gravity, came down on the lever before he continued to fall past his crouching brother and into the water below. The door emitted a loud crunching noise. There was a dull bang, and the iron shot away, missing Craig's head by a fraction of an inch. The door stood open. The force of the exerted leverage had, as planned, ripped the bolt out of its latch.

A short while later, the two wet heroes were standing in the guardroom, puddles forming at their feet. Alex pointed to an antiquated looking switchboard.

"There, that has to be the gate!"

He activated a turn switch. Somewhere a windlass began to whine—music to their ears. The heavy slider slowly began to rise along the lateral rails. The door to the boathouse was opening. The bigger the opening got, the faster the water streamed out.

The twins embraced each other, laughing with relief.

Mesmerized, they huddled over the edge of the doorway above the ladder, and watched the water burble outside. The gate had reached its final position; they could see lights shining in the distance. This was no time to relax—freedom was beckoning them!

"Into the boat! Let's get out of here!" Craig sounded full of fresh energy. He turned and put his foot on the top rung.

A sharp voice cut right to their cores.

"You'd like that, wouldn't you?"

They had never seen the man who was now standing in the guard-room, aiming his pistol at Alex. But his angular, hard face, which was red with obvious rage, did not leave a shadow of a doubt—this guy with the icy stare was a whole different caliber. He would stop at nothing.

"Get against the wall, both of you . . . *Leon!*"

Leon was on the spot with a few bounds, a stupid grin on his face. The bat came down in two expertly aimed blows to the backs of the boys' heads and they instantly slumped to the ground.

"Get these fucking mommy's boys out of my sight!" Bronx roared. "Into the basement! They'll never try a stunt like that on us again, right, Leon?"

"Never again, boss," Leon panted ecstatically.

97

The Spike Corporation jet rolled to its designated spot in front of the Jet Aviation Terminal in the slight, drizzling rain. The Sunday morning atmosphere at Teterboro was one of tranquil lethargy, almost as if no one was quite in the mood to tackle the new day. The steward opened the door and extended the stairs. Finally, a small van came to take the passengers the short distance to the arrivals hall. There was no rush. Leslie peered outside. *Where was the CBP man who was supposed to take care of the visa?* Amira stood in the isle, still and proud. Her dark eyes sparkled beneath her fine, tightly woven veil.

"They're expecting you," Paul Engl informed them, following the two women down the airplane stairs.

A friendly female Border Patrol agent awaited them by the sliding-glass door to the arrivals hall. Leslie breathed a sigh of relief.

"Welcome to New York," the agent said, then grasped Leslie's arm, firmly pulling her aside. "Ms. Palmer? My name is Selma, CBP. I'm here on the First Lady's orders. I have the visa." She pulled the document out of a zippered shoulder bag. "Is this Amira causing any difficulties?"

It was only now that Leslie had a chance to answer.

"Pleased to meet you, Selma. Thank you very much. No, no problems—at least so far."

"Good. I have given passport control a heads-up. Ms. Al Raisi can enter on a visitor's visa. Is there anything else I can do for you?"

"No, thank you, Selma. There will be someone to pick me up. I will tell the First Lady how wonderful you've been."

"Just doing my job, ma'am."

As she said this, her face lighting up with a smile, the little group stepped up to the passport control counter, Amira firmly in their midst. The passport and visa inspection took a minute and two clicks of a stamp. "Have a nice time in New York," the agent said. *Women taking care of business today—I'll take that as a good sign,* Leslie told herself as she walked closely behind Amira through the Club Room, on into the lobby.

And indeed, it was yet another woman who approached them. Only, neither her matronly, no-nonsense figure, which was packaged in a police uniform, nor the nervous yet strict look in her little, round eyes, promised anything fortuitous. Nor did the wall of four grim looking police officers posted behind her look much like a welcoming committee.

"Ms. Palmer? You are under arrest. Come with me," the female officer said. At that moment, her four colleagues stepped forward and parted her from the group—*from Amira!*

"Just a moment, this has to be a mistake!" Leslie protested, unable to free herself from the cops.

The matron waved a piece of paper in front of Leslie's face.

"A mistake? That's what they all say. This here is an FBI warrant."

Leslie stood still, dumbfounded. She stared at the FBI all points bulletin with what was undeniably a picture of her. *Where was everyone? Someone had to help her!*

She saw a flash of Amira's light green skirt outside—uniformed officers were leading her off.

Was this the end? Had it all been for nothing?

"Come," the female officer said, pushing herself and Leslie through the revolving door and out toward the parking lot. Her tone seemed a hint friendlier than it had been.

A few vehicles stood somewhat off to the side on spaces reserved for Port Authority. A parked bus shielded a row of four hefty SUVs with tinted windows from curious glances. Two black and white New Jersey patrol cars were waiting curbside, their motors running.

"My God, did you give me a fright!" a dark-haired officer called as she rushed toward Leslie. She had that flawless, slightly brown skin tone, a soft, narrow face with high cheekbones, silky black hair—it was Jennifer, her daughter.

Leslie was speechless. A strong hand pushed her toward the nearest car as Jennifer signed a form and dismissed the New Jersey officers.

Then her daughter was sitting beside her on the spacious van's light gray seat, talking away at her.

"My Lord, Mom, I happened to see the APB and just couldn't *believe* it! I . . . well, as you can see I was able to fend off the worst of it . . . Thank goodness you informed me of your arrival time . . . I was only just able to organize everything . . . *phew* . . . It would have been a nightmare if they'd nabbed you in the city!"

The women embraced silently. They practically clung to each other, until Leslie suddenly jerked back.

"Amira!"

"Amira al Raisi is in my custody," said a pleasant voice from behind them. "In that vehicle over there."

Leslie spun in her seat. Junior District Attorney Chuck Browne was smiling back at her.

Jennifer set about providing her confused mother with an explanation.

"I called Chuck, of course—what else would I do?"

"You know each other?"

"You gave me his number, remember? I called and asked to meet him. We went to Charles' funeral together."

"How was it?"

"A lot of people, Mom. It was very festive and dignified. Well, I wanted to discuss the criminological insights with Chuck anyway... You were nowhere to be found... One thing led to another, Chuck introduced me to Nassim..."

"Nassim? That sexy rogue of a surgeon...?"

"Don't say it's a small world, Les. *You* were the one who led me to Chuck."

"People, can we go now?" The man asking the question turned around and looked Leslie straight in the eyes. "Howdy. In trouble again, are we? Lucky that the tough guys are ready to help you out..."

Leslie felt herself starting to blush.

"Yes, by all means, go ahead, Nassim," she said pragmatically. *Let's get the hell out of here.*

"What does he know?" Leslie asked Jennifer in a whisper.

"We know each other, Les," her daughter confessed, blushing. "Nassim was with us when Chuck and I went over granddad's study one more time to look for evidence."

The four vehicles approached the on-ramp to the George Washington Bridge. A lovely blue sky was spreading from the south, pushing away the haze that lay over the Hudson River to the north.

"We found a print on a whiskey glass. *Bronx!* We think that he must have moved it to get to the carafe. After he got a hold of it, he must have followed Charles back into the hallway, where he hit him over the head with it. But here's the biggest thing—there was a lot of hair up in the bedroom: on the carpet next to the bed, in the bathroom, in front of the closets... It was Charles' hair. Right. We had all of it examined for DNA. We found some of your hair, too, Leslie."

Leslie gazed forward impatiently. They were on a six-lane highway, approaching the mighty bridge piers.

"We almost missed a single hair, Les."

"Bronx?"

"Exactly. It was in the drawer that Charles kept his woolen socks in. It came back positive for his DNA. That puts him squarely at the scene of the crime."

That's all fine and well, Leslie felt like answering. But her thoughts were focused on other matters right now. The scene of importance was Brooklyn Bridge. It was half past nine in the morning. In two and a half hours, she would finally be shifting the scales in her favor.

Chuck Browne got on his walkie-talkie and transmitted the Lower Manhattan destination to the other two vehicles in their group: *Duane Street, near City Hall.*

The eastern part of Duane Street, not far from Brooklyn Bridge, was almost void of people on this Sunday morning. Parking spaces were vacant along the entire length of the street, so that all three of the black SUVs were able to pull up in a row in front of a brownstone. They all gathered around the open back of the first vehicle.

"Long Bill," said Chuck Browne by way of introduction. "He's allowing us to use his meatpacking firm as our headquarters. Thirty-third Street, this is the exact location." The others murmured approval as he handed Leslie a sketched map.

"Ronnie, our amateur tapping expert, has brought his equipment. He's operating out of vehicle number two—the Grand Cherokee here. And Martin Luther has brought a few little items to help us out in case things get ticklish. He's watching the woman in the last car."

There was a hint of skepticism in Leslie's voice.

"And who is *she*?"

The pregnant redhead said, "Sandy. Responsible for catering."

It wasn't long before a roar began to echo down the street canyon. A swarm of other members and friends of the Pleasure Cruise Riders were booming up—Leslie estimated a good two dozen. This rather impressive force pulled its machines up next to a newsstand and a bunch of public phones on the other side of the crossing.

"The plan is great," Browne praised. "Hostage exchange at noon on the Brooklyn Bridge. Perfect."

"Still—I sense that there may be trouble," Nassim warned. "This Bronx is in a league of his own. Leslie needs a fallback position in case he tries to trick her."

"Oh—and he will," Leslie agreed.

"Exactly. But you, Leslie, are a disguise artist—an expert at mimicking people. I mean..."

Leslie interrupted him.

"I could play Amira, and walk across the bridge as Bronx's mother?"

"Yep, something like that," Nassim said with a grin.

Browne muttered his approval. Sandy contemplatively stroked her stomach, scrutinizing Leslie's face. But Ms. Palmer didn't seem convinced.

"Maybe. I don't know," she said, doubtingly. "It is important that we define stages."

The men looked at each other in confusion.

"You know, I mean, the good old Brooklyn Bridge has two towers. We're on Duane Street, this is our home base—stage one. The Manhattan tower, the one that's closest to us, is where we'll do the exchange—stage two. Are we all clear?"

The men nodded. They were grinning. It was kind of a cool game—a bunch of tough guys enjoying getting bossed around by a tough dame.

"The tower on the Brooklyn side is stage three. Chuck, Long Bill, Ronnie, you're going to be ready to push through to the second tower. I mean that in the military sense. With all of the bells and whistles that you have with you."

"And what's this little boy going to do?" Nassim asked with a sly wink. Leslie remained focused.

"You, Nassim, are going to be on my heels wherever I go. You are going to make sure that I don't lose contact with our base."

The men pretended to be thinking over what she had told them—but of course there were no two ways about it. *This woman knew what she wanted, and she sure as hell knew how to ask for it, too!*

"I'll get your face done," said Sandy into the moment of silence. Seeing Leslie's baffled expression, Chuck explained: "As far as Sandy is concerned, 'catering' comprises everything. Well—let's say *pretty* much everything. She works as a make-up artist on the side. Got your stuff on you, Sandy?"

"I've already thought it through. I just quickly have to get hold of the few clothes that I still need. Half an hour sound okay?"

The question was directed at Leslie, who nodded enthusiastically.

Unbelievable. I've just walked right into a bona fide dream team! And these people aren't even interested in asking any questions about why Bronx has Craig and Alex. As far as they're concerned, Bronx is a killer and that's all they need to know. Nassim may be a bit crazy, and sometimes a little full of himself, but you can certainly count on him. Perfect!

"Then I'll make the call now. Everyone on board?"

"Just one moment," said Chuck Browne. "First let me make sure that Jennifer is where she's supposed to be."

Jennifer had used her sources to scout out a number of buildings along the Brooklyn waterfront that fit the description of the public storage warehouse. She had also found out through the FBI that the Mossad had tapped phone calls—although they hadn't definitively been able to make out a location. The calls always came from the same number—one that could only have been issued by the Secret Service. Probably Agent Frank Sureman, she speculated.

Well, that number's dead now, huh, Frank ol' buddy? She was quite shocked at her own cynicism.

98

That morning, employees had put up a wooden stage on the stairs leading up to New York City Hall. On it, they had put two blocks with one dozen chairs respectively to provide seating for guests of honor.

Further toward the front of the stand, four flags flanked the lectern, which was decorated with the seal of the city's mayor. Old Glory hung limply next to the flag of the City of New York on this lovely wind-still morning; on the other side of the podium the blue banners of the New York Police Department and New York Fire Department—the main entities for which this memorial service was being held—hung side by side.

Sergeant Perez bustled around busily, checklist in hand, going over the seating arrangements, adjusting the four all-weather chairs reserved for the presidential couple, the mayor, and his guest toward the front of the stage. Cleaning crews in green uniforms were polishing the wooden planks and sweeping the stone tiles in front of the broad main entrance. A scrubbing machine was washing down the asphalt on City Hall Plaza, which gave way to the park across from the stage. The visitors' area that was accessible from Broadway was sectioned off with light blue crossbars on sawhorses that read *Police Line*. The 2nd NYFD ladder company had parked a heavy, bright red fire truck on the curb. The truck's impressive, fully extended 75-foot turntable ladder projected well above the small City Hall cupola—the fire engine gleamed, its chrome parts polished to a mirror shine. On its side an American flag was waved above color portraits of the New York firefighters who had given their lives on 9/11.

Further back in the park, the police brass band was beginning to gather in small groups. There they stood in their full dress uniforms, next to their instrument cases—faces of every shade and race mingling in camaraderie, passing time, smoking, chuckling softly, waiting like soldiers before a mission.

The mood was somewhat somber, at least it seemed that way to Avi Leumi. He was sitting behind a bass trumpeter whose strong body was no less lithe and elegant than that of her instrument. Avi's legs were casually crossed, his elbows draped over the backrest, fingers drumming on her highly polished horn, which she had already taken out and stood on top of its case...

"So, who are you playing for today," the Mossad agent asked, looking through the group of musicians and not taking his eyes off the one face that was of principle interest to him this morning.

"Man, you sure know how to ask a silly question!" the African American police officer responded as she extracted her precious instrument from under Leumi's provocatively impertinent fingers.

"For New York's finest?" He asked no one in particular. "Or maybe for our great new president?"

He rose just as Bronx started strolling down the narrow, paved footpath, past low hedges and over to the visitors' section, where he stopped in front of the blue police barrier. In front of him stood the oldest city hall in the United States, just as it had for two hundred years—two stories high, a pillared portal over the broad stairway, and a slender tower topped by a cupola so venerable and beautifully formed that it had served as a model for a spire at Harvard University.

A high-ranking police officer, distinguishable by his stark white uniform shirt and a set of broad, golden epaulettes, stepped across the few stage steps and over to a civilian. They shook hands, then joined up with a third man, who had been standing with his back toward them. Had this particular person turned for even a short moment, Bronx would almost certainly have recognized the distinct features of his CIA colleague Ken Cooper, from Science & Technology. But the police officer and the two men dressed in dark blue suits wasted no time making their way up the long, broad steps to the main entrance and into the lobby. From here, they climbed the grand curved stairway under the gently swaying Calder mobile and up to the first floor, to the New York City Mayor's office in the west wing.

Meanwhile, Bronx's well-trained eye was searching in vain for discreetly positioned security agents. He also noted the absence of the fleet of black Secret Service vehicles that should have been present and clearly visible by now. He glanced over the rooftops, over to the street corners, and to the news vans—the television presence, at least, created a familiar picture of the hustle and bustle that was to be expected before a presidential appearance.

Being the wily tactician that he was, Bronx had one more ace up his sleeve. The white Fendi purse that he had handed Leslie in front of *Victoria's Secret* was, indeed, a masterpiece of explosive technology. Nobody had to teach *him* how to suck an egg. And that included Sheikh Khalid. The purse's lining contained very thin sheets of Semtex. Should Palmer fail her mission, he would detonate the charge with a quick call from his cell phone... There was nothing like a well-thought-through backup plan—or, as he might put it in military jargon—a 'contingent decision.'

The memorial service would begin just two short hours from now. His eyes focused on the four chairs behind the lectern... Bronx pictured Palmer alias the First Lady of the United States—*Cinderella*... stepping from the ashes of the Towers to take her place as, arguably, the most powerful woman in the nation... *Cincinnati* in Secret Service–speak... with the agreed-upon white Fendi... She would rise in the middle of the ceremony, pull up her purse... now she was opening it... the president looks up, astonished... she pulls out the gun, takes aim... screams from the crowd...

Bronx gazed around in gleeful anticipation, imagined the rampant horror, as he looked at nothing but the calm scene of the police band unpacking their instruments.

...and then she was pulling the trigger, and again... the bullets were hitting the president in the head, the heart, at close range... Secret Service agents were tackling the First Lady, throwing her to the ground... too late. A shrill scream rose as one from the many voices of the crowd—then dead silence...

A shot shattered his reverie. Bronx started. *Where the hell did that come from?*

"Sir? Would you please step back!" The cop had a peculiarly inquiring look in his eyes—for a moment, Bronx thought he was staring straight into Howard Young's face.

"Oh... sure, officer. Where did that bang come from?"

Bronx stepped aside. The musicians looked over to the street... it had been a backfiring motorcycle that had further frayed the already tense nerves of everyone present—now the bike was thundering down Park Row toward the Brooklyn Bridge at a speed that might have suggested that the rider with the full-face helmet was embarrassed about the disturbance himself.

Bronx hated these full-of-themselves bikers who didn't seem to give a shit about much of anything. Like that doctor who had pulled Palmer out of the wreckage and draped her across his machine like a rag doll. Hadn't he also been wearing a red helmet? He despised bikers, skaters—all of those freedom-loving individualists on wheels.

Better not attract attention!

Bronx decided to find a better vantage point. He set out at an easy trot, blending into the overall picture of trees, musicians, hedges, and pedestrians.

Avi Leumi had been following Bronx like a shadow. At this moment, he was leaning against the 2nd company fire engine, holding a commuter paper that he had fished out of a trash can sponsored by the charitable *Ready, Willing and Able Community Improvement Project* in front of his face.

Bronx was obviously interested in the security setup.

And then it was as if the earth had suddenly opened up and swallowed him whole. Cursing under his breath, Leumi ran forward and around the front of the truck. He peered across Broadway, searched the park, the sidewalk again—*there!* Bronx was just getting into a car. The tires squealed... *Gone!* Thoroughly pissed off, the Mossad agent flipped open his phone and dialed Ken Cooper...

...the cell phone in Bronx's jacket pocket began to vibrate almost at the same moment. *Leslie Palmer.* About time that the pain in the ass called him!

"Yeah," he growled with professional restraint.

99

It was ten thirty on Sunday morning when Leslie called the cursed number. Bronx's gravely *Yeah* sounded in her ear loudly and clearly almost right away.

"Where are you, damn it? Do you really want your boys to die?"

Leslie waited and said nothing.

"Listen, Leslie, I know, the location has changed. You will accompany the president to Medal Day at City Hall. Everything else remains as planned..."

She interrupted him.

"I know, Bronx. The ceremony will commence. I will be watching everything, and I will do exactly what is expected of me."

She turned her cell phone to speaker.

"Good... err... just a moment! Is something wrong? Did I just understand you correctly?"

At this moment Amira jerked her head toward the hand with which Leslie was holding the phone and screamed something incomprehensible.

"*Hamla salîbiyya yahûdiyya jadîda!*"

"What was that, you old witch? What? What did you just say?" Leslie grabbed for a switchblade and sprung it open.

Amira was silent, but her eyes gleamed in triumph.

"Who... said that?" a halting voice asked over the speaker.

"Your mother, Bronx. I'm holding her hostage. So, tell me, how does the shoe fit on the other foot?"

"I don't believe a word of what you're saying. What are you going to do next—try and sell me the Brooklyn Bridge?"

"Just a moment!"

His shtick was annoying the hell out of her.

Martin Luther handed her a note with a meaningful look on his face. It was the translation of what Amira had just called out in Arabic.

"Thank you... Bronx, your dear mommy just said *'Jihad is the only answer!'* Which pretty clearly outs you as a double agent for Al Qaeda. Amira, why don't you be so kind as to tell him that again—*in English!*"

Leslie held the cell phone in front of the veiled woman's mouth.

"Adil, it's me, your Mama!"

On the other end of the line, Bronx's expression sagged. A knot contracted in the pit of his stomach.

"The American woman kidnapped me from my home. Now I am in this godless city... may Allah... *hamla salîbiyya...*"

Leslie coldly pressed the blade against her neck.

"One more word, bitch, and you're history!"

The woman gurgled, moaned. A hollow scream blared from the speaker.

"Leslie, stop! Please! It didn't mean anything."

"Oh, it didn't? Really? Well that's news! I'll tell you what's going to happen here, Bronx. I'm going to cut off one of your dear mommy's ears, then the other one, then her cute little nose, then I'll bypass her hairy chin and go directly to..."

"Stop it!" Bronx yelped.

"Awww, Bronx, *good* boy, are you begging? Are you losing your cool? Well, well, well..."

"Okay, what do you want?"

"Pay close attention, Bronx. We are going to do a little hostage exchange. Right on Brooklyn Bridge. You have exactly ten minutes to organize everything with your people."

Bronx seemed to be fighting a sudden attack of the whooping cough. Then, "Leslie, I need more time to be able to promise you that."

"You don't have it. Either you're in, or your mother is out. Sound familiar, by any chance? Ten minutes. I'll call you back. And when I do, you will answer promptly and take good note of the directions I give you for the exchange."

Winking amiably at Amira, she pressed the field with the red receiver symbol.

Bronx stepped before his men at the Brooklyn waterfront warehouse with a stony expression on his face. He had trouble voicing what Cinderella had just conveyed to him. *A hostage exchange!* He had to save face. There was no way that he could simply admit defeat. The looks on his people's faces were not making him happy. They were just licking their chops for their infallible, hard-core boss to screw up...

"Chenny, Leon, listen. This is my plan. We will not send Craig and Alex across the bridge or anywhere. We will find two boys that will pass for them, understood?"

The tub of lard rubbed his chin uncertainly.

"What do you mean, boss?"

Practicing a good deal of constraint, Bronx explained patiently, "It's a trick, you idiot. We will not exchange Craig and Alex, but two people who look like them. Are you finally getting me, damn it?"

Leon nodded.

"Okay, boss, so two kids who look like them, same clothes, same height... that's pretty tough."

"Take this picture."

Slant-eyes was faster. He snatched the picture of the Palmer boys and said cockily, "I know where guys like that hang out, boss. Come Leon, let's get moving."

"Wait! You had damn well better do a good job. I'll give anyone who agrees to do it a hundred bucks—what the hell, even two hundred if I have to."

Leon seemed to be searching for a pimple on his fat neck with his left hand.

"What should we tell them, boss?"

Bronx threw his arms up impatiently.

"Just tell them we're shooting a movie and we're looking for extras. That always works. They just have to walk across the Brooklyn Bridge when you tell them to. But I want to take a good look at them first. Now go, get your lame asses moving!"

"Cool idea, boss," Slant-eyes grinned, casually lifting a finger to the bill of his baseball cap.

The two pieces of crap had hardly left the room when Leslie called back.

"Bronx, I hope you're paying attention. I'm going to give you my orders. You will follow them to the letter, understand? Unless, of course, you're not interested in putting your arms around your beloved mommy again in this lifetime—am I making myself clear?"

"Go ahead, if you must," Bronx said through clenched teeth.

"Noon today, Brooklyn Bridge. Dead center. Your mother will be coming from the Manhattan side, and you will send my sons over from Brooklyn. The hostages will start walking from beneath the towers at exactly twelve o'clock. We will compare watches. It is now precisely eleven sixteen."

Bronx tried to think as fast as he could. The towers were about a third of a mile apart. It would be difficult for Leslie Palmer to recognize her sons' faces at that distance. *They would have to wear sunglasses, baseball caps...*

"The time, Bronx? What does your cheap plastic knock-off say—11:16?"

"Yes, 11:16."

"And one more thing, Bronx. Just in case you're thinking of trying anything stupid. I have an AR-15 center-fire rifle with its crosshairs aimed right at the back of your mother's raven-haired skull. A .223 caliber. Hollow point. You'll be watching her head explode like a watermelon, understood?"

"Yeah... Understood. You, you dirty fucking..."

"Shut up, Bronx! It's my turn now. What was it you told me...? 'If you mess up this job, Leslie, your boys will be dead and gone.' So the same thing, exactly the same thing, goes for your good old mama, not even from Alabama, you sorry bastard! And now I want to hear you say 'I understand'—loudly and clear!"

The line was silent for a few heavy heartbeats. Then a pressured voice answered in little more than a wheeze, "I *get* it, Leslie!"

"No, you do not. You weren't told to say 'I get it.' You are to say 'I understand.'"

"I understand," he responded dully.

Before she severed the connection, she said in a firm voice, "Any funny business, Bronx, and your mother will be shot. The same goes if you touch a single hair on either of my sons' heads. Just so that we have this straight: neither my people, nor those disgusting pieces of shit that work for you, will set foot on the bridge. Only the hostages. No police. Remember my sniper! And the back of your mother's head. And think 'watermelon.'"

With that, she hung up. Bronx squeezed his fingers around the handset so tightly that his knuckles turned white.

Over on Duane Street, Nassim was throwing Leslie a look of admiration. An acknowledging smile crept onto his furrowed, unshaven face. There was a hint of affection in his smoky voice when he spoke.

"Where do you want to position your sniper?"

Leslie made a silent gesture with her head, then got out of the car.

11:20. The gray telephone at the warehouse buzzed and blinked. Bronx came to from his frozen state. Sheikh Khalid's slimy voice was unmistakable. Bronx immediately bristled.

"Are you out of your *mind*, calling here?"

"Shut up, Bronx! It's the landline. We'll keep it short. What is the status quo?"

Bronx hesitated. Khalid would not let up.

"Are you having difficulties? My sixth sense tells me that something is not going right."

Bronx squirmed like an eel.

"Well, yes, there has been an unexpected development. Nothing but a glitch on the radar, I... we'll take care of it..."

The Sheikh cut him off sharply.

"What is this *nonsense* you are talking? What happened? You sound like you have shit in your pants."

"Well... Cinderella has taken my mother hostage. I have no idea how... but there is no doubt... now she wants a hostage exchange—her sons for my mother."

Khalid's voice seemed to be dripping with spite.

"Cinderella. So the miserable female has you under her thumb, does she? What do you plan to do?"

Bronx searched for words, for some kind of escape. Should he tell him about the ruse he had planned? Before he was able to regain his speech, the Sheikh was already giving him an earful.

"The two boys are worth more to us than your mother, Bronx. I hope we are clear on that?"

Bronx swallowed. His stomach convulsed and he felt a stream of acid shoot to the back of his throat.

"What happened to the big master of espionage?" Khalid asked sneeringly. "There will be no hostage exchange, and that is an order. It is probably just some stupid maneuver. Whoever is behind this is trying to trap you. Do you hear me?"

Bronx let out a venomous growl.

"Operation Cinderella is your baby, Bronx. So you will see it through to the bitter end. No holds barred, and no exceptions. How did you put it? 'War demands victims.' Exactly! Sorry, Bronx. There is no room for sentimentality—this is a military operation."

Before Bronx could croak a response, the Sheikh had hung up.

100

The mayor struggled to put the final polish on his memorial service speech in the New York City Hall west wing. This was no easy task, since he was somewhat distracted by the security risk factors that the FBI deputy had warned him about. Bill Baker and Ken Cooper were taking up their posts in the mobile NYPD command unit down on City Hall Plaza. The white, windowless bus was parked behind the 2nd Company fire engine.

"A classified target map was found on Secret Service Agent Sureman's body," Cooper recapped. "My agent secured it. We assume that Frank Sureman had stolen it and tried to pass it on to his contact."

Baker spoke up.

"No, I think that he had probably already conveyed the data by phone, and that's why they put him on a slab."

"But the shot might have been aimed at the First Lady or her companion," Cooper continued digging. "Do we even know who the other woman at the scene was? Do we have a picture?"

"Only a skimpy description—black clothing, sunglasses—nothing that's of much use. We have managed to secure a record of the calls placed on Frank Sureman's cell phone—it is blank, except for a single contact. We are trying to establish who the number belongs to."

The police officer with the captain's epaulettes checked his timepiece.

"My people are ready. We have two SWAT teams to back up the mob control units. You fear an assassination attempt on the president? Did I understand you correctly?"

Cooper nodded.

"Avi Leumi from the Mossad is obsessed by the idea that Bronx is acting as a double agent, and that he's behind the whole thing."

Baker was listening intently.

"And what got the Mossad on his trail?"

"I think it has something to do with a past encounter during an operation in Yemen. A personal matter. Leumi is tenacious—apparently the thing kept nagging at him. It was sheer coincidence that he helped me to examine aerial shots when I was looking into the Howard Young murder case. It seems that the car captured by the UAV camera at the site of the murder was exactly the one that Bronx was driving at the time."

"Bronx is a Langley legend, Ken. If he is the traitor that Secret Service Agent Sureman was supplying with target data, then that means that Leslie Palmer is his accomplice," Baker deduced.

Cooper's shrug indicated only lukewarm agreement.

"Leumi spotted Bronx in front of City Hall this morning. What would he be doing there except conducting secret reconnaissance? Meeting forbidden contacts, perhaps? I want all radio signals in the area monitored."

"Electronic tracing is an integral function of our mobile command post," the captain confirmed. "We have already suffered all that we ever want to, sir. May God save us from any further disaster!"

Baker nodded in agreement. The men were all on one page. Now it was just a matter of who would be telling the mayor to cancel the ceremony.

"The Secret Service has already reached its decision, Ken. The president will definitely not be coming to City Hall to attend the event."

"Then I will convey your decision to the mayor," the police officer offered.

Cooper allowed himself a discreet smile that was brought on by Baker's raised eyebrows.

"That's very kind of you, sir. It's good that you're wearing a uniform. As far as I know, the mayor has never attempted to strangle a man wearing a uniform."

101

Bronx came to a stop almost within sight of City Hall. He placed a hand on the cold railing. Many years ago, he had stood at this very spot, marveling at the thick steel wires that started from here to impressively span the soaring towers. His father had explained the basics of this world-famous suspension bridge in his typical, succinct way.

"The entire top of the bridge is suspended by steel cables. The engineer who designed it had to use incredibly precise calculations—and this was over one hundred and fifty years ago. The man had both courage and foresight."

This sentence had stuck with him. He remembered it as if he had heard his father saying it only yesterday. He was painfully filled with a searing longing for the good times of his youth as his eyes followed the steel wires and their meshed pattern up to the broad, sandstone-colored tower, and across the thick steel trusses that distributed weight to the abutments in three places. Back then, he had stood next to his father amazed, filled with pride and confidence, completely assured that this was the land of limitless opportunities. To him, the bridge had symbolized a new and better world—a world of adventure and glamorous careers instead of boring drudgery. He had anticipated being welcomed into America's elite... *Dreams. Nothing but dreams!*

The enormous pylons of this, one of the most beautiful bridges of its time, seemed unshakable in their majesty, inspiring a firm trust in its foundations. And not just in the foundations of the bridge, no—in the very values that the United States were built on. It was as if there were no such thing as Ground Zero, which gaped within view close by. It began to dawn on Bronx that this nation could not be conquered. It was hard to counter the optimistic spirit that pervaded everything, and that enveloped you wherever you went.

The two slender Gothic Revival arches, beneath which the roadway ran either way across the river, appeared like two mighty church windows. They lent the massive 273-foot structure a beguilingly airy elegance. Light flooded through its functional orifices: it exuded a metaphysical, elementary power—it drew the eye upward, to the heavens over the Manhattan skyline. However, the charm that was so inherent in the Brooklyn Bridge, the sense of new beginnings and wide horizons that it conveyed, all of this now seemed dampened. The Twin Towers were missing from the silhouette of the mighty metropolis, as if they had never existed. They left an incomprehensible gaping void. And clouds of smoke were still rising from the ruins of Ground Zero.

Jennifer had taken up position in her mobile command post on the other side of the bridge, in Brooklyn, next to the High Street subway station. She sat in the back of an Army Commando Humvee, her cell phone clasped in her hand. She was undecided. *Should she call now?*

A strong team spirit had developed between her, Ken, and FBI Deputy Baker over the past few hours. They shared a certain understanding. The amassing of suspicious facts against Bronx had finally convinced even the skeptical Cooper. Bill Baker had done good work—he had followed scant trails with professional determination, using the resources of his FBI specialists to full advantage.

"We found the number on Sureman's cell phone and were able to determine the receiving station," Baker had reported. "It's a former CIA safe-house in Brooklyn, disguised as a public storage facility. A SWAT team, backed up by an Army engineer unit, is now on standby close to the location."

The engineer commander handed Jennifer a paper cup of coffee from a nearby Starbucks, then placed a building blueprint on the map table.

"The building is full of residual waste," he explained. "Tons of barrels and containers in the cellar. Our directional microphones are picking up unclear voices. I estimate that there are about a dozen subjects in the building."

"This is all about the two boys. It's important that nothing happens to them."

"Are you sure they're in the building?"

"No—but we'll know within the next half hour."

Jennifer was on pins and needles. Baker had rattled her with his questions. Where was Leslie? Had she been questioned yet? She had evaded his queries by informing him that the woman was under the custody of the competent district attorney. Which was more or less correct. She had to direct the men's attention to Bronx.

"A vehicle is leaving the building. Four occupants. What's next?" a voice asked over the walkie-talkie.

"Give me the details, Sergeant," the commander replied.

"Dark green Dodge van, 6778 XML, New York."

"Let it pass. Do not follow it. Continue surveillance," the commander ordered in response to a clear gesture from Jennifer. It was 11:45.

"The target object is bringing the boys to the arranged meeting place," Jennifer said and got out. She stepped over to the group of motorcyclists to speak to Nassim.

Minutes later the Dodge van reached the approach to the bridge and suddenly stopped. Men jumped out, crossed the road, and ran to the stairs leading to the bridge's pedestrian walkway.

Nassim gave his buddies a sign. Engines howled, and the dozen heavy machines droned toward the approach in loose formation. They caught up with the van halfway across the bridge, surrounded it, and forced the driver to turn onto Duane Street once they reached the other side. Half a dozen of their friends were waiting.

102

Had the grand mission been worthwhile? Bronx gave himself a jolt. His synchronized watch showed that it was 11:58. Without looking back, he gave a signal with his hand and began walking over the wooden planks of the pedestrian and bicycle path toward the tower on the Brooklyn side of the bridge. He obstinately strode in the center, setting one heavy foot in front of the other on the yellow divide. He'd be damned if he was going to sacrifice his mother. Two lanky young men followed. They were taking their roles as extras so seriously that they could easily have been mistaken for the stars of the alleged new television action series. Leon, wearing his crumpled hat as always, had remained behind, as discussed.

That asshole, Bronx pondered grimly to the rhythm of his steps, *that asshole of a Sheikh had more than a few screws loose if he thought he could command him to betray the deepest, most intimate of all relationships.*

Everything would have to go very quickly—Leon, his colossal meaty mass backed up by two guns that he carried in separate shoulder holsters, would cover their retreat.

Hordes of tourists were navigating the famous bridge—just like they did on any other day, and in any kind of weather. They took pictures, marveled, cyclists considerately gave them a wide berth. The crowds suited Bronx perfectly. They would provide the necessary confusion once things got going.

Heavy traffic rushed monotonously back and forth beneath them. More than one hundred thousand vehicles on any given day.

The closer Bronx drew to the tower, the clearer his vision of his mission became to him. Nostalgic memories gave way to harsh reality, feelings ceded to effective tactics. Operation Cinderella could not be allowed to fail. Not at the last minute. *Who did this Palmer think she was? Did this bitch actually believe that she could prevent Rick Bronx, a warrior for Allah, from fulfilling his noble contribution to the righteous cause?*

An observation deck led around the towers on both sides of the pedestrian and bicycle path. The construction history of the bridge, which was opened on May 24, 1883, was described in bronze inscriptions and reliefs that were affixed to the double iron railing.

11:59. Bronx stood by the railing on the south platform, staring down onto the water of the East River. A white tour boat, coming from the southern tip of Manhattan, turned around.

"New Yorkers didn't believe that the bridge would hold," his father had said, as they had stood here, peering across the water for a glimpse of the distant Statue of Liberty. He had told an open-mouthed Adil that the builders had paraded 21 circus elephants across the bridge to prove its weight-bearing capacity. Not that it had really proven anything—but it did make for a great show. Back then, when America was still a teenager of sorts...

Bronx passed a hundred-dollar bill to each of the two young men and gave them their final instructions. "Walk straight across the bridge calmly. Do not stop until you reach the other tower. The cameras are running."

12:00. An elegant figure wearing a long, green skirt set out on the Manhattan side. She stepped from beneath the arches and began to walk the third of a mile long deck that stretched between the towers. The hostage exchange had commenced.

On the Brooklyn side, Bronx elbowed the boys roughly.

"Get moving, will you! Go! Time is money. You're holding up the entire production!"

He brought a pair of miniature binoculars to his eyes, and saw her immediately. Unmistakable. There she was, walking amongst a host of colorfully dressed pedestrians. She held herself so proudly! Her typical, trudging walk, her chubby figure, a striking veil—as always... *Amira! Mother!*

Bronx's heart beat faster. He lowered the binoculars and waited impatiently. His mommy, his everything! She was coming toward him, he would embrace her, just moments away, here on the Brooklyn Bridge—the bridge that represented all longing...

Meanwhile, Leslie was carefully eying the two men that were making their way toward her. They were wearing the typical, loose garb, baseball caps, sunglasses...Leslie studied their gait, the movement of their arms, the carriage of their heads...the rhythm with which they looked up and down...and she knew. A smile stole across her face in spite of the gravity of the situation. Great, lanky boys, those two. But Craig and Alex?

If they're Craig and Alex, then I really am Amira...

103

Leslie didn't harbor the slightest doubt.

The two men that Bronx had sent, and who were now casually strolling across the deck of the bridge, were not her sons. Never in a million years. They were poor doubles. Thank God she had listened to Chuck. She bit her lip. The fight was on.

Bronx felt as if it took forever for the hostages to cross paths, and for his mother to finally, finally, get closer to him.

The elegant woman in her shimmering green, ankle-length skirt was still thirty feet away when he ecstatically spread his arms to greet her.

"Mama, Amira!"

As she came close, she gracefully lifted her fine, black veil.

Bronx stared, paralyzed, into Leslie Palmer's face.

"Son of a bitch!" she hissed. "Get over there!" The heavy pistol in her hand made him think better of resisting. Bronx immediately did as he was told.

"And now you will bring me my sons. Otherwise there won't be much left of your mother's face...Or of yours, for that matter. You have fifteen minutes! Then we will begin to cut off parts of her...think of it as a filleting process."

Her words pierced him like daggers. His body squirmed with pain and anger, as if she had rammed a red-hot poker up his ass.

But he did as she commanded. Immaculately, this time.

He ground his teeth as he phoned. His face was scarlet with rage. He stared at Leslie with raw hatred. She stood before him, completely calm, restricting his field of vision, controlling everything. Chuck

Browne, who had followed her, had seen and heard it all. Then he had called the stage two group waiting beneath the other tower.

Bronx knew nothing of any of this. His world had turned into an evil roar, a threatening darkness that was slowly closing in on him, swallowing him whole. Bronx's world had turned to chaos…

104

Time stood still…

…these were the longest minutes that Leslie Palmer had ever experienced.

Bronx was clutching, rather than leaning against, the railing of the southern platform under the Brooklyn tower. Chuck Browne, the junior district attorney, stood close to him, the muzzle of his Glock Police Special unambiguously poking somewhere in the vicinity of Bronx's kidneys.

Ronnie, who was wearing a ConEdison helmet on his head, was on the opposite, northern platform, pretending to be doing maintenance work. A bright yellow cone that had Keep out written on it kept pedestrians at bay. Long Bill was keeping a watchful eye on Amira, with her long green dress and the black veil covering her face. She was standing in an alcove, still as a statue, her back painfully stiff, her eyes fixed up the East River. Only about sixty feet separated her from her son on the opposite, southern platform of the Brooklyn pier.

Leslie stood in the middle of the pedestrian and bicycle path in a broad-legged stance, like a human traffic divider. Her black cloth bag clamped firmly under one arm, cell phone in hand, she tensely monitored the field of action.

It felt good to have the veil covering her face. She didn't have to worry about anybody recognizing her—particularly the two cops who were sauntering by on patrol. *Had she really seen that female officer giving her a dirty look? Her male colleague, on the other hand, seemed more interested in the curves that hinted beneath the exotic covering… Wow, she had a lot going on under there!*

Jennifer called to say that the boys were on their way. Leslie's stomach tensed sharply. *Would this work out?*

Bronx's nerves were also ready to snap. Like a trapped animal, he was frantically trying to think of a way out of this utterly fucked-up situation. *Leon must have noticed something by now. Had he alarmed the driver of the van? Where the hell were they?* He was not able to see the opposite platform. Uttering a dull snort, he tried to take a step to the side, but a rough prod from Chuck Browne's gun made him freeze again instantly. At least he had been able to shift slightly, so that the annoying bastard next to him was no longer completely shielded by his body…

Jennifer gave the SWAT team the go-ahead from her position in the Humvee command vehicle. *Storm the building, secure all evidence!* The commander of the Army engineers unit had his people advance with their heavy equipment.

This time, there was no doubt in Leslie's mind that it was them. There they were. Alex and Craig—alive and well! She had to restrain herself from calling out to them and running toward them.

Her maternal heart skipped a beat—what bright young men they were. Just to see their upright posture, their smooth, casual gait—as if they knew that the world was theirs for the taking. They didn't seem at all phased by their experience. Leslie couldn't stop staring at their faces…which made her forget to critically survey the people around them.

When she finally noticed the meathead with his battered hat, it was too late. Leon stood by the railing, raised his shining silver weapon as if in slow motion…aimed.

Leslie shrieked.

The sound of the shot ripped through the air.

Chuck Browne staggered, fell.

People were scattering in every direction, running, screaming.

Where were her boys? Leslie had lost sight of them. *This was a nightmare!*

The mountain of lard moved with surprising speed. In just a second, he had managed to rush up and throw Bronx his second weapon.

Bronx felt a rush of adrenaline. This was war. And war was what he was most at home with. They were in the minority. No doubt Leslie had collected her people on the other platform. Now it was a matter of acting quickly—brutally. He had to shut them down before they found their bearings. He signaled Leon to round the tower from the left. He would attack from the right.

Leslie had always known how to handle a weapon. But shooting at human beings was a whole different story—even if it was a matter of self-defense, like now.

Long Bill was covering the right flank... if Bronx attacked from both sides... Leslie wasn't given time to think of a plan. Shots rang out, stone fragments sprayed.

Leslie jumped from her cover, steadying her weapon with both hands as she fired from a crouched position. Bronx ducked away, pressed himself against the wall, and returned her fire.

Numerous shots were exchanged. Leslie's green dress was not only a perfect target—it also hindered her mobility, while Bronx was fast and did not offer much to aim at. This was not going well. She had to regain control.

"Bronx!" she screamed. "Give up! For someone who hates America so much, you don't know us very well. Whatever you think you're going to do here, you can't win. Your mother..."

More shots cut her off cold. Leon was plodding up on the other side, firing his weapon as he went.

The ConEdison man cowered against the railing, seemingly confused. The meathead grinned, swinging his weapon toward the sorry figure. Another sharp bang. Silence.

"He got him," Long Bill called out.

Ronnie had pulled his heavy revolver with lightning speed, shooting Leon smack in the middle of his face.

"Ronnie?" Leslie panted, her back pressed firmly against the wall, her gun up in front of her face.

"No... We have to get to Chuck—Les, cover me!"

"Bronx! Listen to me! Amira, your mother...," Leslie screamed, daring to come out a bit. The slug bit the granite just above her head.

What choice did she have?

Leslie grabbed Amira, who was pressed against the wall in her identical green skirt as if she had grown roots there, staring straight ahead. She tore the veil from her head, pushed her around the corner. "Say something to him, *do* it, anything!"

Amira shook her head.

"Bronx—*Amira!*" Leslie screamed. "I'm coming out with Amira... do you understand?"

She pushed the woman forward.

Bronx was pushed for a decision. He had to eliminate Palmer now. *She could identify him, knew everything...*

His muscles were so tense that they seemed fit to tear. He raised his weapon, peered carefully over the edge. Combat training.

There she was. Seeing a patch of green, Bronx reflexively fired. She swayed—*good!*—he pulled the trigger, again, emptying the magazine into the twitching body. The severely injured woman swayed back, fell against the railing, her eyes wide. Blood flowed from her mouth, over her beautiful breasts, the green dress...

"Fucking whore," Bronx panted.

Then he recognized her face.

Her weapon raised, Leslie Palmer stepped out from behind the pillar in full stature. She stood over the corpse.

"You killed your own mother, Bronx!"

"NO-OOO OO!"

Bronx's terrible scream seemed to reverberate through all of Manhattan.

He swayed forward, threw himself to the ground, leaned over the dead woman. He stammered, whimpered, stroked her face, covered it with kisses...

Junior district attorney Browne laboriously got up. The bullet from Leon's gun was lodged in his upper arm—he was bleeding profusely. Long Bill applied First Aid—motorbikes roared in from Manhattan. Uniformed men and women, led by Jennifer, came running from the Brooklyn side, weapons drawn.

"Les! Les!" she called. But her mother was not moving from where she stood, holding Alex and Craig tightly. Shaking, sobbing. The shock of it all sat deep. But now . . . now everything would finally be all right.

Nassim applied a bandage to Browne's arm.

"You just can't help yourself, can you? Must you always be in the line of fire, old boy?"

He got ready to give him an injection.

"It'll sting a little. Don't faint on me now."

"What's wrong with him? Is it bad?" said Ronnie, nervously turning the ConEdison helmet in his hands. He shot a worried look over at Leon's stone cold corpse, which was lying, grotesquely contorted, on the wooden planks nearby. He waved in its general direction . . . "That counts as self-defense, doesn't it?"

"Not to worry, Ronnie," the doctor said soothingly, "I will be sure to nominate you for a New York City medal of bravery. But help me get Chuck in the saddle first."

EMTs ran up with a stretcher.

"Where is he?" Jennifer repeated. "Where is Bronx, Mom?"

Leslie freed herself from her disguise with trance-like movements—it was as if she had played the role of Amira in her sleep. "Bronx? Don't you have him? No . . . !"

Long Bill pointed his arm.

"There!"

All heads turned.

Amid the general excitement, Bronx had managed to squeeze over the railing. He was now climbing through the bars, across the steel beams, and to the outer edge of the deck.

"Stop! Police! Get back here immediately!"

Jennifer pulled her pistol. Two police officers carefully narrowed in on Bronx from either side. He stood erect, staring over at them with empty eyes.

"Leave him, Jennifer, he's not going anywhere," Leslie said quietly, in a gentle voice. "What has he got left?"

She saw Bronx rigidly holding his cell phone to his ear, his features cruelly contorted. *A monstrous image of a traitor on the edge.*

Avi Leumi spoke. Bronx listened, expressionless.

"What went wrong, Bronx? You were the best agent the CIA ever had. What made you hate your country so much? Answer me! We met in Yemen. You remember. The briefing. For the attack on the USS *Cole.* I'm sure of it now. You're damned good, Bronx. Why are you doing all of this? Where are you right now, physically? Come with me to City Hall, then we can talk about what we'll do from here. Bronx? Why did you betray America? Bronx..."

Leslie felt as if an icy hand was closing around her throat.

Bronx spread his arms in a gesture of surrender. His eyes staring fixedly at the sky, he pushed off the edge with his feet, falling silently backward, his body extended, slowly plummeting into the depths below.

Leslie hurled herself toward the edge, leaned over the railing.

The body swayed, turned, it seemed to take an eternity...then he smacked, no, impacted on the concrete-hard surface of the East River.

Nassim stuck a salmon-colored cigarillo between his lips and lit up.

"No one survives that kind of impact," he noted, matter-of-factly.

A Coast Guard boat curved through the water with wailing sirens.

"Give me one, too!"

He handed her a cigarillo and lit it. She inhaled deeply, the smoke went down the wrong way and she coughed—the raw pain deep inside her chest felt good. Bronx was done. Out of her life. *There could hardly have been a worse punishment for him. He had executed himself! How fitting!* She took a deep breath, blew smoke out across Nassim's shoulder, motioned at his feet.

"What's going on with you—*there?*"

"Oh, nothing—my damn leg is bothering me again."

"What are you doing about it?"

"Downing meds. Painkillers. What else?"

"You should try wearing a higher heel. You're favoring it."

Nassim's light blue eyes grew wide.

"*Favoring?*"

"Yes, you're favoring it slightly, to lessen the pain when you step off of it. I can see that in the hesitance of your motions. You are sparing your leg. What you need is a heel that's a few centimeters higher on the left."

"Sparing, favor! I like that. It speaks to me somehow." The roguish doctor discarded the cigarette butt, tried a few steps.

He looked up.

"You have a wonderful daughter," he said suddenly.

Someone called over that they were searching for the body. It didn't matter.

"We're going back to Duane Street, Leslie called out to everyone. She linked arms with her boys. "Jennifer? Are you coming?!"

Mother and sons marched off buoyantly.

Jennifer was on the phone, gesturing to her family that she still had to take care of a bit of business.

The unit of engineers had stormed the warehouse a few minutes earlier. The commander was waiting for Jennifer there, in the entrance hall. His men had found a box of red papers that belonged to Charles Palmer.

A valiant NYPD lieutenant escorted the group past the massive police barrier on the western bridge entrance in Manhattan. There was a confusion of heavy vehicles, patrol cars, and intimidating SWAT team officers wearing black helmets and bulging body armor. Everyone was on red alert. Television vans directed their parabolic antennae, teams of reporters pushed forward. Leslie adjusted her veil, the boys tugged their caps down over their faces. They had almost reached Duane Street when her vibrating cell phone showed a call from the First Lady.

Leslie answered a simple 'yes,' breathing a sigh of relief. Her sons were with her and safe.

"It's over, Sarah. Everything is alright. Can we meet? Where are you?"

"Still in the city. We didn't go to the memorial service. I simply told my dear husband that never in the history of our proud country had a president of the United States demeaned himself by visiting New York City Hall."

"Excuse me? And he bought that?"

"No, of course not. He claimed that Abraham Lincoln had been there once—in 1861 or something like that. I told him that we all knew what happened to Lincoln. He countered that I was his wife, not his security advisor. As if that hadn't been embarrassingly clear to me for a good while now."

"But he still didn't go, in spite of all of his arguments? Typical!"

"You said it... Know why?"

"For security reasons?"

Leslie could see Sarah perkily shaking her head.

"*Cherchez la femme*—pardon my French. That black hussy, that... well, you know. She dragged him off to Camp David. I can't tell you how badly I wanted to take my elegant little white purse and whack her upside the head with it..."

"Purse?"

The connection was silent for a moment. Then the First Lady said, "I knew that you had no idea."

"Yes, I did. There was a revolver in it, wrapped in a greasy red cloth..." The Pleasure Cruise Riders had gathered around the three vehicles, keeping gapers at a reasonable distance. Leslie waved to the men and smiled as she weaved her way through to the cars with her boys. Sarah sounded dead serious.

"Do you remember where you got *that* particular Fendi bag?"

"Well... *Victoria's Secret*... of course. From Bronx."

"The whole thing seemed fishy to me, Leslie. It's not like I was born yesterday. What was I supposed to do with the damn bag, not to mention the gun."

"And?"

"Was I supposed to sell it on a flea market?" She laughed at her own joke. "No, seriously. So yesterday, I had a chauffeur drive me over to Arlington Memorial Bridge in the dead of night. And there I committed the piece of shit handbag to the floods of the Potomac, right along with the weapon and a couple of handfuls of gravel from the rose garden. Oh, it felt wonderful. No souvenirs left behind."

"Perfect, Sarah! And the president? Did you tell him about it?"

"Him? He doesn't know a thing. He's at Camp David, isn't he? Embroiled in a hot debate on issues of 'national security.'"

It did Leslie good to have a hearty laugh. Sarah was the best! They arranged to meet later that afternoon. Leslie would call her with the meeting place. But first she wanted to get over to Brooklyn with her boys and her loyal friends, to seek out the safety of her father's house. Jennifer would meet them there. *With Nassim? The modern-day knight on a steel steed? With one orthopedic heel?*

She caught herself giggling. *What had good old Shakespeare said so fittingly? All the world's a stage, and all the men and women merely players…*

And in the end, what could be more beautiful than that great old stage?

105

"This Synnx Software really is ingenious," said Cooper once their flight had taken off from La Guardia. "It enabled users to hack into other computers without triggering any alerts. What Ben Heller couldn't have known, is that the Software he used contained a code—because it was a trial version—which would show all of the computers that had been hacked into. Know what's screwed up about that?"

Baker shook his head.

"Bronx knew it. His hard drives—the ones that we found—were practically empty."

Ken Cooper looked silently across the southern tip of Manhattan Island. The Brooklyn Bridge disappeared beneath them as the glistening bay with its elegant Verrazano Narrows suspension bridge drew closer.

"Everything that could have gone wrong, Ken, *went* wrong," Baker grumbled, resigned. "But I said it, and I'm *still* saying it: something's not right with the First Lady."

"You just can't let up, can you? What's the problem you have with her?"

"What was she doing in New York, for one thing? Frank Sureman from the Secret Service, who rescued her on 9/11, is dead. We can't ask him what happened. Then her speech at the Library of Congress. We compared video footage of her appearance."

"To what?"

"Pictures of Leslie Palmer."

"Why to her of all people?"

"Palmer was at the White House at the beginning of the year. There was talk about using her as a double for the First Lady. Their resemblance is baffling. I wouldn't bet the farm that First Lady Sarah Crawford really was the person who held that speech."

"Why should she have asked a double to do it?"

"Ask me something I know, Ken."

"Didn't you tell me that Palmer has been missing since 9/11."

"Exactly. Her disappearance was ingenious. She called her last message in to her office from the South Tower just minutes before the second plane hit. Her office assumed that she had been one of the tragic victims, until someone used her password to access the Navy Intelligence database. It really could only have been her. I believed that she had gone under cover to work for Bronx—that's why I put an APB out on her. New Jersey Police intercepted her at Teterboro."

Jennifer had already informed Cooper about the arrest. The gesture he made with his shoulders signified acceptance, more than it did approval.

"I don't know, man. You shouldn't be driving yourself nuts. Okay, I agree that Mrs. Crawford did some strange things for a First Lady, but I think that she was probably going through a phase that is now over. If she was having an affair in New York, it's likely that it went down in flames, right along with the Towers. What do you think?"

"We'll probably never know," Baker growled. "Leslie Palmer is the only one who could testify in the Bronx matter if she wanted. If not..." Bill made a clueless gesture.

"We need more people with a sense of imagination!" Cooper countered. "Why are we leaving all the grand ideas to the Arabs? We have to tighten and coordinate all of our agencies' intelligence functions. But, more to the point, Bill—what's next for you?"

"I'm retiring after Christmas. Then it's off to California. You?"

"I still have a couple of terrorists to catch. I'll probably end up going to London. The Brits are insisting that I come over to coach their counterterrorism people."

"The Brits aren't squeamish. Operatively speaking, they have a leg up on us. We're just not catching the terrorists, Ken. We're too damn naïve."

The men remained lost in thought for a while. Beneath them, the Atlantic coast drifted by. Cooper felt almost as if he were floating a few thousand feet above the aircraft they were sitting in. He looked into the distance—far across the home of the brave, and the land of the free.

But for how long?

"What?" Baker started. "What did you say?"

"Me? Did I say something?"

"I must have nodded off a bit," his buddy said with a grin. "I dreamed you said 'but for how long.'"

"Well, keep dreaming," Cooper responded with a neutral smile.

They exchanged only few words during the rest of their flight back to Washington.

A few hours later, two women sauntered in cadence over the perfectly manicured lawn, past low gravestones that were set into the soft, green grass. Warm rays of sunshine fell onto their straight, strong backs; their shapely, bare legs glinted discreetly, yet invitingly, beneath dark skirts.

"You wanted to tell me something important," Sarah suddenly said sharply. "Why in a cemetery of all places?"

Leslie stood still under a group of old willows, next to a rough, reddish granite gravestone.

Lights blinked on the half a dozen black limousines that composed the First Lady's escort out in front of Green Wood Cemetery in Brooklyn. Secret Service agents wearing dark glasses and holding miniature radios were guarding the columned entrance gate with uncompromisingly unapproachable expressions on their faces.

"This is where our father is buried," said Leslie.

Sarah Crawford read the proudly raised, golden letters: Charles W. Palmer 1941–2001.

"Your father. I'm so sorry, Leslie."

Leslie took off her dark glasses. The black, silky hair of her wig fell softly over her shoulders. "*Our* father, Sarah," she corrected her quietly.

Sarah looked into Leslie's shining eyes, confused.

"What are you trying to tell me? I know my father."

"You know your mother's husband," Leslie responded in a gentle whisper. "Your mother is not your mother, Sarah."

The First Lady seemed to be slowly losing her patience. She drew her shoulders back and faced her double in a wide stance.

"Are you trying to kid me?"

Leslie reached for Sarah's hand. Her voice had grown strangely compassionate.

"The person you think is your mother suffered a stillbirth on the night of November 4. The night that you were born. A short time earlier, a woman had given birth to twin girls by Caesarian in the operating room next door. She died on the table."

Leslie moved closer to the grave, pulling Sarah with her. She placed a loving hand on the cool stone.

"Charles was desolate about the stillbirth, and so he laid one of the dead woman's babies on the woman's chest. You were that baby, Sarah." Leslie paused for a few heartbeats. "The other twin girl..."

"Was *you*?"

Leslie nodded and hurriedly told the rest of the story.

"It was a stormy night. The chief obstetrician had to be called in. He didn't make it until everything was already over and done."

Sarah gestured, disoriented.

"I can't believe it. That's impossible, Leslie! The stillbirth, the exchange, it would all have to be officially documented, no?"

"No. There aren't any official documents. Charles managed to arrange things so that nobody would ever know. Except Melissa, the nurse assisting him that night."

"See—I'm sure she would have reported the incident."

"Melissa took me in and married my father shortly afterward. I grew up in the belief that she was my birth mother."

Sarah shook her head in disbelief.

"She never told you anything?"

"No. I suppose she probably planned to, but she died young—she was killed in a car crash. I was only ten years old. She took her secret to the grave."

"How do you expect me to believe all of this?"

Sarah's voice expressed serious doubt—and despair.

"Standing at the graveside of my, *our*, father, Sarah, I would never tell you anything except the whole truth, and nothing but the truth. Our mother's name was Fabienne. She was a stunningly beautiful French woman. She was pregnant with Charles' twins—the two of us."

The woman stared silently down at the grave, as if hoping for a sign of confirmation.

Leslie opened her Bordeaux-colored designer purse and extracted a stack of red documents.

"Here. This is the proof."

Now utterly discomposed, Sarah poked the tip of an elegant shoe at the gravestone.

"And him? *He* didn't tell you either?"

"Yes, he did. Of course. But only after he had learned of my mission. The entire thing must have weighed on him enormously. We had a long talk about that night at the Odessa hospital. Then he promised to provide me with this proof, but he didn't live long enough..." Leslie's final words gave way to sobs. She wiped at the tears on her face.

"We found the documents that he wanted to show me among Bronx's possessions. I looked through all of them today, and discovered his final secret—that you were the other baby! Father secured the DNA. You really are my twin sister, Sarah."

"Well, then I suppose that makes you mine. Who else knows about this?"

The pitch of her voice had raised, expressing concern.

"No one. Just you and I... and him." Leslie placed her hand on the gravestone again. "Of course you can take a DNA test at any time, and compare yours to mine..."

"No, I believe you," the First Lady interrupted her. "No wonder..."

"What? That we get along so well?"

"No, that we both also gave birth to twins. Your boys and my girls. It has to be genetic."

The two of them laughed for the first time in a long while.

"Charles really was a man unto himself," Sarah marveled.

"Do you want the papers?"

The First Lady shook her head.

"Better not. We should burn them. Look, over there!"

Leslie's eyes followed in the direction of Sarah's outstretched arm and saw the cemetery-keeper's burning woodpile. Flames licked out of a walled fire pit. They approached. Wood crackled. The fire blazed, fueled by thin twigs and autumn foliage.

"Should we?" Sarah asked. When Leslie nodded, she began dropping the documents into the flames, one by one.

They strolled back. There was a light spring to their step. They stopped at the grave of Charles W. Palmer, their arms wrapped around each other tightly.

A short while later, the First Lady's vehicle convoy set forth with the usual commotion of red and blue lights.

As Leslie got into her mid-class rental car, she knew what she had to do next...

EPILOGUE

Plumes of fog had settled over *Le Milieu de la Fin*.

"How did you happen to meet up with Steve again?" I asked Leslie Palmer.

Steve Quinn added a log to the fire, and responded in her stead.

"The magazine flew me back from Doha, Qatar, on their jet, and then brought me into the city... The truth is that I had an eye on Leslie ever since I did that interview with her. So, there I was—beaten like a dog, and as brainwashed as a babbling parrot—and I thought, if anyone can bring me back to humanity, then it's her. You know what would have happened if I had turned to the FBI or CIA... I would have been treated like a usual suspect. So... we soon agreed that we would work the whole thing out for ourselves, far away from everything."

"He left me a message at Dad's house," Leslie added. "We decided almost right away that we wanted to go to Europe. By the way—the FBI still hasn't retracted the warrant that they have out against me. We made it here via Canada."

"Why here," I asked "in the middle of nowhere?"

"My mother, Fabienne, was French," she reminded me. "Charles left detailed notes on her family and where she came from. Steve and I discovered the location of the family farm, where she was raised until about the age of fourteen. This is it. *La Maison Noire*, in the *Le Milieu de la Fin* valley—and in the end, we finally made it here."

She spoke the last words quietly, looking at me for a long while.

"There's a place called *Les Enfers* not far from here," I said casually, to ease the tension a bit. "This place seems to be full of fateful symbolism."

Steve took up my little reference with a motion of his hand.

"Yes, I know. We went through all kinds of hell. But we have no regrets."

"I have one more question on my mind, Steve. Bronx's number, the one that you secretly memorized from this... Bassan's... cell phone in Tora Bora... That was an explosive piece of information. I mean, the Americans..."

Steve interrupted my thoughts with a gesture of resignation.

"I gave up. The Defense Intelligence Agency investigators lost all interest once they understood that I couldn't contribute to their efforts to find the chief terrorist. They didn't trust me much, anyhow."

"And the First Lady? Are you still in touch with her, Leslie?"

"Of course. Sarah is the fourth member of our secret society. She pays an official visit to our capital once a year, and then we spend a couple of days together. You know that Sarah's daughters are twins. Have you noticed—our mother Fabienne, my twin sister, and I—we all gave birth to twins..." She laughed easily. "It's karmic!"

"And Alex and Craig—do they visit you? Does Jennifer?"

The boys had returned to live in the United States. She did not wish to tell me more than that. Jennifer, she told me on the other hand, her eyes gleaming with pride, lived with the handsome, now no longer limping Nassim.

"They also have two boys."

"Let me guess..."

Her entire face glowed as she nodded enthusiastically—yes, twins.

The one thing I still had a hard time understanding, was why I—of all people—had the honor of hearing her story. Steve tried to enlighten me.

"I believe that Leslie had made her peace with life that night, when she drove into the river," he confided as we stretched our legs in front of the old country manor. "She saw the fact that you saved her as a grace period granted by fate. A bit of added time."

At a complete loss, I asked, "You mean she... she was...?"

Steve nodded. "Six months, maybe less. That's what the doctors say—all the specialists."

"*No*—that's terrible," I exclaimed in an attempt to deny the incomprehensible. "I had no idea—she looks perfectly healthy..."

Leslie Palmer died from complications of the incurable disease three months later. As I write these lines, Steve Quinn still resides at *La Maison Noire.*